The
Girl
in the
Striped
Dress

BOOKS BY ELLIE MIDWOOD

The Violinist of Auschwitz
The Girl Who Escaped from Auschwitz

ELLIE MIDWOOD

The
Girl
in the
Striped
Dress

Bookouture

Published by Bookouture in 2021

An imprint of Storyfire Ltd.
Carmelite House
50 Victoria Embankment
London EC4Y 0DZ

www.bookouture.com

ISBN: 978-1-80019-877-7
eBook ISBN: 978-1-80019-876-0

This book is a work of fiction. Whilst some characters and
circumstances portrayed by the author are based on real people
and historical fact, references to real people, events, establishments,
organizations or locales are intended only to provide a sense of
authenticity and are used fictiously. All other characters and all
incidents and dialogue are drawn from the author's
imagination and are not to be construed as real.

To R. Love you.

Introduction

The Girl in the Striped Dress is a novel mostly based on a true story. I shall go into more detail concerning the authenticity of certain characters and events in the "Author's Note" at the end of the novel but I felt the need to write this short introduction since this story is quite different from what I have learned about Auschwitz throughout the years. I've read countless memoirs and historical studies and most of them concentrated on regular inmates and their sufferings; quite often those were the stories of survival against all odds, which took place in the overcrowded, filthy barracks and in the open-air work details, where the inmates were constantly beaten and harassed by the Kapos and the brutal SS men – in short, the stories of extermination through labor, which the survivors were fortunate to live to tell. Based on those memoirs and studies, this has always been my general impression of Auschwitz-Birkenau. However, Helena's story is quite different and I wished to give you, my readers, a quick insight into her experiences in Auschwitz-Birkenau before the novel even begins.

In the spring of 1942, two thousand young women from Slovakia were deported to the concentration camp in Auschwitz. Helena Citrónová was among them. Not long before that, a wounded Waffen-SS soldier, Franz Wunsch, was transferred from the Eastern Front to Auschwitz after being declared unfit for further active duty. Helena was scheduled to die in the gas chamber on March 22, however, by lucky chance, the day before that, Wunsch's comrades brought her into their barrack to sing Franz a song, since it was his birthday. According to the testimonies given after the war by both Helena and Franz, he enjoyed the girl's singing so much, he demanded that her execution be canceled and instead signed her up to work under his command, in the so-called Kanada work detail.

The last names of the main characters, Helena and Franz were changed; most of the names of the real historical figures who served or were incarcerated in Auschwitz-Birkenau, remained unchanged, just like their personality and actions which I tried my best to transfer into the novel, relying on the survivors' memoirs, historical documents, and different studies conducted throughout the years by different historians.

Most of the action in *The Girl in the Striped Dress* takes place in the so-called Kanada work detail – a complex, which consisted of a number of warehouses and storing and disinfecting facilities. Kanada (original German spelling was preserved for this novel) was nicknamed so by the inmates due to the fact that the sorting detail, to which the new arrivals' possessions were brought to be sorted, was constantly overflowing with clothes, jewelry, and currencies of different countries. They believed Canada to be the land of riches and since, in the Auschwitz Kanada, just about anything could be found, the name stuck. The sorted items were later disinfected and shipped to Germany, while the gold and money went to the Reichsbank. Most of the inmates working there were female and it was one of the most sought-after work details in the entire camp since the labor was not hard and the inmates were allowed to grow out their hair, wear civilian clothes, and take the food and other items for personal use. The women assigned to the Kanada had quite a different life from the women living in the Birkenau women's camp (the Kanada girls' barracks were situated in the Kanada itself, separately from the women's camp) and the living conditions there were considerably different. The Kanada women were also allowed to take showers daily and were hardly ever subjects for selections, which, in contrast, were conducted systematically in the regular camp.

Here's what the survivors had to say about the Kanada:

"The girls who work there have everything – perfume, cologne – and they look as if their hairdos were the work of the top hairdresser of Paris. Apart from freedom, they have everything a woman can dream of. They also know love; the proximity of men, both inmates and SS men, makes this inevitable… Ten meters from their barracks, on the other side of the barbed wire, rise the rectangular chimneys of the crematoriums that burn constantly, burn the owners of all the goods that these admirable creatures sort in these barracks." – Simon Laks and René Coudy, members of the Birkenau orchestra. (credit: "People in Auschwitz" by H. Langbein).

Kitty Hart, one of the Kanada girls, described her experiences in these words: "It was a splendid summer. The sun was hot and we, who had been assigned the night shift, found it hard to sleep during the day. We usually got up in the early afternoon and if the weather was fair, we lay on the grass in front of our barracks, sunbathing and splashing water over ourselves to cool down. Often, we danced and sang and we even formed a little band. We began to laugh and joke again. I spent many hours reading books that those destined for gassing had taken along on their transport to Poland. Our situation was surely one of the most insane in the whole world. All around us were the screams of the dying, destruction, the smoking chimneys that darkened and polluted the air with the soot and the stench of charred corpses. I suppose what we primarily cared about in those days was not to lose our minds and that is why we laughed and sang even so close to the flaming inferno. It is astonishing what body and soul can endure if they have to. One can get accustomed to almost anything." (credit: "People in Auschwitz" by H. Langbein).

What follows, is Helena's – the Kanada girl's – story.

Chapter 1

Germany, 1947

Under the warm yellow glow of the overhead lamps, Dr. Hoffman was leafing through Franz Dahler's *Spruchkammerakte* – Denazification Tribunal folder, entirely ignoring the commotion around him. He couldn't blame his US army colleagues for being excited. It's not every day that such a curious case of this sort was being heard. After the Denazification program had been transferred to the control of the Germans, in March of the previous year, the Americans were only too glad to reduce their role to supervising the tribunals in their sector, instead of presiding over them. They felt they'd done their duty with the Nuremberg Trials; they hanged all the major perpetrators – now, let the Germans sort their own kind into the guilty ones and… *not-as-guilty-as-the-others,* Dr. Hoffman caught himself thinking.

Ordinarily, he wouldn't even have been present here. The Denazification Tribunal for minor criminals didn't require a psychiatrist's conclusion; only the Chairman's verdict usually given after a ridiculously cursory perusal of the evidence and a miserable two-hours-long hearing and that's if the defendant was lucky to get two hours out of the Court. The system was so overwhelmed with these hearings, the chairmen wished to send the defendants on their merry way as soon as it was possible, for, in place of one, forty new former POWs were expecting their turn with their summons to oral proceedings at the ready.

It was all understandable, too, that the American Public Safety Branch supervising them didn't blame the German chairmen for being so quick to hand out "not guilty" verdicts. If the defendant wasn't found guilty of participating in major war crimes or crimes against humanity, he was let go with a mere slap on the wrist and a restriction in employment. *So what that you trashed a Jewish grocer's store in 1938 and reported his neighbor to the Gestapo? No public office for you, for now, my good fellow but by all means, walk the streets free, unlike the said Jew and the neighbor, who both died, not directly by your hand but with your help nevertheless. That doesn't make you a major offender or even an offender who is subject to imprisonment. A follower or a nominal Nazi, at best.*

Dr. Hoffman wondered how soon such "exonerated" followers and nominal Nazis would find their way back to positions of importance once the US Army left Germany to her own devices. He also wondered if this would be the case with this young man, looking out from the photo, attached to his folder, with honest, black-and-white eyes. For some reason, the fellow ignored his right to an attorney, insisting that he could defend himself perfectly fine. The psychiatrist lifted the picture to reexamine Dahler's *Arbeitsblatt* – a worksheet that was placed on top of the file.

> *Last name:* Dahler
> *First Name:* Franz
> *Occupation:* Auto Mechanic
> *Town:* Munich
> *Street address…*

Dr. Hoffman ignored the rest and shifted his attention to the *Vermögensübersicht* – financial statement prepared by Dahler. Nothing noteworthy was here, no buildings or apartments to his name; only a family house in Austria owned together with his mother, in which he didn't reside. A bank account showed just a little over three thousand RM to his name; no artwork, jewelry, or gold listed. In the line "animals," Dahler wrote, *Prinz, an Alsatian,* most likely misunderstanding that he was supposed to list domestic animals which could bring profit and not pets. In spite of himself, Dr. Hoffman caught himself smiling at this, not with malice but with genuine amusement.

Army rank: Unterscharführer SS, SS-Totenkopfverbände
Wartime employment: Waffen-SS (discharged due to injury); KZ Auschwitz, Kommandoführer; Waffen-SS (taken POW by the US Army).
War crimes or crimes against humanity: Not charged

Not charged. Dr. Hoffman closed the case and patted his pocket absentmindedly in search of cigarettes. Most of the former SS men of a relatively low rank sported the same exact verdict – a life ticket, basically – in their papers given to them by the US War Department upon their early release from the POW camps. Only the vilest of criminals was actually brought up on charges. Small fish like Dahler, despite – most definitely – having their fair share of blood on their hands, were simply "not charged." Not "acquitted" but simply "not charged." Because, if the War Department began detaining and prosecuting every single such guard, they would run out of jails and gallows for these former Nazis.

Former or not, that was another question altogether, if Dr. Hoffman were entirely honest. *So, the simple Denazification hearing, it was for Dahler, so that he'd get his clearance stamped and find even better employment and live his life while his victims...*

The psychiatrist lifted his eyes, framed by metal-framed spectacles, to the clock on the wall. Within ten minutes, the session would start. A slight pang of excitement, or giddiness perhaps, prickled his lungs with its icy needles with every drag he took on his cigarette. Unlike the rest of the officers in the room, he didn't speculate on the outcome of the trial; he didn't talk at all. He rarely did, as a matter of fact. His entire life he'd been a keen observer of human character, a scientist taking the greatest pleasure in studying human nature and the deepest layers of a person's psyche.

Words, he had found, a long time ago, were almost always aimed at concealing the truth. He preferred listening to the tone of the voice, watching closely instinctual gestures, noting the slightest discrepancies between what was being said and how it was being said and that was one of the reasons why he was here that day.

Andrej Novák, a former Auschwitz inmate, insisted *that justice ought to be served and not the regular "exonerated" bull-manure one, but the real sort, the pre-war sort,* in his own words. According to him, this particular defendant had to pay for his crimes like no other. Once again, Dr. Hoffman regarded the Slovak closely. One didn't need a degree in psychiatry to notice the young man's agitation. He paced the room as though set on wearing out the carpet that had miraculously survived the bombing and smoked like a fiend. *One ought to feel for him; so young and already so very broken.*

"I don't understand. Why not just arrest him and throw him in jail," Andrej Novák hissed under his breath in his accented English. Dr. Hoffman glimpsed a bulging vein on the young man's forehead. Novák was in his twenties, a handsome fellow in that half-brutish, half-brooding way that was characteristic of his type – the survivors who'd been through hell and were now firmly set on serving that hell back to the ones who had put them through it. The newly emerging Nazi-hunters, the dangerous and eerily heroic types, who instilled both fear and respect into anyone who'd come in contact with them. "Or better hang him at once – he deserves it like no one—"

"It's a Denazification court, not a wild-west lynching," Lieutenant Carter, one of the Public Safety Branch officers, remarked in an even tone. Quite a few medals adorned his chest – a testament to his bravery in action ever since the D-Day landing. Unlike Dr. Hoffman, he was a real soldier, not a pencil-pusher as Hoffman considered himself to be. Carter, dark-haired, virile Carter, almost radiated strength whenever he entered the room, yet everything intellectual he left to his colleague, Dr. Hoffman, for consideration. Just like Hoffman considered himself a pencil-pusher, Carter just as unabashedly referred to himself as *a simple GI, no fancy degrees here*. Carter was one of the first interrogators of the captured war criminals in early 1945; Dr. Hoffman – an analytic, supplied his opinions concerning the said war criminals and signed Carter's reports to the OSS, with his own verdict attached. Carter knew how to get answers out of men and Dr. Hoffman knew when the answer was a lie. They made a good team; everyone around thought so. "I understand that the matter is still raw and personal to you—"

"Personal?" Novák glared fiercely at Carter. "Of course it's goddamn personal. He whipped my back on quite a few occasions and nearly shoved me into the fire pit – alive – once! If that's not personal, I don't know what is! He was detained, along with high-ranking criminals, in a POW camp by your own War Department officers! What I don't understand is why they dropped the charges against him. He's a murderer to the marrow of his bones!"

"And that's precisely the reason why you're here in the first place," Carter countered, unimpressed. "Your being a co-plaintiff and a witness for the prosecution will certainly help us clarify matters. However, we must stick to the procedure. As of now, it's your word against his." Novák was just about to interject something but Carter stopped him by raising both of his great paws in the air. "No disrespect. I, personally, believe you. However, he's bringing his own witness who will be testifying in his defense—"

"A woman who he was abusing systematically while she was at his complete mercy in the camp and whom he forced to marry him to get his Denazification clearance out of you people!" The last words Novák outright shouted.

Dr. Hoffman shifted his weight from one foot to the other. He agreed with Carter completely; bringing former concentration camp inmates into the courtroom wasn't the best idea. Working with them on hunting down war criminals was one thing. In such cases, their help was truly invaluable. However, putting them face to face with their former abusers never ended well. As a psychiatrist, it was his most profound conviction that the less former inmates had to do with their former captors the better. *Let them get their closure from the verdict. If a perpetrator is found guilty and that sets them free; let them rebuild their lives, forget all that nightmare once and for all.* Living obsessed with that grim, all-consuming hatred didn't do them any good. It only corroded them gradually from the inside, the acidic memory of the bloodstained past.

He hadn't always held such a conviction. On the contrary, at the very beginning of his "local" career, when he was first posted here in Germany, an idealistic, relatively young psychiatrist with a fresh diploma and a burning desire to help, he was thoroughly convinced that facing the former oppressors would help the victims. But, having witnessed major relapses after progress had already been made and even following suicides, he eventually acquired a polar-opposite view of the matter. The extermination camp cases were the worst ones and particularly Auschwitz and Mauthausen. Those two, had left no one unscarred.

"I understand your feelings, Mr. Novák," Carter announced in a softer tone, after a pause. "But the court is a court. Will you be able to keep those feelings under control? I don't want this to turn into a circus. Perhaps, it would be better to use your written affidavit instead of facing Mr. Dahler?" He consulted the clock on the wall, much like Dr. Hoffman had done, just mere minutes ago. "It's not too late to change your mind. You are not under any obligation to be present during the hearing."

Novák took a deep breath, seemingly collecting himself. "I only need you to listen to me."

"And we will. But do you believe that you can give a calm, dispassionate testimony?"

Novák's clenched jaw didn't escape Dr. Hoffman's attention. Yet, the Slovak Nazi-hunter steadied himself and slowly nodded. "Yes. I believe I can. I have to. For *her* sake. He belongs in prison for the rest of his life, where he won't be able to hurt her anymore. I will prove it to you that he's a pathological liar, a cold-blooded killer, and a rapist, who manipulated that poor young woman into the position of a slave, first in the camp, and now, as his wife."

His tone dripped with derision as he uttered the last word, *wife*. The Slovak didn't believe it for one second that a former extermination camp inmate would willingly marry the man, who used to be an officer in charge of her sector. Neither did Dr. Hoffman, truth be told. He had met with many women who spoke of SS guards with a tremor in their voice, even two years after the liberation. Their eyes widened in fear, instilled by the months of abuse. Of their own volition, nervous fingers clenched and twisted the material of their skirts. They spoke of those guards either with a fervent tone of accusation and nearly palpable hatred oozing out of their voice or with horror and tears, shaking their heads and trembling with their entire bodies at the mere mention of a certain SS guard's name.

Needless to say, when Carter dropped Dahler's case on top of Dr. Hoffman's desk and announced, in his usual unemotional voice, *I believe this would interest you, as a specialist,* Dr. Hoffman found himself utterly and positively mystified. A former SS guard from Auschwitz, after receiving the Denazification Tribunal's summons for the oral proceedings, wished to bring his wife as his witness to the Court. The wife, who used to be an inmate under his charge. A Slovakian Jew. Oh, that interested him, all right.

"Mr. Novák, I assure you, we will do everything in our power to bring Mr. Dahler to responsibility, if he is indeed found guilty of such crimes," Carter assured his Slovak colleague, who had helped the MPs hunt down and identify not just one Nazi and motioned his head in Dr. Hoffman's direction. "Dr. Hoffman is here precisely for that reason as well. He'll be observing Mrs. Dahler closely as she's giving her testimony and if he finds that she's being coerced in any way to give it, we'll place Mr. Dahler under temporary arrest, reschedule the trial and speak with her in private, where he won't be able to influence her. Would that be satisfactory with you?"

The Nazi-hunter nodded, seemingly pleased with such arrangements. *Perfect timing, too,* Dr. Hoffman noted to himself. One of the MPs opened the door to the conference room and announced that they were expected in the courtroom.

*

The courtroom, one of the many in the State Magistrate's Office, was a small affair, still under construction after the damage it had received in the last months of the war. The paneling was still intact though, much like the floor in this particular courtroom. It was the west wing that had suffered the most from the bombs raining onto the city in the spring of 1945 and the ceiling that now sported multiple cracks in its white surface, as though a soldier scarred by the war.

At last, the door opened silently prompting everyone present to crane their necks. A bailiff looked into the corridor and called out Franz Dahler's name. Andrej Novák pulled himself up in his seat, straightening his back to an almost unnatural, rigid pose.

A young man stepped through the doors. Dr. Hoffman regarded him with a surge of sudden, harsh curiosity. A handsome face; high forehead, sharp, pleasing features, eyes – bright blue and expressive. Wavy, dark hair brushed neatly back. Behind his tall frame, Dr. Hoffman at first failed to see his wife, who trailed after him, until Dahler reached the front of the courtroom where a chair was set up for him. Only then did she come out of her hiding and only after he turned to her and took her by the hand. He didn't release her palm even when the Chairman walked in; only asked to address the Court before the hearing would start.

The Chairman nodded his assent.

"Would it be agreeable with the Tribunal if my wife sat next to me?" His voice was surprisingly pleasant, with a slight accent to it that Dr. Hoffman recognized as Austrian. "Crowded places cause her great anxiety and particularly if she's alone. She would be much more comfortable if she sat next to me. This way, I will be able to hold her hand if she gets... overwhelmed."

Dr. Hoffman looked at Mrs. Dahler, who stood next to her husband, with her gaze downcast. She was, undoubtedly, a beautiful woman, with brilliant dark-brown, nearly black hair, expressive eyebrows, and full, finely-shaped lips which must have looked so pretty when she smiled but which were now pressed into a hard line. Under a tailored suit, her posture was rigid; the facial expression guarded, the skin – unhealthily pale, almost of the color of the pearls around her neck.

Well, at least he dressed her up for this occasion, a thought slithered through Dr. Hoffman's mind, which he took great care to chase off, at once. He was here to be an objective observer and yet he found it difficult not to pass judgment after Novák's passionate speech. *He's a pathological liar, a cold-blooded killer, and a rapist, who manipulated that poor young woman into the position of a slave, first in the camp and now, as his wife.*

"Frau Dahler, would you be more comfortable next to your husband, or would you prefer to sit alone?" the Chairman addressed her directly.

Dr. Hoffman noticed that Mrs. Dahler's fingers trembled imperceptibly. Without looking at her, Franz Dahler gave her hand a gentle pressure. Instantly, she looked up at the Chairman.

"Yes, please. I'd like to sit next to my husband, Your Honor." Her voice was pleasant but vaguely tense; her German – a bit halting and had a slight Eastern lilt to it.

A second chair was brought in and set up next to the one in which the defendant was supposed to be seated. Dahler waited for his wife to take her place and pressed her shoulder slightly before taking his own seat. Dr. Hoffman didn't see his expression when he did so but he found himself a bit surprised at Mrs. Dahler's reaction. Instead of cowering in fear like most victims of abuse would do in a similar situation, she smiled warmly at her husband, as though in gratitude.

Not a silent threat then? The reassurance of a concerned husband? Was she indeed anxious and he was merely looking out for her? Or was it all a carefully constructed performance?

The usual routine followed.

"Defendant, raise your right hand and take an oath… State your full name, please. Birthdate. Current occupation. Occupation during the war. Have you ever been accused of war crimes or crimes against humanity? When were you released from the POW camp by the US War Department?"

Dahler replied calmly and confidently. *Twenty-five years old. Auto mechanic. Former SS guard in the extermination camp Auschwitz. Before that, a Waffen-SS soldier. Dismissed from active duty on the Eastern Front due to injury. Never accused of any war crimes or crimes against humanity. Cleared by the US War Department on December 14th, 1945. Released from the POW camp on the same date. Married Helena the following day.*

Dr. Hoffman thus learned Mrs. Dahler's first name. *Helena.* A fleeting shadow of a smile passed over her face when her husband mentioned the marriage. Dr. Hoffman made a note in his notepad.

After the formal part of the questioning was over with, the Chairman shifted in his seat before addressing the defendant. "Ordinarily, the Tribunal would have given the verdict based on the witness' statements, personal characteristics, and letters of support provided by the War Department – you do have excellent reports here from the officers at the POW camp in which you were detained. However, Mr. Novák has acted as a co-plaintiff and required a full investigation of your crimes, which, according to the prosecution, fall under the category of Crimes Against Humanity."

If Dahler felt uneasy after those words and a pregnant pause that followed, he didn't betray his feelings in the slightest.

The Chairman then pointed at Andrej Novák with his pen. "You *are* familiar with this man, aren't you?"

As Dahler shifted his gaze to one of his former prisoners, Dr. Hoffman observed both men's reaction closely. Novák, his features convulsed with fury, gritted his teeth with such force that Dr. Hoffman could see facial muscles shift under his skin that was shining with sweat. He stared at the former SS man with unmasked hatred, ready to pounce on him if given half a chance.

On Dahler's face, to the contrary, not a wrinkle appeared. He looked at the Slovak with almost fascinating calmness and then back at the Chairman before uttering the letter A and a series of numbers in such a soft voice that Dr. Hoffman couldn't make the exact numbers out.

Novák's veins stood out on his neck. The Chairman scowled slightly.

"You must forgive me, Your Honor," Dahler spoke again, with a fleeting ghost of a smile that passed over his face, without reaching his eyes. "It must have come off as a bad joke. I do know this man but not his name. Just his number. We didn't know almost any of the prisoners' names in the camp; we only called them by the number that was given to them upon their admission into the camp. The one tattooed onto their forearms."

At this remark, Helena Dahler tugged on a long sleeve of her jacket. To Dr. Hoffman, it appeared to be an instinctive gesture. She was embarrassed by hers and was used to hiding it.

"You met your wife in the camp, you said." For the first time, the psychiatrist addressed Dahler directly. Not the regular protocol but he needed to clarify something.

"*Jawohl.*"

"What year?"

"She arrived with the transport from Slovakia on March 21, 1942."

"You have a remarkable memory for dates, young man," the Chairman noted.

Dahler looked down, concealing a smile. "Only because it was my birthday, Your Honor."

"You said you didn't know any of the prisoners' names, just their numbers," Dr. Hoffman repeated. "Did you know your wife by her number only, before the liberation, as well?"

"Of course not." Dahler chuckled as though Dr. Hoffman had asked him something incredibly idiotic. "When I learned her name, she didn't have a number yet."

"How come?"

It was Helena Dahler who answered instead of her husband, once again surprising the psychiatrist greatly by the suddenly confident tone of her voice. "Because I was scheduled to die the next day. They don't tattoo the ones who are to go into the gas chamber. It was Franz who saved me from it. And no, he never, not once, called me by my number. I was always Helena to him."

Chapter 2

Helena

Auschwitz, March 21 1942

What does one do when they are told that they have only twenty-four hours to live?

I, for one, brushed my hair, stroke after stroke, as I was ordered by Rottenführer Wolff, making myself into a pretty, almost-corpse. It wasn't a sickness that would claim my life soon; it was a death sentence for a crime, which I didn't commit. I was a prisoner and this surely was a jail, the worst one that anyone could imagine in their worst nightmares. Did I kill anyone to get here? No. The ones who did, they wore a green triangle on their uniform. Murderers actually left this place from time to time, after serving their sentence, or at least, so I was told.

Just this very morning, while we were still waiting on the ramp, as the SS were deciding what to do with us, a man in a striped uniform announced to us the reason for the wait. The camp administration was congratulating a Kapo on completing his sentence and releasing him back into society with their best wishes, rehabilitated. Apparently, that Kapo (a prisoner supervisor of some sort, from what I had concluded from his explanations) murdered his wife with a butcher's knife, in a fit of jealousy but had been working so diligently as part of the camp team that he had earned himself an early release from Herr Kommandant himself.

The Kapo was a German, needless to say, and his crime wasn't as unforgivable as ours. He was only a murderer. We were Jews and we were scheduled to die as soon as the Kapo affair was over with – a newly arrived SS man announced in a cheerful voice. But then, another one appeared, coughed into his hand in embarrassment and reported that the damned inner walls in one of the crematorium's chimneys had caved in again and the *Aktion* would have to wait until the Sonderkommando had fixed it. From time to time, they looked us over and tilted their heads to one side, narrowed their eyes slightly as though calculating something in their methodical minds – perhaps, the number of bullets needed to off us all and the exact amount of manpower required to dispose of our trembling, miserable bodies.

We stood as they had assembled us, close to each other and in neat rows of five; a resigned little army of shadows, already fading into nothingness. Around me, deathly silence lay. Even the ones who spoke, did so, in undertones. Our transport consisted solely of young women – the second one coming from Slovakia. The SS spoke openly about our fate; women are generally an obedient lot, not prone to revolts and therefore, the soldiers had nothing to fear. All we could do was shiver unmercifully, left to our own devices on the snow-filled ramp and feel the cold spread from our toes to our very hearts, turning them into unfeeling stones, as though all of us had already died. Some cried softly, my friend Cylka included. But she had a valid reason for it – her baby has died from hypothermia on the train. I, for one, preferred this liberating numbness. The interminable wait of one's approaching death was easier this way, not as agonizing.

We still stood on the ramp when a group of SS soldiers, accompanied by the men in striped slacks but civilian jackets with numbers sewn onto their chests strode up to our pitiful column. The men in striped slacks began taking our possessions from us, calmly and very rationally explaining that soon we wouldn't need those. One of them pulled my suitcase out of my clenched fist, looked at me with a sort of momentary pity but I refused to meet his gaze just like I refused his sympathy. I looked straight ahead of myself instead, while cold rage and helplessness battled inside of me, obliterating every other thought.

Distant and indifferent, the sun hung among the remnants of the clouds above the neat rows of barracks in front of us. A flock of birds fluttered their wings against the curtain of blue sky. I followed their progress with envy. How I should like to do the same – up and away from this place. But these birds didn't consider escaping this doomed misery. On the contrary, they crowded over one of the barracks, weighing down the powerlines around it, adorning its roof in gray – the color of SS men's overcoats. The barracks must have been the kitchen and unlike us, the birds had nothing to fear from the said SS. Only the barbed-wire fence didn't attract them for some reason. After regarding its construction closely and noticing a sign with a death head and a sign in German and Polish – *Halt/Stoj* – it occurred to me that it must have been electrified.

Another gray-clad officer trotted over and began demanding that everyone who could sing, recite poems, or dance reported to him immediately. He had a sharp, impatient face and a horsewhip in his hand. The women hesitated for a moment but after he flicked it in a typical manner, characteristic of someone with a short fuse, a few of them reluctantly stepped forward. One of the women pushed me, by accident, as she was passing me by and, before I knew it, I was separated from Cylka and stood face to face with the SS man whom his strange underlings in striped trousers addressed as Rottenführer Wolff. He seized my face in his gloved fingers at once and, in a business-like manner, turned it this way and that. A shawl slid off my head but he pushed my hands away before I could fix it.

"Beautiful mane you have there," he commented in a hoarse voice that betrayed his fondness for smoking and let a strand of my hair run through his fingers. "*Ja.* That'll do. Come."

I couldn't quite believe all this had happened mere hours ago.

Wolff brought us, the few women he had chosen, into a warehouse of sorts – a tremendous affair overflowing with personal belongings and suitcases of all shapes and colors with names and deportation points smudged over their surfaces in chalk. Wolff's underlings threw our suitcases into the same pile unceremoniously. I think it was then that I realized that I would never leave that place again; alive, that is.

"Welcome to the Kanada, the land of riches." He spread his arms in a mock-welcoming gesture and smiled like a snake. "Enjoy it while you can. It is unfortunate that you won't be staying, my ladies."

His orderlies were already snapping the suitcases open and rummaging through our carefully packed clothes and underthings, pulling out the sweaters and stockings with the same indifferent expression that I saw on a butcher's face while he was sorting the hooves and the guts from the good cuts of meat.

"Don't look so sour now." Wolff grinned pitilessly again, perching on the edge of a sorting table and lighting a cigarette. "You should feel honored; all of your clothes will be disinfected and sent to Germany, for the Aryan folk to wear. And your hair, that, too, should not be wasted. Our Kriegsmarine sailors will make great use of it in their socks and Wehrmacht soldiers, in their felt boots. You should be proud that you can make sacrifices for the Great German Reich. Well, now, let me see how well you can dance and sing."

When my turn came, I told him calmly that I couldn't sing or dance at all. If they were going to off us all, regardless, at least I'd spare myself this last humiliation.

"You can't sing? Rot," he countered with a derisive snort. "The *Russki* fellows, or what's left of them here, have a saying that I like. *If you don't know how, we'll teach you. And if you don't want to, we'll make you.* Now take this heap of rags and off you go to change. Just for your attitude, I'll make you the star of the show. And do not come out of there before I fetch you. No need for these rams to get all randy over a show that is not meant for their eyes," he concluded, regarding the men under his charge in a superior and mocking way.

The horsewhip that he demonstrated to me, to emphasize his point, didn't leave much desire for any further testing of his patience. He held it much too confidently for a man who used it only as an empty threat. I gathered the pile of clothes and a hair-brush he shoved at me and went into the room he had indicated.

The time crept on. Gradually, it grew dark. The dusk colored the walls into the shades of rusted steel and I was still brushing my hair, mindless stroke after mindless stroke – a madwoman's repetitious act. At one point, it seemed as though Wolff had forgotten me here. Eerie silence lay everywhere around me; even Wolff's men had long left and I was grateful that they had, for some of them were Slovaks and I understood far too much of what they were saying to each other behind that thin door, to remain blissfully ignorant on account of this place. We had been told that we were being sent to work in the factories, you see. We hadn't been informed that we would have been undressed, shaved, gassed, and burned upon arrival. These men were some special kommando – Sonderkom-mando – that took care of everything, except for the gassing itself, for the SS. I had learned that they were inmates as well. I had learned that one of them had put his own uncle and his little cousins on the crematorium gurney a few days ago.

Suddenly, I heard footsteps on the steel-lined steps outside. The door to the small storage room was flung open. I scrambled to atten-tion and pulled myself up, as Wolff stepped in. He turned the lights on and scrutinized me thoroughly as I was trying to blink away the blinding brightness. He tilted his head this way and that; grimaced slightly as though it wasn't him who had put all this ridiculous outfit together for me earlier, demanding that I get dressed and "make myself look presentable as if I was going to meet the Führer himself."

"Well," he mused out loud as he circled me, "it could have been worse, considering."

He tugged at the sable fur stole and adjusted it over my shoulders. I still smelled faint remnants of perfume on it, the smell of some other woman who was most likely dead by now, just like I would be tomorrow.

"Allow me to ask?" I carefully assembled foreign German words into a sentence. I hated hearing this tremor in my voice but I had also learned a lot about Wolff from his own Sonderkommando and suddenly getting on his wrong side was utterly beyond my desire.

"*Ja?*" He looked at me with semi-interest.

"What is it exactly that is demanded of me?" I made a vague gesture towards my ridiculous outfit.

He had chosen the gaudiest burgundy dress and shoes to match. They were a size smaller and pinched my feet already. I was only hoping he wouldn't make me dance or anything of that sort.

"I thought I told you. One of our comrades celebrates his birthday today. We wanted to surprise him. Normally we'd take him to a cabaret or something of that kind of place but, since we're here, we'll have to work with what we've got." *Which is you,* his eyes finished the sentence for him.

I was too afraid to say that I knew nothing of cabarets, never been to one, and knew no songs that women usually sang there.

"Don't fret," he laughed, far too close to my face and pinched my cheeks painfully. I stilled myself and tried not to wince under his fingers, forcing the blush into my cadaverous complexion. He was in a good mood; I smelled schnapps on his breath. It was my guess that the other women had already completed their performances. I wondered whether they were still alive or finished off already, disposed of by the same hand that was touching my cheek now. "You only have to sing him a birthday song as we bring out the cake. You do know birthday songs, I assume?"

The last words had a hint of a threat to them. *You'd better know them, you Mistbiene.*

"I do know some German songs and some Slovakian ones besides that," I answered carefully.

"That'll do just fine. Sing something to me. I want to hear your voice."

I inhaled deeply and began singing.

"Louder!"

My shoulders jerked involuntarily at the shout. He didn't mean to frighten me but it didn't take much, with me, anymore. I sang louder, applying my best to the task.

He stopped me abruptly with his raised hand. "That'll do. Sing just like that. And smile. I want you to look happy. It's the fellow's birthday and I won't have you standing there with the face of a professional mourner, do you understand?"

"Yes."

"You should reply, *Jawohl,* Herr Rottenführer."

"*Jawohl,* Herr Rottenführer," I repeated diligently.

"I assume it's unnecessary to mention that if he's not happy with your performance, I'll punish you severely."

"I understand, Herr Rottenführer. I'll do my best."

*

Wolff left me in front of the SS barracks and told me that he'd fetch me as soon as the time was right. Shivering in the thin silk material, I pulled my head inside my shoulders, hiding my neck in the folds of the stole. The air outside took one's breath away. I was gulping mouthfuls of its howling wind until my lungs were full of its icy needles. A sentry passed by with a rifle slung over his shoulder. He stared at me uncomprehendingly and paused for a moment but then Wolff stepped outside and grabbed hold of my forearm.

"Showtime," he breathed into my face. Now, in addition to schnapps, I smelled the brandy on his breath.

Inside the SS barracks, the air was warm and thick with cigarette smoke and a roast-meat aroma. The boisterous conversation came to an abrupt halt as soon as I stepped forward. Wolff nudged me so forcefully toward one of the SS men that I nearly fell into his lap. He was wearing some sort of a paper crown they'd fashioned for him, for the occasion. He blinked at me, mystified. His face appeared flushed in the dimmed light of the barracks, either from alcohol or my nearly falling on him. I quickly pulled myself up, caught a glare from Wolff who now stood in front of me and promptly pasted a huge false smile on my quivering face. In a loud voice, just as Wolff had instructed me, I began to sing. Two of the birthday fellow's comrades brought in a cake. Soon, they all picked up and my voice drowned in the veritable roar of theirs.

A round of applause followed. They applauded him, the birthday fellow, of course, not me.

I sang a song in Slovakian next. The birthday fellow was young and dashing, like most of them. Dashing and ruthless and full of hate. His eyes were pale blue. His hair and heart were black. Suddenly, he smiled at me for the first time.

"What kind of a song was that?" he inquired after I had finished singing in my native tongue.

"It's a birthday song that we usually sing in Slovakia," I quickly glimpsed his insignia, same one as Wolff's, "Herr Rottenführer."

"It's nice," he commented with a measure of restraint in his voice. They were not used to complimenting the Jews, that much was obvious.

I thanked him softly.

"*Bitte,* sing something else," he requested. His voice was actually gentle and had a softer accent to it than his counterparts, however, it somehow sounded more commanding than even Wolff's, without his having to raise it one bit. It was the voice of a man who was used to giving orders and having those orders obeyed without any questions. "Sing…" He considered something for a few moments, named a German song but I didn't know it. He named another one but I didn't know that one either. In the end, he raised both hands in surrender. "Well then, sing something you like. Sing your favorite song to me."

I was silent for a moment. I wasn't sure of what to sing. The song that I liked the best was too tragic – about a woman whose beloved dies – and it was wholly and utterly unsuitable for the occasion but my lips parted on their own and a sad, haunting melody filled the room. At one point, one of the SS men pulled out a harmonica and started picking up the notes as I sang. He was very gifted musically, just like Wolff was very gifted with his whip. I finished singing. No one clapped. A vague shadow of tension hung over the room, along with the silver rings of cigarette smoke. I felt Wolff's eyes on me. Most certainly he was already considering the thrashing he'd administer to me for pulling this stunt and I was too afraid of him to even say a word in my own defense, to explain that I didn't do this on purpose.

Suddenly, the birthday fellow was pressing a piece of cake, wrapped in a napkin, into my hands. It smelled so divine that it made my mouth water, a soft wispy cloud of sweet delight in my sweating palms. Just now had I remembered that I hadn't eaten anything in a few days.

"It was a very nice song. And you have a beautiful voice. You must sing for us sometime again in the future."

I wetted my lips. "I'm afraid that will be impossible, Herr Rottenführer. Our entire transport is being liquidated tomorrow. I was told so today. But thank you for your kind words, nevertheless. It warms my heart, knowing that I pleased you on your special day. I wish you a long and prosperous life."

He swung round in his seat. "Is it true?" he asked Wolff.

The latter only shrugged in response, busy munching on a sausage with mustard.

"I want you to exclude her from the *Aktion,*" the birthday fellow said with a sudden authority in his voice, which was rather strange considering that his rank was the same one as Wolff's.

"She's already on the list."

"Well, strike her name out of there then. What's so difficult about that?"

"Palitzsch has already signed it."

"I don't give a brass tack! Strike her name out of there. Why are they liquidating the entire transport when we're so severely understaffed in the Kanada?"

"Go ask the Old Man. He gives the orders here, not me." Once again, Wolff was back to chewing.

In the corner, one of the soldiers was offering round cigars to the others gathered around him; well-fed smiles chasing one another across their faces, entirely oblivious that a human being's fate was being decided at that very moment, between two of his comrades. My head had grown light all of a sudden. For a moment, the floor appeared to have been going from under my feet. The birthday fellow's face swam before my eyes – one of the killers whom I desperately wished to save my life because he liked the way I sang for him.

"But don't you think we could use some women to sort the clothes? These women aren't sick, are they?" He turned to me sharply. "Are you sick?"

I shook my head vehemently, pleading him with my swimming eyes the best I could. *I was healthy, very much so and very eager to work. Just let me show you how good of a worker I can make. I can do anything, Herr Rottenführer, absolutely anything you tell me to!*

"They're expecting a new transport from the Protectorate tomorrow, I think," Wolff commented lazily. "They gave me the order to liquidate today's transport; that's all I know."

"Assign her and the others to our work detail then. I'll sort it out with Palitzsch myself."

Wolff stared at him as though the birthday fellow had completely gone off his head. The latter didn't even flinch, suddenly stern and regal in his paper crown.

At last, Wolff nodded, with a measure of respect.

"Just because you asked me, Dahler."

Now I knew his name. Rottenführer Dahler. He gave me a bright, reassuring smile, a monarch pardoning the person on the gallows at the last moment. On shaking legs, I walked out of the barracks. Once outside, I could finally breathe again. Tomorrow, almost everyone I knew would die but I wouldn't be among them. A sudden urge to scream came over me and I quickly shut myself up with the cake, shoving it down my throat together with tears and wild, animalistic fear. I was too terrified to believe. I was too terrified Wolff would get drunk and forget his promise. I was too terrified Dahler would change his mind. But the morning came and with it, the roll call and Wolff himself signed to me, out of the column, which later marched straight down to the block from which no one had returned.

"Yesterday was Dahler's birthday," Wolff commented as he took me to my new work detail, the Kanada. "Today is yours."

I didn't argue. He was right.

Chapter 3

Helena

April 1942

Another day in the Kanada. I pulled the pocket of a coat inside out, producing a cigarette case. I weighed it in my palm before considering throwing it into the box that stood in the middle of the warehouse for that very purpose – all valuables went into its narrow slot to be counted and registered later by the accountant, Rottenführer Weber. The case was heavy. The coat was good English tweed, yet I hesitated. Sometimes we misjudged these things and threw a fake into the box and received a good hiding for it. Not from Weber himself – he was too much of a bureaucrat to bother raising his hand to anyone – but from a Kapo, that's for sure. Or from Wolff, which was worse.

The beating for getting caught at loitering – precisely what I was doing right now – was usually much more severe but I still stood like an automaton that had run out of power and stared at the case in my palm with glassy eyes. Rochelle, my work detail mate, gave me a prod with her elbow along with an expressive look.

"Get to it," she hissed but only after ensuring that there were no Kapos around to catch us at chatting. "What is it with you today? Barely out of the grave and testing your luck already?"

There were very few of us, women, who had the luck to survive solely due to Rottenführer Dahler's insistence to include us into his Kanada Kommando. Only fifty, to be exact. His authoritative bearing made some sense to me now, after I had learned that

Dahler was a Kommandoführer in this sorting detail and had his superiors' ear but due to what, no one appeared to know. Some inmates speculated that it was due to Dahler being some big-shot's son; some argued that he merely knew how to butter up Rapportführer Palitzsch with a timely bribe; some insisted that he had some dirt on someone in the administration. Whatever the truth was, no one could tell but what they could tell, with enough certainty, was that Herr Kommandoführer was from Austria, that he was not an unreasonable fellow when he wished to be but also that whenever he blew his lid, making oneself scarce was a wise thing to do, for he was such a beast with his whip that he would put even Rottenführer Wolff to shame.

Aimlessly, I started digging into a new pile, rummaging through the pockets as though in a daze. It was an odd sort of a job, searching for valuables and sorting the clothes of the people who were either already dead or sentenced to work here till they dropped from exhaustion and hunger or one disease or the other. On our second day here, I heard an amused snort from one of the women – she had just found her own skirt among the piles and piles of clothes that littered her sorting station. I hadn't found anything of mine yet, only mountains and mountains of other women's clothes, the women who hadn't been as fortunate as us. Yes, the Kanada detail was an odd sort of place for sure. The hours were much too long and the Kapos didn't encourage talking and therefore all kinds of thoughts would eventually start creeping into the mind, corroding it and tainting it like spilled oil spreading over clear water.

"You, girls, don't even comprehend how lucky you are," one of the inmates of the Kanada Kommando told us quietly on the first day.

Just like the members of the Sonderkommando, Kanada men wore striped trousers and caps but made-to-measure civilian jackets with numbers and different types of triangles on their left breast. They were also always clean-shaven and some even wore shoes shined by the less fortunate inhabitants of the camp, in exchange for a piece of bread – scorned by the Kanada men but considered a veritable feast in other inmates' terms. Still dazed and utterly disoriented by everything around us, we nevertheless had enough wits to quickly realize that the Kanada detail was considered to be some sort of elite in the camp's complex hierarchy and the inmates belonging to it, were looked at with reverence and incomparable respect; whenever one needed to procure anything, it was the members of the Kanada Kommando that they bribed – for warm shoes, for underwear, for the much-needed toothbrush – anything really that could make an inmate's life more bearable.

We, the first women, were issued striped dresses after undergoing the disinfection process and, much to our delight were allowed to keep our hair that was unmercifully treated with chemicals and was now covered by the dark-blue kerchiefs. To the Kanada men, we were still some sort of curiosity, something new and amusing, for there were no women at all in Auschwitz before and therefore they didn't demean us as much as they did with the new, wide-eyed male arrivals but instead took a certain pleasure in instructing us on the camp's system of rules and regulations, both official and unofficial.

"We may be sorting dead people's clothing," he continued in the same soft voice, "but at least we have a roof overhead, the possibility to procure food and whatnot, and, what's more important, we aren't made to hurl rocks from one pile to another all day just to hurl them all back into the first pile the following day. Now, what's with the surprised faces?" He smirked. "Never heard of the SS amusing themselves in this manner? *Arbeit macht frei* and all that rot. They'll make you hurl rocks, in a second, just to occupy your hands with something if they don't have an actual task for you that day. So, yes, you're very lucky girls. Be grateful. This is the most kosher work detail in the entire camp. Inmates fight to get into it. You haven't seen yet what it's like for the others," he finished, on an ominous note.

To speak the truth, we did fare much better in the Kanada than other inmates. When the Kapos looked the other way (or stuffed their own pockets with goods), we pulled whatever edible items we could find and ate them right there or concealed them in our mess tins that dangled from our belts to eat them later or exchange them for cigarettes or medicine or even alcohol. I'd found a half-eaten bar of Swiss chocolate earlier that morning. With a faint smile on my face and my mouth pooling with saliva at the mere thought of it sitting snuggly in my pocket, I dreamed of the evening when I'd eat it after dinner – a piece of sawdust bread and a smear of margarine on the palm. What a dessert it would make! I could almost taste its bitter-sweetness on my tongue.

"Achtung!"

Instinctively, I dropped the trousers that I was searching, at the hoarse voice of our Kapo and froze at attention. Someone with an inspection. Someone from the SS and it wasn't Weber, the accountant. He was in his office; I could hear the keys of his typewriter from here.

"Back to work."

I recognized the voice that had given the command behind my back. My savior. Rottenführer Dahler.

Out of the corner of my eye, I watched him stroll among the rows and rows of tables on which the mountains of clothes were rising – the Alps of Auschwitz. I saw a man pull his head inside his shoulders as Rottenführer Dahler passed him by; Herr Kommandoführer must have administered him a veritable thrashing, at some stage, for whatever he'd done and here, we had a dogs' memory for such things. With his gloved hand, Dahler pulled an overcoat out of the pile, inspected it without much interest and threw it back. Moved closer to my station; fingered at the box with piles of books and documents in it before throwing a sidelong glance in my direction.

Pretending to be unbothered by his attention, I shoved my hand inside yet another pocket and fished out a handkerchief with the initial's SM in its corner. Another pocket produced a pack of American Camels. Dahler looked at it with apparent interest. I considered throwing it into the respective box for a moment but then caught his eyes on me again and tentatively outstretched my arm, with the pack in it, in his direction.

From Dahler, an uncertain, wavering grin. He was quiet for a few seconds.

"Not allowed," he said at last. "But thank you nevertheless."

I barely suppressed an indifferent shrug and threw the pack where it belonged.

He loitered nearby even though now I ignored him entirely. Cleared his throat once, twice; sighed, somewhat irritably.

"Anything… special, today?" he finally asked.

I regarded him for some time, working things out in my mind. Special? I found a porcelain doll with a part of its head broken among someone's belongings and it reminded me of my first day in the Kanada. We had just had our armpit and pubic hair shaved; were still sore and humiliated after the SS doctors' personal search for valuables – in the most intimate places, of course, where else – doused with a solution of calcium chloride that made our eyes burn so viciously it was impossible to open them for a few minutes. Along the narrow, barbed-wire-encased passage, we were being marched to our new work detail in our newly issued uniforms. Towards us, a column of women, the ones to which we had belonged just a day ago, was trudging in a different direction, in their wrinkled, dirty clothes, with haggard, pale faces lined with tear stains and resignation – a truly pitiful sight that made one's heart bleed. The longing glances they threw our way made us turn away in shame.

Suddenly, a baby began wailing, most certainly unfed and unchanged ever since their arrival; ever since the baby's mother had boarded that cursed transport, most likely. The baby wailed and wailed and one of the guards, escorting the column, must have been nursing a hangover or was just in a bad mood, not for any particular reason but just on general grounds; who knew what the issue was, with him. We only caught a brief glimpse of him tearing the screaming infant from his mother, swinging him wildly by the legs and bashing his head, with savage force, on the cabin of a truck that was parked nearby. The entire camp must have heard the sickening crunch.

The doll that I found today looked just like the child after the guard had dropped him on the ground; only the doll's head was empty inside.

However, I didn't think that this story would qualify as the something *special* that Rottenführer Dahler had in mind.

I pulled the cigarette case that had caused me such confusion from under the pile of coats and demonstrated it to him. "This thing, I suppose. I wasn't sure if it's gold or not, Herr Rottenführer. It's heavy enough but—"

I came to an abrupt halt as soon as his gloved fingers touched mine as he took the case from me. They lingered on top of mine longer than necessary and I barely restrained myself from yanking my hand away.

Dahler inspected it thoroughly, opened it to examine its dark-brown suede lining, grinned at the sight of a few cigarettes still left inside and quickly emptied the case's contents into his own pack.

"Loose ones are allowed," he explained, as if I'd go and report him to the camp Kommandant for taking a few smokes from the Reich. "Silver, most likely, with golden coating," he announced his verdict. "You can put it into the box. Weber will sort it out later."

"Thank you, Herr Kommandoführer. I would hate to cause any confusion for Rottenführer Weber."

He nodded but didn't take his leave. In his presence, under his curious gaze, I suddenly felt even worse than before, like an animal that had been put in an enclosure in a zoo and was now gawked at by the visitors; a humiliated slave who would end its days in captivity after getting its personal freedom violated on a daily basis.

I took such great pleasure in visiting the zoo when I was a child but now, the mere thought of it was loathsome.

"Have you found any food items today?"

For an instant, cold terror seized me. There it was, the reason for all this idle talking. I should have known, should have sensed the carefully and cruelly constructed ruse. The SS guards never exchanged pleasantries with the inmates. He must have seen me pocket that half-eaten chocolate bar earlier that morning and was toying with me this entire time; made me drop my guard and now he would administer his punishment. Feeling the blood draining from my face, I wondered if he was planning on merely beating me or sending me to the gas along with the next group. The chimney of the crematorium had long been fixed and worked on an industrial basis, day to day, non-stop operation. Surely, he'd find a spot to squeeze me in for the next scheduled *Aktion*. I was almost relieved at the thought – at least, this would end. I'd be alone, forever left in peace and quiet.

"Half of a bar of Swiss chocolate, Herr Rottenführer," I replied without much emotion.

I was resigned to my fate. I was ready for him to free me. Smiling, I extracted the bar from my pocket and demonstrated it to him. Somewhere, behind my shoulder, someone gasped barely audibly. They all thought he'd slaughter me properly now and they were not wrong.

"You kept it?" Before I had a chance to answer, he suddenly broke into another smile. "Good. You can keep whatever half-eaten items you find. The Reich has no need for those."

With that, he calmly set off, whistling a tune. Around me, stunned silence lay.

After a pause, Rochelle found her voice. "Did he mean us all?"

The Kapo administered her a hard blow on her shoulder, "for asking stupid questions."

*

It was still early morning, about six, I think. Across the camp, caught between the barracks, a wet April wind was howling, in search of an escape. The electrical current hummed softly in the wires. We stood still for our morning *Appell* – the roll call. It was ordinarily a long affair on its own but today our sufferings were prolonged even further for our Blockälteste and Blockschreiberin couldn't get their numbers right.

Wet snow melted on my cheeks. It didn't melt on the cheeks of the woman who my bunkmate Esther and I held by her arms. She had died during the night – between us – and now we had to hold her until the *Appell* was over and only then would we be allowed to throw her into the "dead" pile, for the corpse carriers to take later to the crematorium. I silently thanked God that the sparrow-like thing wasn't heavy. Just cold. Like snow. Like snow, she'd disappear soon, only into the sky.

Rottenführer Wolff was growing annoyed with Blockälteste Irma, who kept nervously checking her lists. She was appointed as our block elder solely because her father was a *Volksdeutsche* and that, in turn, appeared to qualify her to wear a red armband with a white label and a block number on it – a sign of superiority over the rest of us, full Jews. I saw her pull that armband upward in anguish, as she, for the first time, must have cursed her fate as the bearer of such a responsibility.

That morning, Irma couldn't seem to place three of the women. They were not among the dead the others were holding; neither did they shout their usual "Present" as she read their numbers from the list. Wolff threw his third cigarette down and stomped on it in irritation. To be sure, it was some sort of a bureaucratic mistake; they couldn't have possibly escaped. There was no place to run from here. We were surrounded by miles of electrified barbed-wire and hundreds of dogs and men with their rifles and steel-capped boots that hurt so much when they connected with one's ribs. The only escape from here was death or madness and I wondered, with cool indifference, which one would claim me first.

Esther, the sad-looking woman with empty, invariably downcast eyes, had already succumbed to this collective Auschwitz madness. Not too long after our arrival, she began whispering to herself long into the night as she stared with her unseeing eyes into the bunk above us, talking to people whom only she could see. I hadn't muttered anything to anyone yet but sometimes, I lapsed into some inexplicable outwardly abstraction while at work or in line for the turnip soup and only a fellow inmate's nudge or a Kapos baton would bring me back to this hateful reality.

Many of us, new arrivals, walked around in a dream-like state, although, a nightmare would be a better word to describe this place. It was our common belief that we had arrived at a place, which one could only leave through the chimney; where every man was for himself and where one couldn't count on such a thing as human sympathy. On the contrary, the weakness of the spirit, just like the weakness of the body was mocked and jeered at by both the ones bearing power and the old-timers, who had only survived because they had turned off everything human in themselves.

Auschwitz was the world where the question, "what happened to my brother and father?" was met with sadistic, in its cruelty, laughter and a Kapos crude response, "they both are coughing; you see, they swallowed a bit too much gas." Auschwitz was a world where death was such a common occurrence that it had transcended, as grotesquely wrong as that may sound, into something ordinary and plain, something expected and unavoidable. Human suffering lost all meaning in this place. Each had their own survival to worry about to be able to consider being charitable to others and that was the reason why Irma was already twisting her baton in her hand, the half-Jew ready to pounce on us, full Jews. If she didn't come up with the missing women, she'd be getting twenty-five lashes on her buttocks and thighs in front of us all as a punishment and Rottenführer Wolff's hand was infamously heavy.

Rottenführer Weber was brought from his warm accountant's quarters to resolve the issue. It appeared the three missing women had been reassigned to one of the SS doctors' infirmary duty and Irma simply forgot to strike them down from her list. Shamefaced in front of the SS, whose favor she was hell-bent on earning, Irma dismissed us quickly and rehabilitated herself by administering a magisterial thrashing to our Blockschreiberin Vera, "whose sole responsibility was to remind Irma of the inmates' transfer." Naturally, the block clerk knew nothing of the transfer order but took both the verbal abuse and the following beating with calm resignation. Wolff muttered *"stupid bitches"* under his breath and stalked off. Because of their mistake, his entire overcoat was wet with snow, he was cold and hungry, and therefore mightily displeased on account of all this.

We dropped our load into the pile of already stiffened bodies and headed to our work detail. Esther was whispering something again. I touched my mouth to ensure that I still was not muttering anything. It wasn't like she noticed it until I told her that she was doing it again. But no, my lips were pursed shut. I was not mad yet, or so I thought…

*

Dahler was here again. I hid behind the pile of coats as he made his rounds, on his long legs, as though searching for something. Or *someone*. I suppressed the desire to duck and hurl all of these sheepskins and furs and raincoats on top of myself, to bury myself forever, as I did with my sister when we played hide and seek. My favorite hiding place was the laundry bin and not once had she found me there. Would he find me if I did so here? Of course he would. They always found us and dragged us out of our hiding places – wasn't that how we all ended up here?

At last, he discovered me in my corner. With a bright grin on his young, clean-shaven face, he made his way to me, this time with purpose, without pretense.

"You changed your regular station," he stated the obvious.

"I was assigned to this one by the Kapo," I lied.

He nodded and surveyed the pile in front of me. The Auschwitz Alps were even higher today – the new transport had just arrived this morning. For some time, he just stood there watching me work.

"Have you…" he began, without looking at me and examining a sleeve on a camel-wool coat, sticking out of the pile, instead. "How do you like it here, in the Kanada?"

I shot him a sharp glare before quickly remembering myself and lowering my eyes. One had to be quite barmy to antagonize the man who was the very reason we hadn't gone up in the chimney. "You have the best work detail in the camp, Herr Rottenführer," I replied carefully before throwing a leather jacket, with a silk lining, into its respective pile. In just a few days, it would be disinfected and shipped to Germany and some Herr Schmitt would be proudly strutting around in it, with his wife on his arm, also clad in a coat stolen from some other murdered Jew. "I don't think I had the chance to thank you for assigning us all to it. We are all very grateful."

My words appeared to have pleased him immensely. He was practically glowing now.

"It was my pleasure. I asked the doctors specifically not to shave your heads during the disinfection, too." He was looking at my head, covered by the blue kerchief. "You have such beautiful hair. It would have been a shame to cut it off. I'm glad they listened to my reasoning. It cost me, of course," he added in a conspiratorial whisper and gave a burst of somewhat nervous laughter before assuming a serious air again. "The workers under my charge don't really interact with the rest of the camp's inmates and the living conditions are much better here, so they don't suffer from lice. I did, however, promise it to the doctors that I'd keep it that way.

Just like the men, you'll have some time after lunch every day to check your clothes and hair for lice. I want to keep the work detail clean. We don't want any typhus epidemics here, do we?"

"Of course not, Herr Rottenführer. Thank you for looking out for us."

He inched closer. We stood a while, much too near to each other. Whenever I moved, the hem of his woolen overcoat brushed the bare skin on my leg. In the uncertain light of the overhead lamps, his face appeared solemn and pensive.

"I don't want anything to happen to you."

He said it very softly, so only I could hear it. Before I knew it, he pressed something into my hand, squeezed my fingers one last time and quickly left without saying another word. Only after he was out of the work detail did I unclench my fist. In it, a small note sat. My entire body began to tremble when I read what it said.

I fell in love with you.

I re-read it once, twice, still not believing the audacity of it. It all surged up in me again – the anger, the resentment, the powerless, maddening ire. How dare he? In this cemetery where we dug our own graves daily, to give it to a Jew he'd watch go up in smoke one day? He was in charge of the work detail that sorted dead people's belongings daily. How dare he even utter the word *love* in this place? How dare he imply that he could feel anything?

I asked the Kapo for permission to be excused to the latrine. She measured me icily but waved me off nevertheless. Briskly, with my nerves strained to the utmost, I made my way to the facility.

It was a joint affair, with rows of holes on two sides, an overpowering stench and a guard who monitored the time we spent inside, men and women together. Two male inmates were sitting with their backs to me. I quickly tore the note apart and dropped it where it belonged, into the hole. If only I could tear apart and throw the memory of it in the same manner.

Love.

Chapter 4

Helena

The morning chill of the unheated barracks woke us up before the block elder Irma's usual shouts. In the second half of April, the camp administration thought it to be wasteful to use the stoves at night but compensated us by shoving more people into our barracks. *Body heat,* Rottenführer Wolff later explained, with owl-like wisdom about him and left us to freeze in the mornings, when the temperatures plummeted below zero and we shivered next to each other on top of our bunks despite the stolen Kanada sweaters, for which we had already gotten a truncheon across the ribs. However, the bruised sides hardly concerned anyone as long as they allowed us to keep the goods. In this cold, it was all that mattered.

Today was Sunday, a day off of sorts. It only meant that we weren't sent to work details but could spend the day cleaning our barracks and around them instead. The breakfast was served late and cold. Stolen newspapers wrapped around our soles to provide at least some insulation from the icy floor, we were patiently shifting from one foot to another while waiting for Blockälteste Irma to distribute the brooms. A new woman – a still unfamiliar face – bumped into me without noticing it. She was too consumed by trying to reach, with her finger, the residue that was left in her mess tin of our "breakfast" – a splash of lukewarm ersatz coffee. I looked at her distressed face.

"What part of Slovakia are you from?" I asked her in my native language.

As though woken up from a trance by my question, she looked up and offered me a wavering smile before shaking her head.

"Czech?" I tried again, this time in German – the camp's official language.

"Polish, from here," she replied, her features twisting into a tearful grimace. It was a common disease of the new arrivals, this extreme, overwhelming homesickness. The mere mention of one's hometown's name was enough to send one howling in tears.

I nodded solemnly. So, they'd begun transporting Polish women here as well now. The tapestry of nations was enriching the multinational KZ each month, it appeared. If I paid more attention to the text of the newspapers that I was shoving into my half-boots when the Kapo wasn't watching, I would have put two and two together sooner than that. But the camp has long taught us new priorities. Warmth came before information and besides, reading was strictly prohibited by the camp rules. I didn't fancy twenty days in the bunker for trying to figure out how the war was going for the Germans. The question of who was winning was clear enough from the sheer number of transports that kept pulling up to the ramp and the growing mountains of personal belongings that would take us years to sort out.

Around me, women began to mutter. They were looking forward to sweeping, eagerness written all over their pinched, blue-lipped faces. I blew onto my cupped hands as well and saw a cloud of vapor forming around them. We all wished for Irma to hurry up with those brooms. Brooms meant sweeping, sweeping meant warmth and we had already grown cold after an offering of coffee that did nothing to provide nourishment or energy but only made one's stomach churn with hunger.

However, they changed their routine this time, it seemed. Irma arrived with stacks of cards and a fistful of pencils, which she set to distribute in the same business-like manner ordinarily reserved for the Sunday brooms. Mystified, we regarded them for some time, turning them this way and that in our hands. One side was lined and there was a place for a stamp. Another one depicted a beautiful landscape with cheerful farmers working the land. *Waldsee,* the gothic letters announced, not Auschwitz.

"Write to your families," Irma instructed us as she stalked across the barracks in her new, tall boots.

Rumor had it that she'd finally wormed her way into one of the SS men's graces despite her doubtful racial status and was now enjoying the full privileges of such a position. Her entire countenance now reflected it; she carried herself almost like one of the new SS female wardens who had begun to arrive from Ravensbrück recently. We had only seen them from afar; the sharp-dressed, stone-faced creatures that strutted around with an air of utter disdain surrounding them. Strangely enough, we were spared from falling under their jurisdiction. Rottenführer Wolff, who wouldn't stop leering at them, was even generous enough to explain it to us that they were here to oversee the outside working details, the women's camp that was being constructed in Birkenau. *The Kanada women were his,* he added with a dirty wink in our direction. It still puzzled me, how exactly he benefitted from having such a female harem under his charge – it's not like he would have ever touched us, *the dirty Jewesses,* but apparently, it somehow made him feel better about himself. Not that we complained; our SS supervisors were at least a familiar evil. The SS wardens, we heard, whipped just about anyone who looked at them the wrong way. We only got beaten for a good reason, in the SS men's eyes, that is.

"Write the following," Irma continued. "*Dear such and such, we're all well and doing fine here at Waldsee. The work is not hard and the food is plentiful. Come see us soon. Yours –* your name here."

A few heads shot up as if to ensure that we hadn't misheard her. Suddenly, we couldn't get our breath. Cold horror crept over us and it was even worse than the April chill that hung over the barracks like a permanent mist. Anxious and ashen with fear, we exchanged uncomprehending glances. *To write something of this sort to our own flesh and blood!* Our senses may have been dulled by hunger and exhaustion but we still had our wits about us to see through the charade well enough. *To lure them into this hell pretending to be one of the tanned, smiling women waving from the golden field, in which we were supposedly working.* They even drew a German soldier next to this travesty, his face almost swimming in kindness. Sure enough, he lacked the whip attached to his hip. Nor did the artist draw a gun on the German's belt. Postcard Germans didn't shoot anyone. They were there merely to supervise. *We were all friends here, after all. You really ought to come to see it for yourselves.*

The same frantic fear that was painted on mine was reflected on my fellow inmates' gaunt faces. Cautiously, one of the women raised her hand with a stub of a pencil in it.

"Blockälteste Irma, allow me to report, please. I have not anyone left at home."

"Write to your friends then. To your neighbors, to your rabbi, for all I care!" Irma waved away her objection with an incredible nonchalance about her. "Everyone must submit their postcards."

How fast she had forgotten her Jewish half, firmly concentrating on the *Volksdeutsche* one! I quickly bit my lip, averting my eyes from her beautifully styled hair. Who was I to judge her? After all, wasn't she only trying to survive, like most of us? Surely, there were other ways to go about it, ways that didn't involve turning on her own fellow inmates, for one, but that's what the slightest hint of power did to people in this place and Irma was, so far, the least corrupted by it from what I saw. At least, she wasn't openly bullying anyone and neither did she try to set the inmates against each other – a pastime, with which some Kapos and block elders entertained themselves. The truth was, Auschwitz was a nightmare but at least Irma didn't make this nightmare worse for us.

She regarded us, the pitiful lot, and suddenly a fleeting ghost of sympathy softened her features.

"If you arrived here with someone and they—" She wetted her lips with a nervous glance toward the door. "You can write to your friends or family *who aren't here anymore.*"

She said the words without saying anything openly. Hope once again ignited in our frozen hearts. Smiling and overwhelmed with gratitude, we set to writing, the diligent little pupils. I arrived alone, without my family but I did have a friend with me on that train and so, I would write to her – the woman *who wasn't here anymore.*

"Dear Cylka." My hand was not steady and the words came out unsure, wavering. We weren't used to writing anymore, only to working and dying.

I summoned her spirit out of the depths of my memory. *Here she is, laughing with her beautiful voice as we head home from school. We are fifteen and two boys follow us, precisely five steps behind. They had just begun doing it a few days ago and the situation still amuses Cylka immensely. They never talk to us, only among themselves, quietly and shyly and the only communication that we get from them is "Goodbye now! Till tomorrow," before we disappear into our tenement apartment house. A year later, one of them will get enough courage to kiss me on the cheek and I would lie without sleep countless nights, imagining that I'm in love with him.*

"… we are all well and doing fine here at Waldsee."

Here she is, in her wedding dress, hugging me tightly as her beautiful eyes are brimming with tears. "Next year, I'll be dancing at your wedding," she says and kisses me on both cheeks. But the next year the war starts and my family sends me to live with our gentile friends. It's easier for me to pass as one of their daughters; unlike Cylka or my older sister Różínka, I'm still unmarried and have no children. They hide my passport and procure false documents for me, for which my father pays unthinkable money to some crook. This buys me a couple of years of freedom.

"The work is not hard and the food is plentiful."

Here she is, rocking her youngest child at the train station as we wait for the transport, guarded by the German soldiers. The cattle car arrives. Inside, there's a single bucket with water. We are told to use it to relieve ourselves after we drink all the water. We haven't seen Auschwitz yet and its communal latrines; we haven't been stripped naked and forced to stand with our legs wide open while an unfamiliar man's hands shave off our pubic hair. We still have our dignity and modesty; we're shy and are trying to hold on for as long as it's possible. Only when one can't stand this torture any longer does she work her way into the "bucket corner" and mutters her "excuse me, please," while another woman is holding a coat in front of her to allow her at least some privacy. The bucket soon begins to overflow and the refuse splashes all around it emanating the most revolting stench but the guards, who travel with us, wouldn't let us empty it, despite all the screams and pleas that it's impossible to breathe inside.

"Come see us soon."

Here she is, still rocking her child, who has died from hypothermia on the train, as she stands on the camp's ramp. An officer walks on it flanked by two oddly-dressed men and we can't help but gawk at him as though hypnotized. His uniform is regal and immaculate and tailored to fit him to stunning perfection. His hand in a leather glove grabs my chin and not hers and he turns to lead me away after himself, leaving Cylka and her dead child along with the rest of the women. Rottenführer Wolff.

"Forever yours, Helena."

I wrote the address. My hand was firm now. They didn't assign the numbers to the ones who were sent to the gas upon arrival and therefore, they would never know that my Cylka was dead. Over my shoulder, Irma grunted her approval before taking my card.

*

Dinner time. I looked at my palm with a miserable smear of margarine on it, at a piece of bread in my other hand and began licking the margarine absentmindedly as I chewed the bread as slowly as possible. Dinner was the most nourishing meal of the day. In the morning, we only got a splash of ersatz coffee and for lunch – the so-called turnip soup. I had learned by now to stand in the middle of the line when they distributed it from two tremendous cauldrons. If one lined up for it too soon, they only got water from the top, into their mess tin. If one was at the end of the line, there was a chance that nothing would be left at all and they'd go hungry till the evening. But the lucky ones in the middle could count on getting a piece of a carrot or an onion, in addition to the vegetable broth – a veritable feast! However, all of these miserable meals only teased our appetite. They never satisfied it.

My stomach was still rumbling when I clambered onto the bunk to lie next to two sisters, Anna and Katarina. They were also from the former Czechoslovakia, only the Czech part of it, the new arrivals. Anna's nails were still painted. I kept staring at them with greedy fascination the entire time during the dinner – a piece of a long-lost life. Katarina was constantly crying; an SS doctor defiled her during the mandatory "search for valuables" upon arrival *and now Jozef surely wouldn't marry her. Who would want an impure bride? How would she explain herself?*

The same SS doctor also shoved his fingers, in a rubber glove, inside me on my first day, only unlike her I knew better than to hope for making it out of here alive. *Who cares if I'm technically speaking not a virgin any longer? Certainly not I.* But I didn't tell her that, just turned to her for a fleeting instant and enclosed a biscuit, which I had found among someone's belongings in the Kanada today, into her hand. She hiccupped in surprise and broke into more tears, thanking me profusely. I felt sorry for her. She was being transferred to the outdoors detail from what I'd heard. I was saving the biscuit for myself for later but she needed it more than I did. Everyone around knew what an outdoors Kommando meant for an inmate's life expectancy – two months, if one was lucky not to catch malaria or typhus or get on one of the supervisors' wrong sides.

They talked to each other softly, the usual sister talk. Rόžίnka and I used to chat the same way, lying next to each other in our bed. I missed my sister dearly after she'd gotten married and moved away and now, I missed her even more so because from time to time and on Sundays in particular, it got so unbearably lonely here in the evenings that one wanted to howl, like a wolf, at the moon. How was it possible to suffer from solitude in such an overcrowded place? Very simple – when one had nobody at all, not a soul to talk to, not a familiar face to look at, not a friendly smile to see one through the day. People died much too fast here and therefore, making friends was a dangerous affair.

Rottenführer Dahler's face suddenly appeared before my eyes. He was one of the few people who smiled at me here. I shut my eyes tightly and willed myself to sleep. I'd rather see grim faces around me than his smile. I'd rather die than smile back at him.

Chapter 5

Helena

Another week passed by. Auschwitz Alps were threatening to overflow. The trucks, often as many as twenty, arrived daily from the ramp, to which new transports crept up carrying their human cargo. The transport Kommando only shrugged apologetically when we began moaning at the sight of yet another truck, belching its contents at our feet. If it continued in the same manner, we'd soon drown in all these clothes.

A day ago, Camp Kommandant Höss arrived in his staff car to inspect our work detail. Waded around, as though through a great sea, poking and prodding at the mountains of clothes, with his whip; shook his head disapprovingly at the SS men and particularly at Rottenführer Dahler – Kanada Kommandoführer – who followed him close on his heels and demanded for the additional warehouses to be built and for a night Kommando to be added, at once, to a day one. It had rained the day before and all of the clothes that had been left outside, for there was not a chance to fit them all into the warehouse, now lay around its walls in pitiful, wet heaps, emanating the faint smell of sweat and damp cotton. Such wastefulness, as the clothes were meant for the Aryan folk, after all, must have caused Kommandant Höss even greater frustration.

After throwing his last, "sort out this mess! All leaves are canceled until you do," at the officers, he stalked off along with Schutzhaftlagerführer Aumeier. Not too far from me, a Kapo pulled his head into his shoulders. A tense silence hung over the warehouse, along with a forming fog. Rottenführer Wolff's hard breathing could be heard even by us, who cowered in our neat lines of five behind the male part of the Kommando. The Kommandant took his dissatisfaction out on the SS men, reprimanding them for the mess; they, in their turn, would take it out on the Kapos using their whips this time. After that, our turn would come and the Kapos didn't have a habit of sparing the ones who got them into trouble with the SS. In the end, it was always our fault. We failed to produce the quota. We were lazy and didn't work hard enough. The very impossibility of such a task to be completed, even if we worked night and day without breaks, didn't seem to cross anyone's mind in this chain of command.

I clenched my fists and mentally prepared myself for a rubber truncheon beating.

As it was expected, it was Wolff who exploded first as soon as Kommandant Höss's car was out of the gates.

"You brainless swine!" He whipped around, already brandishing his horsewhip. "I ought to knock your fucking heads off, right about now!" The first blow landed on the nearest Kapo's shoulder. The Kapo fell down at once, covering his head with his hands, as Wolff pummeled him mercilessly. "Lazy scum! You think you're here on a vacation of some sort?! I'll show you how to work, you filthy lot!"

Just as Dahler turned around to face our Kapo, Maria, she quickly put two and two together and began working her rubber truncheon on us before he would put his horsewhip to work on her. *Better skin off our backs than hers,* she reasoned. Not that it wasn't understandable.

For the next fifteen minutes, the SS were taking their frustration, for the canceled leave, on the Kapos and the Kapos showered us with blows in return. In this competition for the best disciplinarian, Dahler's eyes caught mine as I, after receiving my prescribed beating from Maria, was inspecting my aching ribs gingerly in the hope that she hadn't cracked any of them in her zeal. His hand, with the horsewhip in it, froze midair above the back of some unfortunate man – I couldn't quite make out who it was, for Maria whacked me on my temple and quite hard at that – before he lowered it slowly. I turned away. *By all means, don't stop on my account, Herr Rottenführer. I know you're annoyed with your canceled leave and we, the Jews, deserved it, the lazy scum that we are.*

Moving slowly, I staggered toward my working station and began sorting the clothes without waiting for the Kapo's order. My ears were still ringing from Maria's truncheon. From the corner of my eye, I saw Dahler making a hesitant step in my direction. I turned my back completely on him. I never thought I could hate someone so much in my entire life. I didn't even hate Maria for the thrashing she had just administered to us. At least, she was honest about it. Him, I couldn't even look at. My entire body was trembling with that hatred. It was coursing through my veins, turning blood into acid. If I had a gun in my hands at that moment, I would have shot him without a second thought.

*

Canceled leaves must have been some powerful incentive for our supervisors. After a month only, new additional warehouses had been erected for our Kanada work detail. Inside, new offices for the SS had been installed – Kommandant Höss's special order:

"Whenever I or any of my deputies come here, I want to see you either supervising your workers or doing the administrative job in your own office. Whoever is found missing from his post without a superior officer's permission will be transferred someplace where they will put you to work, if you don't appreciate your current employment. The Eastern Front, for one example."

Now the SS was always on top of us, walking around, tapping the hands that didn't work fast enough for their liking, with the tips of their horsewhips; shouting insults and dealing blows for a misplaced item or for money discovered in the pocket of a jacket that had already been thrown into the "disinfection" pile.

Rottenführer Dahler avoided me the entire time, much to my relief. Soon, however, he began inching closer again, trying his best to catch my eye, purposely walking nearby, giving directions to everyone around, in a voice that was suddenly almost pleasant, with the quality of a request in it, rather than an order. The theatrics were nearly amusing. I could almost believe him, had he not shown his true colors during that inspection day a month ago.

The more he was trying to get my attention, the more I ignored him. At last, he lost his patience. The Kapo delivered his order for me to report to his office, a smirk crossing her face. She was *Reichsdeutsche,* our Maria, blonde and evil like a witch and lacked whatever sympathy our block elder Irma was kind enough to show us. They had just recently begun appointing them, the German women with the black triangles of anti-socials – prostitutes, that is – as our Kapos and most of them took the greatest pleasure in humiliating us as much as possible with the new order of things. We had long grown used to such an unjust hierarchy, where a German prostitute was valued much higher than a Polish physician and where a green triangle of an Aryan criminal held more power than the red one of the political-prisoner, of the same race. We, the Jews, were at the bottom of the food chain. Our lives were not worth anything at all. We were disposable and they made sure to remind us of it daily, Maria sometimes hourly, if not with a blow then with a demeaning, ugly word, that's for sure.

In front of Rottenführer Dahler's door, I wiped my palms over my skirt before knocking. They were suddenly wet with sweat. After receiving his permission to enter, I stepped inside.

Dahler was sitting at his desk, smiling brightly, a typewriter in front of him. I regarded him with a stony expression.

"You wished to see me, Herr Rottenführer?"

"I did. Close the door and sit down, please." He rose from his chair and even went to the pain of moving up a second one for me.

I lowered into it, smoothing my skirt over my knees. Gray ringlets of smoke were rising from a cigarette left in an ashtray. I regarded it closely, thinking that I recognized the design on its crystal surface. It was commandeered from our work detail, no doubt.

"How's the work been?" he inquired, with the same mild grin.

"Even with the second night-shift Kommando, we're still behind schedule," I replied honestly. Why ask me? He spent his days here. Certainly, he could see for himself that the trucks with new items arrived faster than we could sort out the old piles. "The transports arrive daily. We simply can't cope—"

"Yes, yes, I know." He waved me off impatiently. "They're building a second camp – Birkenau – as of now, where the second Kanada is going to be. Don't fret, after a few months, we'll all be doing just fine."

"If you didn't gas all of those people, you would have more workers for the detail," I mumbled under my breath before realizing that, perhaps, it was an utterly moronic thing to do, to push one's luck with an SS man.

Indeed, a scowl replaced his previously bright expression.

"I don't gas anyone," he retorted, with ice in his voice.

"I meant you, the SS, in general, Herr Rottenführer. I apologize for the misunderstanding."

He rubbed his forehead irritably. The conversation wasn't going according to his plan, it seemed.

"I know that you're overwhelmed with work there," he began again, almost forcing himself to sound more conciliatory. They didn't make it a habit of being friendly with us; it was an acquired skill, for any SS man, to be nice to a Jew and Dahler was, so far, a slow student. "That's the reason why I called you here. I imagine you could use some respite from all that sorting business?" He slightly inclined his head to one side.

I merely looked at him, still unmoved and unsmiling.

"I want you to do my nails."

I thought I misheard him for one instant. He had to repeat his request for a second time. He thought I didn't understand his language. No! I simply couldn't believe his audacity.

"Yes, my nails. Sit here with me and file my nails so that I can look at you for a few minutes."

He broke into a beautiful, boyish smile again, seemingly delighted with his own proposition. With my face as hard as marble, I rose from my chair slowly.

"Absolutely not."

His smile faltered but didn't altogether drop. He didn't seem to comprehend that a Jew had just refused him something. "I beg your pardon?"

"I said, absolutely not," I repeated, trembling with my entire body. "Did you know that you beat that man from our detail so badly after Herr Kommandant's inspection that Rottenführer Wolff had to put him out of his misery later that day with a mercy shot to the head? You're both murderers and I'll die before I touch those hands of yours. Don't bring me into this room ever again. No manicures, no nothing. I don't do manicures. And now, if you'll excuse me, I must go back to my work detail."

The legs of the chair scraped sharply on the floor. He was suddenly on his feet, furious.

"No, I don't excuse you! Sit back into that chair right this instant! I haven't dismissed you yet!"

Without turning around, I continued for the door.

"If you walk out of that door, I swear I'll shoot you!" he bellowed.

I stopped. Morbid curiosity got the better of me. Slowly, I turned around. To be sure, he was holding a gun in his hand, aiming at me. In his eyes, I saw it all at once, a man's wounded pride, the certainty of an Aryan man's superiority, indignation, and fury... and fear that I wouldn't obey. I walked up to him once again, oddly calm despite the fact that only his desk separated us and that his gun was still pointing straight at my chest. His hand was steady, the confident hand of a man who was used to pulling the trigger.

"*I fell in love with you,* you wrote to me some time ago, Herr Rottenführer. Only, this is not loving. Love is never forced, only earned. It's given freely, not torn out of someone's heart with threats and blows. You don't know how to love. None of you do. You're all heartless and I'll prove it to you right this moment. I'm walking out because I can't look at you another second. Do what your SS pride tells you to."

With that, I turned on my heels and crossed the room, expecting a shot to ring out any moment now. With a trembling hand, I reached for the door, opened it, and walked out, unmolested. Only when I was back at my assigned place did agony find its way out, streaming from my eyes and falling onto newly delivered trench coats and leather jackets. The spring was raging outside and the new arrivals were dressed lightly.

In the evening, as Rottenführer Dahler was making his last round before dismissing us for the night, he stopped by me and spoke softly above my ear, "You wished to prove me wrong but it will be me who will prove you wrong in the end."

I had difficulty falling asleep that night. For the life of me, I couldn't understand what happened between us that day.

Chapter 6

Helena

Rottenführer Weber, the Kanada accountant, emerged from his office – a rare occasion on its own – just to urge us to work faster. They were getting transports daily now; he was behind schedule with the Reichsbank and "all of those clothes were not going to sort themselves." The Auschwitz Alps were growing and growing and now it wasn't just clothes and shoes and valuables. It was also children's dolls and porcelain dishes and prosthetic limbs. The members of the Sonderkommando brought them here from "the showers" anteroom and dumped them unceremoniously into a pile for us to sort out. Most of us preferred to bribe Maria just to stay out of such a morbid duty.

Some still whispered prayers here. Most, however, had long abandoned their religion. Someone said that Auschwitz was such a terrible place that God himself decided not to go there. To be honest, I couldn't agree more with that statement.

Wolff was making his lazy rounds, yawning. He must have spent his weekend in the nearest town's brothel again. The gossip had it that he had a big interest in that department. The same gossip had it that the Kanada accountant, Weber, scorned the place, preferring the SS chess club, to it. Gossip also had it that out of all three of our supervisors, Dahler was the cruelest one once he blew his lid; *the natural Jew-hater, the man with the horsewhip.* I haven't seen him since the day of our last argument. His office stood closed and empty. I begin entertaining the hope that someone had overheard our conversation, reported it and they'd shipped him off to the Eastern Front.

Wishful thinking, Helena.

There he was, waving off the Kapo, who had us frozen at attention and signing to us to get back to work, without uttering a word. He was oddly pale today; pale and stern and not in the mood for idle chatting, it appeared. He silently pointed at this pile and that and tapped his wristwatch at one of the women, implying that she wasn't working fast enough. Instead of a whip, he held a Thermos in his other hand.

He caught me stealing a sidelong glance at him. I swiftly averted my gaze. He didn't approach me right away, only when my natural turn came, after he'd finished his unhurried round. He began saying something but broke into a vicious coughing fit instead, which didn't stop for a long time. In spite of myself, I made a move toward him. The wheezing noises in his chest were dreadful to listen to. I made a move to slide past him to fetch a doctor but he caught me by the wrist and shook his head negatively while still trying to get his breath. Wolff emerged from his office, undoubtedly summoned by such atrocious coughing and regarded his comrade with visible astonishment.

"Just what are you doing here, you numbskull? You're supposed to be in bed in the sickbay!" He was already pulling on Dahler's hand.

The Kanada Kommandoführer wrung his wrist free out of Wolff's grip and motioned for his comrade to open his Thermos instead. My nostrils twitched at the divine smell of the chicken broth as he took a few careful sips from it.

"I'm fine," he rasped, wiping his mouth with the back of his hand. "I'll walk it off – it's better than in an infirmary." His voice was hoarse and parts of his words were hardly audible.

"I've seen idiots in my life but you certainly take the main prize," Wolff declared incredulously, crossing his arms over his chest.

"Stop berating me in front of my subordinates," Dahler croaked with a grin. The circles under his eyes were as dark as charcoal. "You're undermining my authority."

"Does the doctor know you're here?" Wolff continued his interrogation, utterly unimpressed with Dahler's remark.

Dahler hesitated for a moment. "Yes."

"No, he doesn't."

"I got the chicken broth from the canteen." Another coughing fit. Wolff stepped away and scrunched his face involuntarily. He was quite serious about his health and Dahler was certainly not someone with whom he wished to be associated at the moment. "It'll right me in a jiffy."

"Mhm. Get your fat tail back into the hospital before you make everyone sick."

"I'm telling you I'm—"

"Are you going to get back on your own or would you prefer me reporting you? No one needs your plague here."

"It's fungal pneumonia, not typhoid. It's not contagious." Dahler tried to smile. His eyes, rimmed with red, had an unhealthy gleam to them and I could tell he was running a fever.

"I honestly couldn't care less about your exact diagnosis. Leave." Wolff pointed at the door.

Dahler shifted from one foot to another and threw a quick glance in my direction. Wolff followed his gaze, turned back to his comrade and arched his brow. Dahler tilted his head ever so slightly to one side. Some silent exchange was happening between the two. At last, Wolff heaved a massive sigh and started for his office.

"If you're not gone in five minutes, I'll drag you out of here myself," he threw over his shoulder before shutting the door after himself.

Dahler's chuckles quickly turned into coughing again. He sipped some more of his aromatic broth. I swallowed, in spite of myself, unable to tear my eyes off the Thermos. The broth was the real deal, I could tell; nothing like our miserable "soup."

"How's the work been?" he managed to ask, after all that.

"It's been good. Busier than usual but it's good for you." I kept staring at the Thermos as though hypnotized. All of my thoughts had suddenly turned to my empty stomach. All else had ceased to exist. "More clothes for the people of Germany."

He was about to say something but changed his mind at the last moment. Watching me closely, he put the Thermos onto my sorting table.

"We are happy to be contributing." I had not the faintest idea why I was saying all of these things. All I knew was that the smell of chicken was emanating from the silver container even through the closed lid and I kept swallowing like a dog who's been teased a juicy bone. We desperately hunted for the remnants of dignity still left in us in this place but when one was constantly hungry to such an extent that all other thoughts were consumed only by the desire to find something edible, to do something for a piece of something edible, to steal a morsel of something edible – reflexes transcended all that was left of human pride.

"You're doing a great job," Dahler commented slowly in his halting voice. I was so obsessed with that broth, I didn't hear him at first when he added after a pause and in the softest of whispers, "I missed you, Helena."

I looked up sharply, still confused and unsure whether he really just said it.

"Your hair looks very pretty today," he spoke again, regarding me tenderly.

I caught myself touching the plait that I braided around my head this morning, embarrassed but touched to the marrow. Constantly harassed by the Kapos and guards, we so longed for a bit of comfort, for a single kind word that once it was spoken, it warmed us instantly and made the hell in which we lived a bit more bearable.

"Thank you, Herr Rottenführer." I meant it this time.

"I came out to see you—"

There he was again, coughing even worse than before and struggling to draw in another breath. I reached out to him with my hand – a sheer instinct to help someone who was suffering – and yanked it back at once, remembering myself. Forbidding myself to think of the contents, I began unscrewing the lid of his Thermos.

"You'd better not talk anymore, Herr Rottenführer." *Why did I care if he got even sicker? Let him. Let him die; let them all die.* Yet, I felt sympathy towards him which defied all laws of logic, simply because he had ceased to be *the man with the whip* for one day and had become someone sick, someone, who could barely stand due to the fever, someone who was much weaker than me even and solely because this balance of power had tipped, I was able to feel sorry for him. "You'll make yourself even sicker than you are."

A smile flourished on his deathly pale face. "So kind you are. So considerate."

"Rottenführer Wolff is right. You should go back to the infirmary."

His smile faltered. He regarded me for some time. "Are you afraid to catch it from me? I told you, it's not contagious."

"No, I'm not. I don't want you to harm yourself even more, that's all."

He pondered something for a few moments. At last, he conceded. "Fine. One more day in the cot won't hurt, I suppose." He tried to smile through the tears that still stood in his inflamed eyes after his latest coughing fit. "Walk me back, will you?"

I followed him, stealing a glance in the Kapo's direction. Strangely enough, Maria even favored me with a generous nod. Escorting the sickly SS officer to ensure that he made it safely back and didn't collapse on his way there was certainly an honorable duty in her eyes.

Over the Kanada barracks, hung a lukewarm, pale sun. The wind tossed the treetops indifferently. Rottenführer Dahler shivered against a particularly harsh gust and pulled the collar of his overcoat higher. I clasped my arms around myself, trying to prevent it from seeping under my sweater, thrown on top of my striped dress. For some time, we walked in silence. Just now I noticed that he limped slightly, favoring his right leg. He must have taken great care to conceal it when in perfect health but now, too preoccupied with his sickness, he forgot to put up the appearance of an immaculate Teutonic Knight and suddenly seemed so very human, so convincingly approachable and almost harmless.

We turned around the corner where an empty barrack stood with its door open – to ventilate the premises before the outdoor crews would come back, no doubt. Suddenly, he grabbed me by the elbow and pushed me inside, quickly closing the door after himself. At once, the illusion had shattered into sharp, silver shards. Instantly alarmed, I leaped away from him just to stumble into the brick wall behind my back.

The old Helena in me considered screaming at once. There was only one reason why the guards wished to be alone with young women in this place and I wouldn't think twice to scratch his eyes out before he touched me.

But the new Helena knew better. If I did scream, he'd have all the reason to knock me out cold, do what he came for and shoot me afterward – for an attempted escape or some such. I'd seen such "attempted escape" victims before. I knew how the authorities conducted their affairs here.

I thought of turning away just so as not to have to see his face but then looked him square in the eyes instead, regretting those fleeting few moments during which I felt something remotely close to sympathy for him.

For some time, it was a looking game between us. He didn't move and neither did I. Suddenly, he outstretched his hand, with the Thermos in it, toward me. I regarded it in stupefaction.

"Well, go on. Take it. I saw how you were looking at it," he went on to explain. "I didn't need you walking me back to the sickbay. I made my way back from the battlefield with a shrapnel-shattered knee all by myself." He grinned. So, he'd been to the front then... It was a painful memory, I could tell. "I just thought you might be hungry."

Tentatively, I took the Thermos from him and opened it.

"Wait a second." Dahler quickly extracted a handkerchief from his pocket and wiped the neck of it. "It's not contagious but..."

He didn't finish. He wished it to be clean when I drank from it. For some inexplicable reason, that simple gesture touched me profoundly.

"Thank you, Herr Rottenführer." I barely heard myself as I whispered it.

The Thermos was warm to the touch and the broth itself was pure heavenly manna as I swallowed the first few hungry mouthfuls. *How good it was!* My taste buds exploded from the richness of it. I gulped it greedily and couldn't stop myself even as I tipped it more and more and a frantic realization hit that he'd have nothing left for himself. With an inhuman effort, I tore the Thermos off my lips and licked them to get the last bits of it from the corners of my mouth. I would be licking them for days now, stealing the phantom-like remnants of it from my lips.

"Thank you," I breathed out again. *What a present he gave me!* My lips curled into a grateful smile of their own will. I looked at him almost tenderly.

Dahler shook the Thermos in his hand slightly, splashing the contents inside. "You haven't finished it," he remarked in surprise.

"If I did, there wouldn't be anything left for you. I tried to drink only half. I'm sorry if I drank more than that—"

"What nonsense!" He laughed and coughed and laughed again. "It's all for you. I'll get myself another portion in the canteen. Do you think they don't feed us here?"

My cheeks were burning from the broth, from infinite gratitude, and from the shame – what terrible things I thought were on his mind when he only wished to feed me. I closed my eyes – I couldn't quite face him now – and gulped down whatever was left in the Thermos. He accepted it back, still pale but visibly pleased.

I tried to think of the words to say to him. I had to come up with something better than a miserable, "thank you."

"How can I…" I began and lowered my eyes. It was much more difficult than I thought. I didn't want to offend him or anger him and I had such little idea of what could offend him – my silence or my words. "If I can do something for you… in return…"

He interrupted me at once with a resolute shake of his head. "I don't need anything from you. I gave it to you because you were hungry not because…" He made an annoyed gesture with his hand. "Are you taking the food that you're finding in the Kanada? Are you eating enough?"

I was taking it, it's just that I was giving most of it away.

"Yes, Herr Rottenführer."

He looked at me sternly. He must have suspected that I was lying.

"Franz," he suddenly said quietly.

I looked up at him.

"My name is Franz," he repeated again, coughed into his hand and opened the door outside. "Go back to the barracks. You're dressed much too lightly. We can afford only one sick person at a time."

"Thank you, Herr Rottenführer," I repeated once again, a veritable broken record.

He regarded me with a warm smile. "Already forgotten my name?"

I had just opened my mouth, realized that I could not bring myself to utter it even with the best will in the world and ran past him before he could stop me.

Chapter 7

Helena

In a leather suitcase, with multiple foreign stamps on it – the owner must have been quite a traveler in his time before he took this last trip to the place from which there was no return – I found a newspaper. Throwing a thief's look around, I quickly scanned the headlines. It was in German, the new official language of my former country. It had ceased to be a proud and independent Czechoslovakia, much like we had ceased to be its citizens. The Nazis' knife sliced it in half, into Slovakia and Reich Protectorate respectively, so that the Germans could now "protect" themselves from us, the alien elements. We had to be exterminated to ensure the survival of their superior nation – the official line with which they justified the mass genocide.

From my superficial perusal, nothing good came out. The war was going well for the Germans; production was booming all over Protectorate; the *Hitlerjugend* boys and the SS smiled out from black-and-white photos next to their counterparts from the *Hlinka Guard*. One couldn't even tell them apart from each other any longer, the hateful, uniformed, jackbooted mass. Disappointed, I threw it into the box, the contents of which were to be later taken outside to be burned by one of the Sonderkommando men, Dayen.

I'd never learned whether Dayen was his first name or his last. Dark-haired, painfully thin, with thick glasses and a soft-spoken manner, he never touched whatever goods were possible to procure in the Kanada's riches for *they were not kosher*. All-day long, he stood outside the warehouse and poked the burning pile, muttering softly under his breath. One time, when I carried out yet another box overflowing with diplomas, birth certificates, photographs, Talmuds, and military decorations that their owners would never again proudly display to others, I caught the familiar words of the Kaddish. Some people said he used to be a rabbi in Poland.

Block orderlies brought in the cauldrons with turnip soup. On Maria's signal, we lined up to receive our midday rations. After everyone settled down on the ground to consume them, I gave mine to Olga, a Czech girl who had just arrived with the new transport from the Protectorate and was miraculously spared the fate of her counterparts, most of whom met their end in a gas bunker and later, in a ravine behind it, within hours of their arrival.

As I was observing the Kapos instructing the new inmates brought to our detail earlier that morning, Rottenführer Dahler stopped by the section to which I was assigned that day and straightened out, seemingly proud of himself. His pneumonia was all but gone.

"I delegated your concerns about the lack of manpower to my superiors and they granted permission to allow these able-bodied women to live," he announced. "You were right about gassing each transport upon arrival. It is counterproductive. We need workers for the war effort, not corpses."

I cringed inwardly at his words but forced myself to smile nevertheless. After all, he did, in some respect, help these women escape death. For that, I was grateful to him. "I'm glad your superiors saw reason, Herr Rottenführer."

My words produced the desired effect. He grinned broadly. "You know, if you have any ideas as to… how production can be improved, you can always speak to me. I'm certain that if the ideas are good and implementable, Herr Kommandant will agree to them."

I examined the new workers as they were being directed to their respective workstations by the Kapos. The Kapos were in their element and particularly in the presence of the SS men.

"This is Auschwitz," they announced, full of self-importance and cruel disdain, as they observed the trembling mass of bodies neatly lined up in front of them. "They've sent you here to croak. Anyone who opens his mouth without permission or doesn't keep things in order will leave through the chimney all the sooner."

"Anyone caught stealing, will be sent to the punishment block where you'll make an acquaintance with Political Department leader Grabner's standing cell and later, the Black Wall."

"Anyone caught shirking duty, using the latrine longer than permitted included, will be getting it across the back and prohibited from using the latrine for the rest of the shift." Maria, our women's section Kapo, had a particular aversion for women who used their 'time of the month' excuse to visit the latrine more often than the others. Very few of us still suffered from the monthly ordeal; the stress, malnourishment, and bromide or some other chemical added to the food – or at least such was the rumor – had long ago seen to that. Still, she thought it to be her duty to remind the new women under her charge that they'd better forget any special privileges that came with being a woman. *Women didn't exist here,* according to her. *Only useful workers did and useless eaters.* "I strongly recommend you not to soil yourselves, or you will find yourselves in the outdoor details before you know it, where our delicate noses won't have to put up with your stench."

Next to me, Rottenführer Dahler cleared his throat. I looked up at him, my hand with the silk shirt, still bearing some unfortunate man's initials on its cuffs and the breast pocket, hovering above the sorting table, unsure. *Wrong pile?* I blinked at him, suddenly alarmed.

"Do you," he started again, turning his back completely on the Kapos, "have any such suggestions? I have to go to the Kommandantur with the report to Rapportführer Palitzsch later today. I could delegate them, to him, for his consideration."

I stood, undecided, between the SS man with his own agenda and the women, all so young and helpless and terrified beyond all measure. If he had already saved them from the gas, whatever his reasons for it were, perhaps, it wouldn't hurt to ask him for something else?

It was a strange moment. The Kapos did the talking and he was still patiently waiting.

"Well…" I began and suddenly lost my resolve.

"Go on, I'm listening," he encouraged me, with a quick smile.

"Since there will be more of us living in the same barracks and since you, the officers, that is, work within such close proximity of us, I think it would be beneficial for everyone, to install showers, so we can use them after work, Herr Rottenführer. Overcrowded barracks always produce epidemics of lice and we all know that they carry all sorts of diseases…" I left my thought unfinished, hoping that he would make all the necessary conclusions himself. In our barracks, a rusted faucet provided us with just as rusted water, but it did virtually nothing to keep us clean between the weekly showers. Our skin was covered with a thin film of filth for six days out of seven, our clothes stunk with sweat and it was impossible to breathe at night even in the non-heated barracks. "And if we could get some new dresses perhaps, not these… They're much too rough without any undershirts, like sandpaper—" I quickly remembered myself and dropped my hand that had moved to my tender breasts without my realizing it. We all suffered from painful nipples that all but bled from these uniforms but I didn't imagine it was an appropriate remark to make to an SS man.

I quickly apologized. Dahler only shook his head just as quickly – *oh no, don't be sorry, please* – reddening to the roots of his hair. Just as embarrassed as he was, I apologized again, cursed myself inwardly and began digging into some suit I'd pulled out of the pile just to occupy my hands with something. Since my arrival here, I had long forgotten I was a woman and now, I suddenly remembered it and remembered that I had breasts and that he was a man standing next to me and that he was alone with me just a couple of weeks ago in that barrack and he had told me his name. My hands were trembling.

"You really oughtn't to apologize for anything," he spoke again after a pause. His voice was, too, unsteady. "I didn't realize… I'll try to talk to my superiors."

"Thank you, Herr Rottenführer."

Heavy golden coins began falling onto the sorting table from the torn seam on the shoulder pad. I put away the small scissors that we were allowed to keep for that specific purpose and began collecting them into my palm.

Suddenly, after throwing a quick glance around, he picked up two of the coins out of my palm and dropped them into my pocket.

"Buy yourself something," he whispered to me before adding in a louder voice, clearly meant for the rest of the inmates' and the Kapos' ears, "well, go on. Put it where it belongs. You don't need to count these coins, that's Weber's responsibility. Loitering on the job…"

I felt his hand, with which he'd nudged me, ever so slightly, toward the box with valuables, in the small of my back, long after he was gone.

One coin, I decided to keep. For the second one, I bought myself two triangles of cheese, a piece of sausage, and a poppy-seed cake, from the Sonderkommando men, who gladly traded with us whenever they arrived with the new truck to drop more suitcases at our feet. A piece of that sausage, I also handed to Olga, the new girl, in addition to my soup.

"Aren't you going to eat it?" She regarded me in amazement. "And where did you get the sausage?" She sank her teeth into it at once, devouring it in a few mouthfuls.

I didn't reply anything to her, just went further along the warehouse wall and sat down separately from everyone to munch on a piece of cheese. Turnip soup, made with rotting potato peels, only caused dysentery and if there was any chance of avoiding eating it, I preferred to stay away from it. The cheese was the goods, first-grade stuff, still fresh and impossibly aromatic. Yet, it tasted oddly in my mouth, purchased with the SS man's money stolen from my fellow countrymen. I wondered if my father would have eaten it. No, he wouldn't have. Not a chance. He would starve himself to death slowly, much like Dayen was doing, repeating endless Kaddish hour after hour for each person who went up in smoke and whose memories were going up in smoke, as blackening photographs curled and disintegrated in their death throes in his fire pit. My father was a good person. Me, not so much, judging by the looks of it. I regarded what was left of the cheese triangle in my hand, put it into my mouth and licked my fingers off.

Chapter 8

Germany, 1947

For some time after Helena stopped talking, only the sound of Dr. Hoffman's mechanical pencil on paper could be heard in the perfect, eerie silence. As he raised his gaze to the couple in front of him, he saw that Dahler was still perfectly unmoved and oddly, given the circumstances, serene. A faint blush now appeared on Helena's pale cheeks. Her gaze was absent, lost somewhere in time and space. Outside, a car's horn blared, shrill and impatient. Helena's shoulders jerked. Slowly, she roved her gaze around the courtroom, as though taking in unfamiliar surroundings. At last, her eyes focused on her tightly clasped hands. She blinked a few times and frowned as she regarded her nails. It appeared she was surprised to find them neatly manicured and painted.

With difficulty, she began arranging words into sentences once again. "In summer, we were transferred…"

She paused once again, tragically lost in the cobweb of memories she clearly wished to be no part of, yet, Dr. Hoffman admired her will to continue, the stubborn determination still alive in her dark, haunted eyes. *This was how it must have been for her in Auschwitz,* he thought to himself. *She willed herself to go on after seeing others perish; how unfortunate it was that she now blamed herself for that strong will of hers.*

The survivor's guilt was written all over her face when it betrayed any emotion at all. He wished to sit alone with her at least for one miserable hour. He wished to tell her that she had nothing to blame herself for. The SS was the guilty party here, not her. There was nothing wrong with taking Dahler's money. There was nothing wrong with eating the food it had purchased. People gnawed on pieces of flesh they'd carve out of a recently deceased inmate's thighs at night; he had come across such cases during his two years of interviewing the survivors here in Germany. Starvation and thirst, bloated stomachs ravaged by hunger pangs, the agonizing obsession with food, drove even the men of the highest morals and noblest professions to madness. Who could really blame a young woman for accepting life-saving rations out of the enemy's hands?

"... transferred to Birkenau." Helena's voice found its strength again. The pallid sunlight illuminated her face. Her hair formed a dark halo around it. "This is where I first met Andrej," she finished softly.

Novák's head shot up at the mention of his name. *First name.* His eyes, so harsh and bright with anger before, were suddenly full of some unspoken emotion. He pulled forward, as though willing Helena to look at him directly for the first time but she was reaching for her husband's hand instead. Dahler readily took her palm into his and covered it protectively with his other hand. Novák's eyes grew dark and impenetrable again. He lowered his gaze. Dr. Hoffman's pencil hovered over the fresh page, unsure.

"Is that so, Herr Novák?" the Chairman inquired of the Slovak.

"Yes, that is correct," Novák confirmed. He, too, seemed to be reluctant to talk of that summer. "As a matter of fact, I was the one who was building the future Kanada 2 barracks, before I was selected for the crematorium Sonderkommando, that is. It was in August of 1942. A part of the Kanada 1 Kommando was transferred into the barracks, which were already finished. Helena was among them."

"Weren't male and female inmates strictly separated in Birkenau?" Lieutenant Carter regarded the Slovak quizzically.

"Ordinarily, they were. There was a men's camp and a women's camp; men's Kommandos and women's Kommandos," Novák explained and went on to clarify. "Since our Sonderkommando had special privileges and access to the Kanada work detail, to which we brought the clothing from the gassing facilities, we often had a chance to exchange a few words with the women who sorted them. Sometimes we traded food and other items. Of course, that was when no SS was around. Men worked in the Kanada too, only in separate warehouses."

"And this is how you met Frau Dahler?" the Chairman asked.

"No. Yes. No… I first met her— I beg your pardon, I first *saw* her, when Herr Dahler was beating her in front of the gas bunker. I was on duty that day, which meant that I was to escort the new arrivals into the two extermination centers – they didn't suspect what those were, of course – and instruct them on what to do next. The SS that escorted the new arrivals would assure them that they were only going into the showers but it was us who were with those people until the very end."

He stopped for a moment. A shadow of something subtly aggressive stole over his face; the hardly veiled accusation was audible in his voice that was trembling with indignation. It was only Dahler he bore his unblinking gaze at as he spoke. *Listen to what you made us do. Remember every crime that stained your hands with blood.*

"There were two gassing facilities at that time in Birkenau, Bunker 1 and Bunker 2, called The Little Red House and The Little White House, respectively. They were completely unsuspicious, simple whitewashed farmhouses with thatched roofs – not a soul expected that something horrible could happen to them inside such harmless facilities. Those two structures were the only ones that remained from Brzezinka village that had been demolished prior to Birkenau's construction. The camp administration converted them into gas chambers for the time being, until the construction of the new crematoria would be finished."

The courtroom's air had grown tenser, stuffier, as though thick with a vague threat. For some time, Novák stared moodily ahead.

"It was all very smartly organized. People were starved, thirsty, and dog-tired after the train and the SS promised them warm soup and coffee after the showers. They also told them that their clothes would be disinfected and that they would be placed in quarantine for a couple of weeks before they would be assigned to their respective work details. Some of the SS, particularly inventive ones, even went as far as asking people for their professions. *'Oh, you're a carpenter? That's wonderful. That's precisely what we're looking for. And you're a seamstress? It seems we are in luck today! Those are just the professions we need. Report to me after the showers and I'll ensure that you're assigned to a work detail that suits your profession.'* It was sickening to listen to." He pursed his lips into a thin bloodless line. "Needless to say, all of those people would be gassed within the next twenty minutes, skilled workers and unskilled ones alike. Their bodies would then be buried in the ravines behind those two bunkers. In summer 1942, a new problem manifested itself though. Those bodies began to swell and the earth began to open under the scorching sun. The smell coming out of that opened ground was atrocious. But when some black liquid began rising and polluting the groundwater in the vicinity, the SS ordered us to take chlorinated lime there and pour it on top of the mass graves. When that didn't produce any results, we were ordered to unearth and burn them all. However, that was already in the autumn of the same year."

The Chairman cleared his throat. Next to him, Lieutenant Carter took a sip from his glass. Even Dr. Hoffman himself felt something catch in his chest at such a dispassionate, yet hauntingly vivid description of the extermination process. He wondered how Novák himself coped with what he had seen daily, in what he had participated, unwillingly, yet participated nevertheless. To be sure, at least some of the Sonderkommando men sometimes escorted their own newly arrived relatives and even families into the gas chambers. No wonder the Slovak was so agitated when it came to the hearing of Dahler's case. Dr. Hoffman could very well understand his sentiments on the former SS guard's account.

"You said you saw the defendant beating Frau Dahler, is that not so?" the Chairman continued, forcing his emotions under control.

"Yes. I was walking with a column of men towards Bunker 1. Helena, I beg your pardon, *Frau Dahler,*" Novák bared his teeth in a snarl as he pronounced Dahler's last name, "ran along the women's column that followed in front, in the direction of Bunker 2. Half of the women had already entered the structure. She was trying to get inside when Herr Dahler caught her by the scruff of her neck and pulled her to the side. What followed was some sort of altercation between them. I didn't hear the words, only saw that she was crying and begging him for something. Then he threw her down on the ground and began beating her with his horsewhip, calling her all sorts of names. *Stupid fucking Jew; one more time you disobey me; I've had it up to here with you; I ought to shoot you, you stupid bitch* – that sort of thing. I heard him because by then, he was screaming. One of the superior officers, Hauptscharführer Moll, intervened at this point and told Herr Dahler to take her away and continue with his beating someplace away from the new arrivals' eyes. Moll himself was a first-class sadist but he didn't want to create any sort of panic among those people who were still unfamiliar with the camp. Herr Dahler agitated a great deal of them with that beating."

Dr. Hoffman was watching Dahler closely the entire time that Novák was speaking. Not a muscle moved in the Austrian's face. He remained fascinatingly calm.

At the mention of violence, a failure to display any sort of emotion was characteristic of those suffering from psychopathy, the psychiatrist wrote down in his notepad but then put a big question mark next to it. With the best will in the world, Dahler, for some reason, didn't appear to be a textbook psychopath to him. And the more he observed the couple in front of him, the more confusing the entire affair was getting.

"Defendant, is that true, what Herr Novák just described?" The Chairman regarded the former SS man over the rim of his glasses.

Dahler appeared to be hesitating for a few moments.

"Yes, it is," he finally replied in a mild voice.

Suddenly, his wife pulled forward in her seat. "Your Honor, may I clarify something?"

"Yes, Frau Dahler, you may."

"It wasn't what Herr Novák described. That is… he misunderstood what he saw."

"With all due respect, Frau Dahler, I don't quite see how it is possible to misunderstand an assault. The defendant either beat you that day, or he didn't. There's no way around the fact itself."

"He had to. Otherwise…" She stumbled upon her own words, confused. Her eyes were flashing about in distress, dark, suddenly alarmed. "Otherwise, Hauptscharführer Moll would have put me into that gas chamber, along with my sister, Rózínka. My husband saved us both by his action."

For some time, the room was immersed in such silence, Dr. Hoffman could hear himself breathing.

"Care to elaborate, Frau Dahler?"

"Yes, please, Your Honor. I wouldn't want you to assume something of my husband's actions that were beyond his control. You'll see it for yourselves that it was the only possible solution in that situation. Herr Novák is right, Moll was a first-rate sadist. Franz had to whip me in front of him so that he wouldn't do something worse to me."

"Very well, Frau Dahler. We're listening."

Chapter 9

Helena

Birkenau. Summer 1942

Despite the early hour, the scorching sun was beating down unmercifully. Escorted by the SS and Kapos, we marched in between passages of electrified barbed wire towards our new living quarters. Well, a part of our Kommando, that is – young women only. The men were all left in Auschwitz.

On the border of the two camps, we were stopped on some senior SS man's orders. Near the gates, through which outside work detail groups left every morning, some sort of selection was being held. Accompanied by the orchestra music blaring its usual morning march, two SS officers, with medical corps insignia gleaming on their shoulders, were pulling men out of a work detail group and lining them up aside from the others.

"Strip completely!" The order was given.

As slowly as possible, the pitiful gray skeletons began pulling off their filthy, torn rags on which the blue stripes could hardly be recognized under all the layers of grime covering them.

"Faster, faster! Get on with it!" Another impatient shout from the SS medic.

Instantly alarmed, we began shooting anxious, pleading glances in our SS supervisors' direction. For some time, they observed the unraveling scene with politely bored expressions and only when our nervous shuffling and murmurs had grown too loud to go unnoticed, did they take pity on us.

"No need to worry," Rottenführer Dahler commented quietly. "Those are all *Muselmänner*. They can hardly walk, let alone work."

No one could say anything to that. The severe emaciation of the inmates stunned us into helpless, petrified silence. Under their wrinkled, scaly skin with a cadaverous tint to it, bones protruded to such an extreme that their very ability to stand on their own two feet was a miracle beyond any comprehension. Their shaved heads had lost all semblance to those of actual human beings' – a pitiful parade of skulls with their eyes still glimmering with hope to cheat fate, at the last moment. At the end of the line, one of them snatched his prison garb from the ground and began pulling it on all the while staring at the SS doctors, both of whom were busy taking the selected men's numbers down. A sorry attempt to cheat the Grim Reaper but he still had the fight left in him. The stubborn human will to survive shone in his hooded eyes, rolled in between tightly pressed jaws. A Kapo, the Green triangle, saw him and pounced on him at once, pummeling the poor creature with his club until the latter could no longer raise his skeletal arms in a futile effort to protect himself. After ensuring that the man was dead, the Kapo ran up to his SS bosses and tore his cap off to report "the incident." Without any emotion or even a single look in the murdered man's direction, the SS doctor put his number down along with the others. The rest of the unfortunates were loaded onto a truck that sped up in the direction of Auschwitz, at once. Outside work detail Kommandos were waved off to proceed. The entire affair was over in under ten minutes.

We resumed our marching in silence. Having seen off outside work detail gangs, the camp orchestra were packing their instruments, ridiculous and mocking in their white uniforms and red cords. Behind my back, a few women were sniffling quietly.

"Stop feeling sorry for them," Rottenführer Wolff snarled, annoyed with such an unseemly, in his eyes, display of sympathy towards our fellow inmates. "If we keep wasting food on sustaining *their* miserable existence, it'll mean that good, able-bodied workers will go hungry, such as yourselves. Is that what you want, you feeble-minded cows?"

Rottenführer Dahler marched on my side of the column. Soon, he leveled with our row of five – the standard marching formation here – and kept walking, looking straight ahead, next to me. I kept touching my kerchief – a nervous gesture, which I couldn't control for the life of me after seeing that scene. How sheltered we'd been in our Kanada! How positively blind to the misery of the rest of the camp, in our little paradise. Now, we were suddenly terrified to be taken away from it; terrified, that we should end up like those men in striped garb, starved and worked to death until not only our bodies but our souls were wasted away, withered and covered with countless sores – walking corpses for whom death was a welcoming notion.

I suddenly couldn't get my breath. Cold sweat poured down my back, my very body was oozing with fear. I clasped my mouth to stifle a sob – crying after an SS man explicitly prohibited us to do so was a sure way to get oneself a one-way ticket to the gas.

For a moment, I didn't feel the ground on which I was walking. I only saw the gray sleeve of Rottenführer Dahler's uniform, swinging rhythmically back and forth. He never uttered a word or betrayed a single emotion. Only once did he brush my hand with his, *accidentally,* no doubt. I risked stealing a quick glance at him. A few heads turned after mine, as well – a veritable herd instinct. He was gazing vacantly ahead and his relaxed, almost serene features instilled some certainty into our anguished souls. We felt ourselves growing calmer. It must have been some sort of a mind trick the camp played with one's brain. We had learned to put trust into them much like sheep put their faith into their sheepdogs. To be sure, they were still the enemy, the alien species and could still kill us at will and yet, they wouldn't give us away to the wolves with the SS medical corps insignia on their shoulders... at least, so we thought.

It was better to think so.

It was better to trust them rather than not have anyone to trust at all.

We had to march for quite some time, for our new barracks sat on the very outskirts of Birkenau, surrounded by pine trees and overlooking vast green fields as far as one's eye could see. The road was well trampled on and dusty. On both sides of it, an insufferable number of barracks lay. In the distance, the railroad work Kommando were hammering away at the still unfinished tracks. The air was thick with tar and oil and stale sweat.

Staff cars sped by; trucks with Red Crosses on them; motorcycle patrols with uniformed SS in them, *Lagerpolizei* signs gleaming on their necks and we still marched, marched past endless barracks and work details, past emaciated inmates with hollow eyes and sunken cheeks, past misery and death itself. Some of them still rose to their feet at the sight of the SS men but some had long lost the strength to even lift their heads. With our faces white as chalk, we saw that these new *Muselmänner* wore striped dresses – like us.

"Must be the women's camp," someone commented incredulously under their breath.

We looked closer but with the best will in the world, we couldn't recognize women in those pitiful figures. Same hollow eyes, same shaved heads, same grayish skin and bony fingers stretching out in our direction from behind the barbed wire like an apparitions' transparent limbs – only by those dresses could we tell them apart from the men that we'd seen. More heads began turning, in alarm, toward the SS men. *You aren't taking us there, are you?*

"Take a good look!" Wolff shouted as though on cue, pointing with the tip of his whip in the women's direction. "This is where you will end up if you keep being lazy scum. Take a good look and get it once and for all into your thick skulls how nice you have it with us!"

Instead of looking, we swiftly averted our eyes, shuddering at the thought that this could very well be us, had it not been for some lucky chance that landed us with the Kanada Kommando. Wolff wasn't wrong. We did have it nice, compared to these walking skeletons. To be sure, we looked thin but still human. We were allowed to keep our hair and wear regular shoes and not wooden clogs supported only by leather straps or go barefoot like half of these women. We were able to steal some food found in suitcases and pockets. Women from the women's camp followed our procession with dead eyes. In our turn, we were ashamed to look at them. For whatever inexplicable reason, we felt guilty before them, as though we had betrayed them in some way.

"There will be showers as well." I looked up at Dahler. He announced it to no one in particular but I knew the words were meant for me. "Behind the warehouse, for now."

In spite of myself, I broke into a beaming smile. *There will be showers!* I wished so much to ask him whether we should be allowed to take them daily or if there was going to be a schedule of some sort but speaking to an SS officer without being addressed first, wasn't allowed. Irma, with the red armband reading *"Senior – Block 1"* on her sleeve, marched right in front of me and she certainly wouldn't hesitate to administer her punishment with her club for my opening my mouth without permission.

Dahler, however, seemed to guess my thoughts for he clarified, after a pause, "you can take them as often as you like. As a matter of fact, it would be preferable for us, if you took them daily. We don't need any lice in our work detail."

"*Ja,* shower daily, ladies." Of course, '*ladies*' was spoken with a scornful smirk from Wolff. "If you don't want to end up with your heads shorn off like those cows over there." Another nod in the women's camp direction. "There will be no ugly shaved-head scum in our Kommando. You get lice, I'll see to it personally that you burn, along with them."

As we had reached our destination, at last, the Kapos assembled us once again for the last roll call before sending us straight to work. Inside and in between partially constructed warehouses, mountains of personal belongings were piled up. In front of the sorting stations, men attired in made-to-measure jackets were working – all "old numbers," judging by the insignia on their breast. They must have bought their way into the kosher detail by bribing the SS. Their well-nourished faces, skin gleaming with health, their wristwatches, hair styled with pomade, and shined shoes indicated their belonging to the camp elite who knew how to "organize" things here. In stunned silence, we observed them before the Kapos began assigning us to our stations.

The differences between the two Kanadas soon manifested themselves. The process of "organizing" here had been put on an almost industrial level.

"Anyone need French soap?" One of the men kept repeating his offer as he was making his round from one end of the warehouse to the other, on some suitable pretext.

"I can give you shoe polish for it," a muffled voice replied near my station.

"What kind?"

"Good kind. From Holland. It smells like perfume."

"French perfume... French perfume," a different inmate murmured, following the same route as his counterpart some ten minutes ago.

A hushed offer from the sorting table in the corner. "I'll take your perfume for five dollars."

"Ten and not a penny less."

"You'll sell it to an SS warden for twenty, you crook! Do you think I'm an idiot?"

"Suit yourself."

"I'll give you eight dollars and some stockings to go with it."

"Silk?"

"Nylon! He wants silk! Fathead!"

"One yourself." A derisive grin. "Fine. Have it your way but it's highway-robbery if you ask me."

Like wide-eyed deer, we dug aimlessly at the clothes in front of us as they traded with each other like some Wall Street big shots. The most astonishing part was the fact that the Kapos almost entirely ignored such blatant black-market dealings, yawning, and almost purposely averting their eyes when the goods exchanged hands. At last, after quickly glancing around, one of the girls pulled a pair of underwear from the pile and stuffed it inside her dress. Another one snatched a women's wristwatch while two others were busy stuffing their pockets with food. The old numbers, who had at first ignored us entirely, soon broke into grins.

I, myself, couldn't resist the pair of undergarments that I found among some unfortunate woman's belongings. The old number, who had bartered his French soap for a tin of sardines, snorted with amusement next to me. Blushing copiously at being found out, I thoroughly pretended to ignore him. "You can take pretty much everything from here," he said. "Just don't forget the golden rule of the Kanada; the Kapos and the guards need to get their share. If you don't bribe them, they'll do you in for stealing before you know it."

I made sure to instruct the rest of the girls on this matter. In the evening, our Kapo Maria left the detail with a smile on her face for the first time. Everyone could see her bulging pockets as she walked away from our neat columns, leaving us in Irma's charge.

The SS appeared before us. Under the collar of Rottenführer Wolff's uniform, a new silk necktie was gleaming softly. Rottenführer Dahler was chewing gum like some American actor who'd just jumped off the screen. Both seemed mighty pleased with their new working arrangements away from Kommandant Höss's watchful eye and constant harassment. Here, they were masters and Gods and, so far, things were looking up for us, as well, in view of such lax policing.

"We have another surprise for you," Rottenführer Wolff announced cheerfully. I had a suspicion he had discovered a bottle of some top-shelf spirits among the dead people's belongings. Now that the alcohol had taken its effect, his goodwill knew no restraint. "Block by block, you will now go inside the main warehouse and find suitable clothes for you to wear. No more of this prison garb. Get yourselves some shirts and slacks preferably and comfortable shoes as well. But keep your kerchiefs. We don't need any of your hair falling into the sorted clothes. You're welcome now, tramps. Now, off you go! Make yourselves look pretty."

If it weren't for Irma already prodding us in the backs with her truncheon as she shouted her *"Los, los, los!"* at our small column, we would have thought it was some sort of drunken joke.

"Take off all of your clothes and drop them in that corner over there." Irma indicated where we were to discard our striped dresses.

Naked, we were quickly herded into the showers. The showers were a small affair, dark and dingy, with metal stalls on both sides with pipes running along the walls and showerheads protruding from them and a concrete floor. The water was blisteringly cold but we were just delighted at being able to wash, no matter this minor inconvenience. At least, we could remove all the grime off our skin! It was a paradise, no less.

Only a few minutes were allotted to each block. After a quick but vigorous scrubbing, Irma chased us back into the warehouse where we, naked and still glistening with droplets of water running down our backs from our wet hair, were allowed to select suitable shirts, trousers, and even underwear from the piles of the already sorted and disinfected clothes. One of the inmates carefully marked down the exact number of everything we took – the clothes were already prepared to be shipped to Germany.

"Get dressed! Be quick about it!" Irma shouted again. Two minutes later, but not before we could extract whatever we had "organized" during the day from our abandoned dresses' pockets, she was chasing us toward the exit. Women from Block 2 were already waiting at the doors for their turn.

Only when we were inside our new barrack, inspecting our new attire and boasting who had brought the biggest haul from the new Kanada, did scowls replace the smiles. Brooding silence now shrouded the barrack instead of the cheerful remarks. All this had come off our murdered kin. How could anyone celebrate that?

Chapter 10

Helena

I heard Maria call out my number as she pointed in the direction of a building that was still missing part of its roof. Carpenters were hammering away overhead as I proceeded to my designated area along with a few other women.

"You're on disinfection duty today," Maria barked out, all business as always. "Sonderkommando will tell you what to do."

Anxiously, we looked around. There were no clothes there, only endless clotheslines stretched like spiderwebs from one wall to another. Sonderkommando men, indeed, soon appeared along with their Kapo, who was to be our supervisor that day. We had long grown used to these men, even though we weren't allowed to communicate with them openly. They stomped inside in their usual black rubber boots; no one spoke about it but we all knew that they had to hose off the gassed people's bodies inside the bunkers before bringing them outside for burial or cremation. After that, they would clean the gas chamber itself so it would be pristine and spotless for its new victims but no one talked about that either. Death and food were two prohibited subjects for discussion in the camp and for a good reason.

With their usual efficiency, the Sonderkommando began organizing the working station.

The Kapo, a burly black-haired man with a red triangle of a political prisoner on his chest, began instructing us in his thick, low voice. "So, ladies, here are rubber gloves for you. Now, you each take a basket for yourself. Yes, those ones that the lads just brought in. You take the hair and wash it first in this solution, it'll strip it of all the oils and bugs if there are any. Then, you rinse it with regular water and hang it to dry on these clotheslines. If the hair is too short, lay it out on these newspapers."

The Kapo spoke in German with a thick Polish accent and since most of us girls were Slovakian, we exchanged uncomprehending looks. We must have misheard him, or he must have used the word "hair" instead of something else. Or maybe it was their Sonderkommando slang for something? They did call corpses, "stiffs," after all and the contraband they called, "non-kosher goods," so, perhaps, that was one of those things?

Only when he prompted us to move – *well, go on, grab a basket, those braids won't wash themselves* – did we realize that he was talking quite literally. Piles and piles of women's hair came into view as we looked into the baskets. Blond, gray, curly, braided, long, permed, red, dyed – shorn-off womanhood itself that made us shudder with horror. We were used to sorting and disinfecting the clothes but this was an entirely different matter altogether.

"Well, get on with it!" The Sonderkommando Kapo nudged us in the backs softly. "Don't be so squeamish. At least it's not teeth," he added in a mild voice, as though in an apology.

Two of the inmates under his charge quickly demonstrated to us what was expected of us. Their motions were quick and professional, almost mechanical and utterly devoid of any emotion.

"You must forgive us," one of them whispered softly when Maria was busy talking about something with the Polish Kapo. "Ordinarily, it's our duty to do all the head-shaving and hair disinfection after the gassing but there have been so many of them in these past few days, we don't have enough men left. Half of us are sent daily to the burial pits; all of those stiffs are coming out and the SS said we need to—"

"No jawing!" The Kapo's shout quickly put an end to the conversation.

With shaking hands encased in rubber gloves, we handled dead women's hair all morning. When the time for lunch came and along with it, block orderlies with cauldrons of soup, our group suddenly couldn't even look at it. Not too far from us, the men from the Sonderkommando calmly munched on their rations. We regarded them almost with envy. They had long grown used to it. Death simply didn't touch them any longer. They had invented names for it and mocked it daily, just to get through the day, just to keep their minds, just to desensitize themselves to the point where their bodies functioned like automatons but their thoughts were somewhere very far away, away from the mountains of corpses which they washed, shaved, burned, and buried daily. It was the only sensible solution. No one could blame them for still being able to eat their soup.

*

The man was sun-tanned, well built and with the sly face of a typical profiteer; attired in a white undershirt, black slacks, and the already familiar black rubber boots. His hair was not shaved but parted on one side and neatly brushed back. He whistled to me softly as I was piling the baskets into a separate heap outside the barracks. For some time, I stood undecided. The area adjacent to the warehouse lay deserted; most of the inmates worked inside, away from the heat. But to me, the midday heat meant not the damnedest thing. Here, I could be left alone, in my own company, at least for a couple of hours. When one is constantly surrounded by people, one grows to loathe their company. Women took the risk and disappeared in the latrines' direction at night for that very reason. Just to be alone, just not to hear the others' voices, just to be alone with one's own thoughts. Such luxury was nearly unobtainable in the camp but I had a willing ally in Rottenführer Dahler.

"But of course," he had granted me his permission at once as soon as I had offered to sort the mounting piles of luggage outside.

"Only watch it so that you don't get heatstroke out there. If you feel warm, come back at once."

After an incessant torrent of *Jawohl* and *thank-you,* I nearly ran into the blinding early-afternoon sun, grinning like a cat.

Another whistle from the Sonderkommando fellow. I turned sharply round, brought my hand to my brow to shield myself from the sun and cast a suspicious glance at him. He signed to me to come closer. However, I refused to leave my position for some doubtful business affair he had come to conduct here, no doubt.

He threw his muscular, tanned arms up in the air in the universal gesture of exasperation and disappeared behind the barracks. Not a minute later, he reappeared with a rolled mattress under one arm and a pillow under another.

"Interested?" he shouted to me, annoyed with my skittish ways.

My eyes widened in amazement. *Surely, such lavishness as a personal mattress couldn't have been "organized" here!* Yet, I regarded it greedily as he dropped it down onto the ground that had been swept clean just this morning.

"Well?" he pressed, playing with the pillow in his great paws. "Stuffed with the down; first-rate quality."

I made a step in his direction. "And the mattress?"

"Cotton, my guess. Lots of it. Soft as a feather! Come and feel for yourself."

Before I knew it, I was squatting on my haunches in front of the rolled, striped mattress and digging into its softness, giggling like a schoolgirl. The Sonderkommando inmate dropped the pillow into my lap as well, fluffing it up and arranging it with great care.

"See? Soft as a cloud. You'll sleep like a child, take my word for it. Nothing like a good night's sleep for people in our profession, eh? We all have such mattresses in our barracks. They do make a difference; trust me when I tell you."

The man could sell, that much was obvious. And I was already clutching the pillow to my chest, refusing to part with it. No more miserable straw pallets, so thin that each board of the bunk was prodding and poking at our bony forms at night. I pressed my cheek to the pillow, burrowing my entire face into it and imagining how positively delightful it would be to sleep on such a cloud of long-forgotten softness each night.

I was sold. Sold, through and through and not even ashamed of it.

"What do you want for it?"

"I need top-shelf liquor, as many bottles as you can get your hands on. By tonight."

"By tonight?"

"Well, *ja*. It's an SS man's birthday and one of his comrades wants to make it memorable for him. Stash them all in one of those baskets you were just sorting and bring them to the back of the disinfection facility after your shift." He motioned his head in the direction of the warehouse, from which the clean, folded clothes were taken to Germany every morning.

"How am I going to smuggle so many bottles out of the warehouse?"

He narrowed his eyes slightly. The sly grin was back on his face. "That's for you to worry about. Rumor has it you have your own SS man in the Kanada. Why don't you ask him for permission?"

"Are you mad? He'll never agree to that! One bottle, perhaps, but an entire basket full of them – he'll personally shoot me for it!"

"Stiff luck for you then. It's a good mattress, and these are hard to come by." He patted the striped roll with affection.

I screwed up my face and glanced from the warehouse to the mattress and back. He moved closer. I clutched the pillow tighter to my chest.

"He won't refuse you. Ask nicely. Smile at him. You can risk smiling at an SS man for a mattress; no?"

"How am I going to smuggle it into my barrack?"

"Leave it up to me. Delivery is free; just tell me which barrack and which bunk is yours and I'll even throw in some sheets and a blanket for you, on top of the deal."

I regarded him in amazement. He certainly knew which hands to grease up, if he could make such promises.

"I'll try."

After lunch – even the soup was different here, made of potatoes and not rotten turnips – I knocked on Rottenführer Dahler's office door.

"Oh." I paused at the door, noticing the steaming plate on his desk. "Forgive me, please. I didn't know you were still eating, Herr Rottenführer. I shall come back after—"

"No, no, don't be silly!" He was already on his feet, ushering me in. "Come in. Sit down. What is it?"

For a second, a thought occurred to me that he might have been offended by the idea that I only came to him whenever I needed something. However, judging by his question and the attentive manner in which he'd inclined his head slightly to one side, it dawned on me that he had long put up with such a state of affairs between us. It seemed as though it had been his plan all along, to wear me out with this suddenly kind attitude. He did say that it would be him who would prove me wrong in the end and it appeared that he was stubbornly keeping to his promise. *You want the showers? I'll get you the showers. You want new clothes? I'll get you the clothes. You want food? Take all you like – I will see to it that the Kapos won't say a word to you. You want to work by yourself? Stay out there by yourself until you bore yourself into consumption. I'll let you do anything you want, anything that's in my powers, just for you to keep coming here and asking me for more,* it read in his blue eyes that shone with such bright, fiery passion today, it was suddenly impossible to look into them.

I lowered my eyes and decided to look at his plate instead. It was also soup but different from ours, with pieces of meat in it and even some green onions mixing with yellow circles of fat on its surface. Misinterpreting my gaze, he pushed it slightly towards me. "Are you hungry?"

I shook my head and surprised even myself thinking that I really wasn't. Well, not as hungry as we used to be before, in Auschwitz, where this plate would turn me blind with hunger and never let me concentrate on a single coherent thought as long as it stood, teasing and excruciatingly unattainable, before me. Here, in Birkenau's Kanada, where the stealing was so widespread that we left the work detail every evening with pockets full of foodstuffs, we began worrying about other affairs. We were well dressed and showered daily now. We were turning from animals back into people again.

"A man from the Sonderkommando offered me a mattress." I cast a probing glance in Dahler's direction.

"In exchange for…?"

"Liquor. A basket full of it, to be exact. By tonight." I bit my lip, expecting the worst. He was feared for his temper after all and one could never predict how he would react to such an insolent proposition.

Curiously enough, Dahler's face drew into a wry smile instead.

Seeing my confusion, he shook his head good-humoredly. "That weasel Voss. It's one of their crematoria SS men's birthdays. He could have asked me for it but he knew that he'd have to pay me for it. So, he went about it the only way an arch-crook like him would do, asked an inmate to arrange it for him for free. What do you say to that?"

Smiles were chasing one another across his tanned face. I thought it to be wise to smile as well, even though I had not the faintest idea who this SS man Voss was.

"I say he *is* a veritable crook, Herr Rottenführer."

"It's good for you, though," he continued. "You'll get yourself a new mattress out of the deal. Where did he tell you to meet him, that Sonderkommando fellow?"

"Behind the disinfecting facility."

"*Gut.* Don't go there by yourself. I'll send an inmate instead."

I regarded him in confusion. *Was I not an inmate?*

"A man," he clarified. "A basket full of liquor is much too heavy for you to carry."

I thanked him quietly and, after a moment's hesitation, extracted a wristwatch with a golden face, out of my pocket. I had procured it beforehand and thought it to be a suitable thing to offer him. "Thank you again, Herr Rottenführer." I slid it quickly across the desk toward him.

He tensed at once, pulled himself up and folded his hands on his lap, offended.

"Do you think I do this to profit somehow?" He pushed it back toward me in indignation. "Take it back. I don't want it."

"It's not a bribe, Herr Rottenführer."

"It looks oddly like one." There was ice in his voice.

"It's a present. For you," I tried to explain.

For a few moments, he was staring blankly at me, utterly confused. "A present?"

"Yes. A present. You always give me something. Now I can finally give you something in return. It's not... a payment, it's a... gesture. Forgive me, please. It was never my intention to offend you." I passed my hand over my forehead, nervously searching for the right words. "I can't explain it all to you in my bad German but I'll just say that if you take it, it'll make me feel better. Make me feel like I can give something. It makes people feel better when they can give something to others."

He looked at me for a very long time.

"Yes, you're right," he finally spoke, after a pause, his voice faltering and turning strangely melancholic as if I had just reminded him of some long-forgotten, universal truth the sight of which he'd lost a long time ago. "It does. Giving is better than taking."

He took his SS-issued watch off and put the new one onto his wrist. "Help me, please."

I wanted to ask him jokingly who usually helped him put on his watch every morning – surely it was just a trick for me to touch him, even if in passing – but then didn't.

"There, Herr Rottenführer." I even helped him adjust his cuff. "It looks very nice."

"Yes, it does." He examined it with a smile. "Thank you. I shall never take it off."

Dahler did arrange everything as he promised. That night, I slept on my new mattress covered with bedsheets and rested my head on a pillow stuffed with down. It was bliss, pure bliss that made one forget and that's all that mattered for me at that moment. I could almost forget that all of this came from a murdered people. I could almost forget that we survived only because the others were dying in their thousands.

But really, what choice did we have? Starve ourselves to death and wear rags and go filthy out of solidarity? That would only turn us into the dreaded *Muselmänner,* and the SS would have more of us to kill off. No, we were firmly set on surviving this hell. We were firmly set on making it out of here at some point, if only to tell the world of its horrors. If that meant to trade murdered people's belongings, so be it. If I perished one day, I would be perfectly satisfied with someone trading my "riches" for a piece of bread and prolonging their life by one more day. It wouldn't hurt me at all, some other Jew surviving off what's left of me. It would hurt me much more if some Party-badge-wearing Aryan benefited from it instead. That was KZ life for you. We only did what we had to, to survive.

Chapter 11

Helena

The wind blew from the fields these past two days, bringing with it the suffocating stench of death and putrefaction. We, the Kanada Kommando, suffered worse than other inmates from it, as our barracks and work detail were within walking distance of the ravines. Even our SS supervisors began grumbling their discontent for they also had to breathe the same putrid air daily.

"They really ought to do something about those stiffs." Wolff spat on the ground, squinting in the direction of the two bunkers behind which mass graves lay. "It gets worse by the day."

Rottenführer Dahler preferred to mask the stench with cigarettes. Just as he had finished the old one, he lit a new one and inhaled deeply, regarding his comrade a trifle mockingly. "Will you be the hero who bravely brings it to Moll's attention?"

Wolff didn't reply anything but his expression said it all. Not even they wished to have anything to do with the dreaded Hauptscharführer, who reigned over the Sonderkommando and was officially in charge of most extermination operations taking place in the two bunkers. Unlike the sweet-talking, sleek-mannered Obersturmführer Hössler, whom the Sonderkommando rightfully called "Moshe Liar" for his ability to pacify even the most anxious crowds of new arrivals, Moll was a sadistic murderer who drew perverse pleasure from others' sufferings. We, the Kanada Kommando, only heard about him in passing but couldn't stop wondering how wicked a man must be, if his actions didn't sit well even with our SS supervisors who didn't shy away from violence, by any means.

It was the beginning of September but an uncharacteristically warm, even sultry one. The roof of the warehouse, in which we currently worked, was finished but the doors stood open on both sides to allow the air to circulate inside. While the new accountant, Rottenführer Gröning, was busy counting foreign currency in his office, Wolff and Dahler preferred to loiter in the warehouse with us, either bored or in the hope of pocketing some valuables to send home later. We regarded the new SS man with suspicion at first – all changes in the camp signified danger for us – but soon realized that Gröning didn't differ much from his unassuming predecessor, Weber. Just like Weber, he was blond and very young. His bespectacled blue eyes were alert with intelligence; he didn't speak much and preferred desk work to loitering around the warehouse with his fellow SS men. In fact, we hardly saw his tall frame at all, only when he came and went at different hours with a suitcase full of foreign currency and when one of us had to deliver the box filled with valuables into his office. Even then, he was invariably polite and indifferent – a typical bureaucrat with no interest in anything besides numbers and the camp's sports club; at least that was the rumor.

Wolff stifled a yawn. He was growing bored with our monotonous sorting. Just his misfortune, nothing valuable or curious seemed to be found that day. The latest arrivals were from a ghetto from what we had learned. Their valuables had long been traded for food within its walls. They had nothing to offer to our Kanada.

"Time to check the perimeter," he announced, after consulting his pocket watch, with the air of an aristocrat about him.

It was golden, with a beautiful face and a long golden chain, thick as one's finger. To be sure, he hadn't a waistcoat to attach it to, so he kept it in his pocket, thoroughly ignoring the idea that such a bourgeois accessory went against their very neo-Germanic ideals. Just like Rottenführer Dahler's new wristwatch, it came from the Kanada riches. His own watch Wolff had long thrown into the wristwatch box without even bothering to conceal this fact from our eyes. Those would later head to Sachsenhausen for repair and from there be sent to the front for the troops to use.

Wolff made towards the exit. Dahler paused a moment before making a reluctant step after him. For the past few weeks that was all he did, lingered somewhere near my station, made only very short remarks in passing and mostly concerning work matters – there were far too many people around to have any semblance of an actual conversation – and risked dropping a golden ring, a dollar, or a biscuit into my pocket from time to time.

Recently, he was growing imaginative with his presents and soon, the oddest items began finding their ways into the pockets of my black slacks. At first, I puzzled over a small, round, mother-of-pearl powder case with a mirror inside that he gave me. It wasn't expensive and had no real value on the local black market. However, he must have come across it and remembered that women liked their mirrors, in a normal world. I thanked him warmly, in a hushed whisper, the next time I saw him. It was a very dear present, indeed.

A few days ago, he managed to smuggle a corn poppy into the warehouse and hid it under the suit he told me to check, as *it looked expensive. There must be some valuables hidden inside.* There was undoubtedly a precious thing hidden, not inside but under it. Twirling the flower – *a flower!* – which I hadn't seen in months, in my fingers, I broke into the broadest smile before quickly hiding its red velvet luxury in my pocket to press and save it later, right under my pillow. From the corner of my eye, I saw Dahler quickly hiding a smile too, looking most satisfied with the effect his little gesture produced.

Today, with Wolff around, he couldn't find any excuse to approach me and so, he only threw a last glance, full of longing, in my direction before setting off after his comrade. It was then that I realized that I had pulled something familiar from a suitcase that had just been delivered by the Sonderkommando men. The SS men's steps still echoed on the concrete as I turned a small child's shirt this way and that, hoping to find proof that I was mistaken. But there couldn't be any mistake. I embroidered a smiling bear's face into its front with my own hands before gifting it to my sister Rózínka for her newborn son.

"This will be my present to him for his very first birthday," I told her, rocking the beautiful, fussing wrap in my arms as she looked on, smiling, the proud mother.

That was in August 1941. My nephew was exactly one year old and it was his shirt that I was holding. It was neatly packed, along with other baby clothes, his and his big sister's, in the suitcase that bore Rózínka's married name. Next to the baby clothes, her favorite dress lay, pressed and also neatly folded.

A cold wave of terror washed over me. *My sister was inside the camp. My sister was among the people heading to the gas chambers.* My hand, with the baby's shirt still clutched in it, was wet with sweat. Before I knew it, I was running toward the exit, gasping for air and feeling as though my nerves would snap any moment now.

"Just where do you think you're going?!" Maria's shout didn't stop me; neither did Irma's hand that reached out to grab my arm as I charged past her to the outside. Narrowly escaping her grip, I set off along the narrow passage framed with barbed wire in the direction of the two bunkers.

Rózínka, my dear, sweet sister! Don't listen to Moshe Liar, don't take your clothes off, don't go inside the "showers," I repeated like a prayer in my head that was pounding with fear.

Soon, I caught up with them. Desperately searching for Rózínka in the column, I could hear Moshe Liar's – Obersturmführer Hössler's – regular speech.

"This is not a holiday resort but a labor camp," he spoke in measured tones as he walked along the column, in his sweet, cultured voice that never failed to instill security in the new arrivals. "Just as our soldiers risk their lives at the front, you will have to work here for the welfare of a new Europe. The chance is there for every one of you. We shall look after your health and we shall also offer you well-paid work..."

Frantically, I twisted my head from one end of the women's column to the other, craning my neck to locate my sister who was listening to all of Hössler's sickening lies and marching straight to her death, lulled by the SS officer's reassurances.

"After the war, we shall assess everyone according to his merits and treat him accordingly," Moshe Liar continued spinning his tales, as part of the women's column was obediently walking inside the gassing facility. "There's a changing room in the showers. All of your clothes must be disinfected. This is for your safety; we don't want any epidemics and needless deaths. Would you please all get undressed and undress your children also? While you're taking a shower, they will all be cleaned and returned to you after you're finished. When you've had your bath, there will be a bowl of soup and coffee or tea for all. Oh, and before I forget, would diabetics, who are not allowed sugar, please report to staff on duty after the bath."

I shuddered at how convincing he sounded. Even I began doubting the fate of the columns that were currently being swallowed into the dark gaping mouths of the two bunkers. They even separated them today by genders. And I still couldn't locate my sister!

She must have been already inside, undressing her children and pacifying them with soup and warm tea, promised by the *kind Herr Offizier*. Just as I turned on my heel, ready to run inside the bunker – I didn't quite think what exactly I would do once inside and how I would be able to save Rózínka and her children from a horrible death – a hand gripped me tightly by the scruff of my neck, pulling me out of the line.

"Just what are you doing here?!" a voice hissed above my ear.

It was Rottenführer Dahler, not Maria or Irma, and he looked both mad with fury and genuinely terrified.

"My sister is inside," I whispered back, tears spilling down my cheeks. "Herr Rottenführer, please let me go to her…"

"Out of the question," he hissed through his teeth in a most categorical manner. "You go inside, you'll die along with her. Go back to your work detail before anyone sees you."

His concerns were justified. Obersturmführer Hössler already regarded us with interest, no doubt wondering what was going on. Dahler was pulling me away from the column. My entire body shaking with sobs, I clung to his tunic and dug my heels into the ground, positively refusing to take another step.

"Herr Rottenführer, I beg of you, help her," I implored him. I didn't see anyone around any longer, just his face, which was as unyielding as a wall. He wasn't looking at me but in the opposite direction, his scowl growing deeper.

"Hössler is coming," he muttered, more to himself. I felt his hand, in which the collar of my shirt was still balled, faltering. His gaze darted toward the bunker, then back to Hössler, then back to my face.

"Franz, please!" For the first time, I called him by his first name, hoping that at least this would touch him in some way, make him change his mind. "Save my sister! I will do anything you want… Anything, without any questions; whatever you say, I shall do from now on. Any wish of yours, any desire I will attend to without any reservations. You won't hear a word of protest from me ever again. I shall forever be your most faithful servant. Just please, I beg you, help her!"

He hesitated for an interminably long moment, gazing helplessly somewhere above my head. "I'll try," he finally conceded. "Tell me her name, quickly."

"Różínka Feldman. She has two small children with her—"

"Children, that's an entirely different matter. Children can't live here. *Scheiße!* Moll has seen us!" He looked at me in desperation, almost tragically. "Forgive me, please, Helena. That bastard will never buy simple words—"

He didn't finish his sentence, only hurled me to the ground. Cowering at his feet, I glimpsed both Hössler and Moll heading towards us from both directions.

"Stupid fucking Jew!" Dahler's tone changed as though by magic. It wasn't a desperate whisper anymore but an enraged shout; neither was the first blow of his whip a pretense by any means. "How difficult is it to understand my orders?!" Another blow landed parallel to the first, stinging through the cloth. "I ought to knock all of your teeth out, you stupid fucking bitch!" Pain radiated from each spot where his horsewhip had landed. I'd never been whipped, *really whipped*, before and just now understood why the horsewhip and cane were considered to be the most feared punishments among the inmates. Each blow felt as though it lacerated the skin to the bone, yet, I took the beating silently, only dug my fingers deeper into the ground and stared at the entrance of the bunker, by which the women paused, no doubt horrified by the unraveling spectacle.

"Rottenführer!" Hauptscharführer Moll was the first to reach us. It was him who seized Dahler by his wrist. "Just what the fuck are you, numbskull, doing?!" These words Moll hissed through gritted teeth, pulling the whip out of Dahler's hand. For one instant, I thought he was going to hit him with it. "Have you completely gone off your head?! Do you want all of these two thousand people to start panicking and running about? Who's going to stop them if they begin to trample us all? There are only fifteen of us, SS men, supervising the *Aktion,* and a miserable number of Sonderkommando men. Have you considered this, you *verdammter Arschloch*?!"

"My sincerest apologies, Herr Hauptscharführer. She's one of my workers. I sent her here to fetch part of the belongings but she decided to go inside to see her boyfriend from the Sonderkommando instead, when I spotted her. I warned her about her whoring ways before but these Jew-bitches only understand the whip from what it seems."

"Of course, that's all they understand! But be so kind, next time take this tramp someplace else to administer the punishment instead of doing so in front of these people. They're like a herd of sheep. If one starts running, the rest will follow and it'll take us all day to restore the peace and catch them all. And then you try and put them into that damned bunker after what they've seen."

I still lay curled on the ground that was trampled by many feet. Three pairs of boots surrounded me now. Hössler was next to us, also. Moll quickly assured him that everything was taken care of.

"Ladies and gentlemen, please, proceed to the showers!" Hössler began speaking again, a broad smile on his face. "There's nothing to see here. This woman stole something and our SS always take it a bit too close to their hearts when someone steals from the Reich. She's going back to her working place now to think about what she's done. Go into the showers, please! The soup is getting cold."

"Herr Hauptscharführer, another worker from my Kommando is in there too, I think," Dahler cast a probing glance at Moll. "Allow me to go fetch her? She's a very good worker…"

"Be quick about it. And give them both the cane, not this childish business." He thrust the whip back into Dahler's hand. "They have all grown immune to it. Now, the cane, that ought to teach them how to obey. Next time I see your bitches running about here, I'll send them both to the gas, good workers or not. Understood?"

"*Jawohl*, Herr Hauptscharführer."

"Dismissed."

Leaden with fear, I waited where Dahler had left me. Only when he reappeared with my sister in tow did I force myself back onto my feet, weeping with relief and happiness. As he marched us both toward the warehouse, I couldn't stop whispering my most ardent thanks to him, *the savior, the protector, the kindest soul on earth*. It was madness to think about him in this regard; I understood it and yet I was suddenly overcome with such powerful emotion for him, such incomprehensible gratitude that it utterly trumped all common sense that was left in me. All I knew was that he brought my sister back to me. He saved her, for me. At that very moment, I felt no pain from his blows. Suddenly, I nearly worshiped him.

He brought Różínka to my station and quickly explained to her what to do.

"Your Kapo," he motioned Maria over, "will put your name on the list and will take you to the showers later and process you as needed. I have to take your sister to the medical block." He cast another concerned glance at my gray shirt, which was stuck to the wounds from which the blood was slowly seeping in places where his whip broke the skin.

"What about my children?" Różínka held her breath, awaiting his answer.

Dahler had just opened his mouth to tell her not to worry about her children anymore but I caught his hand and pressed his fingers in an imploring, fleeting gesture. *Take pity on her! She's new to the camp, she won't survive the truth, not just yet…*

He was silent for a moment but then heaved a sigh and even forced a smile onto his face. "Did you see the Red Cross trucks parked in front of the showers?" Those were the trucks that delivered the gas to the bunkers but she didn't know that yet. "Your children will be taken by nurses to a special children's *Lager* that we have here. They will be taken care of."

"When will I be able to visit them?"

"Soon, my good woman. The sooner you fill your quota, the sooner you'll be able to see them."

She smiled at him brightly and took to her task with commendable, heart-breaking eagerness.

Chapter 12

Helena

He didn't take me to the inmates' infirmary but to some strange whitewashed barrack, to which I'd never paid attention before. As soon as we stepped through the doors, the inmate doctor jumped to his feet and froze at attention, propelled by sheer instinct, instilled by months of submission to every SS man's whim. He was a man of about forty, with the face of an intellectual, prematurely gray hair and a Jewish star sewn on top of a white gown. With infinite longing, I eyed a book which he had been reading and which now lay open on top of his desk. *What I wouldn't give to be able to read a book, at least for a few minutes a day! Just to forget all this horror, just to lose myself for a few precious moments...*

Next to me, Rottenführer Dahler cleared his throat, unsure of how to begin. "I need you to check one of my workers."

The doctor picked up the glasses, in a thin metal frame, from the desk, looked at me and then back at him, inquisitively.

"Yes, her." Dahler shifted from one foot to the other.

"Am I looking for anything specific, Herr Rottenführer?" the doctor asked him carefully in his correct but slightly accented German, fixing the gaze of his intelligent eyes on me once again.

"Yes, erm... Take a look at her back. I think it needs some tending to."

The doctor's eyes barely touched upon Dahler's whip to express his understanding and condemnation at the same time. *No need to clarify, Herr Rottenführer. Familiar business.*

"Would you please sit over there and remove your shirt?" the physician addressed me directly for the first time.

I sat where he indicated me with my back to both men and began pulling the shirt off. Some of the blood had already congealed and I winced, in spite of myself, while tearing it off the flesh to which it was stuck. Yet, I didn't make a sound, unlike one of them, whose sharp intake of breath indicated that the picture before their eyes was not at all pleasant, by any means. Both should have been used to such sights, so the reaction surprised me, whoever it came from.

"Well…" the doctor began, with uncertainty. "I suppose I could clean the wounds, that's the least I can do to prevent the infection from setting in."

"Is that all you're planning on doing? I could have sent her to the showers for the same effect. What kind of a physician are you with such suggestions?"

"I'm a pathologist, Herr Rottenführer," the doctor replied calmly. Just now, I realized that I was sitting on a dissecting table, which was still wet from hosing off. "In ordinary circumstances, I would have cleaned the wounds, applied the disinfectant, then some vinegar-soaked bandages to draw the heat from the wounds and allowed her bed rest at least for a few hours before cleaning them again and bandaging them. But as I understand, you just wished to ensure that she wasn't bleeding profusely and could be cleared for work?"

"What do you, *Mistbiene,* understand about my wishes?!" Dahler was suddenly incensed. "I told you to tend to her wounds. Tend to her wounds as needed! As you would have tended to your wife's wounds!"

"My wife has been gassed upon arrival, Herr Rottenführer," the doctor announced in the same cool, unemotional voice.

I turned to look at Dahler. For a moment, I thought that he would backhand the doctor across his face for speaking out of turn and of matters that were strictly *verboten* from discussing in the camp and with the SS officers, even more so. However, Dahler caught my pleading glance and exhaled slowly, seemingly collecting himself.

"My condolences," he said curtly after a pause. "Now, do tend to her wounds, will you?"

"*Jawohl,* Herr Rottenführer." The doctor inclined his head respectfully, walked to the medical cabinet and began digging in it, for the needed materials.

"Do you have everything you need or shall I fetch some supplies from the SS doctors if you…" Dahler hesitated before continuing. Such concern for an inmate's well being was far too suspicious and the doctor was already regarding him with interest.

"Thank you for your generous offer, Herr Rottenführer, but I have everything I need. Dr. Thilo's office keeps the experimenting and the dissecting facilities well-supplied."

"Can you give her something for the pain?"

Now, the pathologist outright stared at Rottenführer Dahler, positively mystified.

"She's a good worker," Dahler murmured, as though in his own defense.

The doctor brought along a roll of aspirin along with bandages and the rest of the medical supplies and made me swallow two of the bitter pills. After that, he turned to Dahler once again. *Satisfied?* his gray eyes said. Condemnation was still visible in them, despite all of the doctor's attempts to keep it curbed. *It wouldn't have been needed had you not done all this damage in the first place.*

Dahler wouldn't leave the room even when I had to lie down on the dissecting table, positioning my shirt under me to keep at least some barrier between my bare skin and the cold metal. I preferred not to think of who – or what, to be exact – lay here before me, concentrating on the doctor's gentle, cool hands instead.

"You don't have to be here if you have duties to attend to, Herr Rottenführer," the doctor said, trying to sound respectful. A physician to the marrow of his bones, he couldn't bear to see the tormentor right next to the victim, it seemed. "I'll keep her here till the evening and after I dress her wounds, I'll bring her back to the barrack myself, if you like. I wouldn't want to take up any of your precious time. I know how busy you all are."

Despite the tone being coolly polite, the sting was there. Dahler circled the table so that he could stand right in front of me. I lifted my head from my folded hands, on which it was resting, to look at him. He parted his lips as if to ask something but then remembered the doctor and willed his face back into an unyielding mask.

"Give her more aspirin if she asks for it. Or, better, morphine if she's in a lot of pain. Buy it from the Sonderkommando if you don't have it," he said, by means of goodbye he quickly shoved a few dollars into the stupefied doctor's pocket and walked out of the room hastily.

A good minute passed before the doctor spoke to me in my native language. "Are you in any sort of relationship with that man?"

"He's my work detail's supervisor," I replied softly.

"Just that?"

"Just that."

"What did he beat you for?"

I thought of a good reason to offer him, for much too long, I guess. He snorted softly. "For nothing, then. As always."

I grinned in spite of myself. How nice it was, ordinary human interaction, despite the circumstances that brought me here; how positively refreshing and delightful! For a few moments, I could almost persuade myself that I was merely an ordinary girl visiting an ordinary doctor for some positively trivial reason. In my mind, we were back in Slovakia. He even spoke my language, the wonderful, kind-hearted doctor and just like that, the fantasy was complete.

"Do they often send you people with such injuries?" I asked him.

He was silent for a few moments. "You're my first case."

I turned my head to see his face, to see if he was joking. He finished dabbing at the last wound where the skin was broken and discarded an alcohol-soaked cotton ball into the metal container that stood next to me, along with the pincers. His eyes met mine; no, he was very much serious.

"Ordinarily, the only living patients that I have are either the SS men whom I am permitted to attend to, the Sonderkommando men, or..." He quickly caught himself before he said something that he was clearly strictly forbidden from mentioning to anyone. "But never mind that. Let me just apply these bandages now for some time and you should be as good as new by the evening. I would still strongly recommend sleeping on your stomach at least for a few nights. You're from the Kanada, aren't you? I thought so, judging by your clothes. Do you have two-person bunks in your barracks, like the Sonderkommando?" After I responded affirmatively, he nodded in satisfaction. "Good. A lashing can be a death sentence to anyone from the regular camp, due to the infection and unsanitary conditions. But you should be just fine. Do you think your supervisor will allow you to come here tomorrow to check if everything is healing nicely?"

"I can't say with all certainty but I think he will."

"I think so too. He looked like a wet hen when he just brought you here. Whatever did you do to him to provoke such a reaction? Refused his SS advances?" He smirked cynically.

"No." I looked away, ashamed for some reason.

"If I didn't know the SS, I'd say he looked almost guilty after what he did."

"He found me where I didn't belong," I finally offered by means of explanation.

"With a suitor?" This time his eyes wrinkled with mischief. "I can see how this could have upset him."

"With my sister." I didn't owe him an explanation, but the words tumbled out of me before I knew it. "She was being led to the gas chamber. He saved her from it."

His grin suddenly dropped. The doctor regarded me in stunned silence for some time.

"Please, don't tell anyone," I whispered, lowering my eyes.

"Of course, I won't, child." I felt his palm stroking my hair gently – a fatherly gesture. I wondered if his daughter perished here along with his wife. "Now, rest. Who knows when the chance will present itself again, just to rest, eh?"

*

I must have drifted to sleep after he'd covered me with a thin blanket and left me lying on the table. A man clearing his throat next to me woke me up. My head still foggy with sleep, I looked up and blinked a few times in an effort to clear my vision. The man was young, in his early or mid-twenties perhaps, with a dark stubble of closely-cropped hair under his inmate's cap, warm brown eyes and the typical attire of the Sonderkommando – striped trousers, a civilian shirt, under a decent jacket, with his number sewn onto it under the yellow star, and rubber boots.

"I'm sorry for waking you up." He smiled at me gingerly. "That SS man who beat you told me to bring you this." He extracted a clean shirt from under his jacket. "Can I have your old one? He told me that that one was ruined and that I would have to sew your old number and a star onto the new one."

Without saying a word, I pulled the old shirt from under myself and handed it to him. He thanked me and sat, cross-legged like a Turk, right on the floor with both of my shirts on his lap.

After observing him for some time, the curiosity got the better of me. "How do you know that it was he who beat me?"

"I saw it," he replied, without taking his eyes off his work. He was operating the needle quite professionally for a man, I had to give him that. "He's always much too fast to apply that whip if you ask me. The veterans from your Kommando all know to make themselves scarce whenever he blows his lid."

"He's not too bad," I said quietly.

"Not too bad?" he repeated, lifting his brows in disbelief and barked a laugh. "Compared to whom? Hitler?"

I grinned, in spite of myself. "Compared to Rottenführer Wolff. Or Hauptscharführer Moll."

"Well, you've got a point there," he agreed with another broad grin. "But it still doesn't excuse him for what he did. Beating a woman, with a whip, like some animal…" He shook his head, casting a sidelong glance at the blanket covering my back.

"It's all right. It doesn't even hurt that much. The doctor dressed it and gave me pain pills."

"He's still a sadistic SS bastard and that's all there is to it," he concluded abruptly, with sudden harshness in his voice.

I didn't argue.

When he spoke again, his tone was much softer. "My name is Andrej, by the way."

"Helena." I offered him my hand.

He reached out from the floor and shook it, smiling warmly.

"Your new shirt is almost ready. And if you need anything, our barracks are just around the corner. Tell anyone you're looking for Andrej Novák, or just give them a note with whatever you need. I'll try and get it for you."

"That's very generous of you, Andrej. Thank you."

"We all need to help each other the best we can to survive, don't we?" He bit off the thread, smoothed out the seams with his fingers and got up from the floor. "Here's your shirt. It was a pleasure to meet you, Helena."

"You, too, Andrej. Take care of yourself and thank you for your help."

He winked at me before setting off.

Chapter 13

Germany, 1947

"That's how I first met Herr Novák," Helena Dahler finished in her soft voice.

The testimony was long and tiresome; giving it, she looked just about everywhere but the panel of judges before her. Dr. Hoffman suddenly recalled himself in college; he also could not bear looking at his professors when he had to present his thesis. He was much too afraid that he'd forget something if he did. The audience's eyes had the oddest ability to destroy a person's confidence in the most crucial of moments, whereas floorboards and walls were much safer in this respect. They never judged. They were just there, stable and unmoving and impartial and perhaps that was the reason why the father of modern psychiatry Freud suggested that his patients lay on the couch and observed the ceiling, instead of forcing them to look into the psychiatrist's eyes.

The court recorder leaned back in his chair, taking a well-deserved respite as he flexed his fingers. Carter fidgeted in his seat for the first time. He must have just remembered that he hadn't had a smoke since the beginning of the hearing and now looked as though he would give his life for a Camel. Dr. Hoffman, meanwhile, went on watching the couple for a while. He had to give Helena that, she was rather well composed for an extermination camp survivor. Her voice didn't betray itself with trembling even when recounting such an emotional situation as watching one's sister's column being led straight to the gas chamber. Neither did she falter when recounting her own beating.

Dahler's face remained impassive almost the entire time that his wife spoke. Only a slight shadow passed over it when she was describing the whipping itself. He clearly did not enjoy being reminded of it and in front of the courtroom, even less so.

"My husband apologized to me after that incident countless times, of course…" Helena added as if in an afterthought, perhaps not wishing to upset her spouse.

Andrej Novák only snorted and rolled his eyes emphatically.

The Chairman looked at him over the rim of his glasses. "Herr Novák, did you know the circumstances of that incident? The fact that it concerned Frau Dahler's sister?"

"No. Helena never explained the details to me back then, which leads me to believe that it was Herr Dahler who invented the whole story and coached his wife how to tell it convincingly in case anyone asked. I knew that her sister arrived in the camp but Helena never told me back then that it was Dahler who saved her from the gas chamber."

"You didn't see the defendant emerge out of the bunker with Frau Dahler's sister?"

"No. I was already inside the second bunker watching the order. I only saw him beat Helena and that's all."

The Chairman exchanged glances with Lieutenant Carter. Dr. Hoffman, meanwhile, observed Dahler closely. The young man remained enviously calm, not protesting any of the accusations that Novák was hurling at him. *A silent admission of guilt? What else could it be, such intentional ignoring of Novák's claims?* Still, something just didn't seem right to the psychiatrist.

"You can ask my sister who brought her out of that bunker," Helena Dahler spoke quietly instead of her husband. "She came, at my request, from Palestine specifically, for this very purpose, to clarify any doubtful claims. My husband has included her on the list of witnesses for the defense and it was approved. We have submitted her affidavit but she came here in person in case you wish to question her properly."

"I don't see why we shouldn't interview Frau Feldman – her name is still Frau Feldman, isn't it?" After getting an affirmative nod from Helena, the Chairman went on to clarify. "We still have things to sort out with your testimony, Frau Dahler and with Herr Novák's but if we don't have enough time today, we'll definitely hear Frau Feldman's tomorrow."

Helena Dahler nodded and was back to studying her white, narrow palms.

The prosecutor called up his witness, Andrej Novák, who was only too glad to take the stand. "Herr Novák, you also said that the defendant used that whip on you, isn't that so?"

"Yes, he did. It happened not that long after that episode, in late November if I remember correctly. A part of our Sonderkommando was burning them by then, the corpses that the SS ordered us to dig out and cremate in the open pits. The most atrocious substance was seeping out of that soil in which they were buried and the SS didn't want it to poison their water supply, or spread some sort of plague around the camp. They were afraid for themselves, of course, not for the inmates. I remember my comrades saying that Moll was rushing everyone with his whip, like a slave driver during that last month. They had to finish fast because the temperatures began plummeting at night and the ground was difficult to turn the next day. So, it must have been around that time because it was then that I was ordered to join it, that part of the Sonderkommando, that is."

"Would you describe the circumstances to the court?"

The Slovak was quiet for some time, obviously gathering his thoughts. "Helena got very sick around that time. That is, at first it was a regular cold but as you can imagine, no one treated such things in the camp and so, it quickly took a turn for the worse. It went straight into her lungs. I had easy access to the Kanada warehouse due to my working with the Sonderkommando – prior to my reassignment, I was still a part of the transport Kommando. Every day we would deliver personal belongings left in the gas chambers' anterooms to the Kanada, so it wasn't that difficult for me to smuggle some medicine for Helena. We're both from Slovakia, you see. We had many things in common and it was nice to speak one's native language among all that German barking that was required of us. Over a matter of a few weeks, we developed a friendship of sorts. We weren't allowed to talk to each other but it was still possible to exchange a few words when the Kapos weren't watching. One day, Herr Dahler caught us talking and apparently, it displeased him quite a lot since he considered Helena his property." He shot Dahler a glare. "What incensed me the most about the entire affair was not the fact that he beat me for it. It was the fact that, with all the resources available to him, he didn't lift a finger to help her when she was as sick as a dog and on top of that, prohibited me from ever approaching her again. He didn't care one way or another if she died, as long as his pride was satisfied."

"Could you describe exactly what happened between you and Herr Dahler?" the prosecutor inquired. "What did he do?"

"In front of Helena, nothing," Novák declared, looking at Dahler derisively. "That's another reason why I advised the court on account of his character. Herr Dahler has always been extremely cunning. He knew that being the sensitive person that she is, Helena would be appalled if he began beating me in front of her. So, he told me to follow him and only when we were in the open field, far beyond both bunkers, did he begin working on me with his whip and then beating me just with his fists, when the whip wasn't enough of a thrill for him, I suppose."

"Was it just the two of you in the field?"

"No. He brought me near the ravines next to where the unearthed bodies were being burned. Part of my Sonderkommando was there, along with a few SS officers supervising the process but, needless to say, none of them paid the slightest attention to an SS man beating a Jew. It was such a common occurrence, it didn't impress or interest anyone."

"What happened next?"

"After he beat me within two breaths of my life, he took his gun out and stood over me with a smirk on his face. Dragged me near the edge of the big pyre and turned me, by my collar, towards it, saying, 'Well, waste of life, tell me which I should do now – shoot you first and then throw you in there or throw you in there alive?' I was terrified he'd actually do it, so I began begging him for my life. Finally, he dropped me onto the ground, kicked me one last time in the stomach and said, 'You're assigned to this part of the Sonderkommando from now on. You'll be burning these stiffs until we run out of them and after that, you'll be burning them in the crematorium that we're building. You'll be burning bodies until you kill yourself or until the time of your Sonderkommando comes' – they would kill off almost the entire Sonderkommando every four to five months, leaving just a few people to instruct the new Kommando on what to do. They didn't want to leave any witnesses to their crimes. I guess Herr Dahler hoped that it would be my fate also. He also warned me that if he ever saw me speaking to Helena again, he wouldn't be asking me any preferences as to how I would like to go into the pyre, dead or alive."

The Chairman shifted his attention to the defendant. "Is that true, what Herr Novák just described to the court?"

"Not entirely. I did beat him and I did ask Kommandoführer Hössler to assign him to the part of the Sonderkommando that was in charge of the cremation. But I never threatened him with my gun or any burning pits. That's a blatant lie," he announced dryly.

"Of course, you would say it's a lie," Novák said poisonously. "You wouldn't want your wife to learn the truth about the many things you did."

"I don't have secrets from my wife and what you just described certainly doesn't fall into the category of the things *I did*." Despite his tone being coolly polite, the derisive look he threw Novák's way spoke volumes. "I haven't said a word against anything spoken in this courtroom that was true to the fact. I'm not trying to paint myself better than I am but I will not sit here silently either and listen to your lies. If something that you say is not true, I will let the court know it. I regret if such a position upsets you."

"It doesn't upset me," Novák replied sweetly. "Quite the contrary; it's you who will have to live with yourself for the rest of your days knowing the crimes you committed against innocent people."

Dr. Hoffman concentrated on the couple in front of him. Helena visibly stiffened, while, next to her, Dahler took a deep breath, seemingly bringing his emotions under control. After a moment, he was back to his politely uninterested self. Dr. Hoffman almost applauded such self-control.

"I am very well aware of my part in the Holocaust, Herr Novák," Dahler began slowly, carefully measuring his words. "It is not my intention to minimize it in any way. I know that my participation in what was proclaimed and rightfully so, a crime against humanity, will be forever on my unclean conscience. In no way is it my intention to deny my responsibility for being a part of that collective mechanism that brought death to millions of innocent people. Do I regret the part I played in it? Absolutely. With all that said, I won't be taking the blame for something I didn't do. I hope that you will respect this court as much as I respect it and treat it accordingly. Speak the truth that is. Otherwise, this entire procedure is pointless. Besides, if we're talking about throwing people into burning pits, it's you who is guilty of this crime, not me."

All of the heads turned to the Slovak. All the blood seemed to leave his face at once. "What lies are you spreading now, Herr Dahler?"

The emphasized use of the German form of address didn't escape Dr. Hoffman's attention. He was mildly surprised that Novák didn't address him by his full military rank. He almost expected a jab of this sort from the Slovak.

"Not lies, facts." Dahler shrugged, unimpressed. "Wasn't it you and your comrades who shoved an SS guard alive into the crematorium's oven during one of your revolts?"

An eerie silence hung over the room. Dr. Hoffman could hear himself breathing. Blood rushed back to Novák's cheeks, painting them in crimson patches.

"Do you know how many people he killed? That man deserved it!" he cried, trembling with his entire body.

Dahler was the picture of composure. "Again, blatant lie. That guard was no Moll by any accounts. He was one of those apathetic guards that didn't care one way or another as to what's going on around them as long as the work gets done. He was much too indifferent to beat anybody, let alone derive any sadistic pleasure from it. He just happened to be there, alone with you and you used the chance to take your revenge out on at least someone wearing the uniform you all hated so much. Let's call a spade a spade, Herr Novák. You killed an innocent man; sentenced him to die a horrific death in an oven. Of course, it's now my word against yours but judging by the fact that out of the two of you – the man, whom you and your friends burned alive and yourself – it's you, who's lived to tell the tale. That makes you the sadistic killer, not me. I didn't throw you into any burning pits, otherwise, we wouldn't have been having this conversation right now."

"How dare you call me a killer?! You, who wore the SS uniform, who sent millions to their death, who savagely beat the woman he claimed he had feelings for, how dare you call me a sadistic killer?!"

The Chairman hit his hammer, calling Novák to order. "We won't be having a circus here with a shouting contest, Herr Novák. Calm down, please. As a matter of fact, I think it would be wise for all of us to take a little break. I'm announcing recess and I'll see you all here in one hour precisely."

Chapter 14

A State Magistrate's Office's cafeteria was a simple affair but it was functioning and that's all that mattered to the harassed-looking court members and American MPs. An outline of an eagle was still visible on one of the walls even through a hasty whitewash job the German POWs had managed to complete last year, with whatever miserable resources were available to them. Lieutenant Carter and Dr. Hoffman chewed their lunch in silence, each immersed in his own thoughts. Ever since the end of the war, they'd had to plow through thousands of denazification cases, yet neither of them had ever come across anything of this odd sort.

Andrej Novák barely touched his food. Instead, he shifted his gaze from the psychiatrist back to an MP and back again, growing more and more agitated.

"You're not actually considering believing that Nazi, are you?" He'd finally had enough of that silence. "You do understand that he brainwashed his wife into saying all of those things, don't you?"

Lieutenant Carter stopped chewing and looked at Dr. Hoffman. The latter put down his fork. With the Slovak sharing their table – a co-plaintiff, he had the right to sit with them – the quiet lunch, it appeared, would not happen. *Might as well talk about the elephant in the courtroom.*

Dr. Hoffman fidgeted in his seat uncomfortably. A torrent of accusations would pour down onto his poor head after what he was about to say but he was here to observe and give his verdict and so, here it went. "I don't think he did," he announced quietly, after a pause.

"No?" Carter regarded him with curiosity. He took the announcement much better than the Slovak, who slumped back into his chair in stunned, furious silence. But Carter had long grown used to relying on the psychiatrist's opinions concerning even much higher-ranking war criminals; to Novák, Dr. Hoffman was just another American uniform in glasses who didn't know the SS from his elbow. He hadn't had time to earn the Slovak's respect, as a specialist, yet, so such mistrust was only too understandable.

"No," Dr. Hoffman repeated. "Based on the behavior that I observed, it is my profound conviction that Mrs. Dahler hasn't been coached in any way for this testimony. It doesn't have a 'learned' quality to it. One can easily tell when a person has been coached to give a certain testimony. It's invariably stilted, often repeats itself as though to drive a point across; it lacks emotion and doesn't stray away from the subject. In short, it sounds like a recited lesson. Mrs. Dahler's story was her own. I don't believe that Mr. Dahler influenced it in any way prior to this hearing. However—"

"I can't believe you have actually fallen for his lies!" Novák had found his voice again. He made a gesture of despair with his hands before dropping them helplessly onto his lap. "I have warned you that he's a snake – a veritable snake, yes! – who belongs on the gallows! That woman, whom he calls his wife, is a victim! All that he does, starting with all that, *can she sit next to me* business, is manipulation through and through! How you, a psychiatrist, can't see through it? He has frightened her into submission! And do you know what? Perhaps you're right and he didn't have to specifically prepare her for this hearing. She's so afraid of him, she'd never dare think of saying something against him! She's terrified of him and he's only using her as a means of getting that denazification clearance certificate from you! Who knows what's going on in their house, behind the closed doors? And you're planning to let him walk away free and keep tormenting her throughout her entire life? Or, maybe, she won't have to suffer any longer. If you clear him, he won't need her anymore. Do you understand that he may kill her?"

A mild smile spread slowly over Dr. Hoffman's face. The Slovak was certainly passionate about Helena Dahler's safety. Or, most likely, Helena herself.

"I doubt he will kill her, Mr. Novák."

"I don't. Not for a second." The Slovak crossed his arms over his chest defiantly. "Because I know him. His real face. You only know the one that he wanted you to see."

"I apologize for the interruption but I did hear a 'however,' if I'm not mistaken." Carter stepped in to save his colleague from Novák's passionate rebuke.

Dr. Hoffman grinned in gratitude.

"As I have already stated, I don't believe that Mrs. Dahler was coached to give this testimony. However," he looked at Carter, who smiled broadly in return, "there's something wrong with Helena herself."

"Wrong? As in…"

"As in, psychologically." Dr. Hoffman's gaze concentrated on the ruins outside.

The glass in the windows had all miraculously been replaced, wherever the city administration bartered it from. It was the view that was the same as everywhere in Germany. Shambles and shards of the former life; pitiful gray piles of dust and concrete and former glory. It was all swept aside from the main roads and carefully stacked alongside them. All around, a former shell of a city lay, thoroughly pretending that it was all right and very much functioning when, in reality, it still crumbled whenever the clearing brigades pulled the wrong brick out of the pile.

In front of Dr. Hoffman's eyes, the faces of his recent interviewees materialized in place of the ruins – the victims, not the perpetrators. How similar it was with them – a seemingly functioning façade, but once he touched the wrong brick, provoked the wrong memory or asked the wrong question and the whole person collapsed, tumbled, and disintegrated into a totally destroyed, obliterated mass. Too much internal structural damage. It would take years to rebuild them anew if it was even possible to rebuild them at all.

"Care to elaborate?" Carter's voice brought him out of his reverie.

Dr. Hoffman regarded his notebook but didn't open it to consult his notes. He looked pensive and lost for a moment, unsure of where to start. "Some of her emotional reactions to certain events are far too strange. For instance, when she was describing the lashing that he gave her and what followed... Have you noticed how she repeatedly stated that she hardly felt any pain and instead was overwhelmed with this profound feeling of gratitude? How she minimized the harm that was done to her and praised Dahler instead for such a wonderful deed? I understand that he saved her sister but... if you look at the things logically, he and his compatriots are the reason why that sister found herself in that camp in the first place. An ordinary person's reaction would be suppressed anger, silent condemnation, definitely emotional and physical hurt... Mrs. Dahler, instead, declared that she almost loved him at that moment."

"Because he told her to say it!" Novák cried in desperation once again. A few heads from the neighboring tables turned in their direction but the majority ignored the shout entirely. Such outbursts were nothing new in this place; lawyers and prosecutors were particularly prone to them.

"I doubt it was his doing." Dr. Hoffman shook his head. "I firmly believe that she did feel love for him but why, that's what I'm yet to understand."

Carter sipped his coffee. "When you say that there's something psychologically wrong with her, does that mean that she's unfit to stand trial, as a witness, or..."

"Oh no, she *is* fit," Dr. Hoffman quickly replied. "She's not clinically unsound or anything of that sort but... she definitely suffers from one sort of dissociative disorder or the other."

"And you, a Stanford graduate, don't know what it is?" Carter's face drew to a wry smile.

"I'm afraid, no," Dr. Hoffman admitted, spreading his arms in a helpless gesture. "How can I better put it for you to understand? Imagine that I'm a nineteenth-century physician who has just noticed the beginning of sepsis in a patient. I know that something is wrong with the patient but have not the faintest idea as to what has caused it or how to cure it. Nowadays, we would blame the bacteria, give him penicillin and he'd be like new in a couple of weeks. But just a hundred years ago, I would be absolutely and utterly helpless. Same with Mrs. Dahler, I'm afraid. I can tell that there's something wrong with her but I can't tell what. There are no described precedents like that when a victim would willingly defend the perpetrator and even go as far as declare love for him. It's simply unheard of. I don't understand it and I have not the slightest clue as to what caused it and even less clue as to how to treat it. If it's treatable at all, that is and if such treatment would be beneficial for her."

"Why wouldn't it be?"

"Sometimes, a psychiatrist can do more harm with such treatments. Forceful conversion therapy for homosexuals is just one such example. It does absolutely nothing to change their nature but causes an appalling number of suicides. Sometimes it's better to leave the things as they are if they don't harm the patient."

"You're saying that she'll off herself if you separate her from Dahler?" Carter arched his brow just enough to express utter disbelief.

Dr. Hoffman pondered something for a long time. "To be honest with you, I wouldn't be surprised. She appears to be dependent on him to an unhealthy degree. She searches for his hand each time she struggles with words. He said it himself that she prefers to be next to him at all times. At first, I thought that he only said it in order to control her and what she says but then I noticed that she does it on her own. And the way she entered the courtroom? My first impression was that she was a typical victim following her abuser who, by not allowing her to walk in first, reminds her of her place, once again. But now I think that it was her initiative. She was *hiding* behind his back. She definitely brought a lot of issues with her from the camp, severe social anxiety is one of them, depression and perhaps even certain elements of trauma-related psychosis. With all that, she doesn't see Dahler as an abuser but as a protector. I have not the faintest idea why, but there you have it."

"Perhaps, because he was the only person who made her feel safe, to a certain degree, I mean, in the camp?" Carter suggested.

Dr. Hoffman nodded slowly. "That was my impression too. I do believe that if it was that other SS man, whom she mentioned, Gröning; if he were kind to her, she would project those emotions on to him. Or the previous accountant, Weber. Or whoever else was in control and on whose decisions and favor, her and her sister's lives depended."

"Our friend Novák?" Carter insinuated in jest, motioning his head toward the Slovak. The latter's cheeks instantly assumed a deep blush, only confirming Dr. Hoffman's guess concerning Andrej's true feelings.

"Mr. Novák didn't have enough power to make any life or death decisions," he mused out loud. "No. We're talking only about SS men. Not even Kapos. It had to be someone who wore the uniform."

"So, she doesn't actually love her husband then?"

Dr. Hoffman inclined his head to one side, chewing on his lip. "I believe that *she believes* that she does. Like a schizophrenic believes that he is made entirely of glass. This is how he sees reality and no amount of therapy will persuade him in the opposite. I believe that she had persuaded herself that she loved him because it helped her survive. That lie, into which she forced herself, eventually became a reality for her. I do believe that she's fully dependent on him but whether she would have fallen in love with him during normal circumstances? I can't tell you that with any degree of certainty. It's all just a theory, of course," he added quickly, giving

Carter a somewhat apologetic smile. "I can't diagnose something modern psychiatry has never had to deal with before. Or perhaps, she does love him after all and I'm searching for an illness where there isn't one."

He stopped abruptly when he saw Franz Dahler escort his wife into the cafeteria. With his palm positioned firmly on the small of Helena's back, Dahler was pointing at an unoccupied table positioned in the furthest corner. Through the general buzz of the cafeteria, Dr. Hoffman could barely decipher the German words – apparently, the couple's official language.

"Why don't you go sit over there and I'll grab us something to eat? Unless you want to stay in line with me?"

Helena replied something much too softly for the psychiatrist to hear. Dahler laughed at her response. His white teeth glistened in the bright light of the overhead lamps. "Point taken. Do you also want me to take sauerkraut if they have it? And something sweet, too? Coffee, as usual?"

It was then that the Austrian's gaze fell on the table, which Dr. Hoffman shared with Carter and Novák. He acknowledged the psychiatrist – the only one out of the group who was facing him – with a somewhat stilted, embarrassed nod and whispered something to Helena. She turned to Dr. Hoffman, offered him a small wave and quickly made a hasty escape toward the corner table where she sat facing the wall instead of the room. Dr. Hoffman smiled wistfully at such a strange choice of seating arrangements, as did Dahler, when he approached the psychiatrist's table.

"I'm sorry." This time, the Austrian offered the same apologetic smile to everyone around the table since now it was all three men observing him, two with curiosity and one with unmasked hatred. "She's a bit skittish. She was afraid you'd ask us to share the table with you and she's had enough people around her today. She'd rather stare at the wall and my ugly mug."

Dr. Hoffman smiled in understanding. "I very well imagine she could use some respite from us all."

"I'm sorry," Dahler repeated again, gestured to his watch (Dr. Hoffman had the impression that he would stay there and apologize some more had his time not been limited) and quickly headed to the end of the line in front of the food court.

Carter snorted softly in amazement. "What do you know? The stony-faced Teutonic Knight can actually smile when caught unawares."

"I believe that Otto Ohlendorf, who annihilated the entire Jewish population of South Ukraine and Moldova, was smiling at you too when you were interviewing him," Novák commented poisonously.

"He did," Dr. Hoffman conceded surprisingly easily. The Slovak regarded him with suspicion. The psychiatrist, however, only nodded a few times to some thoughts of his own, before repeating quietly once again, "He did."

Chapter 15

Helena

Auschwitz-Birkenau. November 1942

Rottenführer Gröning was seeing off the newly promoted Unterscharführer Dahler, all smiles and countless back pats. They had become fast friends in the course of a mere couple of months, most likely owing to the fact that Dahler shared much more in common with the new accountant than with his other comrade, Wolff. Surrounded by the grinning inmates of the Sonderkommando, Gröning helped his new friend adjust the backpack on his shoulders, bursting at the seams with all the goods the inmates had stuffed there just that morning – *unbeknownst to Unterscharführer Dahler, of course. Let it be a surprise for him when he opens it on the train. From the Kommando, with love; so that when he comes back, he'll say a good word, for us, to Voss and we won't be sent to the gas, as our four months expiration date approaches.*

No one spoke of it but the SS men serving in the regular camp went on leave with a change of clothes and a single, mandatory, camp-provided food parcel. The Kanada and Sonderkommando supervisors went on leave like kings, weighed down with the murdered people's possessions and all sorts of delicacies, thoroughly pretending that they had not the faintest idea of what their inmates had shoved in their pockets and backpacks and sewn into their uniforms' seams.

I watched them say their farewells from my sorting station with sudden alarm. Unterscharführer Dahler was still here, yet with a sudden harsh lucidity, I sensed his absence from the camp. Wary-eyed, I observed my surroundings in a futile effort to persuade myself that nothing horrible was truly happening. The "old numbers" had ceased their transactions just to renew their black-market trading as soon as the two SS men were out of the warehouse. All around me, the girls were still sorting the clothes; Maria, with her Kapo armband and a club at her hip, waited for her masters to leave just to resume her chatting with the inmates who were on kitchen duty that day. After lunch, Rottenführer Gröning, with a box full of foreign currency, would come out of his office and smoke in the doors as he waited for the staff car to arrive and drive him to the Kommandantur. Sonderkommando men would still hurl suitcases from yet another truck into a pile next to the warehouse – everything would once again become so ordinary and mundane. Only, along with Dahler, the very sense of security would be gone. Throwing yet another frantic look around, I suddenly realized that I had no one to turn to if anything happened.

As though sensing my unease, Unterscharführer Dahler caught my glance and offered me a barely perceptible nod before turning back to Gröning and quickly saying something in his ear. The latter looked at me closely through his lenses but nodded stiffly nevertheless. And just like that, after a final parting handshake, both were gone – Dahler, to the truck that would give him a ride to the train station, Gröning, back to his office – and I suddenly couldn't get my breath, for never in my life had I felt so utterly abandoned and alone, even with Różínka by my side.

She was oblivious to my mood, just like she was oblivious to everything around her. That day, she worked as diligently as always; she had the strongest incentive, after all. *Herr Unterscharführer had told her that if she worked hard enough, he'd grant her the permission to visit her darling babies in the children's Lager. Perhaps, when he comes back from his leave and hears Kapo Maria's report about how hard she had worked—*

"What children? Are you mad?" Just her misfortune, Maria overheard Różínka's usual murmurs and there was no Unterscharführer Dahler around anymore to stop her cold, mocking laughter. "Your children have been feeding the worms for months now, you half-witted *Scheiße-Jude!* The Sonderkommando are burning what's left of them in pits. Yes, those very ones in the field, behind the bunkers."

For an instant, Różínka had lost her very faculty of speech. She stood there and blinked at the sneering Kapo like an owl. "But Herr Unterscharführer said—"

"Herr Unterscharführer lied!"

The entire barracks stood still after that shout.

On the verge of tears, yet still refusing to believe Maria's cruel words, Różínka whispered, "But why would he—"

"Because the SS love inventing lies like that to taunt you, on purpose. It's funny to see the look on your faces afterward."

Without saying another word, numb with grief, Różínka turned slowly back to her sorting station and resumed her work. She didn't say another word throughout the entire day. In the evening, she refused her bread for the first time. A week later, I woke up in the middle of the night just to find her side of our two-person bunk empty and, having burst out of the barracks against all regulations, had just made it in time to pull her away from the wire, to which she was so resolutely crawling. Self-imposed starvation wasn't killing her fast enough, and thus, she decided that the electric wire would do the trick instead.

"What are you doing?!" I whisper-screamed in her ear, hurling myself on top of her body and pressing her into the snow. "Just what do you think you're doing, you stupid, stupid—" I gasped and suddenly couldn't bring myself to utter another word.

Then, the tears came; mine, not hers. Stroking her black hair, now streaked with mourning gray, I sobbed my heart out. Only then did she still herself and stop her suicidal crawling, right near the guard's tower, across the death zone. The camp's rule for the guards prescribed shooting any inmate who had entered it but the guard above us, with the mouth of his machine-gun pointing downward, only regarded us sorrowfully with his head tilted to one side and from time to time took a pull on his cigarette. I remembered Dahler saying that they had begun conscripting elderly men to take over the young SS men's duties after the latter had all been sent to the Eastern Front. Highlighted by the glare from his searchlight, he eventually motioned for us to get up and get lost before all three of us would get in trouble. I wondered if he had daughters of our age at home.

After that incident, Rôžínka was back to her slow self-starvation, still positively refusing to exchange a single word with me. To be sure, she was still alive thanks to Unterscharführer Dahler's action, but it appeared that now a part of her died along with her children and without them, she was as good as condemned to death, refusing to eat, moving like an automaton and simply waiting for the life to abandon her body that was wasting itself away day by day. Through my new acquaintance from the Sonderkommando, Andrej, I managed to procure some sort of pills for her that he had suggested could help but they only succeeded in numbing her senses enough to prevent her from going to the wire. However, they did nothing to remedy a mother's heart torn to shreds in such a brutal manner. And so, she sat next to me staring vacantly ahead, a mess-kit, from which she had poured the contents into mine, lying forgotten in her limp hands.

I ate my soup and tasted the salt of my own tears in it. The silent treatment stung the worst. Perhaps, it would have been more merciful to have let her die along with her children but I was a selfish sister and couldn't bear to imagine being alone in this place any longer. Little wonder she now despised me for my selfishness.

"Rôžínka, you must eat something," I spoke to her quietly. "If you don't eat, they will send you to the gas. The monthly disinfection is coming up. If a doctor sees how thin you are, he'll mark your name on the list and it'll be over for you. No one will help you then, not even Unterscharführer –"

I suddenly stumbled over the familiar name. *He isn't even here, you stupid sow. Should have appreciated him better when he was. Murderer's hands, my foot. Who else here cares if you die tomorrow? Not a single soul.*

I clutched my mess-kit tighter, just to hold onto something tangible, solid; just not to feel the ground go from under me.

"Unterscharführer Dahler?" She gave me an odd, cold look. "Perhaps I would have preferred it that way. Has that thought ever occurred to you?"

I stared at her in disbelief. "But how can you possibly say that?"

"You're not a mother," she replied without emotion and turned away. "You won't understand."

"That's a fine thing to do, to throw that in my face," I argued bitterly, tears welling up again.

"You've changed a lot, Lena."

"The camp life does it to you," I barked bitterly back.

"Conspiring with an SS man in such a manner, behind my back—"

"No one conspired against you! He only invented that Children's *Lager* tale because I asked him to, to make it a bit easier for you in the very beginning! Would you have rather heard it from him the same way as Maria did it to you, on your very first day? Like they do with the rest of the new arrivals when they point at the crematorium chimneys and tell them to wave goodbye to their relatives that go up in smoke? Would that have been more merciful?"

"More merciful would have been to leave me with my children so that I could have held them in my arms while they were dying, as any mother should. And you two robbed me – and them – of that."

She could have stabbed me in my chest with the same effect. I stifled a sob. I hardly ever cried here, but now I suddenly felt it coming. I thought I had grown used to this, to this unbearable isolation and solitude among the faceless crowds, to the constant fear of death that prickled one's spine at the slightest of provocations, to the savage dog-eat-dog world that prompted a young son to rob his elderly father of the last piece of bread just to get caught by the Kapo and get clubbed to death along with his old man, to the corruption that was the second universal language after German and to the hope that perished daily in the gas chambers along with each new transport and tasted like ashes on one's bloodless tongue.

It was coming in waves now, surging up and choking me with the severity of it and scratched against the back of my throat like barbed wire. My own sister wished nothing to do with me any longer. I had no one left in this entire, hostile world.

Franz, a hateful and uninvited thought came, and I clutched at my own hair just to rip off the very thought of him out of my mind.

"I'm sorry that I asked him to drag you out of there, Różínka." I wiped my face with my sleeve and made a move to get up. "I'm sorry I was so selfish. Go ahead and slowly kill yourself, so that I lose not only my nephews but my sister as well, in front of my own eyes. Leave me all alone here. That's a good sister."

I hurled all of these childish screams at her when I should have begged for her forgiveness but the environment here did strange things to one's psyche and when one only thinks of survival for months, to no apparent end, should it really be expected of such a damaged person to do anything logical or decent?

She still caught my sleeve before I could set off back to my work detail and pulled me into a tight embrace instead. Tears streamed down my cheeks. My entire body was shaking with sobs.

"It's me, who should be apologizing," she finally said with a sigh. "I should have thought of you. Of course, I won't abandon you, my poor little darling." She was only ten years older than me but I was always her little darling. She was my second mother, my most intimate friend and I almost lost her – twice. "I'll start eating, I promise."

She kissed the top of my head, covered with a blue kerchief. From the safety of her embrace, I caught Maria regarding us with a mocking expression, full of cruel scorn.

*

Exposed and vulnerable, we waited for our turn in the disinfection facilities – a pitiful sea of naked bodies. While our clothes were being sprayed with some sort of chemicals, which invariably caused unbearable itching and irritation, we lined up in front of the men with shears, for our monthly ritual. It was Różínka's third time only – she had to undergo a mandatory disinfection process as soon as her name was officially on the list of the Kanada Kommando – but she still couldn't overcome her emotions that such a humiliating treatment brought. That's precisely how one could tell the new members of the Kommando from the old ones. The new ones still stood covering their breasts with their arms and were red with embarrassment. We had long gotten used to the procedure; to the SS doctors present, to the female SS overseers rushing us, to their male SS counterparts standing there and watching the whole spectacle just for the entertainment. We, Kanada women, were well-fed compared to the others. We were allowed to keep our hair. We were still attractive to them due to all that.

When my turn came, I obediently stepped in front of a political prisoner, a Red Triangle. I raised my arms, jerking briefly when the cold metal touched my armpits. In a few moments, it was all over with.

"Open your legs, please."

From his accent and polite manner, I deduced that he was, most likely, Polish intelligentsia. I grinned bitterly in spite of myself at the entire rotten business around us. A university professor or some such, shaving off Jewish girls' pubic hair. He looked equally embarrassed by such a sad state of affairs.

I had just stepped in line waiting in front of the doors that said *Bath and Disinfection* when one of the three SS doctors present called me over. I never learned his name but recognized him at once, as he never missed a chance to conduct *personal searches* on the inmates that caught his eye. That would make sense with the fresh arrivals who might have smuggled some valuables that way but with us, however, it was a pure whim of his, from which he drew his sexual pleasure. That was the only explanation for his actions, for no one heard of a single case when he would find something on us, the Kanada Kommando, that is.

I stared straight ahead of me as he gripped my hips with his cold hands covered in rubber gloves and shoved his probing fingers inside of me. It took all the will in the world not to wince in disgust and to keep one's face impassive during such revolting, invasive searches, for one single twitch of an eye could be interpreted as utter disrespect for the Master Race and the doctors were the ones who decided who would live and who would die here. Antagonizing them in such a manner would certainly earn one a one-way ticket to the gassing facility and we all were aware of it. Perhaps, lost in his indoctrination and propaganda-induced illusion, he considered it a great honor for us to experience an Aryan man touching us in the most intimate manner. To keep our lives, we had to pretend that it was.

With utmost relief, I stepped away when he finally released me. Another inmate, a Jewish doctor this time, rubbed my head and pubic area with a solution of calcium chloride. After thoroughly rubbing it all over myself and ignoring my burning eyes, I felt at least somewhat cleansed of the SS doctor's touch. In spite of myself, my thoughts turned to Dahler again. One thing he never did was force himself on me despite making his feelings more than clear in his note. Not once did he touch me in a disrespectful way. Not once did he make me shudder with revulsion at the mere thought of his touch.

I looked at my bare body shivering with cold after the shower and was suddenly overcome with such mad longing for his return that it caught my very breath in my throat. I tried swallowing the lump that now lodged itself there but it refused to go away. Hot tears sprung to my eyes again as I was pulling the shirt, still warm and smelling strongly of disinfectant, over my head. I couldn't remember myself crying so easily here before. Now, it was all I did.

Różínka moved to pacify me, muttering her quiet curses on the doctor's account but it was not him who was on my desperate, anguished mind. I wanted Franz back.

Franz, Franz, Franz, I repeated his name like a prayer in my head but not a whisper flew off my tightly sealed lips. Różínka would never forgive me if I admitted this to her.

Chapter 16

Helena

Appell. Fog rolling in from the north. Coffee, which had lost its steam long before we had a chance to warm our shivering bodies with it. A new SS guard demanding something from Wolff. Wolff rolling his eyes and motioning for Maria to deal with the problem which was clearly not his. Nothing in the Kanada was his problem unless it involved looting the freshly murdered people's possessions.

I should have guessed by the malevolent look Maria threw my way that she had something in store for me after her short exchange with the second SS man.

"You, *Scheiße-Jude!*" It was a new form of endearment from her. When Unterscharführer Dahler was here, I was just 'you.' His absence was noticeable even in such minor details, which weren't really significant if one would stop and rationally think about it but which cut to the quick nevertheless just by the sheer power of their unnecessary cruelty. Not life-threatening at any rate, yet it stung nonetheless and one couldn't help but feel it. "Come over here. Faster, will you? Lazy ass!" I broke into a trot. "I have a job for you."

I froze at attention diligently. The new SS man gave me an evaluating once-over.

"Is she clean?" He looked at Maria with suspicion.

"*Jawohl,* Herr Rottenführer. They are all treated for lice every fourth week of the month as a preventive measure. Anyone who gets caught scratching is sent away at once. These women are all clean."

"Do you understand German?" This time he addressed me directly.

"*Jawohl*, Herr Rottenführer."

He nodded in satisfaction and motioned for me to follow him. We walked in silence for some time – me, the usual three steps behind him – until he either grew bored with it or decided that he must instruct me, after all, concerning my new duty.

"Jehovah Witnesses usually work in the officers' quarters but those fanatical halfwits refuse to touch anything military-related. Religious views or some such. Even the Kommandant can't set them straight. Well, no matter. The point is, while they clean the living quarters, you'll need to work on Hauptscharführer Moll's uniform, boots, belt, and holster."

At the mere mention of the dreaded name, my stomach churned in horror. Moll, the sadist; Moll, the torturer; Moll, the terror of the entire Sonderkommando detail, who once beat an inmate to death only because the inmate dared to kick Moll's Alsatian in the snout and no matter that the dog had been set on that inmate by Moll himself, solely because he was bored that day and wished to see some entertainment.

The SS man, meanwhile, continued talking in his phlegmatic manner. It's not like he would have noticed the blood leaving my face at once – he walked too far ahead of me to see the cadaverous tint my skin had taken on straight away. "The uniform needs to be brushed, the boots polished, the belt and the holster oiled. I'll give you everything you'll need."

By the time we reached Moll's quarters, I could barely restrain my body from trembling openly. Far too many stories we had heard about him, even in our "safe haven," Kanada. He was the man who killed just for the thrill of it and I was to oil his belt!

I breathed with difficulty. The sky itself was no longer a sky above my miserable head, it was a coffin lid, indifferent and closing.

"Herr Rottenführer—" Such a pitiful whisper against the November wind. I was ready to dig my heels into the ground and beg for the SS man to send me to the quarries for all I cared but not into that serpent's pit. I would rather turn soil with a shovel all day, or I would rather hurl bricks until I dropped with exhaustion than face that evil incarnate.

It was no use to call him. He didn't hear me.

The SS barracks stood empty and silent, with only a few inmates darting dutifully around it, cleaning equipment and with piles of laundry in hand. Some of them sported the shined boots just like the SS wore – the highest class-distinction amongst the camp's elite. After the typhus outbreak, the SS were wary of admitting just about anybody into their personal quarters. Only the "old numbers" were deemed worthy of such an honor. Almost none of them wore the striped garb and their faces gleamed with health, too.

Moll must be at his work detail also; very far away from here, in that field behind the bunkers, I tried persuading myself, taking deep breaths as I set one foot before the other. The air was suddenly gone out of the entirety of Poland and I struggled to find any for my failing lungs as I stepped through the door of his personal quarters. *He's not here. I won't see him. I'll just do what is asked of me and leave.*

We reached the end of the long corridor. The SS man knocked on the door and I nearly fainted with terror. Moll was here after all. The last hope had been lost.

"Herr Hauptscharführer, the Kanada girl is here. Shall I let her in?"

A lazy *"Ja,"* sounded from behind the door.

If the SS man didn't prod me in the back, I would have never made that step inside. He shoved past me, saluted his superior officer who was seated at his desk and asked for permission to *arrange things.* Much to my relief, Moll ignored me entirely, consumed with papers littering his desk.

"Come over here." That was meant for me. I dashed past Moll's desk to the other side of the spacious room as fast as I could, head pulled into my shoulders, trying to make myself as small and invisible as possible. The SS man held out the brush for me. "Start with the uniform." He indicated the jacket and jodhpurs, waiting for my first few uncertain strokes, before growling in exasperation at my incompetence and grabbing my hand, with the brush in it. "Not like that! You'll never get the lint out of it if you stroke it like a cat. Don't be gentle with it. Hard, strong strokes, do you understand?" He forced my hand up and down the front of the jacket, pressing it hard into the gray material. "Do it yourself now."

I imitated his strokes as best as I could. After I didn't get bashed on the head, I realized that he found my work satisfactory.

"Do you know how to polish the boots or shall I show you also?"

"I know how to polish boots, Herr Rottenführer."

"Do you know how to oil the leather?"

"How hard can it fucking be, oiling the leather?" Moll's irritated shout made me drop my brush. This time I didn't escape a clip behind the ear from the SS man, accompanied by the *clumsy cow* whispered under his breath. "I have a report to write and I can't do it while you two are jawing like you're at a fucking market! Leave her alone. If she has half a brain, she'll figure it out. If she doesn't, tough luck for her. You'll have to find a new one."

"*Jawohl*, Herr Hauptscharführer." The SS man clicked his heels and took his leave. I watched him go with envy. He could escape Moll's wrath but I was a mere slave here and a disposable one at that. I quickly resumed my brushing just to avoid his gaze, just not to think about the entire, *'you'll have to find a new one',* veiled threat.

Moll wasn't even thirty yet, however, he already had hundreds of lives on his conscience. He had a face that suited him perfectly – round and brutal, a former pig farmer's one, whom the SS reoriented from slaughtering pigs to slaughtering humans, with astounding ease. His strawberry-blond hair was brushed away from his freckled forehead. Low-hanging brows hid the small, cruel eyes, one of which was said to be artificial. I never looked at him closely enough to find out. Few people did and even less lived to tell the tale.

That morning, he smoked and issued curses, under his breath, after every other drag on his cigarette. He was in a foul mood that day and cursed before picking up the phone and during the conversation itself. No one could escape his sardonic remarks, neither his orderlies, not the Kommandant himself, whoever it was that he was talking to.

"Pompous fucking raven. Where am I going to get three hundred new men for the Sonderkommando?" The pencil scratched the paper angrily. In a mocking voice, apparently impersonating Kommandant Höss, *"Surely you don't want any witnesses to remain alive, Hauptscharführer? Surely, you understand the situation. I'm only following the protocol myself."*

A loud bang on the wooden surface made me jerk involuntarily. Still clasping an empty brandy glass in his paw, he listened to the person on the other end of the line and snorted in disdain. "Like they will go to the gas willingly. Another fucking machine-gun squad that I'll need to request. Another three hundred to train. Out of them, about one-third will off themselves after they drag their relatives out of the gas chamber by the ankles. Another new group I will have to find and train. And whose problem is it? Herr Kommandant's? Of course not. Herr Kommandant *only follows the protocol,* the old sod. And who has to take care of all the dirty business? Hauptscharführer Moll, no doubt. Let's hang it all on Moll. Moll is tough. Moll will sort them all out fast." More huffing and fidgeting. Suddenly, "You!" I nearly jumped and swung round to face him, pressing the brush to myself. "How long are you going to mess around with that uniform? It's clean. Polish the boots now."

"Yes, Herr Hauptscharführer."

I had already located the polish and the brush in the corner of the closet and pulled them out but halted as soon as I realized that the SS man who had brought me here didn't set out the boots for me. Nor were they in the closet. My gaze quickly darted to the richly upholstered sofa next to which a coffee table stood. No boots there either.

Moll was still busy with his paper and phone conversation but the wait was growing interminable. *As soon as he sees that I'm not working, it'll be off with you, Helena.* I cleared my throat and made the tiniest step forward. "I'm sorry to interrupt you, Herr Hauptscharführer, but I can't seem to find the boots…"

After a quick goodbye and a *Heil Hitler,* he hung up the phone. The withering gaze that he threw at me made me wish for the earth to open and swallow me right that instant. Reddening to the roots of my hair, I waited for his answer. He seemed to be waiting for me *to guess* where the boots were. Or he simply enjoyed torturing me with his silence.

"Are you really that dense?" he finally uttered, punctuating each word.

Hot tears filled my eyes despite my intention to keep my face impassionate.

"Come over here."

I obeyed, stopping in front of his desk.

"No, walk over to me and kneel."

Stiff with unspeakable terror, I shuffled over to his chair and lowered down to my knees. Before I knew it, a hand grabbed me by my hair, forcing my head down.

"Still can't see the fucking boots, you dumb bitch?!"

He shoved my face into the black leather on his feet. To keep my balance, I instinctively clung to his legs, before he kicked me off like a dog, hitting me painfully in the chest. It took me all my powers not to wince or press my hand to the throbbing flesh.

"Forgive me, please, Herr Hauptscharführer. I didn't mean to touch you." I scrambled to open the tin with the shoe polish and began applying it on the foot he had generously stuck from under the desk, half-twisting in his chair for my convenience.

Suddenly, he pulled my head up by the hair again, looking at my face closely.

"You look familiar. Have you been here before?"

"No, Herr Hauptscharführer."

"Where have I seen you then?"

"I work in the Kanada, Herr Hauptscharführer."

"Obviously." *Obviously.* Otherwise, my head would have been shaved clean and he would have nothing to hold me by. "Where have I seen you, though?"

I opened and closed my mouth, too hesitant to speak the truth. I didn't have to, though, judging by the smirk splitting his face, he remembered the occasion of our only meeting.

"*Ach,* you're that tramp who goes with the Sonderkommando. Your SS supervisor was supposed to give you the cane for that."

"*Jawohl,* Herr Hauptscharführer."

He pulled closer. There was something odd in his watered-down, blue eyes – one of them terrifyingly unblinking. "Did he punish you properly?" He licked his lips like a snake.

I risked another quick glance at him. He sat, pulled forward, his breath suddenly heavy with excitement. He wanted not just an acknowledgment but details.

"He did, Herr Hauptscharführer. Twenty-five lashes, as you ordered and then some more, on his own initiative. And no food for the entire day."

Judging by his wolfish grin, it was just what he had wished to hear. "Are you still sneaking out to see your Sonderkommando boyfriend?"

"No, Herr Hauptscharführer."

"He taught you a good lesson, didn't he, that young sod? What's his name?"

"Unterscharführer Dahler, Herr Hauptscharführer," I quickly supplied the name. It felt oddly good to utter it, as though a safe word against the evil. "Yes, he did."

"That's right. Dahler. That snotty-nosed sod will go far, mark my words." He looked like a proud father, despite having hardly seven or eight years on Unterscharführer Dahler. "He has no pity for you lot, as it should be." He finally released my hair. Somehow, the mention of Dahler's name had put him in a pleasant disposition. "Why would you go with the Sonderkommando anyway? They're rotten as they get, the ones who work long enough, that is. Have you seen them? They drag a stiff with one hand and eat with another. They don't care it's their own kin they're burning. Do you really enjoy going with them?"

I slowly shook my head. The tears were back, only this time from such humiliating assumptions.

"Why, then? Because they give you food?"

I nodded, just to escape any further interrogation.

"You're ready to do anything for food. A German woman would never humiliate herself in such a way."

A German woman is not forced into a concentration camp against her will, I bit back the thought, *and even when she is, even when she's a prostitute or a murderess or a political, she is still a Kapo, a privileged one and still far above us, 'the Jewish vermin.'*

Moll tapped his foot on the floor. It was a sign for me to resume my duties. He was back to writing, seemingly losing all interest in me. He did, however, throw a pack of cigarettes at me after I finished oiling his belt with its holster. I thanked him quietly and only allowed myself to cry after I was out of there, trailing after the already familiar SS man back to my work detail.

"Where have you been? What happened? Did someone hurt you?" Różínka desperately tried to pry the details out of me during the lunch but I only shook my head quietly and wiped the silent tears that wouldn't stop streaming down my face.

One thing I knew; I never wanted to go back there. And so, knowing Maria and her sadistic ways, I smiled brightly as soon as she suggested that I return to Moll the following day and proclaimed that I would gladly volunteer for such an enjoyable task, for Hauptscharführer Moll treated me so very nice and even gave me some cigarettes and bread for my service. She glared at me and shoved some other girl toward the same SS man who had come here yesterday. That girl never returned from Moll's quarters. The SS man returned for a new one the following day.

Maria still got her revenge.

"Counting days till Herr Kommandoführer's return, you sow? Don't bother. He asked for a transfer to the front; must have had enough of you filthy lot." Having thrown those words at me much like she threw the news about Rózínka's children at my sister, she walked away, satisfied.

I looked up at the sky, violet and brimming with snow. The lid had closed for good now. All that was left for me to do was to die.

*

The boy resembled an elf from a fairy tale more than anything, with his enormous green eyes and chiseled, almost feminine features. His hair wasn't shaved either but neatly parted in the middle and smoothed with water. Fifteen or sixteen years of age at best but with the weary gaze of a truly old, exhausted man who had seen far too much for his years. We all knew him. He was Kapo Schwartz's *Pipel* – his personal servant of sorts who traded his fresh-faced beauty and innocence for life. The boy himself wasn't a pansy but the Kapo was and the boy wanted to live and not just survive on turnip soup and sawdust-bread but perhaps make it out of here alive someday and for that, one needed food and a protector. Schwartz looked after him, more or less. It wasn't a single-case occasion, in the KZ and even the SS guards were buttered up enough by the said Kapos to look the other way.

"You're Helena? From Slovakia? This is for you then," he said quickly, in his high, still-unbroken voice, handing me the parcel and promptly disappearing from our barrack.

Finishing what was left of my dinner – Różínka and I managed to smuggle some sausage and crackers from the Kanada today, on which we now feasted – I turned it this way and that in my hands, mystified. It did have my name on it and an insufferable number of postage stamps, with Hitler's face glowering from them in different shades of blue but I didn't have anyone to send me parcels. Różínka scooted closer, poking at the brown wrapping paper.

"There's something hard inside."

"I'm afraid to touch it," I admitted.

"It has your name on it. Maybe it's from the Red Cross?"

We did receive the Red Cross parcels just last month but this looked nothing like it. The return address was also torn off and quite deliberately at that. Someone inside the camp must have done it.

At last, I tore the paper off and found a small box inside. It had Christmas motifs on it – a bit early for that but I suppose they sold these things in Germany already. Around the box, a red ribbon was wound and tied into a nice bow.

Różínka and I exchanged uncomprehending glances. Was this some sort of a joke?

Slowly, I pulled on the red ribbon and lifted the lid. The most heavenly smell filled the space around us, instantly summoning the rest of the girls from their bunks on which they were resting. Surrounded by a great swarm of bodies, I extracted a cookie out of the box – one of many, neatly stacked one on top of the other. A small note was visible in between the cookies and the side of the box. Różínka quickly pulled it out and hid it in her pocket as I set to distribute the contents of the box among my exhilarated fellow Kanada girls. Only after we ate and only after I responded to all of their questions and inquisitive looks with shrugs – *no, I have not the faintest clue as to who sent it to me* – did I ask Różínka for that note.

I miss you.

That was all it said, in German, in printed letters as he didn't want to run the risk of someone recognizing his handwriting. I pressed my trembling hand to my mouth and bent in half, consumed by uncontrollable, yet silent sobbing.

"Who sent this to you?" Różínka's whisper was uncharacteristically cool.

Who sent you a parcel from Germany? That was the question which she didn't dare to utter for she was certainly very afraid of the answer.

"Franz," I barely whispered in reply. "Unterscharführer Dahler."

An interminable, pregnant pause followed. "Why do you call him by his first name?"

"He told me I could."

My face was still covered with my hands. I didn't see but felt her pull away from me in astonishment. She suddenly didn't know her own sister anymore.

Suddenly, I didn't know myself any longer.

The following morning, I was knocking on Rottenführer Gröning's door as it was my duty to deliver the box with valuables and foreign currency to him that day. He told me to sit down and wait while he was opening the boxes – such was the protocol as only he, the accountant, had the key to them. I watched him as he carefully separated each country's currency into neat stacks and couldn't help but marvel at how many countries were represented there. There were American dollars and German marks, Polish zloty and French francs, and so many others which I didn't even recognize. Gröning counted them on his adding machine that stood on his desk and put the numbers into the narrow columns in his accountant's book.

Without looking up, he suddenly asked, "Did the boy give you the parcel?"

I started momentarily but then quickly collected myself. "Yes, he did, Herr Rottenführer. Thank you."

"It wasn't from me."

"I know who it was from. Thank you for delivering it to me. I know it mustn't have been easy."

He didn't acknowledge my words in any other way, only opened the second box and began separating the wedding rings from diamonds and silver.

I chewed on my lip anxiously but gathered enough strength to ask him at last, "Herr Rottenführer, is it true…"

Gröning looked up, shifting the glasses on the bridge of his nose. Words suddenly failed me.

"Well? What?"

"Is it true that he asked for a transfer?" I barely whispered, thoroughly hiding my eyes.

"Yes. So did I. Both requests were denied," he announced abruptly. "No front for us. Not even the Eastern one. He's out of commission with his knee and I can barely see my hand in front of myself without my glasses."

I looked at him, positively mystified and, making use of his good disposition, decided to ask another question. "Why would you ask for a transfer to the front? Isn't being here better? Safer?"

"Safer, yes. Better? Hardly."

"Why?"

He looked at me as though I asked something incredibly idiotic. "Come now. Do you truly think anyone wants to see *this* every day?" He gestured vaguely around himself, indicating the camp, no doubt.

I suddenly understood why he hardly ever left his office. Gröning pulled himself up as though he'd let on more than he initially wanted to and pushed the empty boxes towards me. "You may go."

Chapter 17

Helena

Much like all people who had no personal achievements to their name, Maria prided herself on her nationality. She possessed neither outstanding – or even mediocre – intellect, nor any talents except for inventing new ways of making life harder for us, inmates. However, she took immense pride in her blonde hair which she wore in braids wrapped regally around her head – owing to the neo-Germanic ideal, no doubt and, in her "stately," as she referred to it, figure. She was particularly proud of her wide hips that "any German woman of childbearing age would be envious of." She, herself, had no children and had never been married (owing to her former profession, was our common guess) but even this ironic contradiction had not once prevented her from regarding us mockingly up and down before wading through our, *miserable twigs*', ranks, like a battleship in between the flimsy yachts.

She was a most pathetic mediocrity, a former farmhand turned streetwalker, whom the new Reich had placed above professors, physicians, opera singers, journalists, and just decent human beings solely due to her "superior Aryan blood." It was pitiful and unjust to them but to her as well, for once the Great German Empire will have fallen, she would be left with nothing at all, except for the shattered illusions that *she was once someone* even though it was in the camp, even though it was only due to her armband of the Kapo, even though it was only due to the fact that we had been forced into the position of being her slaves, just because some madman had decided that a mean-spirited and, unburdened by intellect, German prostitute was somehow better than even the most brilliant, accomplished Jew.

Out of the entire camp population, I hated and pitied her the most. She could have used her position to help us but all she did was take pleasure in humiliating us, for Maria belonged to the type of people who could only elevate herself by putting the others down. Rottenführer Wolff whipped us only when "the occasion called for it" – quickly, harshly, but without any glee. Maria, on the contrary, acted with the sly vindictiveness characteristic of the naturally sadistic women who demean for the sake of demeaning and not out of a desire to punish for a sloppy mistake.

Hundreds of baby prams of all shapes and colors had accumulated in the Kanada warehouse in the course of the past couple of months. The transport was about to arrive from Germany to take them all to the Reich and Maria had us lined up outside, in the freezing cold, forbidding us to fetch any warm clothing for ourselves from the barracks. I doubted that Rottenführer Wolff would have permitted us to venture outside without any outer clothing – SS or no SS, they did know what was good for them and always ensured that we were not only clean but healthy – but he was still eating his lunch in his office and, therefore, Maria could do as she pleased.

"No time to go back to the barracks to fetch your coats, my tender lambs." She smiled sweetly at our neat rows of five – the usual formation; only, this time we were a pitiful parade of childless women peering tragically into the empty prams that our freezing hands were holding onto. Maria herself was clad in a warm overcoat and a scarf to make the joke complete. "If you move your lazy tails fast enough, you won't get cold. Now, make it snappy before I help you find your legs."

By the evening of the same day, half of our "baby pram Kommando" was wiping their noses on their sleeves. The following morning, many of us woke up with a fever. Not that it would change anything in our daily routine. In the KZ, a common cold simply meant that one was to work through it instead of staying in bed and drinking tea with honey. Half-heartedly heated warehouses and constant drafts didn't contribute to one's already failing health either. I did work through the fever itself, but after nearly a week, I suspected that it went into my lungs and ended up as bronchitis. Hopefully, it was not something worse.

"You ought to go to the infirmary with that cough," Rottenführer Wolff commented, observing me closely as I was struggling to get my breath under control.

I looked at him pleadingly with my inflamed, tearing eyes. It was everyone's biggest fear here, the infirmary. To the infirmary, people went to die, not to get cured.

I forced the brightest smile onto my face, feeling my dry lips cracking with the effort. "I'm all right, Herr Rottenführer. It's nothing serious. It'll go away in a couple of days."

He regarded me with suspicion. "Watch that it does."

Naturally, it didn't. If anything, it had gotten worse and I didn't know what upset me more those past few days, the fact that I could hardly breathe without nearly choking myself with this dry, barking coughing, or the fact that I kept the entire barrack up at night. Not one of the girls complained or reported this, for which I was extremely grateful but my condition was not so easy to conceal during the day and particularly in front of Rottenführer Wolff.

I watched his boots approach as I was sitting on the ground, trying to get at least some air into my lungs.

"You can't even breathe, let alone work. I don't know what plague you have but I don't need you spreading it here. Go to the infirmary. Well?" He nudged me on my shoulder with the handle of his whip, propping me up in an upright position. I managed to get back onto my feet yet would not stop coughing into my hand even with the best will in the world. "Off you go, I said! Do not come back until the doctor says it's all right."

With my throat sore from the fit and my eyes still tearing, I snatched the first coat I saw from the sorting table and stumbled my way out of the warehouse. It was snowing outside. Heavy, leaden clouds hung so low they risked entangling themselves in the high-tension wires. For some time, I stood undecided. I knew nothing of the SS doctors in charge of the infirmary, only that very few of their patients made it out of their quarters alive. There was a chance they could offer me treatment if I had something to offer in exchange. I stuck my hand into the pocket of my slacks and rubbed the golden coin, Unterscharführer Dahler had given me some time ago, between my fingers. How ridiculous and positively terrifying it was, the very idea that such trivial matters as seeing a doctor could have been a gamble with life and death here in the camp!

They could take the gold and still put my name on the list.

They could take it and give me something for my cough and very well save my life if I only implied that there was more where that coin had come from.

They could report me for bribery to the Political Department.

I shivered against the cold and threw a glance, full of longing, back at the warehouse. There was no going back there now – Rottenführer Wolff had made himself more than clear – and I was too much of a coward to try and steal my way into our living quarters to conceal myself there and hope for the best. With my lungs, fat chance I wouldn't be discovered within ten minutes, by anyone *diligent*.

Trembling violently, though not from the cold this time, I headed in the direction of the infirmary. In the distance, the women's camp lay. A few of the inmates were digging aimlessly into the frozen ground under the supervision of an SS warden clad in a warm gray overcoat. Her Alsatian's breath was coming out in the form of crystal-gray vapor clouds. As soon as my gaze locked with the inmates, I at once chastised myself for cursing my fate. Their bare legs, in wooden clogs with a single leather strap on top, were blue with cold under their striped dresses. As if on cue, one by one, they turned and looked at my coat, woolen trousers, and warm half-boots, with infinite longing. They envied me and I – them. They weren't coughing; not a big deal, at any rate, under ordinary circumstances but a death sentence in the camp. Under the great fluffy flakes landing softly on top of my head, I dragged myself toward the infirmary.

"Hey!" A familiar voice made me halt in my tracks. I swung around and smiled in spite of myself. It was Andrej, my new friend from the Sonderkommando. He had outfitted himself with a nice sheepskin jacket as well. "Where are you off to?"

He leveled his steps with mine but walked some distance away from me. We weren't supposed to be talking.

"I was sent to the doctor," I croaked and cleared my throat once again.

His smile fell at once. "You're sick?"

"Bronchitis, I think. I hope."

He cursed in Slovakian under his breath. "Go to *our* doctor, will you? And I'll try to fetch you something later."

"He's a pathologist…"

"What does it matter?" He lowered his voice to whisper as we passed a guard's watchtower. Not that he would hear us but it was a reflex in us, to hush ourselves in front of the SS. "He's a Yid, just like us. He won't sign you off at first glance like those Nazis in the infirmary. The SS cure your cases with a shot of phenol into the heart. Surely, you don't want that kind of treatment, do you?"

I slowed my steps, hesitating between following Wolff's order and Andrej's advice. Sensing my uncertainty, Andrej walked over to me, took me by the elbow and marched me straight to the barrack that housed the Slovakian doctor's quarters and the dissection facility. They knew the universal rule of the camp, the Sonderkommando; act as though you belong here, walk with a purpose, and you'll be all right. With the same unshakable confidence, he led me inside, saluted the doctor and reported that my supervisor ordered him to bring me here.

The doctor put away the report he was writing, removed his glasses and regarded me closely. Recognition flickered in his eyes.

"Would that be the same supervisor who brought you here the last time?"

"No." I grinned, shaking my head. "A different one. I have a bad cough."

"Ah. That's not good."

"No, it's not," I agreed and broke into yet another fit.

The doctor listened to the wheezing noises in my chest with a telling scowl and mouth pursed into a thin line.

"I already told Helena that I'll bring her something later." Andrej appeared to understand him without words as well. "Shall I be looking for anything specific?"

"A cough syrup would be helpful but unlikely you'll find one among—"

"The SS has it in abundance," Andrej interrupted him calmly. The doctor was just about to object to something but Andrej waved that objection aside. "I won't steal it, don't fret. I have a man there who will sell it to me for a few dollars."

"Well, if you say so."

"I'll go at once."

The doctor produced the stethoscope out of the medic's leather bag that still bore his name sewn onto its silk lining – surprisingly, they allowed him to keep it – motioned for me to pull my shirt up and listened for my breathing for a good minute. *Front. Back. Cough. Breathe through your mouth...*

"Not good," he announced his verdict. "Not good, but not deadly. Sounds like bad bronchitis. Lots of phlegm." He regarded me for some time. "We could risk having your X-rays done." He tapped his pencil on top of the papers pensively.

"Would I have to go to the infirmary?"

"I'm afraid so."

"Is it true that they inject sick people with phenol there?"

"Not all sick people," he replied hesitantly. "It really depends on the doctor in charge."

"In that case, I'm not going."

"It would be best to ensure that it's indeed only bronchitis—"

"I'm not going there," I repeated, staring at the floor under my feet.

The doctor looked at me sympathetically. "All right. Let's hope its bronchitis. Is your superior expecting you back any time soon?"

I shook my head. I doubted Rottenführer Wolff wanted me back at all.

"I have a room where I sleep, over there in the back. Why don't you rest on my cot while I'm working here? In the evening, I'll send you back to your barrack again. We can do this every day until you get better. Herr Doktor hardly ever comes in here. Ordinarily, it's the medical clerks that bring in the bodies. They're all reliable fellows. They know how to keep their mouths shut."

I found his hand and pressed it in a surge of gratitude. "Thank you, Doctor."

He only smiled wistfully and patted my hand slightly. Perhaps, he did have a daughter my age who had died here.

Chapter 18

Helena

After a week, I was back with my Kommando. Never before had I thought that I would be so ecstatic to see the warehouse, never before did I fold the clothes with such ardent enthusiasm to demonstrate my goodwill to whatever superior might be watching. *Just to be back with the living, just to show that I'm useful again!* Even Rottenführer Wolff refrained from his disdainful remarks and kindly permitted me to keep the bottle with syrup which the doctor had provided me with – well, according to the version which I offered and he accepted.

Andrej managed to trade positions with someone in his Kommando and could visit me daily now whenever he arrived with the trucks and unloaded the suitcases for us to sort. Each time, in addition to syrup, he succeeded in smuggling a few mints or French bonbons for me to soothe my throat. No matter how I begged him to accept at least some payment for his services, which, I knew for certain, cost him dearly, he positively refused to take even the smallest trinket from me.

"Just get better. It'll be the best payment I can possibly receive," he merely said, with a timid smile, carefully hiding his gaze.

Today, he brought me more bonbons. Another transport from France must have arrived. I was in the middle of thanking him for his concern when his hand flew to his cap and he tore it off his head before freezing at attention.

I swiftly turned around as well and instantly broke into a beaming smile at the sight of an SS man in a gray overcoat. Unterscharführer Dahler was back.

Only, he didn't smile in return. As a matter of fact, he had not once acknowledged me with a single look, boring his gaze into Andrej instead.

"Jawing at work?" He looked at Andrej derisively.

My smile faltered and dropped eventually. I was suddenly afraid of him again, much like I was in the beginning. He wasn't Franz at that moment, he was *the man with the whip*. I saw it twitch in his gloved hand.

"Follow me. We'll take a little walk in the woods," he barked at Andrej and stalked off without waiting.

Andrej threw an odd look at me, full of longing and unspoken goodbyes and trotted to catch up with the SS man. I made a step after him but quickly realized that it was no use. Unterscharführer Dahler, no matter how romantically my clouded memory pictured him in the past few weeks, was as moody and erratic in his behavior as they came and I was suddenly not too certain if he, in a fit of rage, wouldn't do me in, along with Andrej, in those woods. Who knew what he had imagined himself from our friendly conversation and my friendly smiles?

He confirmed my suspicions when he returned soon after. He barked, "In my office!" at me as he passed my station by and locked the door as soon as I crossed the threshold. His eyes were mad with fury.

"So, this is how you repay me for all I've done for you." It was not a question he hissed at me but an accusation and a guilty verdict wrapped in one – typical Nazi-served justice. How slender and tall he was in that gray overcoat, how imperious and positively terrifying! "You're too proud to touch *my murderer's hands* but you're not too proud to touch the hands of a Sonderkommando pig, who drags corpses out of gas chambers daily. *That* you don't find repulsive. *That* is acceptable to you because he's a victim of the cursed Nazis and, therefore, is a much better person just due to that fact. A veritable martyr and a God-chosen man on top of things. Now, that's a match, every girl dreams of, is it not?!"

His entire body was shaking with rage. I began trembling too but out of fear that he'd hit me. Out of the corner of my eye, I saw his fists clench.

"Well?! Why are you silent?" he bellowed.

He didn't have to force his voice under control. Shouting at the inmates was not against the camp's rules.

With the best will in the world, I couldn't squeeze a word out of myself. I wanted to ask whether he killed Andrej or just beat him – his gloves were off and his knuckles were freshly bruised – but didn't dare.

The silence didn't go down well with him. "I asked you a question!"

I pressed myself into the door. The sweat was pouring down my body.

"I'm sick, Herr Unterscharführer."

"You seem fine to me." He looked at me with his cold eyes.

"I have a bad cough. Andrej was only bringing medicine for me." I extracted a small bottle of syrup out of my pocket and demonstrated it to him along with the bonbons. He regarded it all with suspicion. "Rottenführer Wolff ordered me to go to the infirmary, but…"

I didn't finish. Unterscharführer Dahler knew perfectly well what the infirmary meant for the inmates.

"It was just that, Herr Unterscharführer. Because he works in the Sonderkommando he can organize these things; surely, you understand…"

"Oh yes, *surely I understand*," he repeated mockingly. "I understand all too well how those rats steal everything they can from the Reich."

I looked at his watch that I, myself, had given him but I wasn't stupid enough to bring it to his attention that he and his comrades were helping themselves to everything they fancied from the dead Jews as well.

"And how did you pay him for going through all these pains?" He spoke with a cruel, sardonic smirk and crossed his arms over his chest. "They don't do anything for free, those pigs."

I could take a lot from him – the shouting, the scornful, cold-hearted remarks, anything really but not such a disgusting, suggestive insinuation. Hot tears sprung to my eyes.

"You can stop that performance right this instant. Tears don't work on me."

"Of course, they don't," I replied bitterly. "Why would they? All human emotions are below you, the master race." The dam was broken and I suddenly couldn't stop the flood of accusations that was pouring out of me. "All you know is how to be cruel. That's why you can't see the good in other people because there's none in you!"

"None in me?" He paled and stepped away as though I had slapped him. "How short your memory is. After everything I've done for you."

"No, it's not short!" I wiped my face in helpless misery. "I've been waiting for you like a dog. Every single day, every passing hour in this hell I kept thinking about you and yes, about how kind you were to me. Every time Maria would berate me, I would think about you and all her words would instantly lose their power. When I had to go to Hauptscharführer Moll's quarters to clean his uniform and he began tormenting me, guess who I was comparing him to and thinking what a different person you were. Even with an SS doctor and his revolting personal searches during the disinfection, even him I could survive because I kept telling myself that you'd be back soon and just one kind look from you would be enough to wipe all those memories out. No, Herr Unterscharführer, my memory is definitely not short. There wasn't a minute when I wasn't thinking of you, there wasn't a second when I wouldn't hope to see you again. And now, you're back and I wish you weren't because whatever I was beginning to feel for you, you destroyed. You may as well take me to the woods and kill me, as you did with Andrej. I won't survive here alone."

He let me cry silently for some time, suddenly ashamed of his childish behavior and unsure of what to say to me. I began coughing again. For a few moments, I almost wished for some blood vessel to break inside my lung and kill me right there and then because for the life of me I couldn't accept the fact that the last person who I had faith in had just turned his back on me in such a cruel manner.

"You're really sick." His warm hand was on my back in an instant while the other one was already digging in the pocket of my slacks. "Drink your syrup! *Gott*, you sound horrible." He nearly forced the bottle into my mouth, suddenly concerned. I made a few soothing sips and waited for the medicine to take its short hold, sniveling quietly.

"I didn't kill him."

I looked up. Dahler shook his head again, seemingly calmer now. "I didn't kill him. Just swiped him a couple on the snout and told him to stay away from my Kommando."

"From me."

"Yes, from you."

"He was just trying to help. He wouldn't even take any money as payment."

"Because he pursues other interests." The smirk was back onto his face, but at least it wasn't malicious like before.

"You're imagining things. He doesn't pursue anything."

"I saw the way he's looking at you."

"Herr Unterscharführer, you can't control the way people look at other people."

"No, but I can control the people themselves and what happens to them if they disobey my wishes."

"But that's precisely what I'm saying!" The attack had passed. I wasn't afraid of him any longer but infinitely disappointed instead. He was no different from the others. He was just like the rest of them. "You are cruel and selfish and think that you're better than others just because of your Aryan blood! You treat people like they're mere things!"

"What rot are you saying now?"

"Rot? Just how is it rot, Herr Unterscharführer? Don't you control us all? Look at you; you're mad with fury because I dared to smile at someone other than you. How is such tyranny not cruel? Isn't it a sure sign of how you consider me merely as your possession? I don't know why you bother with all these theatrics at all. Why all the presents and sweet words… You don't have to court me. I'm not German. I'm not a human in your eyes. You want me to be yours – you don't need me to reciprocate your feelings for that. Just do like your comrades do. Take whatever you want; it's not like anyone would ever punish you for it. You are the masters of the world. We're the slaves. You made your position more than clear and I owe you for my sister anyway."

He pulled away from me in horror. "What blooming nonsense is this? What is it, an invitation to force myself on you, at any rate?"

"You don't need any invitations."

"I don't deserve being spoken to this way."

"And neither do I."

The silence hung over the room. For a long time he had not budged and then he suddenly turned on his heel and marched over to the window. To my astonishment, I noticed him wiping his eyes subtly, with his back to me.

That was the last thing I had expected. "Herr Unterscharführer…" I made a hesitant step forward. "Forgive me, please. I didn't mean to say any of that."

"Yes, you did." His voice was cool and controlled but he still sounded like someone mortally wounded.

I cursed myself and my long tongue. But who would have expected that he could actually feel anything under that uniform of his, let alone be so affected by some Jewess' words?

"I'm glad you said it all," he continued, staring blankly through the glass. "Now I know exactly how you feel about me. You may go now. I will never bother you again."

I looked at the door, then at his stiff back and slowly wiped my forehead. "You know nothing at all about me, Herr Unterscharführer."

"I know that you think me to be cruel and vile."

"Just cruel." I sighed. "What else am I supposed to call you? A knife cannot take offense at being called sharp, just like a cruel man cannot take offense at being called cruel, else he shouldn't act like one. The only difference is that the knife can't control itself while a man is perfectly capable of choosing how to behave. I suppose it's not your fault though; sentimentalism, compassion, and understanding have long been considered un-German among your kind."

"What kind?"

"The SS."

"We're not all the same," he grumbled in self-defense. "I'm no Moll, by any account."

"I know you're not. That's why it upsets me so when you act like him when I know that you can be so very different."

He turned around and regarded me tragically. "I only want you to love me. Am I asking too much? Do you really find me so revolting?"

"No, of course, I don't, but…" I made a desperate gesture with my hands. "Look at this; this is not a normal relationship between a man and a woman. I'm afraid to touch you. I'm afraid to even talk to you sometimes because I never know how you will take things."

"You're afraid of me?" He blinked in astonishment.

I nearly laughed in response. "Is it really so surprising?"

"Quite so. Just why would you be afraid of me?"

I shrugged. "You're the SS. We're all afraid of you."

"Nonsense." In a few long strides, he closed the distance between us. He looked at my hands, took them suddenly in his and placed them on his cheeks. His eyelashes were still wet. "There. See? Same flesh and blood as you. I'm just an ordinary human under this uniform."

Now, you're saying the very right thing that your own leaders can't seem to get through their thick skulls, Herr Unterscharführer.

He slowly removed his hands from the top of mine in the hope that I'd keep them there of my own accord but I dropped them at once. It was a strange moment and I didn't quite know what to make of it. His skin was so unexpectedly soft but touching him still felt unnatural. He was still the SS.

He had caught on to that and now stood before me, suddenly vulnerable and irresolute.

After a while, he began talking. "While on furlough, I wished for nothing more than to come back here and hug you. Can I hold you just for a few moments, Helena?" he asked and, I could swear, held his breath awaiting my reply.

I nodded, much too quickly. He thought it to be the instinctual inmate's compliance and didn't move.

"You don't have to agree just to please me. I would never do anything to you against your will. If you don't want me to touch you, nothing will change between us. I will still protect you and look after you."

"You can hold me if you want to. It would do you good. I don't think your mothers hugged you enough there, in the Reich and that's the reason for all this now."

A fleeting ghost of a smile passed over his face. I guessed by the pitiful sight of it that I was not far from the truth.

"Did your mother hug you a lot?" he asked.

"Daily. As often as she could."

Slowly, he wrapped his arms around me and rested his chin on top of my head. Unsure of what to do with my arms, I let them hang by my sides. He didn't seem to protest or take offense at that.

"I was raised differently," he admitted softly. "We were to be little soldiers from the beginning. No coddling was allowed, just strict discipline only. When I fell off the bicycle and twisted my ankle, my father beat me with a belt. For crying, not for the ankle. I never cried in front of him after that. Only after he died at the front."

"How old were you?"

"He was killed only a year ago. So, nineteen."

"No. When you fell off that bicycle."

"Eight."

What was one to say to that? Overcome with sudden emotion, I lifted my arms and wrapped them tightly around his waist. He froze at first and then nearly choked-up, with the unexpected joy of being embraced. For a few moments, we stood without moving, without breathing even and marveling at how insanely, maddeningly nice it was, just to be held like this in this hell of a place where no human emotions were allowed for either side and where love itself went up in smoke from the industrial oven's chimney.

"How nice…" he sighed, echoing my emotions and rubbed his cheek softly on top of my hair. "If only we could stay like this all day."

I didn't argue.

He stroked my back gently. "I don't like the way you breathe. I can hear it. Did you go to the doctor at all?"

"To the Slovakian one. The pathologist you took me to."

"What did he say?"

"Nothing. He told me to drink whatever syrups were available and hope that it's not typhus." I smiled weakly.

"Do you have red spots on your chest?"

"No. I check every day."

"You do have a fever, though."

"A slight one. It was gone before but it's returned again."

"Any abdominal pains?"

They were well trained to detect the first symptoms of typhus, the SS. Yet, I was grateful that he didn't move away from me even after I voiced such a possibility.

"They may be just hunger pangs."

"You lost weight while I was away." He regarded me with concern.

"I didn't have an appetite."

"You'll be all right, Leni." In spite of myself, I was touched, to the marrow, at the unexpected term of endearment, be it just a short German version of my name. "I'll see to it. Don't fret. I'm back now and nothing will happen to you while I'm here. I'm an old, watchful soldier."

Chapter 19

Helena

The SS doctors appeared unexpectedly, before the morning roll call even and began their usual rounds, checking the general state of the inmates. We, the Kanada women, looked much healthier compared to the camp's general population but they still weeded out anyone, who had the misfortune to sport scabies, sores, or who was foolish enough to break into coughing in front of them, much like I did.

"Lift up your shirt."

I silently obeyed, unsuspecting and still groggy with fever and sleep.

The SS doctor quickly stepped away.

"Typhus. Out. Now. The entire barrack – to the quarantine for two weeks."

In disbelief, I looked down at my chest and stomach. Yesterday still white and clear, today – a map of red dots. My head swam, struck by the suddenness of it. *Just like that, one day you are alive, and the next…*

I didn't remember being led outside.

I was oddly calm when the doctor's orderly pointed me to the truck with the red cross, which they used for driving the inmates to the gas chambers. I only regretted that I didn't get a chance to exchange shoes with Różínka, whose sobbing was still ringing in my ears as I was climbing inside the truck. My half-boots were much better insulated for winter than hers and out of the two of us, she still needed to survive it. I also regretted not being able to say goodbye to Unterscharführer Dahler but the officers hardly ever rose before the roll call. Someone would tell him later what happened to me. I only hoped he'd still find it in himself to be kind to my sister after my death.

The drive was short and morbidly silent. Everyone knew where we were heading and not a single person uttered a word or a cry. I appeared almost like an outsider among the group of striped uniforms and emaciated faces but even then, no one paid any heed to me. In no time, the SS and the members of the Sonderkommando were herding us out. One of them recognized me as a Kanada girl and pressed my hand sympathetically as he escorted our pitiful procession in the direction of the familiar bunker. "Don't be afraid. Today is a good day, dry weather. It'll be over quick. Sit right under the hatches in the roof and take deep breaths. You'll lose consciousness before you know it and won't suffer."

I thanked him and followed him inside. It was comforting to have familiar faces around during one's last minutes. We removed our clothes, men and women alike. When no SS was looking my way, I discreetly motioned the familiar Sonderkommando man over and pressed a golden coin – the one that Rottenführer Dahler gave me before going on his leave and which I didn't spend but kept as a sort of talisman – into his hand. "Could you please give my boots to my sister Różínka? She also works in the Kanada—"

"I know your sister. Don't worry, she'll get them." He quickly stepped away and pretended to give commands to the others.

Soon, we were stripped bare, a sea of emaciated, gray bodies. I was the only one with hair. One of the Sonderkommando men asked his SS supervisor if it would be wiser to shave it off first. The latter only waved his hand languidly.

"Later, in the crematorium." He stifled a yawn. "Teeth, that too. Let them worry about it. Not our responsibility."

The door to the gas chamber opened. The Sonderkommando began herding us in. It was almost surreal how calmly everyone went to their death. Perhaps, unlike the new arrivals, we all knew all too well that no amount of protesting or pleas would help things or we were simply too exhausted from our endless ordeal and simply surrendered to our common fate, welcoming it almost with relief.

Don't be afraid. It'll be over quick.

Still, in the last moment, I caught the familiar Sonderkommando man's sleeve. "Has anyone ever survived it? The gassing, I mean?"

He looked at me as if I were mad.

"I'm only asking to make sure… Is it possible that I'll just lose consciousness and then when… in the crematorium…?"

That was my biggest fear – to be burned alive in a furnace. He realized it and smiled softly, a veritable bear of a man with such sad, sorrowful eyes. "No one ever survived it. But if you like, I can wring your neck before they put you on a gurney. Just to be safe."

"Yes, just to be safe." I smiled at him warmly. "Thank you."

Reluctantly, I let go of his arm.

The chamber was shrouded with darkness. I looked up and located a few square hatches in the roof, through which the light had slipped inside and through which the SS would throw the gas in later. I sat right under one, remembering the man's words. *Take deep breaths. You'll lose consciousness before you know it and won't suffer.*

I closed my eyes and waited for the SS to call the Sonderkommando men out and lock the airtight door.

"Helena! Helena Kleinová!"

Startled at the voice frantically calling my name, I didn't think about getting up at first but someone was already shoving the bodies around me aside until Unterscharführer Dahler materialized in front of me. His hair was tousled, the uniform in disarray and the overcoat lacking. He was deathly pale. His eyes were wild with fear.

"Here you are!" Still out of breath as though after a sprint, he grabbed my wrist and yanked me onto my feet. "Up with you! Out of this rat trap – now!"

One of the SS men in charge of the *Aktion* was blocking his path in the door.

"Where are you taking her?" He regarded us both with suspicion.

"She's not supposed to be here. Didn't you see her clothes? Why haven't you alerted me that one of my Kommando people was here?"

The other SS man opened and closed his mouth, seemingly thrown off track with Dahler's rebuke.

"Well… why would she be here then?"

"Because she clearly ran off in the hope to off herself with your help, you Sherlock with chevrons!" Dahler pulled me forward so that I'd stand directly in front of the officer. My arms flew up to my chest – not so much out of modesty but to cover the rash. "Does she look like someone who didn't pass selection to you? Look at her! She's twice the size of any of these people!"

That was certainly a stretch but I didn't look like a walking skeleton, that much was true.

The officer still wasn't persuaded. His eyes gleamed eerily in the semi-darkness of the gas chamber. "Why would anyone want to gas themselves?"

"Her boyfriend kicked the bucket a few days ago. She's upset over it."

"That seems to be true, Herr Unterscharführer," the familiar Sonderkommando man stepped in to help Dahler. So, the two officers were of the same rank, that explained all the authority challenging. "I saw her. She sat right under the hatch to kill herself quicker."

After muttering a curse on my account, the second officer finally moved aside, allowing us to walk out.

"Where are your clothes?" Dahler asked me sternly, taking care to turn me away from the spectators. He, too, was afraid they'd notice the telling red spots. Unlikely that he worried about them ogling at me with this greater worry in sight.

I pointed to one of the hooks where I left my belongings.

Under his SS comrades' prying glances, he shouted at me, "I ought to have you walk naked back to your work detail for the stunt you pulled!" Unceremoniously, he shoved me in the direction of the clothing. "Get dressed and be quick about it! And get it into your stupid head once and for all – here, we decide how long you stay alive, not you!"

The door to the gas chamber closed and the lock turned with a dull sound. Under the eyes of several SS men and the Sonderkommando team, I was hastily pulling my clothes on with shaking hands.

"Should have left her there if she wants to die so much," the same Unterscharführer commented to Dahler.

"She's a textile expert in my unit. Who's going to do her job? You?" Dahler countered mockingly.

A few SS men guffawed. As I was buttoning my shirt, one of them gave a signal to the orderly who stood in the door leading outside. The orderly, in his turn, waved to someone on the roof. Just a few moments later the commotion began behind the airtight door, first the coughing, then – screaming, as many fists pounded the steel door from the other side. Next, cries and frantic pleading came. The Unterscharführer in charge checked his watch, the same, bored expression back on his face.

"Where are you taking them after?" Unterscharführer Dahler asked, motioning his head towards the gas chamber.

"To the crematorium."

"I thought it was no longer in use because of the chimney? Wasn't it the reason for all those outdoors pyres for the past couple of months?"

"They've fixed it for now. We are to use it while they're building the four new ones."

"Those monstrosities next to my Kanada?"

The other Unterscharführer grunted his affirmation. "Those are said to be industrial type, not that sorry affair in Auschwitz that is crumbling after each use. There will be two stories, with the bunker and the elevator to transport the bodies from the gas chamber below to the cremation facility upstairs. I saw the blueprints," he added boastfully. "Five ovens, each with three chambers. There will also be a Kommandoführer's office," he finished with dreamy notes in his voice, clearly in the hope to be promoted to the said Kommandoführer in the nearest future.

"You mean like the offices that we all already have in the Kanada?" Dahler asked sweetly.

The Unterscharführer shot him a glare. "Take your Jew-girl and piss off back to your Kanada, you self-important veteran of the wars! I ought to have locked you both in there so that you wouldn't wag your tongue next time!"

Dahler laughed carelessly, seemingly delighted at his words hitting a sore spot and grabbed my elbow to lead me out of the anteroom. His face betrayed nothing at all. Only his hand trembled on top of my arm.

Outside, the snow-covered field shimmered under the sun. It blinded me instantly. I was so weak all of a sudden, so positively exhausted. Without realizing it, I began sinking into the welcoming, soft snow.

"No, no, no, we're not having any of that, Leni!" Dahler propped me upward at once and shook me slightly. "We need to walk, little soldier. No sleeping yet, the enemy is watching."

It was odd that on the verge of losing one's consciousness, it was only an SS man's order that kept us going. I saw it so many times before with the *Muselmänner* and now, much like them, I found myself placing one foot in front of the other despite not having any strength to move.

He held me fast. To an outsider, it would appear as though he was dragging me someplace where they administered punishment to our kind whereas, in reality, his steely grip was the only thing that kept me upright.

But soon even he couldn't march any longer.

"Do you mind?" he asked quietly after we had walked some distance away from the bunker. "I need a smoke."

I barely stood on my own but still, mechanically picked up the lighter that he had dropped into the snow. His hands were shaking worse than mine. After a third attempt, he managed to light the cigarette and swallowed a few times as though he were physically sick.

"I've never seen it before." He tried laughing as though in excuse for his ghostly pale face and the beads of sweat that broke out on his forehead despite the negative temperatures outside but receded quickly and swallowed again. "The process itself, I mean. The medics assured us during the orientation that they die instantly; that the gas paralyzes airways within seconds…" He looked at me at a loss and added, a strained touch of anguish in his voice, "Maybe they didn't drop enough gas? Maybe he did it on purpose? He seemed like a veritable bastard to me, don't you think so? Arrogant dung heap with epaulets! Botching an *Aktion* on purpose! He ought to be reported to the Kommandant!"

I almost felt sorry for him and the desperate look he gave me. I knew that they always screamed. Andrej told me that much.

Dahler knew it, too. The trouble was, it was much too painful to admit it to himself that his kin was murdering mine on an industrial basis and in such a barbaric manner at that. Perhaps, he needed to see someone he cared about there to finally be incensed about it.

He looked back at the bunker almost with hatred and took me by the forearm again. "Let's go. No need to loiter here."

With great effort, I parted my lips once again. As long as I was talking, as long as I pretended to be in control of my faculties, I could still walk to wherever it was he was taking me. "How did you know, Herr Unterscharführer?"

"Irma, your block elder, ran all the way to our barracks as soon as they took you."

"Irma?"

It was a pleasant surprise. She didn't have the reputation of someone particularly charitable among the inmates, but who knew whether she was simply too careful to show it? Perhaps, there were some other lives she'd saved and no one was any the wiser?

Dahler only shrugged in response. "I think she knows I'm in love with you," he replied simply.

The snow crunched under our feet as we walked side by side, shivering with cold.

"Where are you taking me, Herr Unterscharführer?" I asked at last.

"Back to the Kanada, where else?" He tried to smile but the grin came out as miserable as they get.

"I have typhus."

"I know. Irma told me."

I looked at him, positively confused. "The entire barrack was sent to the quarantine because of me."

"It's the standard protocol. They want to make sure that it doesn't spread."

Was he purposely avoiding the direct answer?

"But where am I going to go then?"

"Officially, to the infirmary."

"And unofficially?"

"Stop talking. We're getting close to the gates."

I fell a few steps behind him as we neared the checkpoint – the usual way the inmates accompanied SS guards. The guard on duty yawned, offered Dahler a half-hearted salute and motioned us through without bothering to ask for a reason why an SS man was strutting around without his overcoat and with an inmate in tow. Fortunately for us, he appeared to be more interested in his morning coffee than the camp's discipline. They pounced on us, the inmates, at the blink of the eye; to their fellow SS colleagues, an entirely different set of rules applied. I stumbled after Unterscharführer Dahler, applying my all to appear bursting with health.

From a distance, we saw that Rottenführer Gröning was already instructing a new group of women prisoners in the detail where my Kommando ordinarily worked. They were brought from the women's camp, much to Wolff's displeasure. He kept observing them, their striped dresses, scrawny bodies and shaved heads under the kerchiefs, with a sour look on his face as he sipped his coffee from the Thermos. With both of his colleagues busy with the new arrivals, Dahler had no trouble smuggling me into his office unnoticed.

"Well, now…" He looked around, suddenly at a loss.

It had become clear then why he so positively refused to discuss his plan with me. He didn't have one.

I kept looking at him, almost with pity. He was much too impulsive for his own good. Sure enough, he dragged me out of the gas chamber, he brought me here but now what? I had virtually no place to go, not even back to the barrack which was being disinfected according to the protocol. The camp administration was quite paranoid on account of typhus after last July's outbreak during which a few SS men were unfortunate enough to catch it.

Dahler brought me to his desk and pointed at the space between the two sets of drawers connected by a solid panel. "You'll have to stay here for now. I have to go report for duty but I'll be back soon with some food and blankets. Do you still have your syrup?"

"Yes." I pulled the half-empty bottle out of my pocket. I just wanted to lie down and be left in peace.

"Good. I'll try to get you more, later. And," he stumbled upon the request, a bit embarrassed, "could you try and be quiet while I'm not here? Try to cover your mouth when you cough as much as you can, please. I don't want anyone finding out that you're here. I'll leave the radio on but still, try to be quiet, all right?"

"Of course, Herr Unterscharführer."

He gave me a bright smile, turned the radio on and left, locking the door after himself.

Chapter 20

Helena

He returned by lunchtime and dropped a mountain of fur onto the floor before kneeling in front of my hideout.

"How have you been, little soldier?" he asked, signing for me to come out from under the desk.

"Good." I crawled out on shaking legs and arms, feeling the sweat pouring down my body from the sheer effort to move. My head was pounding something horrible. The muscles, which had grown stiff from the cramped sleeping position, were in agonizing pain. I tried to smile at him through it.

"I organized you some goods," Dahler declared, with pride in his voice and immediately set to arranging a sort of sleeping nook under the desk, piling up a few fur coats and sheepskins one on top of the other. He even procured a small embroidered pillow from somewhere. "There. This way, you won't have to sleep on the bare floor."

"Thank you, Herr Unterscharführer."

He looked at me more intently. "You look like you're running a fever." He touched my forehead. "Are you cold?"

"A little." I closed my eyes against the light. It was much too bright, almost blinding. I made a motion to crawl back into my nook and rest some more. Just to shut my eyes and not feel anything.

Unterscharführer Dahler stopped me at once. "Not just yet, Leni. Here, drink this. I got you some chicken broth from the canteen." He produced a Thermos, a standard affair from which they, the SS, rarely were parted in winter. "You need to get some food into you first."

"I'm nauseous."

"I know. The doctor, your compatriot, said that you need to eat even if you are."

"You spoke with him?"

"Of course I did. I need to know how to care for you, no?"

I regarded him with infinite gratitude. "But what if I—"

"What if you what?" He got up, crossed the room and fetched a bucket that the inmates used to wash the floors in his office. "If you get sick, you get sick. I'll empty it later. But it is imperative that you eat, Helena. The doctor said so."

I roved my gaze around the office, as though seeing it for the first time. I was suddenly aware of my surroundings – of the camp around and the barbed wire; of the rows and rows of barracks that housed far too many people who only died and died and died again and turned into ash and buried us all, the survivors, under it, until our turn would come to die as well. The earth itself was poisoned here, festering with far too many corpses that had been killed far too many times by the SS men's hand – gassed, shot, buried, then burned as though they wished to wipe our very memory off the face of the Earth by killing us multiple times. Everything around was hostile and treacherous – the gray-clad guards and their Alsatians, the *Muselmänner* who terrified us for they were our very future, someone caught between life and death itself and, worst of all, the agonizing loneliness among the hundreds of thousands of people. We were all so very alone here, crammed together, yet impossibly alone, with nothing, no one to rely on…

A rush of anguish passed through my veins. Across from me sat an SS man. His image blurred and swam before my eyes. *I oughtn't to accept anything from him. These were the murdered people's coats. The food was taken from the starving. I had no right to use any of that. I never had the right to sleep on a dead man's mattress. I never had the right to wear a dead woman's clothes. I never had the right to survive while the others were dying by their hundreds.*

Slowly and with effort – yet with sudden harsh, lucid resolution – I pushed the Thermos across the floor back to him.

For over a minute, Dahler made no sound, only regarded it coolly. "What is it, Leni? A revolt? Defeatism among the ranks, what?" He pushed the Thermos back to me. "Drink."

After I didn't make a motion to pick it up, he opened the lid and almost forced the Thermos into my hands, cupping them with his own. "Do you want to come out of here or not?"

I regarded him in stupefaction. *No one of my kind was leaving this place. Surely he knew it well enough.*

"Things are not going too well for us in Stalingrad. Our entire army group is getting encircled as we speak. The Reds counterattack more and more and their Siberian divisions are aiding their regular army now that the Japanese are busy with the Americans. And speaking of the latter, with them now joining the war and leasing all of those aircraft and transports and food supplies and just about anything to the Russkies, fat chance the affair will turn out victorious for us. It's a matter of time only, how much longer you'll have to suffer here. Two, three more years perhaps… Do you not want to come out of here and… live? Because I really want you to live, Leni."

"With you?" For some reason, I found it to be the thing of paramount importance to ask him this question. "After the war? Do you want me to live with you?"

Dahler only shrugged. His long eyelashes were covering his eyes and it was impossible to see anything in them. "With me, without me, with that Sonderkommando pig, if you like. It matters not. I only want you to survive, that's all."

I suddenly choked and could almost persuade myself that it was only the cough. I gulped the broth, fighting nausea, the pain, the guilt until I felt warm once again – from the broth or his words, it also mattered not. I had reached the stage where I could no longer fight him. He watched me breathlessly and with the most tender emotion welling up in his eyes and had forever ceased to be the enemy to me. With tremendous effort, I'd searched for the last shards of resistance in me and had found nothing. I was sick and dying and he was the only person who stood guard between me and death and I loved him for it.

A warm smile was back on his face once again.

"I got you something more substantial too." He dug into his pocket and extracted a thick square wrapped in a newspaper. "Liverwurst sandwich. The real sort, Austrian-made, not this sorry camp stuff from the kitchen. I brought it with me from Drasenhofen. *Mutti* makes liverwurst herself, so trust me when I say that it's the goods... And the honey, this too. It'll help with your cough." A jar found its way into my hands, which were already overflowing with all the riches. "The carafe with water is over there, on the windowsill, if you need it. I would stay here with you but those new women are hopeless and it appears we'll all have to watch them all day since they have not the faintest clue what it is they're doing. I'll be checking on you from time to time when I get a chance. You rest now, will you? I'll bring you more food and medicine later. And now, eat. It's an order, so get on with it. I want nothing left here when I come back."

*

I awoke to someone calling my name and shaking my shoulder. Still heavy with feverish sleep, I tried to unglue my eyes to see Unterscharführer Dahler's shadowy form against the light of the pocket flashlight he left lying on the floor.

"Leni? How are you feeling?" His tone was thick with worry.

"Still alive." A pitiful croaking came out instead of my regular voice.

He snorted softly. "I said the same thing to the medic after I crawled back from the battlefield, with my knee shot up before I passed out on his table." His palm felt cool against my burning forehead. "Your fever is getting higher."

I made no reply, only looked around in search of water. My throat was like sandpaper and every breath was a struggle. Dahler quickly handed me a new Thermos, a smaller one. "I made you *Glühwein*. It should warm you up a bit. Good for your throat, too."

I made an effort to lift the Thermos with both hands but it appeared as heavy as a concrete block. Dahler held it to my mouth, much to my relief.

"Your clothes are all drenched," he declared after removing his hand from my back. "We ought to change you into something dry and warm. Wait here, I'll go fetch something."

By the time he returned with the clothes, I was barely awake. Just keeping my eyes open seemed like hard work. Dahler hesitated a moment before kneeling in front of me again.

"Can you change yourself?"

I didn't think I could but I still nodded, propped myself up, with his help, and began working on the buttons on my shirt. I only got to the third one when my hands dropped onto my lap of their own volition. I didn't feel as exhausted after a twelve-hour shift as I felt after undoing those three miserable buttons.

"You should have left me there, in the chamber, Herr Unterscharführer," I whispered with my hoarse voice. "I won't make it anyway."

"Rot. You'll pull through." He took my face in his hands. I felt his warm breath on my lips as he spoke. "If you remember, I told you just this morning that we decide how long you shall live. You can't die for one simple reason, Leni; I prohibit it."

He got a pained smile out of me. "I doubt that is how it works with typhus, Herr Unterscharführer."

"We'll see about that."

He began undoing my buttons one by one. I tried helping him by moving my arms out of the sleeves but in the end, it was he who did it for me, just like he had to remove the rest of my garments. I was much too weak to offer him any assistance. My undershirt, all soaked through, joined the heap of clothing on the floor. I thought about covering myself up to preserve at least some of my modesty. After all, it was improper and a horrible sin on top of things, to allow a man – a man who wasn't my husband – to undress me and touch my bare body but I was too delirious and feeble to dwell on such trifles. Besides, there was nothing sexual about the manner in which he handled the situation. If anything, his hands, his entire thorough, clinical manner resembled much more that of a doctor tending to his patient rather than that of a soldier taking a chance to paw at a naked, defenseless girl.

He fetched some water, wetted my old shirt with it and began gently wiping the perspiration off of my body.

"This should bring the fever down a little," he commented, gently pressing me against his chest to clean my back. I rested my head on his shoulder, hearing my own labored breathing.

"You shouldn't be so close to me, Herr Unterscharführer. You'll get sick too. It's very contagious."

"Lice transmit it, not people. And stop talking. You're irritating your throat."

I waited for him to finish and used the rest of my strength to help him dress me into the new warm shirt and slacks. He also managed to procure warm woolen socks for me, which he dutifully pulled onto my feet.

"You really ought to be going, Herr Unterscharführer. Your comrades will be looking for you…"

"My comrades are getting pissed as we speak as they usually do after the shift is over and won't notice even if the camp goes on fire around them."

He rearranged the furs so that they extended from under the desk for the nighttime, gently lowered me down and lay next to me, cradling my head on his arm. "Now, sleep, Leni. You need to rest."

*

Several times during that night, I awoke and each time Unterscharführer Dahler held me through the worst coughing fits, fetched
me water with honey in it and wiped my forehead with a wet rag.
I tried smiling at him and putting on a brave face but after the
stomach pains came, sharp and vicious, each like a knife stab in
the gut, I suddenly couldn't hold myself together any longer and
began crying as I clutched onto his clothes in desperation.

"Hey, old comrade, what's with the tears?" he tried pacifying
me as he stroked my hair. "Are you in that much pain? Shall I go
fetch you some morphine?"

"Yes... No. I'm only scared..."

"What are you scared of?"

Death. Wasn't it an obvious answer?

"I'm here. You'll pull through and that's that." He wrapped
me even tighter in his arms. Strangely enough, I found myself
somewhat pacified as though death itself wouldn't dare touch me
as long as I was under his protection.

"I don't want to die," I admitted, at last, hiding my face in his
chest.

"You won't die." He was so positively calm about it, so very
assured of his own words that even I began believing in them.
"Tonight, is the worst night, is all. The fever must break, that's
what the doctor said. In the morning, you shall feel better. Why
don't you rest some more?"

"I'm afraid to fall asleep. I feel I shall die in my sleep. If I'm
awake, it won't get me..." I grew agitated again, sweating with fear.

Strangely, he didn't find such superstitions ridiculous, only
regarded me with infinite patience, much like one would a child
that was frantic with unfounded worry. "Just lie down then and
I'll hold you and tell you stories so that you stay awake till the
morning. What do you say to that?"

Still unconvinced, I nodded nevertheless. He pulled the sheep-skin over us and wrapped his arms around me. "What would you like to hear?"

I considered for a few moments. "Tell me about your native town."

"Drasenhofen?" he asked, somewhat surprised. "I wouldn't call it a town. A village is more like it." He laughed somewhere into my hair. "It's in Lower Austria and it actually stands right on the border with Czechoslovakia."

"Really?"

"Really. We're neighbors, old comrade."

He kept his word and not once did he let go of me or stop talking. Through my delirium, I heard him speak about his mother and about his father, who had perished on the Eastern Front, about his childhood friends and his love for horses and about the SS recruiters who came into their town right after the Austrian Anschluss. He spoke of the war and his comrades, of the Ukrainian steppes and his dog Prinz who he missed dearly and of the house in which we were going to live after the war. Perhaps I dreamt that last part and he never said anything of the sort; one couldn't rely on their hearing in such a feverish state.

He touched my forehead from time to time and reached for the wet rag whenever he felt the fever climbing too high for his liking. But not once did he let go of me and at last, I fell asleep in his arms. In the morning, when I opened my eyes to the sound of a roll call fanfare and made a motion to get up – sheer camp instinct – I indeed felt slightly better. Still extremely weak but the void was gone, along with the strange darkness that was threatening to consume me just a few hours ago. I still clutched at Dahler's uniform when he made a motion to get up – a gesture, which seemed to please him immensely judging by the look on his face. I kept him up all night with my coughing and all that storytelling and yet he was smiling as though he didn't mind one bit.

"I have to be there for the *Appell*," he said, gently removing my fingers from his sleeve. "But I'll be back with breakfast soon. Sleep some more. The morning has come. Nothing to be afraid of."

I stuck the hand under my shirt and began feeling for the red spots. "It's still there, the rash," I announced, disappointed.

"It'll stay there for some time. It spreads all over the body, too."

I touched my face self-consciously.

That got a chuckle out of him. "Don't fret about your pretty face. It doesn't spread there. It's not measles."

"You should have been a doctor."

"I should have," he agreed surprisingly easily and kissed me softly on my forehead. "I love you, Leni."

"I love you too, Herr Unterscharführer," I muttered without thinking.

"Franz."

"Franz," I repeated.

With visible reluctance, he rose to his feet. As soon as the door locked after him, I fell asleep once again, dreaming of the border-town between Austria and Czechoslovakia, about the dog named Prinz and the house in which we were going to live someday.

Chapter 21

Helena

The nightly routine didn't change. He would come to the office with his pockets stuffed with goods commandeered from the SS canteen, leave the flashlight on the floor so that the overhead electric light wouldn't attract any unwanted attention and spoon-feed me until I regained enough strength to hold my own spoon again. He would sit cross-legged and dark against the meager amber light and entertain me with army anecdotes until my eyelids would grow heavy with sleep after all the food and warm tea that he'd give me. Then, he would arrange the fur coats around us and hold me as he did on the very first night and breathe softly into my hair, sending shivers down my spine.

More than a week had passed, perhaps more than that and I had grown so used to sleeping in his embrace that I wanted to know nothing different from that time on. With him, I feared nothing.

"How come your comrades never question your staying out every night?" I asked as we shared our small supper consisting of an SS-canteen-issued stew and sausage with bread.

Dahler's face pulled to a wry smile. "After the camp administration raised the rations for schnapps, they've been getting pissed nightly. I doubt they even notice whether I'm in my cot in the barrack or not. Do you know that we used to get back to our quarters in such a state that if we couldn't get our behinds off the cot to turn off the light, we would shoot at the bulb instead?"

"You're joking, most certainly." I even stopped chewing for a moment.

"It's true. As true as I'm sitting here. Nobody checks on us. We can do as we please for the most part. That includes all the comings and goings at night."

"You're not the only one who sneaks out?"

"Oh, no. But the others…" He squirmed uncomfortably. "Well, let's just say, they pursue not such noble goals, as tending to their sick lady friends."

I kept looking at him, mystified until he rolled his eyes in desperation at having to explain it to me. "They're all young men, and there are very few female guards here. So, they barge into barracks, pull a few girls of their choosing and… Do you understand?"

I suddenly wished I hadn't asked.

"I never did any such thing," he added quickly.

"I wouldn't think you would."

"I'm serious. Not even at the front."

"I believe you."

He was quiet for some time, immersed in his memories. "There were fellows who would though… at the front. But we had a good Untersturmführer. He saw to it that such men were prosecuted for their crimes. There were two friends there, both from München, sons of some Party functionaries or some such… Arrogant swine, both of them, if I ever saw such! Always drunk, always up to no good but when the attack would come, we never saw them. One time, they caught a girl, some ordinary peasant's daughter and… well, no need for you to know the details of that nasty business but after our Untersturmführer learned about it from the locals who came to him to complain, he told those two bosom friends to shoot themselves if they didn't want to get shot by a firing squad on his orders. He didn't care one way or another about their fathers' getting upset about such justice. They did get quite upset, to tell you the truth, those Party bigwigs. He was quickly transferred somewhere, our commander. I don't know what happened to him after that. The new one that replaced him was a bastard. Fortunately, I was wounded soon after so I didn't have to serve under his charge for too long. Yes, there are different men everywhere, I suppose." He reflected for a long time before adding in a soft voice, "Wolff is one such example. Sometimes he can't be bothered to go into town and pay for it, so... he finds it elsewhere."

"In Birkenau?" I had difficulty believing such a thing.

Franz shook his head slowly. "Here, in the Kanada," he whispered almost without moving his lips. "Kanada women still look like real women. They wear perfume and have hair and breasts. Birkenau ones, he wouldn't touch. He finds them disgusting."

I put my food away, suddenly losing all appetite for it. How many of the women that I knew did he abuse in such a despicable way? Lashing, that I could still understand and forgive. This was a different matter entirely.

"He doesn't actually force himself on them; he gives them money and all sorts of favors for it," Dahler added, visibly embarrassed, "but..."

"But, despite the illusion of choice they can't exactly say no to him, can they?" I said what he couldn't.

"I don't know how exactly he conducts his affairs," he replied quietly and lowered his eyes.

"Why are you still friends with him if you know that he does such things to people?"

"I'm not friends with him. We're comrades. It's different."

"Just how is it different?" I almost laughed at such ridiculous logic.

"It's hard to explain." His brow clouded as he desperately groped for the right words. One could see how it was a difficult task to rationalize something of this sort. "We were conditioned this way from the very beginning. The Führer and the SS brotherhood are above all. An SS man must obey orders without questioning them. It's our sacred duty to follow our leaders. Thinking is harmful to us – Obergruppenführer Eicke's famous words. An SS man must only follow orders. Doubts are harmful. There's no place for doubts among SS ranks. Our SS brothers are above our own blood ones. Our leaders know what is best for us. We must follow them. Unconditional loyalty is above all."

As his voice slowly gathered conviction, as though finding the foundation on which he could finally stand, his eyes had suddenly grown dark and unblinking. There was a mechanical quality in his speech when he was repeating all of those postulates. They came much too easy out of him, the poisonous, hateful untruths repeated far too many times.

I swallowed with difficulty, suddenly afraid that it was too late for him to untangle them from his own thoughts. They had penetrated too deeply.

"Even against your better judgment?" I probed him cautiously.

He rubbed his forehead. "An order is an order. An SS man's duty is to obey without question," he repeated, once again.

"Even if you know that you're doing something wrong?" I looked at him closely. "Something that goes against your conscience?"

Dahler scrunched his face and drove the heels of his palms into his eyes. "Lingering feelings of compassion are caused by the trickery of the enemies of the state. They appeal to our pity in an attempt to pursue their malicious goals. If a superior gives an order, it must be correct, even if we don't understand it. We mustn't question a superior's authority. It's dangerous. It's treason…"

"Franz, look at me, please." I pulled his hands away from his face that he was carefully hiding from me as though desperately wishing for this interrogation to end. "I'm a Jew. *I am* the enemy of the state. Why did you pull me out of the gas chamber then? Why are you hiding me now? Doesn't it go against your orders?"

"It does but—"

"But what?"

"But… I couldn't have let anything happen to you." He regarded me tragically.

"But I'm Jewish. You're not supposed to protect me."

"I know."

"What of your sacred orders then?"

"Nothing. I love you. I can't help it." He looked as though he was going to cry at such a predicament.

I shifted closer to him and took his hand into mine. It was still odd, touching him first and without asking for permission but I knew how much he enjoyed whenever I did so.

"Your Führer is a hateful human being," I said quietly, looking him straight in the eyes. He pulled back in horror but didn't begin protesting and kept my hand in his, even though I noticed how his entire body tensed at such words. People got shot for less in this place and here I was, testing his loyalty to the man they all swore to die for. "But you are not. I know you're not. I want you to be good, not for my sake or the other inmates' but for your own. Hate only destroys everything. It's love that heals. Aren't you happier now, here with me, than beating some unfortunate prisoner and getting drunk with your comrades like you used to?"

He was silent.

"Weren't you feeling better about yourself when you saved my sister from the gas chamber than when you were listening to people suffocate inside?"

He nodded, very slowly and with great uncertainty, but he did.

"Maybe, it's because you know deep inside that you're doing the right thing? Maybe, that's why you prefer to be friends with Rottenführer Gröning and not Wolff because Rottenführer Gröning never hits or rapes anyone and doesn't ask any questions as to why you would want to send a package to an inmate while you're on leave?"

His lips twitched slightly and curled into a wavering smile.

"You made me feel so secure with you, Franz. With you, I know that nothing will happen to me. I grew to trust you; I grew so fond of you in these past two weeks, and only because you allowed me to see your real face, not that uniform that I hate so much. I know that you can be kind and caring and I know that you do have a heart. All I'm asking is for you to start listening to that heart of yours and not that garbage that your superiors are putting into your head. When you feel inwardly that something is wrong, it's wrong. That's your moral compass guiding you. Do what feels right."

He sat still for some time. Suddenly, he leaned forward and planted a quick kiss on my cheek. "This feels right."

A grin spread slowly over my face. This was already something, better than all that insufferable parroting of SS doctrines. "So it does."

After a moment's consideration and sensing no protest from my side, he drew closer and pressed his lips to the corner of my mouth. I closed my eyes. Our knees touched. Slowly, I moved my hand out of his and put it on the back of his neck, so soft and exposed under the stiff collar of his uniform. He took my face in his hands and covered my mouth with his and I let him kiss me, really kiss me for the first time.

My mother's voice was still repeating somewhere in the back of my head that my kisses and my body were for my husband only and that it was my husband alone who was entitled to the greatest gift – my virtue that I would offer him on our wedding night and not sooner. But the SS doctor had already taken that gift for himself on my first day here. I might as well give whatever was left of former me to someone who would at least appreciate it.

I didn't stop him when his caresses grew more insistent as he explored my body and I didn't push his hands away when he began unbuttoning my shirt. I waited for the shame to come and for resentment – I was raised differently too – but quite a different emotion was in place, from what I had expected. There was no shame and there was no guilt when I allowed him to lay me down and pull my slacks off of me. On the contrary, his hands all over my bare skin felt as though they belonged there, as though I was always his and that he was merely claiming what was intended for him in the first place.

He was impatient with his kisses and with the way he touched me – my breasts, my stomach, between my parted legs – but still asked me in a hoarse whisper if I'd ever been with a man before, so he'd know to take it slowly, in order not to hurt me. I only smiled sadly and told him not to worry about it. The SS doctor had hurt me long before that. I wanted him, Franz, to make me forget it all. Perhaps, I'd make him forget his past also.

Chapter 22

Germany, 1947

Dr. Hoffman watched Helena Dahler lower her gaze and grin softly. "So, yes, as you can see, it was all very consensual between us. My husband never forced himself on me or any other inmate for that matter. I understand why Mr. Novák would make such allegations though." She was staring toward the window, red with the sunset, so as not to look at the judges' panel as she spoke on such an intimate matter. Franz Dahler's thumb gently stroked the back of her hand without him noticing it. Dr. Hoffman couldn't help but smile at the gesture. "As you can probably conclude from Herr Wolff's example, the inmates didn't particularly have a say when it came to any SS man's wishes. Naturally, Herr Novák must have assumed that my husband was the same type of man... you understand. Someone who forces himself on women. I can assure you that Franz never did anything of this sort, not to me, nor to anyone else."

The Slovak was staring at the opposite wall the entire time that she spoke, his mouth pressed into a hard line. Contrary to Dahler, who appeared relaxed if somewhat pensive, Novák's back was rigid with tension.

"Herr Novák, have you ever *witnessed* the defendant having forced relations with Frau Dahler?" the Chairman asked.

"No, of course I haven't. As you can imagine, the SS liked their privacy in such cases. I'm only repeating what the others were saying."

"What precisely, were they saying?"

"That the defendant was having a relationship with her."

"Non-consensual? You ought to be more precise."

The Slovak made no answer.

"Herr Novák, you will need to respond to this question. Do not forget that you are under oath."

"It was implied," Andrej Novák barked back irritably. "No woman prisoner would voluntarily go with an SS man. Don't you think so?"

"We are not here to have opinions. We are here to state the facts," the Chairman explained patiently. "As a co-plaintiff, you brought up serious charges against the defendant, among which was his having a forced sexual relationship with the witness, Helena Dahler. It is our duty, as a court of law, to prove or disprove it. So far, whatever you've brought up in relation to that particular charge is considered hearsay and particularly taking into consideration the fact that Frau Dahler herself is denying such a thing ever occurring. Now, had you witnessed it personally, that would have been an entirely different matter. Hence, my questions."

"No, I have not personally *witnessed* such a thing occurring," Novák snapped, struggling to keep the anger from showing on his face.

"Defendant, just for the record, does this mean that you also deny ever sexually abusing the witness?" The Chairman pointed with his gavel at Helena.

Dahler sighed as though he had to repeat the obvious for the hundredth time. "As my wife has already stated, I never as much as touched her without her consent. So, no, I never sexually abused her or any other inmate. I'm sure that my sister-in-law, Różínka Feldman, will attest to that fact even though her general opinion of me is such that I'm nothing more than a common scoundrel." The courtroom chuckled. "You can interview the entire Kanada Kommando survivors – they will all testify in my defense. Rape is the most despicable thing a man can do to a woman and I've always despised the scum who would lower themselves to such a level. I wouldn't be able to look at myself in the mirror if I ever did anything of that sort to my wife. I never denied beating her that one time, but that…" He shook his head vehemently.

Dr. Hoffman believed him.

"We shall interview Růžínka Feldman tomorrow," the Chairman announced. "I am rather curious as to what she has to say about all this."

"She will be your most reliable witness, Your Honor," Dahler announced in the same jesting tone he had adopted when he previously spoke of his sister-in-law. "She doesn't fancy me one bit but she's an honest woman; will speak only God's honest truth and, unlike my wife, she doesn't care one way or another if I end my days in jail."

Once more, the courtroom was thick with mirth at Dahler's expense.

A charming fellow, when he wants to be, Dr. Hoffman considered. But again, in his practice, he had come across criminals who were crafty as foxes when it came to deceiving others.

*

Past dinner time. Outside, a silent city bathed in the rain. Apart from an occasional yellow smudge of a lamppost, the streets stood dark, still only partly habitable. The water glimmered against the stone as if the city was washing itself of its blood-smeared past. The time was dead once more. Only the streaks of rain against his window were alive, all else stood still.

His dinner, half-eaten and forgotten on the windowsill – in the army, he had long lost the habit of eating properly at the table, always on the move, always consumed by something important – Dr. Hoffman checked his wristwatch. It was much too late to call on his colleague now but he knew that he wouldn't be able to sleep if he hadn't talked it out with someone from his field. The case drove him to distraction like a mosquito in a countryside, stinging him with unanswered questions until he felt himself going mad from their abundance.

And how simple it all looked at the start! A former Nazi brings his wife as a witness to the court in order to save his neck. Co-plaintiff Novák's version was so cut and dry; Dahler was a rapist and pathological liar, a natural Jew-hater and a cold-blooded killer. And Helena – poor Helena – is just an unfortunate victim who had to endure abuse, first in the camp and now, as Dahler's wife. Dahler's motive was only too clear. What would look better on his new resume than marriage to a former concentration camp inmate?

Yet, the way she looked at him, with such profound tenderness, with such obvious fondness couldn't have been faked under any threats. She loved her husband, genuinely and deeply and that's what bothered Dr. Hoffman to no end. Because, how could she? How could she have fallen in love with him? After all, it had started so grimly between them. She had admitted it herself that she didn't want to know him in the very beginning. She tore his love note apart. She was certain during those few weeks after their meeting that he couldn't love, that he had no heart. What changed?

No, he knew what changed exactly – Helena recounted the story in simple enough terms; small favors, odd acts of kindness, her sister saved by him, then – she herself. But that would have caused gratitude in any typical case. Logically thinking, one didn't fall in love with a person who rescued them from drowning. One didn't fall in love with a jailer who allowed you to use a second blanket at night.

And Dahler, he was no hero by any stretch of the imagination. Yes, he did put his life at risk for her but even that goal was self-serving. He wished to keep the woman he loved for himself and only for him. He never pulled anyone else out of the gas chamber, besides her and her sister. It was likely he couldn't have been bothered about those other Jews' fates, only Helena's. So, how could she genuinely love someone who murdered her own kin in such cold blood? Not personally, per se, but he was still complicit in it.

After staring moodily ahead for quite some time, Dr. Hoffman glimpsed his watch again and resolutely walked over to the black telephone that stood on his desk. His fingers drummed impatiently on its surface while he waited for the familiar voice to answer.

There was four of them, graduates of the same Alma Mater, working here as psychiatrists and gathering material for their future academic works. Since Will Hutson was highly praised, by the Stanford professors, for his thesis on the jailer/prisoner relationship, he was Dr. Hoffman's first and most natural choice. In Dr. Hoffman's eyes, it was close enough to the Dahler's case.

"Will?" His face lit up as soon as the line came alive with the familiar and eager, *Dr. Hutson here.* "Did I wake you up?"

"No, I'm still working. What do you think of that damn weather outside?"

"I have a few professional questions if you have a few minutes." Hoffman ignored the unrelated question and dropped the cord, which he hadn't noticed he'd begun twisting in his fingers.

"For you, always. Has something interesting come up?"

That's certainly one way to put it. "You interviewed camp survivors, didn't you?"

"Yes, sir."

"It may sound strange but… have you ever come across a case where a former inmate would… fall in love with an authority figure?"

"You mean, an officer?"

"An officer, a regular guard, a Kapo… anyone above them in the hierarchy."

"Do you mean trading sexual favors for food?"

"No, I mean an actual romantic relationship."

There was a long silence on the line. Dr. Hoffman was chewing on his lip, awaiting a snort of laughter from Hutson any moment now.

"Romantic relationship?" Dr. Hutson asked, once again.

"Yes. In fact, they're married now."

"Who?"

"The former inmate and the guard."

Another long pause. "For the papers, most certainly?"

"Well, from his side, that would have been understandable, right? But I swear to you, the wife appears to have the most genuine affection for him."

"Huh."

"Yes. I know. Hard to believe but here we are."

"And she was in the same camp, with him?"

"Yes, in Auschwitz. She worked under his charge in the Kanada Kommando – the sorting place."

"Lucky girl. A kosher place, from what I've heard."

"Yes, she didn't complain about the conditions."

"How on earth did you find them?"

"He received a summons for the Denazification Tribunal. Another former inmate, who knows him from the camp, swears that the man is the devil incarnate."

"But the wife doesn't?"

"No. The wife appears to be genuinely in love with him."

Another *huh* from Hutson. "What do you make of him?"

"A likable enough fellow. Very charming, as a matter of fact, but only after he relaxes a bit. At first, he was extremely aloof and I had the greatest difficulty in trying to decipher his manner."

"That's certainly a first, in my experience but…" The psychiatrist hesitated.

Dr. Hoffman's interest was instantly awakened. "Whatever it is, even if you think it insignificant, tell me!"

"I had a case with a teenager I treated," Hutson started reluctantly. "Also, from Auschwitz, by the way. He was one of those unfortunate young fellows who were too handsome for their own good, a bum boy; *Pipel* in camp jargon. Have you heard of such?"

"Yes. As a matter of fact, Helena, that's the wife, she mentioned one in her testimony."

"So, you know the deal then. The boy would allow the Kapo to do whatever that Kapo pleased to do with him and in return, he would be clothed, fed, protected from the others; generally, well looked after." Hutson paused.

"Well?" Dr. Hoffman demanded, his breath hitching in his throat.

"Well, when I was interviewing him, he was stating with the most incomprehensible obstinacy that his abuser – the Kapo – was, in fact, a grand fellow without whom he wouldn't have survived. Whenever I pointed out the fact that the Kapo was using him in the most disgusting way, he would begin protecting him with such feeling, you'd think the Kapo was the hero of the day and a statue ought to have been put up in his honor. Numerous times we had this conversation and not once did he budge. His position was set in stone. The Kapo was a grand fellow and he, the boy, owed his life to him. I even asked him whether he was a homosexual but he said no, not at all. He was attracted to women very much and not once did he look at a man that way. I asked him again about the Kapo and again he refused to see any reason and continued proclaiming that the Kapo had his vices but he was a good man because he saved his life when he didn't have to."

A hopeful smile slowly grew on Dr. Hoffman's face; the smile of a scientist on the verge of a major discovery.

"Go on, please," he barely whispered.

"The boy's conclusion was, *'He could have just used me and killed me but he treated me as best as he could. How can I hold a grudge for such kind treatment? Without him, I would have been dead. Only his affection kept me safe. My fellow inmates didn't treat me as well as he did. I will forever be grateful to him for keeping my life when he had absolutely no reason to.'* The logic escapes me personally but there we are."

Hoffman laughed softly into the phone. "Do you know what Helena Dahler said about her husband? Almost the same exact thing. *'He was the only person who cared about me; I owe my very life to him,'* and much more, to that effect. What do you think is wrong with them?"

"Psychologically?"

"Obviously. Don't you think they suffer from some… personality disorder or some such? This is not a normal reaction to abuse, by any means."

"A protection mechanism of some sort?" Hutson mused out loud. "A subconscious survival technique? I came across different ones when watching the prisoners but those were… not in the same class at all. However, the idea is similar."

"That was part of my theory. Still, how does the developing of an affection fit into it?"

"Perhaps to minimize the trauma? What I mean is, the Jews, unlike German inmates, for instance, they were already sentenced to death, if not an instant one, then surely one through work, disease, or starvation. They were aware of it. They had nothing to hope for. In most cases, they had lost their entire families right after their arrival and themselves were being abused daily. Then, an authority figure, on whom their very lives were dependent, suddenly showed interest in them. They grabbed onto it because it meant survival, no matter for how short of a period. They understood that the authority figure was still an abuser but to protect themselves from further trauma by submitting to that abuser's will, they taught themselves to see the abuser in a completely different light, as a savior, which made them seem better as well."

"A sort of voluntary dissociative disorder?"

"Not as severe a case as a split personality but in the same spectrum, I'd say. They purposely confused themselves in order to protect whatever was left of their fragile psyche. By normalizing the relationship with the abuser, they weren't as emotionally burdened by such a necessity as they would have been in any other case. Most victims of abuse recognize themselves as such – victims – and they suffer from such things as psychosis, depression, different neuroses, phobias, and so on and so forth. My teenager, though, appeared much calmer and more stable than the victims of group rape, for instance. Hence, my conclusion. What of your 'wife'?"

"She seems calm when the husband is around. She definitely suffers from certain conditions which had developed during and after her incarceration – agoraphobia and social phobia are just two of them – and that's according to the husband himself. But yes, in his company, she appears to be surprisingly calm and collected. Ordinarily, the victims break down during their testimonies. I had cases when they fainted even but as long as he held her hand, she was fine. And you're right about another thing, she doesn't see herself as a victim. Of the fascist regime, yes; but not of Dahler, that's for sure."

"Quite a subject for research is shaping up, eh?"

Dr. Hoffman chuckled. "Too few research subjects, unfortunately."

"Is the case still open?"

"Yes. Helena's sister will be testifying tomorrow."

"I'd like to be present if it's possible."

Somehow, Dr. Hoffman had expected to hear that request. "Of course, Will. And, thank you."

Chapter 23

The lusterless sunlight tinted the courtroom with pallid gold. The well-polished benches creaked busily – everyone arrived early that morning, well ahead of the scheduled hour. There was something subtly different to the voices exchanging their usual pre-hearing chatter that day; the apathetic and slightly annoyed undertone, so characteristic of harassed Denazification tribunal lawyers, was absent from them. Ten minutes to nine. Lieutenant Carter, in a fresh uniform, was staring at the clock without blinking.

Near the window, Dr. Hutson sat on an empty spectators' bench, his form partially hidden in the shadows. Dr. Hoffman concealed a grin at the sight of his colleague, whose face was alive with impatience. He only stopped his fidgeting when the Chairman had walked in and announced the court session open.

Różínka Feldman was scheduled to take the witness stand first. Dahler and his wife sat next to each other as before, his hand atop of hers. He smiled at his sister-in-law and muttered a quiet greeting when she passed him by, to which Różínka replied with a cool, curt nod. Helena's face showed every emotion she felt – it was a damnable business dragging her only surviving family member into this courtroom but Helena had no choice.

Dr. Hoffman had learned by now that Różínka was ten years Helena's senior but if he hadn't, he'd probably take her for Helena's mother. Whereas Helena was pale and fragile, her appearance resembling more that of a porcelain doll – infinitely delicate but smooth and eternally youthful; Różínka's eyes alone told the story of a life their owner wouldn't wish upon anyone. Two pools of liquid gloom, dark and brooding, crisscrossed by wrinkles and marred by the shadows that would forever haunt her, no matter how many years separated her from what she had been forced to endure. Two deep, bitter lines framed her mouth, pinched and unwilling to speak. Only the hair was perfectly black but Dr. Hoffman had a suspicion that the blackness was of the bottled type, for, without it, the woman's head would have been entirely gray.

She regarded the Bible a bit quizzically but placed her hand on it nevertheless and diligently repeated the oath. The first superficial questions followed.

"State your name to the court, please."

"Roza Feldman."

"Age?"

"Thirty-five."

Dr. Hutson regarded her with sympathy. She looked so much older than that.

"Your address?"

She uttered something unpronounceable in Hebrew or Yiddish, from which Dr. Hoffman only recognized, *Palestine*.

"Marital status?"

"Widow."

The judge spared her the question about the children and Dr. Hoffman was grateful for that. She spoke a little about her life in Slovakia, about the German occupation, about the *Hlinka Guard*, about the new anti-Semitic policies imposed, and about the day when she learned that her sister went to register with the Germans.

"She lived with our parents before that. As soon as they heard rumors that the Germans would be taking young women to work in camps, they sent her to live with our gentile friends. Many families did so, in fact, to protect their children, but…" Róžínka sighed. "The Germans began terrifying the local population. The posters were plastered all over the country, saying that whoever was found guilty of hiding Jews would be prosecuted and sent to the work camps as well. So, Helena, not wishing to cause our friends any trouble, went and registered with the German office. Our friends later gave us the note that she left before she had run off with her suitcase. From it, we learned that she thought that she was indeed going to a factory or some such, where she would be working and helping the German war effort... It was all propaganda and lies, of course, but some people, who were naïve and believed everything that the Germans said – Helena among them – thought that their families would be left alone if they volunteered. They thought the Germans would think them to be useful. None of them suspected that they would be taken to a place like Auschwitz."

Dr. Hoffman threw a sidelong glance at Dahler. The former Auschwitz guard was stroking his wife's hand absentmindedly, his gaze fixed on the floorboards without actually seeing them. He was listening, no doubt but his thoughts were lost in the past. Dr. Hoffman would give all his money just to learn what precisely he was thinking.

There was one particular question that bothered him immensely. Would Dahler want for Helena to remain free and spend the war in hiding but which would have resulted in the two never meeting, or would he have preferred for things to remain as they were? He almost itched to break the protocol and ask Dahler that. Yet, he remained silent.

"When did you receive a summons from the government?" the Chairman asked.

"In summer 1942. A few months after Helena was deported."

"Was that summons for your entire family?"

"The government passed the law that all Jews must register with the office in 1941. So, in 1942 they began routinely sending such summons to everyone's addresses. We received ours – my husband, I, and our children, that is, and my parents received theirs at their address. But theirs was for a different date from ours. After the war, I learned that they were taken to Treblinka instead of Auschwitz, where they were gassed upon arrival." Róžínka recounted the events with admirable self-possession. Her eyes were dry and dark.

"And you arrived in Auschwitz with your family?" the Chairman asked again.

"Yes. On the ramp, they separated us at once. Men had to stand in a separate column from women. The officer who was in charge of the selection asked me if I wished to keep my children. I thought it was a ridiculous question – what mother wouldn't want to keep her children?" Her laughter reverberated through the courtroom, dry and bitter. "Later, the inmates explained it to me that had I abandoned my children, he would have sent me to the other column, which was selected for work and not a gas chamber." She regarded her nails for a moment, growing pensive. "It didn't matter, really. Even if I'd known that back then, I still would have never abandoned my children, regardless, not even to save my own life. I only left them there, in that place—"

That was the first time when she choked, quickly bringing her hand to her mouth, to regain control over her emotions. Her fingers were trembling slightly. At last, she took a deep breath, collecting herself.

"I only left them because I thought we were indeed going to the showers. They were very persuasive, the SS. They kept exchanging small talk with us and explaining what work we shall do after we take our shower, asking what qualifications we had. It all sounded frighteningly plausible!" Suddenly, she was terribly excited. "I was undressing my son when an officer appeared in the room and began calling my name. I walked up to him and indicated that I was Rózínka Feldman. He took me by my forearm and told me to follow him. I didn't speak German too well, so I only understood that he was saying that my sister was looking for me and he would take me to her. I pointed at my children but he told me not to worry about them. I thought that I'd be back to them later." She quickly brought a handkerchief to her eyes. There was no talking about it without tears, not just yet. Too little time had passed. The wound still hurt.

"Who was that officer who took you out of the gas chamber?" the Chairman inquired after a few moments, allowing her to collect herself.

"Franz Dahler." Without hesitation, she pointed at the former Auschwitz guard. The gesture had the quality of accusation to it. It appeared to interest Dr. Hutson, who marked something quickly in his notepad. Victims pointed out the perpetrators to the police in the same manner during lineups.

"What happened after that?"

"I saw Helena outside. She was crying, but she appeared to be relieved to see me. Herr Dahler shoved us both, rather unceremoniously, forward and didn't allow us to hug or even talk until we were away from that place. Then, Helena pressed my hand and told me that everything was going to be all right and that we shall be working together. I asked when would I be allowed to go and get the children, to which Herr Dahler told me that they would be taken care of in a special camp for the children. That I'd see them later."

As her sister spoke, Helena Dahler was gradually lowering her head until Dr. Hoffman could see her eyes no longer. She also leaned closer to her husband as though in search of protection he couldn't offer her, apart from a fleeting kiss he quickly planted on her knuckles before covering her hand with both of his. A thief's gesture, but for some reason profoundly touching in its helpless sincerity. They were both guilty before Różínka, in different respects but guilty nevertheless and they only had each other to turn to.

"Was it the defendant who told you the truth about your children?"

"No. It was one of the Kapos, Maria Krupp. I didn't believe her at first but then other inmates confirmed it. The last person who did was Helena. She explained that she wanted to shield me from the truth for as long as possible so that I wouldn't go mad or do something to myself. She was terrified at the thought that she would be left alone in that place, so she wanted to keep me by her side at all costs."

"Is it true that you worked along with your sister under the defendant's command?"

"That's correct, Your Honor."

"What was your impression of him? How did he interact with the inmates?"

After casting a probing glance in Dahler's direction, Růžínka pondered her reply for some time. Dr. Hoffman caught Dr. Hutson's look. The latter motioned his head ever so slightly in Dahler's direction, lowered his eyes, then looked back at Hoffman and raised his brows in a meaningful way. Hoffman nodded his acknowledgment. He also noticed that Dahler purposefully kept his gaze down. This time there was no guilt in his face, only a respectful desire to keep from intimidating the former inmate by staring directly at her face. In spite of himself, Dr. Hoffman admitted a newfound respect for the man. Rarely were criminals so courteous. Ordinarily, they chose to exercise their power over their victims until the victorious end. Dahler seemingly allowed her to talk, to say whatever she felt she was entitled to say, without any reservations.

He also noted how differently he acted around Novák.

"He was… temperamental. Difficult to figure out, unlike some other guards. Rottenführer Wolff, for instance, he was cruel. One didn't want to get on his bad side. Rottenführer Gröning, on the other hand, was Wolff's complete opposite. I've never seen him raise his hand to anyone. He was mostly locked up in his quarters. He didn't particularly like being among the inmates and preferred desk work to supervising the warehouse. But we liked him nevertheless. He was more or less easy-going. As for Herr Dahler…" She paused again. "He could be both. When something would set him off, it was better to be away from him. He never hit me personally, though, only reprimanded me verbally on a few separate occasions but never touched me."

"When you say, 'he could be both,' could you be more precise?"

"He could be cruel, but he also wasn't deaf to the inmates' pleas. He could be agreeable like Gröning when he wished to."

"Like with you and your sister?"

"My sister was an entirely different case altogether. He was in love with her. Naturally, their relationship differed greatly from his relationships with other inmates. He was very different with her, like a different person."

"For the record, you're saying that he wasn't physically or sexually abusing her?"

Dr. Hoffman cast a probing glance in Novák's direction. The Chairman's question stemmed from his testimony, after all. The Slovak was staring at the top of Dahler's head with cold hatred.

"Goodness, no." Róžínka shook her head emphatically. "I only learned that he beat her with his whip on the day of my arrival after she returned from the doctor's quarters and told me about it. But it was something he had to do. If he didn't, it would look much too suspicious to his superiors and who knows how it all would have played out in the end. He didn't have much choice in that particular case."

"Did he ever hit her after that?"

"No, never. And never before that, from what she told me. As a matter of fact, he was very protective of her."

"Is it true that he saved her from the gas chamber?"

"Yes, in late November or early December of 1942. I'm sorry, I don't remember the exact date. We didn't have a calendar there." She paused a moment, then went on. "Helena contracted typhus and, during an unexpected inspection, the SS doctor sent her to the truck. Everyone knew where those trucks took the inmates who didn't pass the selection. I thought I had lost her when Herr Dahler came to me later that day and told me not to worry and that Helena was safe. He didn't tell me where he was hiding her but he said that he would take care of her. In the following days, he'd stop by my station sometimes and inform me about her condition in a few words. *Helena's doing all right*, or *Helena's fever is going down* – things such as those and nothing more but I was extremely grateful even for that information. At least I knew that my sister was alive. He brought her back after the New Year and said something about the new vaccine that the SS doctors tested on her, which supposedly helped. People believed it. Or, rather, they weren't stupid enough to ask an SS officer any questions. His comrades didn't seem to care."

"Did any of them know about the nature of Herr and Frau Dahler's relationship?"

"Helena told me that Rottenführer Gröning knew. Not *knew* per se but rather, pretended not to know what was going on. He didn't inform on Herr Dahler, that is. But he did know, yes. Wolff, I don't think he did. He was the type that would report something of this sort to the Political Department."

"There were rumors that Herr Wolff had forced sexual relationships with inmates. Are you aware of such rumors?"

"I heard things and I know why you're asking me that." She smiled briefly. "If he was doing it himself, why report his comrade Dahler, right? But, you see, here's where their views differed greatly. While Wolff thought it to be perfectly acceptable to misuse women whenever he wished, the thought of having an actual ongoing relationship with one was against his SS moral code, or whatever he called it. Herr Dahler, obviously, thought differently."

"When did you first learn about your sister's involvement with the defendant?"

"Well, I began suspecting things right after I arrived. My sister had changed a lot, after the first few months of her incarceration. I remembered her as a happy, carefree, outgoing girl who always smiled and loved to sing. The Auschwitz Helena was very different from that girl. She was very… closed off, aloof even, people-shy, and also extremely vulnerable emotionally. For instance, when she noticed that I wasn't eating properly, she broke into hysterics. I was still very depressed after I had learned the truth about my children, you see and... to be truthful, she scared me that day. I admit, I did think of committing suicide but Helena terrified me so much with that erratic behavior that it occurred to me that if I indeed died and left her alone to fend for herself, she would break within days. She was very fragile, mentally. Many people were but I didn't want for my only sister to go mad like some of them did. I had no one else left, so I told myself that it was my duty to look after her to make sure that she survived. But, you see, with the best will in the world, I couldn't protect her even if I wanted. And so, she turned to the only other person who could."

"What you're saying is that hers and the defendant's was a relationship of convenience, for the sake of survival?"

"At first. I don't think she did it consciously. We were all like dogs there, kicked far too many times and starved to near death. Naturally, whoever showed us at least a bit of kindness, we would cling to that person. It was called, to be 'inmate-savvy.' Prisoners formed relationships with the Kapos or block elders to improve their situations at least a bit. Young boys surrendered their innocence to the Kapos for a favorite's position. Skilled workers bribed the guards; the guards favored certain inmates who were useful to them. It was a very complicated hierarchy. But Helena, she was much too innocent to think within those terms. She grew genuinely fond of Herr Dahler. But it was after she returned in January of 1943 that I noticed a change in her." Różínka paused again. "She became almost obsessed with him."

"What do you mean, obsessed?"

"What I mean is, she positively refused to see the reality around her. All she wanted to know was her Franz and her books."

"Books?"

"Yes." A hint of a sad smile touched upon Różínka's lips. "After her illness, she was still very weak to work full shifts, so Herr

Dahler would take her daily to his office and lock her there alone on one pretext or another to allow her some rest. Supposedly, she was cleaning there or doing some other chores but in reality, he'd let her just sit there and read books he'd bring from the Kanada instead of burning them. In the evening, when we'd return to the barrack, she would lie next to me and whisper about the stories she read, in my ear. For the first few days, I thought she had actually gone mad from the fever while she was sick with typhus. She didn't want to talk about the camp or anything else. Only about the books and Franz."

"What would she say about the defendant?"

A smirk, also melancholy. "About their plans for the future." She sighed, before elaborating. "That was one of the reasons why I thought that she'd gone mad. She told me, with that scary, blissful smile on her face, that Franz wanted to marry her after the war and she'd said yes. That they would live in his native Austria with his mother before they would buy their own house. That she couldn't wait to meet his dog, Prinz, because *she missed nice dogs, not the camp kind* and that she couldn't wait to start a new life with him. I thought she had invented all that. I knew that he liked her, but... that kind of talk, I just couldn't associate it with an SS man, do you understand? It was too inconceivable that he would make plans of this sort with an inmate. Soon enough, though, I believed it."

"What made you change your mind?"

"It wasn't just me. By the summer of 1943, the whole Kanada knew about their relationship. They were just too obvious."

"In what respect?"

She gave a small shrug. "He would constantly loiter near her station. Talk to her whenever he could, about innocent enough things but if you were in Auschwitz, you'd notice right that instant, how unnatural it looked, an SS guard speaking to an inmate about the quality of the material of a certain jacket, for instance. He would find excuses to touch her, *'to show her how to properly fold something'* for example. He was always near her. And she always looked at him in that certain way… You know, the lovesick glances and half-smiles. Sometimes, they exchanged notes. She would stay past curfew time and he would later bring her back into the barrack. No one would ask him any questions, of course, as to where she was but everyone knew. It would have all been considered very discreet in any other case but in Auschwitz, they might as well have announced their engagement to everyone in writing. So, yes, inmates certainly knew."

"Did you ever speak with her directly about their relationship?"

"I tried but abandoned the idea rather quickly. It wasn't doing anyone any good."

"What do you mean?"

"I mean, as soon as I would try to say something about him…" Różínka rubbed her forehead and exhaled in irritation. "God, he was an SS man and she was an inmate and a Jew. Do you understand how atrocious it all sounds? To me, personally, it was like a slap in the face. He wore the uniform of the people who killed my children. Our entire family! And here she goes, proclaiming her undying love for him. I wanted to shake her until I'd bring some sense into her. If she did it for survival only, I'd understand. I really would. But she was so genuinely in love with him, she was disgusting me with it!" She waved her hand dismissively. "There was no talking to her, anyway. As soon as I'd try to put some reason into her head, she'd become all hysterical again. *How could I accuse her for loving the only person who cared about her? How could I not wish her happiness, whoever it was with? How could I not be grateful – after all, we're only alive thanks to him?* That sort of thing. Mad talk. But she didn't understand what she was saying. As I said, she became dependent on him to the point of obsessiveness. Without him, the world would end. She still thinks this way. She can't even leave the house unless he's with her."

The glance that she cast her sister, who still sat with her eyes downcast in shame, was full of sorrow this time, not an accusation.

It was a parent reprimanding a child who doesn't know any better. *Or a psychiatrist, looking upon a patient that would never get well, with sympathetic regret,* Dr. Hoffman thought to himself.

"Is that her wish or his, concerning leaving the house alone?" The Chairman immediately jumped on the statement.

"Hers and hers alone. He had tried multiple times to encourage her to go on walks or shopping or whatnot but Helena gets panic attacks in the street. I tried going with her once and she just…" She sighed. "After only a few minutes outside, she became so overwhelmed, she dropped down on her knees and couldn't get another breath in her. She actually fainted and an American soldier helped me carry her back to the apartment. I didn't try to take her out afterward. When she's with her husband, she seems to be all right though. She even manages to enter a full movie theater and sit there through the whole motion picture but only as long as he holds her hand. She constantly needs to know that he's near, otherwise, she completely loses her head. As I said, she's dependent on him to an unhealthy degree. She was this way in the camp already. Although, I suppose their relationship wasn't such a bad thing after all. He began to change too but unlike Helena, he grew much calmer with time, more controlled. He wasn't jumping on us with his whip anymore and generally became nicer to inmates."

"In what respect?"

"Well, Helena would give away a lot of things whenever she could. Since we worked in the Kanada, we had access to, well, everything really. Sometimes, when the workload became too overwhelming, they would send help to our Kommando from the women's camp. They were all extremely malnourished compared to us and lacked the most basic of necessities. Helena always tried helping them the best she could. She'd give them whatever food items she'd find, underwear – they didn't even have that – good shoes to replace their wooden ones. Toothbrushes, medicine, money to buy something on the black market – you name it, she'd give it to them whenever she could. Mostly, it was Dahler who supervised her sector and so, he would just look the other way whenever she distributed the goods. He knew what she was doing and pretended to ignore it entirely. So, he was helping in his own way."

"Would you say the defendant was anti-Semitic?"

"Well, he belonged to the type of the guards that believed that orders concerning the extermination of the Jewish race must have been correct even if they didn't understand them. They believed that if their Führer said so, then it must be the right thing to do even if they personally had doubts about it all. Later, he began thinking for himself at last and even started helping the inmates… It all takes a very gradual change."

"Would you call him a natural Jew-hater?"

"No. I would call him a very confused human being. But he didn't hate us like Wolff or Moll or the others, so, no." She paused. "I ought to be grateful to him solely for keeping my sister alive. Not just physically saving her but staying by her when she needed all the support she could use mentally. Those two times that they were separated in Auschwitz, I genuinely feared for her life."

"Separated?" Lieutenant Carter pulled forward, shedding his role as a mere observer, for a moment. "Are you talking about that time when the defendant went on leave?"

"That would make it three times." A faint semblance of a grin from Różínka. "No, I'm talking about when they were forcefully separated in 1943 and in early 1944. The first time was when some commission arrived from Germany to investigate corruption and he got temporarily arrested. The second, when they both got arrested. But I believe my sister is better qualified to tell this story."

In the front row, Dr. Hutson was all attention.

"We'll definitely listen to Frau Dahler's testimony after the recess." The Chairman reluctantly banged his gavel, dismissing the court for lunch.

Chapter 24

Helena

Auschwitz-Birkenau. Autumn 1943

The *Appell* was an odd affair that morning, with only Rottenführer Wolff present. I kept throwing concerned glances in the direction of Franz's office, which remained locked as the hours slipped by. Next to me, Rôžínka was recounting the best family recipes. *What a feast she would cook as soon as the Allies liberated us!* We were still too afraid to believe it, yet couldn't help hoping, dreaming, whispering about it. After the German loss in Stalingrad, which the entire camp discreetly celebrated with hushed congratulations and renewed hopes, the tide of the war had turned for the Germans. The camp was alive with rumors, most contradicting each other. Some were delivered by the new arrivals who were selected for work; some – overheard on the clandestine radios that some barracks had managed to put together from stolen parts and which for concealing, that entire barrack would be executed. However, they cared not one whit for such trifles. The hope was more important to us than the constant threat of death. To the latter, we had long grown used. It had become a part of us, as real and permanent as the tattoos on our skin.

"But the best part is the glazing on the baked fish," Rôžínka continued, oblivious to my mood, which was heavy with worry. Lately, such talks had become our usual entertainment to pass the day but that afternoon, I barely heard her murmuring, my eyes glued to the closed door of Franz's office. *Where was he?* "If you mix the onions and the mushrooms together and add just a bit of—"

She quickly dropped the dress she was folding and pulled herself up to attention. I did the same, secretly hoping for Franz to walk in and greet Wolff with a smirk and the usual, *"How goes it, you old mushroom?"*

Instead, a delegation of several uniformed men marched straight past our section and toward the offices of the SS. Recognizing Kommandant Höss and Untersturmführer Grabner from the Political Department, my heart sank even deeper, burying itself somewhere in the pit of my stomach. A wave of nausea washed over me, as soon as they demanded from Rottenführer Wolff if he had spare keys to the two other offices. He insisted that he didn't and remained near the door of his own as the newly arrived SS men were virtually turning it upside down. From where I stood, I caught sight of the drawers being pulled out entirely and tapped at, as the men checked for double bottoms, floorboards poked and prodded at; even the walls didn't escape the SS men's attention. Behind my back, one of the inmates barely whispered an astounded, "What's going on?"

No one knew, not even Wolff; suddenly pale and terrified beyond any measure, judging by the sheen of sweat which broke out on his forehead.

Only after the verdict of *"Alles in Ordnung,"* did he seem to release the breath he was holding. The SS men had already shifted their attention to two other offices.

"Who occupies these two?"

"Rottenführer Gröning and Unterscharführer Dahler," Wolff promptly supplied. "Gröning is responsible for currency and valuables and Dahler is the Kommandoführer in charge of the entire detail and also the leather factory."

Someone had already obtained the spare keys with typical German efficiency. In mere minutes, the fate of Wolff's office, was caught up to by the other two.

"What are they searching for?" Rόžínka asked breathlessly, suddenly alarmed.

"Who knows?" I replied, unable to tear my eyes off the unraveling scene. For some reason, the entire action had a faint echo of something sinister and disastrous to it, the effect of which couldn't be averted with the best will in the world. We knew very well what such searches meant for us, the Jews, however, we had not the faintest idea that the dreaded SS were susceptible to the same treatment and just that thought alone terrified everyone around, worse than any barrack search.

"Where is Rottenführer Gröning?" Grabner demanded from Wolff as the delegation emerged from the office, leaving it in horrible disarray.

Wolff pulled himself up even more. "He's in Berlin, Herr Untersturmführer. Delivering the money and valuables to the Reichsbank."

Kommandant Höss nodded his affirmation, his face impenetrable. Grabner turned to another man, who watched the entire search from the outside, flanked by two SS men of a lower rank. "Herr Obersturmführer, since he's not here, perhaps it would be—"

"When is he coming back?" Herr Obersturmführer not only interrupted Grabner, one of the most feared men in the whole of Auschwitz, but ignored him with such astounding nonchalance about him that it had become clear to everyone present at once, who was the authority with superior strength. Even the Kommandant stood a bit aside from him, positively aloof yet visibly watchful of every movement Herr Obersturmführer made.

"In a few days, I believe, Herr Obersturmführer." Wolff shot a quick glance in Höss's direction. *Help me, will you? You're in charge here; I haven't a clue how to talk to these people and how to respond so as not to get all of us in hot water,* his eyes seemingly pleaded. The Kommandant thoroughly pretended not to notice his urgent looks.

"He doesn't inform you of the exact days?"

"No, Herr Obersturmführer. Only approximately. With all the recent bombing, the train tracks—" Wolff quickly bit his lip and paled even more at the annihilating look the Obersturmführer threw him after those carelessly uttered words. "I meant to say, sometimes the trains get delayed, so he can't tell exactly when he's going to be back," Wolff carefully corrected himself.

"For how long has he been employed here?"

"A little over a year, Herr Obersturmführer."

"Would you say he's an honest and conscientious worker?"

"With all certainty, Herr Obersturmführer." Wolff diligently inclined his head in confirmation of his words.

"How do you know that he's not pocketing the money?"

Wolff's head shot up at the unexpected and brutally straightforward question. "How do I know?"

"Yes."

"It's…" Another pleading sidelong glance in the Kommandant's direction, also thoroughly ignored. "It's physically impossible, Herr Obersturmführer. The process of collecting and processing the valuables is such that it excludes all possibility of appropriating even one dollar."

"Care to elaborate?"

"All of the valuables and money that inmates find during the sorting are dropped into a wooden box with a slit in it, which stands in the middle of barracks. As soon as it gets full, the inmate who's on 'box duty' that day takes it into the accountant's office – Gröning's, that is. There, they stay with him until he counts all the money, transfers the exact sum into his accountant book, and writes down all valuables – their weight, metal type, etc. – into another book. Only then does he return the box to the inmate."

The SS interrogator suddenly turned on his heel to face us. "Who was on box duty right before Gröning's departure?"

My heart stopped beating entirely. Wet with sweat, I stepped forward. "I was, Herr Obersturmführer."

"Name?"

It was an odd question in Auschwitz. We were numbers to them, not people any longer. I blinked once, twice, but supplied him with the name. He motioned me closer.

"Was the process that Rottenführer Wolff has just described always conducted in this manner?"

"Yes, Herr Obersturmführer."

"And you never saw Rottenführer Gröning slip anything into his pocket?"

I shook my head vehemently. I really didn't.

He stepped even closer, grinning faintly this time. "And he never offered you money to keep your mouth shut?"

"No, Herr Obersturmführer!" I protested louder than I intended. "They would never do that..."

"Do what?" he asked very quietly. His face was almost next to mine now.

"Conduct any sort of deals with the Jews," I replied, lowering my eyes instinctively.

"*Ach*. I see." He pulled back, seemingly satisfied with the answer. "Are there any non-Jews here?"

A few women stepped forward – all of them Polish with red triangles of political prisoners sewn onto their clothes.

"Have any of your SS supervisors ever offered you any bribes in exchange for your silence?"

Their *nein* came out in a commendable unison. No wonder, when Wolff was staring them down behind Obersturmführer's back with such intensity that it turned even my stomach in knots. The interrogator appeared to catch on to that collective fear. He was smiling kindly again.

"You needn't worry about your fate if you make a confession of accepting such bribes from your immediate supervisors. On the contrary, for aiding the investigation, you shall be not only protected by my personal authority but rewarded with an instant release from the camp."

Kommandant Höss scowled slightly and was just about to object when the Obersturmführer shot him a pointed glare. Some sort of a silent exchange passed between the two – *just go along with me if you know what's good for you, will you?* – and Höss stepped back, visibly satisfied. Only, the inmates were much too well-trained by Auschwitz to recognize sweet lies fed to them with such ease and particularly the Kanada Kommando. Everyone wisely remained silent.

"If you make such an admission, you shall be immediately transferred into the main camp, where my officers will sign your release papers as soon as we finish writing down your testimony," the interrogator made another attempt to untie a few tongues. Unsuccessfully, much to Wolff's relief.

Of course, they were all corrupted. We were all corrupted, only where we took food and necessities for ourselves, the guards took money and gold and both parties pretended to look the other way. I had personally sewn a few golden coins, diamond bracelets, and dollars into the lining of Wolff's jacket before he would go on his leave. It was an unspoken tradition in the Kanada, "an inmates' goodbye," of which the SS pretended to be blissfully ignorant, only to discover a few hidden "presents" in the safety of their homes in Germany. They returned, beaming and in a good disposition and we were allowed to eat whatever we could find and weren't beaten by them any longer. Fair barter is all.

No, we weren't stupid enough to betray them to whatever SS higher powers arrived to wreak havoc on our somewhat stable lives. We could survive because they were corrupted. We depended on them and were ready to supply them with found money and whatnot so that we'd remain safe and protected by them. Because who knew who this Obersturmführer would appoint in their place? Some ideological fanatic who would slaughter us all just for the idea.

Not a single inmate made a sound. In the background, Wolff hid a satisfied grin. The delegation left empty-handed, sealing the offices with official seals.

Not a word was spoken about Franz and that terrified me more than any interrogators put together.

"Where is he, Różínka?" I kept whispering all day and all evening just to get the same, somewhat sympathetic, *I don't know, Lena,* from her.

She was relieved that he was gone. Feeling utterly abandoned and infinitely alone, I cried myself to sleep at night.

Chapter 25

Helena

New transport, new suitcases, new books – once again, in a foreign language. The door to Franz's office was still sealed. Silence lay all about the Kanada detail, oppressive and full of torturous uncertainty. Not a word from anyone, not even a hushed rumor to allow at least a pitiful semblance of hope. We worked, quiet and subdued, under some new SS man's charge who had been sent to aid Wolff until Franz… I drove the heels of my palms into my eyes, rubbing the tears away in anguished desperation. The truth was, no one knew *when* and *if* Franz was coming back at all.

"Keep stalling and I'll leave you without lunch." The tip of the new guard's whip stung the skin on the back of my hands. I quickly pulled them off my face and rubbed the welts instinctively before resuming the folding. I hadn't been hit in so long, the gesture itself hurt worse than the whip.

Franz hadn't used his whip on anyone in months.

Franz allowed us to eat whatever we could find.

Franz permitted us to take warm cardigans and sweaters when Polish autumn, with its mists, occupied our parts.

Franz. Franz. Franz…

I wanted to howl from that uncertainty, from the sight of the sealed door, from the new man's offending presence, from the fact that I was on my own, so very weak and at anyone's mercy.

Another night. Another pillow soaked with tears. Franz allowed us to take pillows.

Franz!

*

A familiar face appeared in the warehouse. Andrej, who was prohibited from approaching our part of the Kommando after last year's incident, stood beaming in front of my station, making use of Wolff's and our new supervisor's watching the unloading of the trucks. In his grimy, outstretched palm, a piece of fresh, thick sausage lay – a reunion offering, no doubt.

"For you and your sister. Hide it, quick! I went through such pains smuggling it here. Not because of the SS but because my fellow mates smelled it like first-class hounds and wished to commandeer it for themselves but I saved it for you."

I stared at him, cold horror washing over me, one wave after another. Never before did I notice the stench of burnt flesh that clung to his clothes and skin itself, it seemed; never before did I feel so nauseated at the sight of the food and such a generous offering as this. My eyes welled with tears in spite of myself and he beamed even brighter, misinterpreting my emotions in an entirely different way.

"Don't cry, Helena," he cooed, consoling me. My entire body jerked in protest from the alien touch when he slipped the sausage into the pocket of my slacks. "That fascist dog is gone now. He won't hurt you anymore."

He reached out to wipe the tears off my wet cheeks but I recoiled in horror from his hand. The stench of death clung to it along with smeared ashes. He didn't bother washing his hands anymore after burning the corpses.

"Don't touch me."

He blinked in confusion but then smiled again. "It's all right, Helena. You don't have to be afraid of him anymore. He's not coming back."

My hand flew to my mouth to stifle a scream that was ready to tear off my lips. *He's not coming back.* Streams of sweat poured down my back. I could barely hear him talk as my entire body shook with silent sobs, "I shall take care of you now. You won't need for anything, you can take it from me. Like back in the good old times, what?"

I yanked my arm out of his hand and backed away, rushed outside before he could catch me and, still short of breath, pleaded with Rottenführer Wolff to allow me to go to the latrines. He gave me an odd look but waved me off generously, nevertheless. Inside the facility, curled into a ball in the corner, I bawled so hard, my head and lungs began hurting from desperate, spasmodic sobs.

He's not coming back.

Outside, the daylight had died.

*

"Rottenführer Gröning is here!"

I looked up at Różínka in confusion. She patiently waited for me to acknowledge her announcement with at least some words but none came. Something broke in me a few days ago and now the thoughts just wouldn't function right. In fact, there were no thoughts. Empty, mechanical movements had replaced them, completely and entirely devoid of any purpose. When I was told to line up for the *Appell,* I lined up. When Różínka nudged me to get my ersatz coffee in the morning, I followed her into the line. But unless she physically forced the bowl to my lips, I wouldn't think to drink it, just like I wouldn't drink soup at lunch or munch on the piece of bread in the evening. The oddest thing was, for the first time here in Birkenau, I didn't feel hunger. I didn't feel anything at all.

"Lena! Did you hear what I just said?"

"I did."

"Well?"

I turned away from her and resumed my mechanical folding. I spent the next few hours in the same manner until she shoved the wooden box under my nose and made me take it into my hands.

"I'm on duty today but you bring it to him. Well? Go on! Go ask about your damned Dahler. I can't stand looking at you, walking around like a zombie, another moment! You're like one of Mengele's guinea-pig girls, only the white apron is missing."

But the eyes are the same – dead. She didn't say it but it was clear enough, what she thought.

I brought the box to the familiar office, from which the official seal was now gone and knocked. Upon hearing the familiar "Enter," something stirred inside, some distant memory, an association with someone infinitely dear, who had turned into memory as well.

Rottenführer Gröning's desk was once again in perfect order. I shuffled to it and deposited the box on its surface. Not a word was exchanged between us while he was going through the familiar movements. Money – into one stack, diamonds – into the other. He had no parcels to ask me about this time. The link, once connecting us, had vanished.

He looked up in surprise and confusion when a drop landed on one of the dollar bills. I brought my hand to my face and examined my wet palm in numb wonder. How could one not notice their own tears?

"Go back to work," Gröning said quietly.

I didn't stir. I had to ask him one single question but the words wouldn't come and so, I stared at him silently, watched him count the money like he always did and pretend not to notice me.

"What happened to Rottenführer Dahler?" I even touched my own lips, unsure if I indeed had just uttered those words.

He had quite the talent to hide his eyes behind the glasses, behind all those accountant books and machines.

"Nothing. Go back to work."

"Is he gone?"

He threw the pencil down and looked at me in annoyance. Then, something softened about his features; some unknown emotion passed through the blue, lens-framed eyes. He took pity on me.

"He's in jail, here in Auschwitz. Along with the others. The SS investigated them all on corruption charges."

"Are they going to kill them?"

His shoulders shook with barely concealed chuckles. He seemed almost amused by the terror in my eyes.

"No, they're not going to kill anyone. Even Palitzsch, the former Rapportführer, is said to be heading to a camp in Brünn instead of the penal battalion and he was guilty of not only enriching himself quite handsomely from the stolen goods but having a Jewish inmate as a mistress, after the death of his wife. Dahler is accused of having unauthorized items in his locker – a few dollars and a pocketknife or something ridiculous like that. Hardly he'll get punished worse than Palitzsch. Now go back to work. We have tons of things to go through and we're expecting a transport later today."

I collected the box from his desk, feeling smooth wood under my fingers, hearing the floorboards creaking under my steps. The world was slowly coming into focus once again. I was actually breathing, consciously and with immense relief, as though after emerging from under the murky water in which I had all but drowned.

But it was only when I saw him for myself, the familiar outline of an overcoat during the *Appell,* the familiar gait with such a slight limp that only I knew to notice it and the face, the dearest and most handsome face in the entire world, did I realize that I was alive once again. The smallest hint of a smile as our gazes locked after such a torturous separation was enough for my heart to explode in ecstasy in my chest.

He's back.

He's back. He's back. He's back!

"You're back." I touched the rough wool of his overcoat with uncertainty. We stood in his office, to which he'd summoned me during the lunch break. He was pushing a sandwich that he had saved for me into my hand but I wanted nothing, just to touch him and ensure that he was alive, still breathing and with me once again.

"Of course, I'm back. You thought they'd ship me back to the front and you'd be rid of me, didn't you?"

I didn't laugh at the joke, as it was all too much. He couldn't uncurl my fingers that were digging into his sleeves even with the best will in the world. I clawed into him like a cat, which would rather see its nails pulled out, before considering letting go.

"Leni, please." His whisper was soft and apologetic. "The investigators are still here. They still stalk about the camp and open doors at the worst possible moments. Nothing against your native Czechoslovakia but I don't fancy sharing a train with Palitzsch one bit."

He managed to pry me off of himself but the more he tried to push me away, the harder I clawed and the louder I begged until he sighed and took me in his arms, cradling me in his embrace while I sobbed my heart out.

"Promise to never abandon me, please," I kept repeating against all of his reassurances. He had tried to calm me, tried to speak to me logically but it was of no use. The horror had seized me and now, I suddenly felt as though I would fall completely apart, disintegrate into the smallest bits and pieces if he was not there to hold me together. "Please, never leave me alone. I shall die without you."

"You won't die—"

"No, I shall die."

Something in my voice made him grip me stronger. He stroked my hair, pensive and suddenly grim. "What happened to you while I was away, Leni?"

"I don't remember anything. The world was gone. I worked."

He looked at me with sudden fear and pity, like at a madwoman. Perhaps, that was the very thing that had happened. I had gone mad and didn't notice? Only he did, just now and that's what has frightened him so.

He pulled me close again, a tender gesture full of sorrow. "I won't leave you, Leni, I promise. I shall forever be by your side."

"You promise?"

"I swear. As long as I'm alive."

Chapter 26

Helena

December 1943

Animated, even though still subdued, chatter breathed some air into the ordinarily deathly-silent warehouse. With the appointment of the new Kommandant – Obersturmbannführer Liebehenschel – the semblance of a somewhat tolerable working camp replaced the suffocating desperation of the extermination facility. Rumors were still exchanged concerning the reasons for Kommandant Höss's removal but whatever the truth was, there wasn't an inmate inside the perimeter of the camp who hadn't greeted such a change with open arms.

We still couldn't quite take it in, how one man could bring such a change in such a short period of time. Hardly a month had passed since Kommandant Liebehenschel had first toured the camp, inspecting every nook and cranny with admirable thoroughness and actually addressing the inmates and diligently putting their remarks down in his small notebook and we suddenly weren't beaten by the Kapos any longer for doing nothing wrong whatsoever. The Sonderkommando wouldn't stop bragging about the new reward system that had been introduced as an incentive to improve the production. Even the SS teased the lucky Polish members of the team, in a purposely loud voice and in front of us, Kanada women, about their recent trips to the newly installed brothel.

"Hey, *Dummkopf!* Did I hear it right that you spent the allotted fifteen minutes of happiness *talking* to the broad? What's the matter? Couldn't get it up or forgot where to put it, you miserable *Arschloch?*"

Amid guffaws of the SS and the heads of the Sonderkommando men hanging in embarrassment, it was a miracle of its own; the very fact that the SS deigned to jest with the inmates, laughing if not with them, then at them but laughing after all, instead of showering them with insults and blows. The men, unloading the trucks for us, were more than satisfied with such arrangements and soon gathered enough confidence to probe the waters and throw an occasional quiet, "She wasn't all that pretty is all," back at the SS, which invariably prompted more guffaws and back slaps from the uniformed guards.

"You look at them, cheeky Poles! We give them ass and they're still being picky about the quality of it."

The SS roared with laughter and grins broke out on the Sonderkommando men's unshaven faces. Even we found ourselves giggling – not because Birkenau had overnight become a tolerable place to be but from the exhilaration that *we were allowed to giggle* and exchange remarks and not be beaten to death for it by an enraged Kapo. I suppose, after being surrounded by death and gore at all times, one grows to appreciate even such small changes; that must have been the reason why my suggestion to organize a Christmas celebration for the new Kommandant was met with such enthusiasm from my fellow inmates.

Right after lunch, I approached Franz and asked him if he thought it would be agreeable with Kommandant Liebehenschel if we, the inmates, prepared something nice for him and his staff in gratitude for his treating us so well.

"I don't see why he would refuse such a generous offer but I suppose we still ought to ask him personally," Franz replied and checked his watch. "As a matter of fact, he must be in the Kommandantur now. Do you want to go and plead your case in person?"

"By myself?" I stammered, mortified.

Kommandant Liebehenschel was no Höss by any comparison but walking into the Kommandantur full of high-ranking SS was utterly beyond my desire.

"Of course not." Franz regarded my startled reaction with amusement. "You can't wander around without proper authorization. I'll take you."

Turning sharply round, he shouted to Wolff that he was leaving to see the Kommandant. Wolff merely waved him off, even more relaxed and unbothered now, under the new command, than he used to be. Only one person hadn't seemed to have fallen under the spell of the collective exuberant mood. Andrej, who had rejoined the delivery Kommando in charge of the trucks in Franz's absence, watched us depart from the warehouse, like a hawk. His face was a mask of cold, grim hate. Franz spoke of removing him from the work detail as soon as he saw him but after I pleaded with him to leave the man alone – surely, no one wanted to spend their days shaving the heads of the corpses or burning the bodies of the gassed people – he reluctantly agreed to let him be. I was grateful that Andrej was sensible enough not to muddy the waters and try and chat to me when Franz was present but he wouldn't stop grumbling curses in the latter's direction, wondering *why the Gestapo didn't off that SS swine, as he deserved.*

Just like I pretended not to hear those hateful words, I pretended not to see his sharp gaze following us until we left the warehouse. Outside, blinded by the fresh snow and finding myself alone with Franz, I instantly forgot about him.

"Whose idea was that? About the performance?" Franz inquired, leveling his step with mine.

I was used to trailing behind not only SS-men but Kapos as well and such a gesture on his part touched me to the marrow.

"Mine."

"I think he'll like it."

"Herr Kommandant?"

"*Ja.*" Franz threw a glance over his shoulder, then at the guard watchtower ahead, ensured that the man was looking the other way, and caught my fingers in his for a fleeting second.

That short but such a meaningful gesture, made my heart catch in my throat from the tenderness of it. All around us, the snowflakes were falling softly and gently. The diamond dust crunched under our feet. The trees were heavy with it as we passed under them. With each new gust of wind, more of the shining crystals flew in our faces. We minded not one bit, walking side by side in agreeable silence. If it weren't for the barbed-wire fences surrounding us, one could have imagined themselves on a stroll in a park. If I looked only under my feet, I could almost persuade myself of this illusion.

"I would so love to hold your hand now," Franz confessed, softly and with sudden emotion.

"Me, too."

"Once the war is over, I will take your hand and never let it go."

As we were nearing the guard tower, I was suddenly aware that I was smiling and quickly pulled the scarf over the lower part of my face. No need for them to get curious about such an unnatural expression on an inmate's face.

"Do you think it shall be over soon?"

"It shall be over someday," he replied pensively.

"Who's winning?"

"So far, the Ivans."

I nodded, greedily taking in any bits of this new information he was willing to supply me with. Despite all the plans for our common future, I knew it all too well what a personal blow each defeat was for him. It was his country, after all, that was losing the war. He had all the natural right to be upset over such a turn of events.

"Yes, someday it shall be over and we shall go and live in Vienna as free people," he murmured again, after exchanging a quick salute with the guard overhead. "There won't be any more Nuremberg Laws. We'll marry and no one will be able to say a word against it."

"In Vienna?" I turned to him. His eyes, with a faraway look in them, were gazing straight ahead, as if he thought it possible to see the future if he looked hard enough.

"Yes. I haven't told you, have I? They gave us an apartment in Vienna. To me and my mother, that is. She has already moved; I have just received her letter."

"That's nice. For your service?"

He was silent for some time, then shook his head slowly. "The previous owners were Jewish. They were resettled a few months ago."

"Deported," I murmured and bit my lip at once, guilty, and annoyed at the same time and not knowing what to make of my own emotions.

"Deported, yes," Franz suddenly agreed. "If I didn't take it, someone else would have. You know how it is. A damned sorry excuse, I know, but at least you shall live there with me and I thought that somewhat balanced things. Do you not think so?"

I nodded, not quite knowing how to respond to it right. Was there a right answer to such a question?

"I assume your sister won't have any place to go after the war either. She can stay with us for as long as she wants."

"Thank you, Franz. That's very generous of you."

"It's not generous," he argued louder than he should have and threw an annoyed glare at the people shuffling behind the barbed wire – half-frozen, stiff almost-corpses. We had reached the main camp. "It's all… *Scheiße,*" he finished, or, to be exact, didn't finish his thought, with an emphatic curse and oddly enough, it suited the situation just fine.

When we reached the Kommandantur, I paused in front of the entrance despite it being quite simple and unguarded. Franz's palm softly lowered onto the small of my back – such a needed gesture of silent support – prompted me forward. Still, I whispered, "You go in first," and caught an amused grin from him. I hid behind his back as we walked along its corridors, which smelled of freshly waxed floors and woolen uniforms and did my best to blend in with the wall when he stepped inside the Kommandant's anteroom, leaving me alone behind the padded double doors, much to my horror.

I fretted without any reason, as no one paid me any heed. Two officers strolled past me, discussing the latest motion picture they'd seen in the officers' quarters and didn't even glance in my direction. An inmate did, though, a beautiful, busy-looking woman with a stack of files straining her arms. I'd never seen her before but knew of her. Her name was Mala, a Jewish woman from Poland, who had a privileged position as an interpreter and messenger, due to her ability to speak multiple languages and her sharp, analytical mind. She was a legend of sorts in the camp, the only other woman who was allowed to keep her hair, apart from us Kanada girls. She greeted me with a quick, friendly nod and I replied with the same, feeling strangely reassured by her presence here. I was still gazing after her with admiration as she walked, straight-backed and dignified, along the corridor, when Franz opened the door and signed to me to come in.

Kommandant Liebehenschel received us in his office, furnished with dark wood, simple and welcoming without the dreaded Höss behind its desk. The new Kommandant was a relatively young man with somewhat sad dark eyes, dark hair, and a high forehead marred by premature wrinkles. His thin lips smiled surprisingly easily, at Franz at least. He motioned for us to step closer after the usual exchange of the salutes and once again, Franz prodded me gently in the back.

"My adjutant says you have some plans for Christmas, Unterscharführer?"

"*Jawohl*, Herr Kommandant. One of my Kommando girls suggested an idea to organize a performance for the SS and I wanted to ask your opinion on this matter."

Kommandant Liebehenschel shifted the gaze of his brown eyes to me. They were big and not unkind. I smiled gingerly. "Herr

Kommandant, we, the inmates, would like to thank you and your staff here in Auschwitz-Birkenau for everything you've done for us lately. If it is agreeable with you, we would like to perform for you and the SS staff as part of Christmas celebrations…" My voice faded on its own. Just then, I heard myself and how utterly strange it sounded, coming from a Jew.

He still smiled easily, interested. "I think it's a splendid idea. What exactly do you think to perform?"

"Songs, traditional ones; some girls can dance very well…" I paused again and then, reassured by his so far non-hostile attitude, looked up at him again. "A play, perhaps?"

"A play? A play should be fine, too. What sort of a play?"

I turned to Franz helplessly. That's what we should have been talking about on the way here and not how we were going to hold hands once the war was over. Grand organizers that made us – nothing to say.

"Something classical, perhaps?" Franz was quicker than me at improvising. He had nothing to fear from the man behind the desk, not that I did either, as he was by no means the same sort as Höss but it was still a habit, to be afraid of anyone high-ranking. One never knew what could set them off, the SS. "Or, even better, something humorous? To lift the spirits of the comrades?" He beamed at the Kommandant. "Something with Krampus, with your permission?"

"With Krampus?" Kommandant Liebehenschel arched his brow in surprise but then laughed, the easy laughter of a man who did it often. "You're from Austria, then. I should have guessed by the accent. Which part?"

"Lower Austria, Herr Kommandant. But my family now lives in Vienna."

"Your wife?"

"My mother."

"You're not married?"

"No, *mein* Kommandant."

"Good for you. Despite all the propaganda, it's the biggest mistake a fellow can make."

Franz's body quivered with silent chuckles.

"Why Krampus, though?"

"He's funny." Franz shrugged.

"He's the devil, is he not?"

"He's the good devil. He looks terrifying but he's actually a kind-hearted fellow. People just misunderstand him."

"Is that how you folk see him in Austria?"

Franz shrugged again, another smile warming his face. "Children wait for him more than they wait for St. Nicholas, believe it or not."

"He's supposed to whip them, put them into his sack, and drag them to hell! What sort of children do you raise there in Austria that they are thrilled to see him?" the Kommandant asked, laughing.

"The fearless future leaders of the Reich, apparently." Franz's face drew into a wry smile after he threw a pointed look at the portrait of the Führer on the wall, his compatriot. Judging by the Kommandant's delighted reaction, it was a smart answer. "They're thrilled to see Krampus because he only punishes the bad children and besides, all that affair with the whipping and the kidnapping and dragging them to hell is not real and they know it. It's play-pretend. That's what makes it fun. They all know he's only playing."

"I'm sold. Stage your Krampus, future leader of the Reich."

"Not me, Herr Kommandant. I don't have the requirements for it. Now, the play-writing suits me much better."

The Kommandant's shoulders were shaking with laughter again. He liked Franz. "Off with you, Shakespeare with chevrons! Prepare a detailed report for me with the exact date, time, and place."

"May we use the officers' mess, Herr Kommandant? So that it's not in the warehouse…" He glanced over Liebehenschel's smart uniform. "Unseemly for you and other officers to sit there, in a sorting facility."

"Yes, you may."

"Thank you, Herr Kommandant."

As soon as we stepped outside, Franz, bursting with ideas, began his excited speech on *what costumes we absolutely must put together and how exactly we should decorate the stage and what to use for Krampus' horns* when he suddenly stopped and regarded me quizzically.

"Why do you look so upset? He agreed to everything and more. Do you not like the idea with Krampus? It doesn't have to be Krampus. We can stage *The Nutcracker* for all I care…"

He didn't seem to understand my downcast gaze and my silence. Finally, we could chat openly, in front of everyone, as we now had a good enough excuse for it. We could spend days together planning and rehearsing everything. What else was one to ask for, if not such, almost freedom?

"I like the idea with Krampus," I replied quietly. "It was so nice, the way you described it. It just reminded me…"

"What?"

I sighed. "I wish it was all play-pretend here too. The whipping and the hell-dragging. How nice it would have been, if it was all one big joke and all the kidnapped people suddenly returned."

Now, he was silent too. Silent, and visibly upset, just like me. I almost wished I hadn't said anything at all. What was the point of it?

We wandered through the white, sparkling day. In this part of the camp, on the very outskirts of Auschwitz, the barracks and the prisoners and even the old crematorium were no longer visible, only the great fluffy waves of snow piled around us, as though in a fairytale. I slowed my steps. I wasn't ready to be back in Birkenau yet. In Birkenau, it was all going to become real again, the death, the walking skeletons, the chimneys.

As though on cue, Franz stopped as well and lit a cigarette. He stood in such a way that he shielded me with his body from the wind as he took deliberately slow drags on his smoke, looking somewhere over my head, covered by the thick scarf.

"Me too, Leni." His voice came in the form of a grayish, translucent cloud against the frost. "I so wish to wake up and realize that I only dreamed it all. This whole…" He made a vague gesture around with his gloved hand. I looked at his young, pale face. Suddenly, he looked at me with determination. "But not you. I would have died if I woke up and didn't have you."

But me and this place were connected together in such a tightly twisted knot that it was impossible to separate us any longer. This time, I held my tongue so as not to upset him any further. "You do have me. You always will have."

This place broke me, broke me to such an extent that I couldn't imagine life behind its walls anymore. With frightening clarity, I suddenly realized that he was just as connected to this place as I was and without him, I would have died too. Even if the war ended, even if indeed I became free again, I couldn't imagine taking a single step without him next to me. I wouldn't be able to step through a single door without the reassuring weight of his hand on my back. I wouldn't be able to hide from the others behind anyone else but him. I needed him even more than he needed me. He needed me out of love but I needed him because, without him, I wouldn't survive.

He smiled at me and blew the smoke away from my face. "Krampus it is, then?"

I nodded readily and, full of contentment, stepped onto the cleared path after him.

Chapter 27

Helena

Weighed down by the bundles of clothing that would serve us as costumes, we waited reluctantly in front of the officers' mess while Franz was communicating the Kommandant's orders to someone inside. It was alien territory, an enemy territory held by the SS and we instinctively longed for the familiar comfort of our warehouses and barracks.

Two SS wardens walked out of the mess but halted in their tracks as soon as they saw us, the pitiful bunch of tramps shifting from one foot to another under their scrutinizing gazes. We rarely saw female SS wardens in our Kanada detail. The women's camp in Birkenau was their domain. Wolff talked about them, mostly in salacious innuendos; Franz only remarked once, coolly and in passing when I asked him about them, that they were the Ravensbrück's rejects and that it would be wiser to stay away from them.

They stood before us, gorgeous and disdainful, their round, healthy faces full of icy, cruel scorn.

"What is this Gypsy gang?" one of them asked. Her hair had a platinum shine to it in the cold winter sun. Her uniform was gray and tailored to her slim figure under her cape, which was still unbuttoned.

"An SS warden just asked you lot a question." The second one pulled herself up. Her hair was styled in careful, onyx curls which matched her polished boots. We were all staring at their tips, afraid to lift our heads to meet their mocking gazes. "Shall I help you find your tongues?"

"They're here on Kommandant Liebehenschel's orders."

We all breathed out in relief at the sight of our Kommandoführer who had stepped out of the mess with two men in tow. One of the SS wardens, the blonde, turned to face him.

"Are you setting up another Gypsy camp in our own headquarters now?" She tilted her head to one side, a coy smile curling her lips.

"We're staging a Christmas play for Herr Kommandant and his staff," Franz replied without any emotion.

"Shouldn't they be working instead of performing?" The same blonde motioned her brilliant head in our direction.

"Shouldn't you mind your own affairs instead of sticking your noses in your superiors' business?" came the intentionally rude reply.

We all held our breaths. To say something of this sort to the SS wardens in front of a group of inmates! But Franz was an SS man and cared little for his female compatriots' feelings judging by the looks of it. Not paying any heed to the couple, he calmly motioned us inside and told the two men, accompanying him, to take our bundles from us.

They had already cleared the space for the stage and arranged the chairs around it in neat rows. Later, we discovered that they were the inmates who worked as waiters in the officers' mess – another highly coveted and privileged position, which every single inhabitant of Auschwitz would have killed for. In hushed whispers and amid work, they inquired if we needed anything to be "organized" from the canteen. We thanked them profusely and took whatever they slid in our pockets, with gratitude. Not for ourselves; later, we would share it with the girls from Birkenau, who had to replace us for the time being. All of them were from the women's camp and didn't have much meat on their bones under their striped dresses. Neither could they bring themselves to pocket anything from the abundance of the Kanada riches – some, out of personal values and some, out of fear of finding themselves on the wrong end of the

Kapo's stick. They were beaten much more than us and even under the new Kommandant's command, they couldn't force themselves to overcome the old fears.

One of the waiters, who was busy slipping a triangle of the SS-canteen cheese into one of the girls' pockets, froze in his place as Franz turned around when the waiter had least expected it and caught him red-handed. Holding his breath, the waiter stepped away from the young woman slowly, awaiting the punishment any moment now.

"What are you doing?" Franz demanded in measured tones. "Distributing Reich's property?"

The waiter blinked once, twice; it was a nervous twitch more than regular blinking. What could one answer to that? Before he could open his mouth and dig himself a deeper grave, the SS man threw over his shoulder, "I don't want to see this happening again," before turning his back on the couple.

Do it if you must, but not in front of my eyes. I have no desire to explain why I allowed this to the Political Department, even though Grabner is no longer in charge of it.

Wet with sweat from such an unexpected lucky break, the waiter applied his best to decorating the stage to the best of his abilities and even managed to commandeer a few rolls of insulation from somewhere – perhaps, even the roof of the mess itself – *"To make the snow under Herr Unterscharführer's tree look swell."*

Rolls of yellowish cotton-like clouds made the latter arch his brow skeptically.

"I'll put it back right after the performance, Herr Unterscharführer," the waiter rushed to reassure his favorite new superior. "No one will even notice anything."

"Take care that they don't. I'm responsible for all this. If something goes amiss or—"

"On my mother's grave, Herr Unterscharführer!" The inmate even rolled his eyes to emphasize his point.

SS guards – mostly men and a few wardens among them – came and went, invariably stopping by our improvised stage just to be chased off (as long as their rank was lower or that of his own) by Franz, who guarded the play's contents with the fearlessness of a true playwright.

"Quit your spying, you louts!" he shouted at them, half-serious. "I'll report you to the Kommandant for interfering with official SS business!"

"You've got yourself set up nicely, with that official SS business!" one of the SS men was quick to see the joke.

"Do you need more actors in your gang?" another one chimed in, his teeth shining white in the artificial light.

"Yes, I need more vagabonds and you look just the part!" Franz bared his teeth in a snarl in reply to all the taunts. "Now, change into those rags and step on the stage and my girls will carry the duty for you, in the meantime. They look more capable at any rate."

"Capable, you say?"

"And much more pleasant to look at, than your silly mug!" Franz finished someone off, with a charming smile full of incomparable sarcasm.

Amid such an exchange of pleasantries and the guffaws invariably following them, we stood, smiling, in our costumes.

We did have two men with us; Krampus, a huge, towering Pole with fierce black eyes and a build to match, whom Franz had borrowed from the Sonderkommando and also St. Nicholas himself. It was St. Nicholas who caused quite an argument between Wolff and Franz when Franz had just brought him in from the back of the Kanada.

"You're taking Dayen with you?" Wolff looked over the former rabbi incredulously.

"I am. I need someone to play St. Nicholas."

"Should you really take him then?"

"Surely someone else can burn all of those books and documents in his absence," Franz only shrugged.

Wolff waited for the punch line to the joke. When it didn't come, he cleared his throat once again. "He's a Jew."

Franz regarded his comrade as though the latter had just said something incredibly moronic. "In case you didn't notice, they all are. Do you want to ask the SS for the volunteers to act in the Christmas play? So that it would be Aryan enough to suit your taste? Or would you like to be St. Nicholas yourself? I don't care one way or another. Just say the word and I'll dress you up in a red coat and glue a cotton beard on your face."

Wolff bristled. It was not something SS comrades would say to one another. He wished to reply something and he had already opened his mouth but suddenly realized that he didn't know what exactly to say. There was an unmistakable treasonous quality to his comrade Franz's words, something vague and imperceptible and rogue, yet on which it was impossible to put one's finger, for Franz didn't say anything openly hostile to the regime or to the SS or even to the racial theory. He merely thought it to be all right, for a Jew and a rabbi to be St. Nicholas. What could have been said against that? After all, he was in charge of the play. The new Kommandant entrusted him with the full rights to do whatever he pleased with it. At last, Wolff's Party loyalty triumphed. If the Kommandant said it to be all right, he wasn't the one to question superior orders.

"Do what you must." He looked somewhere above Franz's head as though the mere idea of looking at his comrade's face was repulsive to him. Franz stood much too close to those Jews. They clung to him much like sheep to their sheepdog. Wolff felt momentarily disgusted with such a trusting attitude. He didn't like one bit how those Jews looked at Franz. He didn't like one bit how Franz allowed them to look at him that way.

Something changed in their relationship from that day on. Some wedge drew itself between the two guards and now, not only Andrej but also Wolff, was following Franz with the same eyes – steady, watchful, waiting for something.

*

Elza was from Slovakia, a recent addition to our Kommando. Her entire family had been gassed upon arrival – mother and father for being too elderly and frail and sisters for being too young – and she resented everyone, who had any relatives left, for this very reason. Not that she was to blame for it. Everyone copes with such enormous grief in their own way; some go mad, like Zosia, who started screaming one day in August of 1942 and didn't stop until Wolff dragged her outside the barrack and shot her. Some turn into *Muselmänner* despite lucking out and making it to the Kanada detail where the chances of survival were much higher than in the regular camp. They simply stopped eating, much like Róžínka did when she had just learned about her children and slowly wasted away, withered without having anyone to care for them. Or because they had no one to live for... One can never tell with those silent types.

And then, there were people like Elza, who lived, obsessed with grim hatred for people like Róžínka and me just because we had each other and she didn't have anyone, anymore.

She was the first one to scoff at my idea to stage a play for the new administration even before I had voiced it to Franz. However, her contempt soon transformed into something much darker, just like her eyes, at the sight of us, the Acting Kommando, appearing just before the evening *Appell* and still chatting in excitement among ourselves. She watched us silently as we lined up next to the girls from the women's camp and discreetly slipped our daily rations into the pockets of their striped dresses. She watched us as we resumed our rehearsing after receiving our dinner in our barrack. She watched us as we laughed and shouted our lines and wrapped the blankets around ourselves as capes. She watched us and finally, she'd had enough of such merriment.

"Aren't you ashamed of yourselves?"

Her shout cut through our chatter like a sharp knife through butter. Silence descended upon the barrack, much like at the SS doctors' arrival for the inspection.

"Prancing around like a bunch of tramps," she continued, satisfied with the effect her words had produced. "Are you really so excited about pleasing your SS masters then? Have you no pride left in you at all? Dressing up and jumping around like monkeys, in a circus, for their pleasure! A truly honorable calling. Nothing to say!"

I felt for her. I always had but for some reason, her accusations, which she chose to direct at all of us, prompted a response from me which I couldn't quite explain to myself. I stepped in front of the group to face her.

"Kindly spare us your sentiments on our account. When was the last time we were allowed to do something to make us smile in this place? An opportunity comes at last for us to do something – anything – that is not digging through the murdered people's belongings daily and you ought to object to that? You have no right! You simply have no right!" A previously unknown feeling, some dark, overpowering rage welled up inside of me, uncontrollable and roaring, which made me shout without any regard to the regulations. "Some of us have been here for years. We have seen it all – the death, the beatings, the disease, the selections – and you wish to preach to us that we are not allowed to pretend, for a couple of short weeks only – that there's something else beyond that, in this world? You blame us for our desire to remember what human emotions are like? You blame us for our desire to dress up and pretend to be someone else just to escape the horror of this place for a few moments? You're not the only one who lost everyone, Elza. You're not the only one whose feelings are to be considered.

We want to live the best we can and you have not the right to tell us that we can't!"

Momentarily, she grabbed my elbow and pulled me, still wrapped in the colorful blanket, towards the door of the barrack. She shoved it open and pushed me into the snow-shrouded outside. A gust of wind hit me in the face, along with her words.

"I have not the right?! Look!" She pressed my jaw into her vice-like grip, directing my face toward the crematorium. "Look at the chimney, you idiot! People are being burned there as we speak. People are being burned there daily, our own people, our own families and you tell me that I have no right?! You wish to celebrate it by dancing and singing! You wish to thank the good Herr Kommandant for his kind treatment of us! You wish to thank the SS for being so considerate!"

"It has gotten better under Kommandant Liebehenschel's command," I muttered stubbornly in my defense. "You were not here before, when Höss was in charge. You have not the faintest idea of how bad it was then. If there's anything we can do to keep in Kommandant Liebehenschel's good graces—"

"Just like you keep in Dahler's good graces?" She stepped in front of me. Shadows played on her face, provided by the light of the stove, lit inside the barrack, distorting it and twisting it into a grotesque mask.

I did not say anything to that. I *had not* anything to say to that.

"You say I have no right! No, I say, it's *you* who has no right. You have no right to call yourself a Jew after what you did. You're a disgrace to our ancestors who suffered but endured in the name of God. You're a disgrace to our history. You're nothing but a dirty tramp who sold herself to the SS." Her face almost touched mine. She repeated, articulating every syllable, "Dirty. Tramp." The words stung more than the back of her hand with which she'd hit me across my mouth. I sensed it coming and didn't turn away, didn't try to dodge it.

She was right. I was a dirty tramp and I deserved it.

Elza was long gone and I still stood in-between the darkness and light, between the madness and sanity, between the life of the barrack and death of the chimney, belching reddish clouds of smoke towards the indigo, indifferent sky. It was December, yet no one shouted for me to shut the door like they ordinarily would have. It was Rôžínka who took me by my shoulders and brought me inside to the suddenly quiet barrack and whispered in my ear the only consolation she could offer me, "She has no right to tell you how to survive. She's mad at you for having me around, is all. Don't take it to heart."

Elza kept glaring at me the entire morning before the roll call, peering almost greedily into Franz's face which had clouded over and grew dark and wrathful as soon as he laid eyes on my face. Out of the corner of my eye, I saw Elza straighten in her place trembling with some emotion I couldn't explain. She wished to prove something to herself that morning, hoping for everyone to see the degree to which I had fallen and wishing for me to point at her, as soon as Franz asked me the expected question, "What happened to your face?"

Looking somewhere past him, I replied softly, "I slipped and fell, Herr Unterscharführer."

He stepped closer to me, forcing me to look him in the eye.

"Who hit you?" he repeated, purposely rephrasing the question.

"No one, Herr Unterscharführer. I slipped and fell," I repeated, louder this time.

He had just started saying something when Wolff spoke abruptly behind his back.

"The clumsy broad has already said it fifteen fucking times that she fell on her face! Can we get on with the roll call or do you wish to call a doctor for her?!"

Franz turned on his heel and glared at him with all the venom in the world but said nothing.

Chapter 28

Germany, 1947

Helena reflected for some time after giving her testimony. The Chairman didn't rush her, respectful of her past.

"I don't know who reported us in the end," she summarized at last. "As you can clearly see, far too many people were aware of our relationship already by Christmas. And then at Christmas, after the play, Franz made the mistake of thanking me a bit too warmly in front of the Kommandant and the officers… It was nothing really, just a natural human reaction; he wanted to thank me for the idea with the play that earned him the commendation from his superior and… Kommandant Liebehenschel only laughed it off and turned it into a joke but several others from his staff began looking at Franz with suspicion from that moment on. By the time Kommandant Höss arrived in May of 1944 and took over the command once again, the whole of Auschwitz, if not knew, then suspected that something was going on between us." She sighed. "Someone reported it."

She grew pensive, her eyes, clouded with memories, fixed on the floor on which the story of her life unraveled, invisible for the others. Her hands lay limply on her lap now. She seemed oddly serene to Dr. Hoffman, blissfully lost in her own world into which he had no access.

The Chairman cleared his throat and probed her gently, with a soft, "What happened next, Frau Dahler?"

Helena pulled her head up with an effort, looking a bit dazed and confused as if she didn't expect to find herself in the courtroom but someplace entirely different.

"One day, we, the Kommando that is, were being marched from work back to the barrack. A Kapo approached me – I didn't know him – and told me to follow him. I didn't know what it was all about until he brought me to Block 11, the punishment block. One of the political SS officers took me to the cell and locked the door without saying anything. Kommandant Liebehenschel got rid of the standing cells but now, with Kommandant Höss being back in the camp, the regular 'dark' cells were back in use. Those were just concrete chambers, with no windows and no lights whatsoever; only with a bucket in the corner for the prisoners to use. Sometimes we would receive water. Very rarely, some soup."

Helena regarded the hem of her skirt, which she kept twisting in her fingers mechanically. Dr. Hoffman saw her struggle with piecing together the memories which she most certainly had tried to avoid ever since the camp's liberation. Hardly anyone wished to relive their experience with the Auschwitz Gestapo.

"They kept us prisoners, there, for quite some time before they would begin the interrogation – as a means of psychological torture," Helena continued – calmly, rationally, carefully picking out the words and arranging them into the needed pattern. "At first one didn't realize it but within hours it began driving people mad, the darkness and the silence. The worst part was that it was impossible to tell whether it was day or night; one couldn't even hear the roll-call fanfare from there. It was dark and cold and quiet like in some cave into which one falls just to die in there. With time, it began to feel that way, as though the light would never come."

A paper slid off Franz Dahler's lap and glided softly toward the floor without him noticing it. Dr. Hoffman saw that the former guard was gazing at the floor with the same haunted look about him. In spite of himself, the psychiatrist pulled forward, a bit unsure if the Austrian would hear him.

"Were you imprisoned in the same bunker, Herr Dahler?"

The former SS guard looked up sharply at the mention of his name – a purely military instinct. He allowed himself a quick smile as if in apology for his absentminded state before confirming Dr. Hoffman's suspicions with a quiet, "Yes."

"I have a record of it here." Still not quite back in the courtroom, still a bit lost in the twilight of his cell, Dahler began searching for the needed document in the stack of files that he kept on his lap.

A bailiff stepped forward and picked up the fallen paper off the floor before handing it to him. Dahler muttered his thanks with another bashful smile – *forgive me please, I'm not myself today* – and motioned a bit timidly in the direction of Dr. Hoffman. The bailiff understood the gesture and placed the paper in front of the psychiatrist. Dr. Hoffman gave it a peripheral perusal and moved it towards the Chairman and Lieutenant Carter. A simple document in German with a sheet of a verified translation attached to it and simple facts enumerated with typical German bureaucratic meticulousness: *name, rank, date of detention, the reason for detention, released due to the lack of evidence.*

The paper looked good enough for Dahler's defense. The grounds were particularly favorable for this hearing: *detained on suspicions of having a consensual sexual relationship with an inmate of the Jewish race.* "Consensual," underlined in red by someone from the political office in Auschwitz, must have been a particularly shameful charge for the said SS officer in question. Rape cases were dismissed mostly with an oral reprimand – that much Dr. Hoffman knew already. But *consensual,* as though an accusation of betrayal of one's blood, the betrayal of all the ideals the German Reich and the SS stood for, that they couldn't let go of for almost a week, keeping both Franz and Helena in their cells next to each other and interrogating them separately, in the hope that at least one should break and speak.

Yes, the paper was good if Dahler had the need to persuade the court that his feelings for his wife were genuine and not some ploy to get himself a release form from the court. But somehow, Dr. Hoffman sensed that the court had long moved past the need for such persuasion.

"They kept me there for almost a week… I think." Helena scowled, unsure of her date of detention or release. Unlike her husband, she didn't have any papers recovered from the Gestapo archives. No one wrote such documents for the inmates. Inmates were disposable, not even technically people, in the camp administration's eyes. "Every day they would take me out of that cell and demand me to sign the paper, to confess that a certain SS Unterscharführer Dahler was having relations with me. I kept insisting that nothing was going on between us and the more I insisted, the more annoyed they grew with me. Soon, Schurz himself – he was the one appointed in Grabner's place – came to interrogate me. This time, they actually took me outside, he and his men and brought me to the Black Wall. The one, next to which they used to shoot prisoners in the early days…"

She sniffled quietly. Her eyes, though, were dry. "They told me that if I didn't confess, they'd shoot me right there and then."

Another long pause. A breath hitched in Dr. Hoffman's throat despite his knowing the outcome of the interrogation, despite seeing Helena very much alive and breathing in front of him. The tension was still palpable, dark, tense.

"I told them that they might as well. I said that I had nothing else to tell them."

Helena looked up at the panel of judges and Dr. Hoffman found himself wondering at the sudden determination shining in her black eyes. She must have regarded Schurz the same way, wrathfully almost, empowered by her own newfound strength. A protector, an all-forgiving martyr perhaps, but surely no longer a victim.

"I still don't know why they released me. I should have been dead, guilty or not," Helena finished, frowning slightly, as though still confused by such an outcome.

Dahler's hand flew to hers and clasped it – a somewhat nervous, spasmodic gesture of a man groping for his wallet in which he carried the check with all of his life's savings. *Still there. Not lost.* Dahler's face relaxed visibly. He allowed himself to lean back into his chair and offered Dr. Hoffman yet another weak, apologetic smile. He wasn't doing too well that day. All of his self-control was out of the window now that he wasn't defending himself anymore, merely recounting his story, along with the woman who shared it with him. Dr. Hoffman caught himself thinking about how tragically youthful his face looked now and yet, how heavy with guilt the eyelids… He would get off the charges simply due to his date of birth and low rank – *a typical brainwashed follower,* according to the Denazification court's categorizing of the former Nazis; he must have known it. Yet, Dahler was looking at him with such searching eyes, as though in desperate need to convey something, to make him, Hoffman, understand something that could only be felt deep inside one's heart and utterly impossible to translate into words.

*

"I still insist on your speaking with Helena Dahler in private," Andrej Novák announced, cutting into his thoughts, during the recess. "He had just acknowledged it to the court himself, the fact that he was quite a gifted storyteller." The last word came out mocking, cruel, cold. "He made her act in front of his superiors and he's making her act before the court now. And you're all buying it and paying triple at that."

"I don't think—" Dr. Hoffman started, just to be interrupted by Novák once again.

"I'm a co-plaintiff in this case. I demand you separate her from Dahler and speak with her privately. And I wish to be present during the conversation."

Dr. Hoffman exchanged glances with Dr. Hutson.

"Separating her from her husband and making her undergo what technically may be considered interrogation, after everything she had just said, could cause potential trauma," Dr. Hutson began uncertainly, shooting a glance in Lieutenant Carter's direction. The latter only shrugged helplessly. If the co-plaintiff wished for the witness to be interrogated separately, there was nothing he could do. *The law is the law.* Dr. Hutson looked at the Slovak again, with apparent reproach. "I respect your rights as the survivor and co-plaintiff in this case. All I ask you is to think of the victim—"

"I *am* thinking of the victim," Novák replied harshly. His eyes glimmered black in the deceiving light of the room. "As a matter of fact, I feel as though I am the only person who is acting in the victim's interests in this court. Separating her from her husband and letting her tell her story as it is, without his oppressing presence, is only going to help her, not harm her. She'll finally be able to talk freely."

The psychiatrists exchanged looks but there was nothing one could do in this situation.

"As you wish, Mr. Novák. We'll ask the Chairman to grant permission for a separate interview and we'll inform you as to where it's going to be conducted."

*

"Would you like some coffee? Tea? Water, perhaps?" Dr. Hoffman put on his best *I'm here to help you* smile and positioned his chair in such a way that Helena wouldn't feel crowded in his presence.

Dr. Hutson moved even further away, into a shadowed corner where he turned into an immobile statue as soon as he took his seat. Despite all these precautionary measures, both couldn't help but notice the immediate change in Helena's countenance as soon as the door closed after her, leaving her husband outside. Dr. Hoffman was grateful to the young fellow for making it as easy for them, as possible, under the circumstances. *"I'll be right outside that door, Leni." His voice was low and comforting, his hands, on top of her shoulders calm and reassuring. "If you need me, Dr. Hoffman will fetch me at once." She only nodded to that, the mistrust of an animal being led to slaughter, evident in her eyes.*

"No, thank you. I'd like to get this over with." Helena pulled the hem of her skirt so sharply over her lap that Dr. Hoffman had a fleeting fear that the cloth might tear.

"We'll only ask you a few questions—"

"I don't understand the need for all this secrecy." She avoided looking at him, shooting subtle glares at the closed door instead. This would not go well. Dr. Hoffman rubbed his forehead, cringing – an unwilling interrogator. At least Novák was still absent. "It's not like I have something to say to you that I wouldn't say to the court."

"Herr Novák requested the interview." The accusation was, for some reason, easy to throw. "He has the right, as the co-plaintiff."

Helena nodded slowly once again. Her right leg was twitching slightly. Dr. Hoffman couldn't rid himself of an image of a wild animal cornered by the humans. She wished to be out of here, there was no doubt about it.

As though on cue, Novák walked in. Oblivious to her tense posture, he smiled brightly at Helena. She didn't even see him, trying to steal a glimpse into the hallway instead before he shut the door after himself.

"Shall we begin?" Dr. Hoffman flipped his notebook open.

"I'm ready," the Slovak announced with far too much enthusiasm for Dr. Hoffman's liking.

Dr. Hoffman shot him a glare. "Frau Dahler?"

For the first time, she looked up at him. The psychiatrist looked down, unable to hold her gaze for some reason.

"How long have you been married to Herr Dahler?"

"Since December of 1945. He was released from the POW camp and we got married right after."

"Whose initiative was that?"

"Mine." Her voice was firm, defiant almost. "I ran away from the Red Cross facility for displaced persons after the end of the war and searched for him until I finally found him in September through the Red Cross. I lived in the American officers' quarters near the camp; they gave me a job there because I wouldn't go away. I slept near the barbed-wire enclosure at first. I, on one side and Franz – on the other. We held each other's hand through the fence. The guards tried to chase me away but after they learned my story, after I showed them my tattoo and papers the Red Cross gave me, they took pity on me. Also, they had to transfer Franz into a separate facility, along with high-ranking criminals."

That was one of the points that Novák kept bringing up, implying that the Americans were investigating Dahler as a war criminal and that they only released him due to the insufficient evidence.

"Why did they transfer him there?" Dr. Hoffman asked.

Helena gave a small shrug. "His own comrades from the SS turned on him as soon as they learned about me. They beat him up something terrible, almost killed him, in fact. The Americans interfered and transferred him to solitary confinement to keep him away from the others. Franz has a paper from an American colonel in charge of the POW camp, which confirms this. You can ask him to show it to you."

Dr. Hoffman nodded. "Frau Dahler…" He cleared his throat. "I feel awkward asking you this, but my duties require it. Has your husband ever been abusive to you?"

Helena looked at him as though he'd just asked her something incredibly idiotic.

"Of course not," she replied sharply. "He's never laid a finger on me."

"Except for that lashing in the camp," Novák inserted venomously.

Dr. Hoffman barely stopped himself from cringing openly.

"I think I have already explained the circumstances of that event to the court," Helena said quietly.

"Circumstances or not, he's a violent man." Novák crossed his arms over his chest. "He beat you that day. He called you all sorts of unimaginable things."

Helena's expression was unreadable, however, her knuckles turned white as she clasped the cloth of her dress, in her fists, even tighter.

"You don't have to protect him before this court, Helena," the Slovak continued, softening his voice. He stepped towards her as though wanting to pick up and hold her hand but Dr. Hoffman stopped him in time by catching his sleeve, at the sight of Helena's pale face tensing even further. "I know that he coerced you into this whole affair. You think that if he got his teeth into you back in Auschwitz, he wouldn't let go now until he breaks your very spine but it is not so. It doesn't have to be this way. Just tell these men the truth and your suffering will be over with. You shall be free again. Free from him, forever—"

"That's enough, Herr Novák." It was Hutson who gave him voice, out of his obscurity in the corner. "Undue influence on the witness."

"I'm only trying to help her break this cycle of abuse," Novák argued. "You're psychiatrists. You must know how difficult it is for the victims to openly confront their abusers. Some can't even testify against them out of fear, which is still too great in them. I have seen it in court before. One woman fainted when—"

"With all due respect, Herr Novák." Dr. Hoffman would have none of any such speeches. "You're here as a witness to the interview only. Please, let us conduct it, as the Chairman ordered." He regarded Helena Dahler with concern. Her breaths were fast and shallow, as her hand flew to her mouth to cover it. But it was her eyes that frightened him the most. They were brimming with unshed tears and almost wild with fear. He reached out for her as slowly as possible. "Frau Dahler, are you able to continue?"

She clasped her mouth tighter. Novák took the gesture for something different though.

"Tell them everything, Helena. Don't be afraid. He won't be able to harm you any longer."

"Why are you doing this?!" Her voice came out in a raspy cry. She was staring at Novák with horror.

"To protect you, of course! Just like I reported him to the Gestapo, first for stealing and later, for forcing himself on you. I wanted him to be arrested, shot – whatever, just so he'd be away from you."

Helena released a short, pained cry of someone mortally betrayed. Her shoulders shook with silent sobs.

"Just say the word, Helena. Just tell these men—"

"What did I ever do to you?!" she cried again, trembling with her entire body. "Why are you doing this to me?! Do you want me dead?!"

Novák's face darkened at once. He shook his head vehemently. "He won't be able to do anything to you, won't be able to take his revenge if you only speak the truth now. Don't fret, he's not behind this door. He's in a separate, locked room guarded by the bailiffs. If you just give this testimony now, you won't even have to face him ever again—"

"That's enough!" Dr. Hutson was suddenly on his feet.

Dr. Hoffman motioned for him to sit down, his face twisted in a silent plea.

"Stop shouting, both of you, for the love of God!" he hissed at both men. "Do you not see what you're doing?!"

However, it was too late. As soon as the Slovak announced that Dahler, the only buffer between the somewhat strained but possible interview and a full-blown panic attack was away from her reach, Helena suddenly couldn't hold herself together any longer. She released such a wild, pained cry that something caught in Dr. Hoffman's chest. He grasped her shoulders before she could double over and bury her face in her lap completely and asked for Dr. Hutson to fetch water and a sedative. He was familiar with fits like hers. Without medication, it would be next to impossible to manage it.

Now, Novák was squatting next to him, clutching Helena's hands and saying something in his language. She only began screaming louder in response. Those were horrible, piercing shrieks of someone who was being skinned alive, no less.

"Leave this room at once!" Dr. Hoffman shouted wrathfully at the man, pushing him off Helena with more force than he intended. "Do you not see that you're only making it worse?"

The Slovak looked up at him uncomprehendingly. Dr. Hoffman released an annoyed sigh. *Damn that Slovak, he truly believed that he was trying to help.*

"Please, leave, Mr. Novák," he repeated in English, softening his voice a little at the sight of the man's hurt expression.

Dr. Hutson appeared in the door with water and a syringe in his hand. Without much hesitation, he shot the dose of sedative into Helena's forearm – wartime-like, through the cloth. Dr. Hoffman didn't reproach him for his haste. It would hardly be wise to begin peeling Helena's jacket off of her while she was in such a wild state.

It took the sedative longer than usual to take hold. The dosage his colleague shot in her forearm would suffice to put a horse to sleep but Helena was still very much alert, just not screaming any longer, only rocking back and forth slightly and eerily repeating, with her wet lips, "I want my husband," like a demented, broken record.

It was amazing how she kept herself awake, just to sit there and repeat those words until they would grant her wish. The two doctors exchanged glances. *Shall we try?*

A scientist's curiosity gleamed in Dr. Hutson's eyes. "I'll go fetch him for you, Frau Dahler."

Left alone with the woman, Dr. Hoffman wasn't sure if she'd heard Hutson's words, as she was still mumbling the same mantra under her breath. Her eyes had glazed over, yet she positively refused to allow herself to fall asleep in a stranger's presence. Grimly, Dr. Hoffman watched that living miracle and wondered how severe her trauma must have been if that was the result of it.

He felt infinitely guilty for the same psychiatrist's interest that he had seen in passing in Dr. Hutson's eyes; for his desire to see how she would react to Dahler's presence under such obvious distress, yet this was precisely the situation, in which it was impossible for anyone to act. It was the rawest of scenes, which was impossible to rehearse even with the best will in the world.

Dahler stepped inside, accompanied by Dr. Hutson. A fleeting shadow of panic at the sight of his wife passed over his face. Dr. Hoffman almost applauded the young man's ability to curb his emotion and take it under control at once. Dahler walked over to his wife – not too fast, not too slow – sat on his haunches in front of her and gently covered her closed fists, with his own hands.

"Leni, *Liebchen,* how are you feeling?" His voice, despite betraying itself with a slight tremor, was soft and tender.

Helena's unseeing gaze focused on her husband's face. Dr. Hoffman released a breath he didn't realize that he'd been holding when her lips stopped moving along with the rocking that had also come to a stop. Helena's tense shoulders slumped visibly. A faint smile warmed up her white, sweat-covered face.

"Do you want me to hold you, *Liebchen?*" Dahler inquired in the same mild voice. He didn't stand up though until she nodded her agreement, her eyes growing heavy with sleep.

He took a chair next to her and effortlessly arranged her body on his lap, cradling her in his arms as one would a sick child. He even began rocking her slightly in the same manner, murmuring something softly to her in German. She pressed her head into his shoulder and sighed – contentedly this time. Soon, her eyes were closed. At last, she was asleep. Next to Dr. Hoffman, Dr. Hutson snorted softly, shaking his head at such an instant transformation.

"Incredible," he murmured.

Franz Dahler looked up at the two psychiatrists, the same apologetic smile back in his face.

"I'm sorry." His voice was no louder than a whisper when he addressed them. "I should have warned you that this could happen. My wife is very sick, you see…"

"You did warn us." Dr. Hoffman returned the smile. "It's us who should be apologizing. The situation got out of hand. However, it was our duty to see to it that it wouldn't happen."

He couldn't help but note to himself that Dahler had not once asked him what had prompted such a reaction, or what precisely it was that Helena had told them. For some reason, he smiled wider.

It was his colleague, who stepped forward this time – the scientist to the marrow of his bones, who wished to milk the opportunity dry just to eliminate any possible doubts, not that Dr. Hoffman personally had any left.

"Your wife *is* very sick, Herr Dahler." Dr. Hutson lowered his gaze sorrowfully, *a concerned specialist, not a court spy, by any means.* Dr. Hoffman almost shook his head at the trick that he himself had used quite a few times in the past. "I shouldn't be saying this to you but I hope it will remain between us. It's almost a sure thing that you could be released today. Perhaps, certain restrictions shall be imposed on you – no public office for some time and no jobs in press or education – that sort of thing but you shall walk free."

Dr. Hutson followed up the words with a meaningful pause. The former SS man's face betrayed nothing, yet Dr. Hoffman saw it that Dahler was listening carefully.

"It is an admirable thing that you're taking such good care of your wife. But do you not feel that she would be better off with the people who can actually help her? There are very good facilities in the United States and I could sign the form for her admission into the best, most modern clinic that my most esteemed colleagues practice at. I assure you that she would receive the best care and—"

"Institutionalize my wife?" Finding his voice after a few moments of shock, Dahler repeated the American's suggestion with indignation as though he couldn't believe that someone actually suggested such an atrocity to him. "I would never do that!" He pulled Helena closer to himself – a protective gesture which, for some reason, made Dr. Hoffman nearly choke with the instinctive sincerity of it. "Helena may be sick but she's not..." He desperately groped for the right word. "All she needs is to live a normal life, to go to parks, to the movies, to cafés, and for someone just to be there with her. That's all she needs. Not different doctors prodding and poking at her daily with all sorts of instruments and needles and feeding her all sorts of pills. She just needs someone to love her," he finished, with a tone of accusation, in his suddenly broken voice.

Tears shone in the corners of his eyes. He wiped his face quickly on his shoulder, clearly not wishing for the men to see him in his moment of weakness. "It's all my fault, the fact that she's in such a bad way."

Instinctively, Dr. Hoffman pulled himself up.

"My fault because I was a part of the regime that did this to her. My fault because I wore the uniform of the men who had set on annihilating her entire race. My fault for not doing something for her, more than I actually did. I really didn't do anything for her. I could have done so much more..."

Dr. Hoffman was staring at his shoes. He couldn't look at Dahler's face just now, the face of an infinitely guilty man who was trying his best to glue together what his entire country had broken into tiny, sharp shards. The Austrian's face was wet with tears. He clutched at his wife's body as one would at a corpse of someone infinitely dear, who had passed away much too soon.

"I just want her to be happy," he repeated softly. "She deserves to be happy after everything she's been through, don't you think? I appreciate your generous offer but I am not signing any authorization for her institutionalizing. Even in the event I shall go to prison, Różínka shall stay with her and look after her while I'm away. But I'm not committing my wife to any hospital, no matter how good you say it is. I shall take care of her myself. I know how." He pursed his lips defiantly.

Dr. Hoffman only smiled again, not arguing with that last statement. *He did know how.* Hoffman had witnessed it firsthand.

As he turned to the half-opened door, he saw Andrej Novák standing there and observing the couple with a strangely melancholic expression on his face. Slowly, as though with effort, the Slovak tore his gaze away from Dahler still cradling his wife on his lap and smiled at the psychiatrist gingerly. Dr. Hoffman had made a move toward him but the Slovak only shook his head slightly, offered him another apologetic smile, turned on his heel and quickly walked along the passageway.

Chapter 29

The conference room was gray with cigarette smoke. Dr. Hoffman pushed the window open and stood motionless for a few moments, leaning onto the ornate windowsill. Soon, Will Hutson joined him. Resting his weight on his elbows, he also peered vacantly ahead. For some time, both watched on as women – it was always mostly women these days – sifted through the rubble left of an obliterated tenement building across the street, collecting together the pieces of their own former lives, broken by their own men.

Dr. Hutson sniffled quietly. "What are you planning to tell the Court?"

Dr. Hoffman gave a shrug. "The truth. The witness is fit to testify and she's not being, in any way, coerced by her husband to do so."

Another pause hung in the air, slowly uncurling itself like a ringlet of smoke.

"Do you think Dahler shall get off as a mere *follower?*" Dr. Hutson used the official term, which had allowed far too many guilty men to walk free by now.

Gradually, German Denazification Tribunals were replacing the American Military ones. They were still supervised, of course, but both Americans had the most profound conviction that even more former Nazis would get off with an "acquitted" verdict after the change came to a full effect. Despite the new German judges being mostly former Social Democrats or even Communists, hardly was there a person in the entire country who hadn't had someone die in the battle, someone called up against his wishes, someone in the family complicit in the same collective crimes that they were to judge them for. Besides, the quiet sentiment of

Victors' justice was growing stronger and stronger as the time went by, sometimes leading to open mocking of the American system of the Denazification.

Dr. Hoffman turned his back on the street and regarded the opposite wall as though searching for the correct answer on its panels. A square outline, untouched by the bleach of the sun, was still recognizable there. He wondered whether it was a portrait of Hitler that used to hang there. Most likely, it was. It had to be. For twelve years, it was he who represented justice for the Germans. The court of law had ceased to exist replaced by the People's one – a Spanish Inquisition of Nazi Germany. It would take time for the people to adjust to the actual law once again. Dr. Hoffman heaved a sigh and pulled on his cigarette, which had almost burned out, forgotten in his fingers.

"Things are looking good for Dahler. If he proves today that he wasn't actively serving on the ramp during the Hungarian action, he'll get off without a charge. If he can't prove it, or if the prosecution brings a witness or a document, which proves his involvement, he'll be recognized as an offender and subject to imprisonment but since the Military Government granted an amnesty to anyone born after January 1st, 1919, he'll still get off without a sentence due to that amnesty. You know how they consider them – *brainwashed children of the Reich* and all that. Not guilty no matter what, unless they personally tortured or shot hundreds of people somewhere in Eastern Europe as part of one *Einsatzgruppe* or another. If they did kill all those hundreds or thousands, they'd probably get five, maybe ten years. You see how they walk free after serving only three. Besides…"

"Besides, what?"

"Besides, unlike the others and I've seen far too many of them while serving here, Dahler is the first one who openly expressed remorse concerning his actions. And also, dyed-in-the-wool Nazis don't fall in love with Jewish inmates, do they?"

"He loves her." Dr. Hutson grinned. It was a statement this time, not a question.

Dr. Hoffman nodded and narrowed his gaze at the square on the wall once again. "The entire Denazification system is flawed, there's no doubt about it. They should all be serving their time. All the criminals of lower rank, whom we have already exonerated, the 'minors,' whom we granted the amnesty, the 'simple guards,' who didn't personally kill anyone – like Dahler." A sad smile appeared on his face. "But unfortunately, we don't have enough prisons in the entirety of Europe to hold them all. There's such a backlog with all the POWs who are still in camps and who are still being processed that it will take years before their cases are heard. They all need to be fed, clothed, looked after. Of course, the Military Government decided to set all low ranks free summarily. Of course, they hardly bother to investigate *a simple guard*. Of course, a regular Denazification procedure takes merely a couple of hours. Dahler is being tried like some Feldmarschall, with his two days of glory." He chuckled sardonically. "And, of course, there's a ninety-nine percent chance that he'll walk away as a free man after today's hearing. But do you know what? If I'm entirely honest with you, it is my personal feeling that if we acquitted or granted amnesty to so many criminals already, putting the one, who actually showed remorse, in jail, would be the height of hypocrisy. He's still guilty as sin in my eyes – everyone who wore his uniform or set their foot in one of the camps is, no matter if they physically killed anyone – but it is my profound conviction that he shall spend his life atoning for his sins, at least by standing by his wife to the end."

"How categorically he refused to institutionalize her, though!" Dr. Hutson was grinning again.

"Oh, quit it. You're just upset that you're not getting a new patient for your research."

Dr. Hutson chuckled but his smile was a bit unsure this time. "To be truthful, I don't know how I would have treated her even if I got her as a patient. I'm not sure if she needs my treatment, that is. I mean, she seems to be doing perfectly fine when Dahler's around. Maybe, the young fellow is right. Maybe, love really is all she needs to heal."

"Have you noticed how composed he always is around her? And everyone described Dahler as being extremely erratic and moody in the camp. It's like as if he knows that out of the two of them only one can afford to be emotional and purposely keeps himself in control the entire time just so she'd have someone stable to rely on, someone who shall pacify her whenever she's panicking."

Both paused, immersed in their own thoughts. Suddenly, Dr. Hutson turned to his colleague. "Can I see your notes?"

"My notes?"

"The ones that you've been taking about her."

A grin appeared on Dr. Hoffman's face. "Why? Want to compare?"

"Why?" Dr. Hutson mocked. "Are you afraid that I'll point out the wrong diagnosis you drew for her?"

"You're the guard/prisoner case specialist here. Criticize away," Dr. Hoffman surrendered, unexpectedly quickly.

For some time, Dr. Hutson chewed on his lip, leafing through his colleague's notepad.

"A personality disorder (question mark), which is characterized by an irrationally tight bond between a guard/captor and inmate/captive seems to require the following conditions to manifest itself," he began reading out loud. *"No previous relationship between the captor and the victim. A relatively enclosed space in which the interaction between the victim and the perpetrator is unavoidable. A constant risk to a victim's life, which seems to transform the feeling of resentment into positive feelings towards the captor (but only the captor who demonstrated some sort of goodwill towards the said victim). The gradual development of sympathy towards the captor as a means of survival and desire to*

please the captor/captors (Christmas play)." Dr. Hutson looked up and grinned. "Can't argue with that one."

After catching an answering smile from Dr. Hoffman, he continued reading. *"Sympathy and general positive feelings towards the captor seem to transform into a pathological dependency under extreme threat to the victim's life (typhus and gas chamber).* Seems logical, too." Hutson nodded his approval. *"Further physical and psychological effects appear to manifest themselves in the following way: post-trauma – confusion, panic attacks, flashbacks. In captivity – aggression and fear towards fellow captives, lack of trust towards fellow captives, refusal to align oneself with the fellow inmates/captives (Elza, Andrej), which seems to promote further dependency on the captor. Social anxiety, estrangement (including one's relatives – Różinka), extreme cautiousness concerning one's surroundings, agoraphobia/ claustrophobia (perhaps? Not enough material to diagnose). Refusal to accept the reality of events."*

Dr. Hutson arched his brow after reading the final line.

A scowl appeared on Dr. Hoffman's face. "What? Do you think I'm mistaken concerning the reality perception part?"

"No. No, I didn't say that. But… if she doesn't perceive the reality as it was, does it make her suitable to testify in court?"

"She perceives it differently but it doesn't mean that she distorts it for the others. She simply sees Dahler better than he was. *A savior, a defender,"* he repeated Helena's terms and smiled. "She defended him for lashing her but never said that the lashing itself didn't occur. She doesn't lie about the facts themselves, only presents them, through her own lenses. So, yes, it is my opinion that she is fit to testify. Besides, how can I say that she's not? She's not clinically insane. And this condition… it's not in any psychiatry book. No one has come across it yet. Or, simply didn't bother to observe and record it properly. Psychiatry itself is a relatively young science. Perhaps, in the future, there will be a name for it."

"Hoffman's syndrome," Dr. Hutson smiled.

Dr. Hoffman only shook his head. "I hope you don't mind, but I don't want my name anywhere near it. The recess is about done. Let's get this over with, shall we?"

*

Franz Dahler took his seat before the court. He threw another quick glance in Dr. Hoffman's direction. The latter offered him a reassuring smile. His colleague Dr. Hutson would stay with Helena while she slept. Dahler refused the offer to reschedule the hearing for the following day. "Better, get this over with sooner rather than later," he had remarked. "And besides, I don't want my wife hearing this particular testimony. *I* still have nightmares about it and with her present state…" He didn't finish, but Dr. Hoffman understood.

The Chairman shuffled through the heap of documents on his desk. The court recorder flexed his fingers. The silence descended upon the courtroom again.

"Defendant, were you in the camp during the so-called Hungarian action?" The Chairman began his interrogation.

"Yes, I was."

"What were your duties during spring-summer of 1944?"

"The same as before. Kommandoführer of the Kanada work detail."

"Were you aware of the upcoming action against the Hungarian Jews?"

"Yes, I was. Our superiors gathered us right after Kommandant Höss's arrival and announced that we all would have to work double-shifts due to the upcoming influx of the new arrivals."

"Were you aware that most of those arrivals would be gassed upon their admission to the camp?"

Dahler paused, considering his answer. For some inexplicable reason, Dr. Hoffman held his breath in his seat, almost wishing for the Austrian to lie.

"In a way," Dahler replied at last and cleared his throat. "That is, they didn't say it to us openly – their plans, I mean – but the camp administration took certain steps to... raise such suspicions in us."

"Would you please clarify which steps?"

"Yes." A sharp wrinkle creased Dahler's brow as he searched his memory for the right place to start. "I'll start with the construction of the pits if the court allows me to." He slightly tilted his head to one side, searching the Chairman's face for permission. The latter motioned for him to proceed. "We knew that something was in the works when Kommandant Liebehenschel was replaced by Kommandant Höss once again. I suppose, they considered Liebehenschel to be too... soft for the sort of thing that they had in mind. After Liebehenschel fought with Berlin in his attempts to prevent a few transports from the gassing, he fell into disgrace with the higher-ups there. There were rumors that Reichsführer Himmler himself ordered his transfer. In any case, Höss was back. At once, he had appointed Hauptscharführer Moll to be in charge of the preparations, for there was no human being who could rival him in being so sadistic, cruel, bloodthirsty, and fanatical to fulfill the idea that Höss had in mind."

It was odd to hear such characteristics from a former SS man concerning one of his superiors and particularly expressed with such unconcealed disgust and revulsion. Dr. Hoffman smiled. This was a refreshing change from the regular *we were only following orders* excuse he'd heard countless times in Denazification courts and at Nuremberg.

"I first noticed that something was amiss when the Sonderkommando men didn't appear in my work detail one day. Usually, it was they who drove the trucks with all those clothes from the crematoria and emptied them for our Kanada women to sort. I believe it was on the twelfth of May when they didn't show up. I went to clear up the matter with their Kommandoführer, Oberscharführer Voss, only to learn that he had been relieved of his post in favor of Hauptscharführer Moll. The reason was the same as with Liebehenschel – he was much too nice to his subordinates to keep in Kommandant Höss's good graces. Unlike Moll, Voss was a good-humored fellow, who loved his drink and who was known to be rather lenient to his men. Quite often he'd laugh and joke and talk about trivial things with the members of the Sonderkommando and had an overall good reputation with them. You may ask Herr Novák if you wish. I'm sure he'll confirm my characterization."

Strangely enough, the Slovak only lowered his gaze as though in agreement – the first time when he didn't openly argue with Dahler. "Voss was a corrupted fellow but he could have been easily bribed with enough gold stolen from the dead. Bribes and alcohol never failed to put him in a good mood," the former Sonderkommando man commented. "It is true that out of the entire SS crematoria leadership, we did consider him the least inhumane."

Dahler nodded. At least they agreed on something.

"Moll changed the entire chain of command in the crematoria department," the Austrian continued. "He replaced anyone who committed a mortal sin – in his eyes, that is – of not being a brutal slave-driver with the inmates and appointed only the most callous and merciless men in their place. Unterscharführer Steinberg was put in charge of Crematoria 2 and 3. Soon, however, even he wasn't despotic enough to suit Moll's taste and Moll replaced him with Oberscharführer Muhsfeld, recently transferred from Majdanek. Muhsfeld, in his turn, chose Rottenführer Holländer and Eidenmüller to work under his charge. Unterscharführer Eckardt was put in charge of Bunker 5 and there was a reason for that, as we soon learned. Eckardt was born in Hungary and spoke Hungarian as perfectly as he spoke German. Along with his comrade Kell, who came from Lodz and could speak not only German but Polish and Yiddish, he was ordered by Moll to listen closely to what the people were saying on their way to the gassing facilities. Due to the sheer number of new arrivals and the insufficient number of SS men guarding them, Moll wished to ensure that he'd be warned in case of the slightest signs of a revolt or insubordination. Two more SS men were also added as reinforcements to Crematoria 4 and 5, Unterscharführer Seitz and Scharführer Busch. Before that, the crematoria were managed only by Unterscharführer Gorges and Sturmann Kurschuss. All of these changes were the first signs of something major underway. Needless to say, Moll told me to get lost with my request for his Sonderkommando men. He had no one to spare, he said and that he'd give me one truck but as for people, I would have to make do with the few male inmates that I still had working in the Kanada, all mostly 'old numbers.' As a matter of fact, Moll soon enlarged the Sonderkommando to a 450-people team," he paused before adding, "a number, which he soon doubled for they simply couldn't cope with all the corpses."

A shudder ran through Dr. Hoffman. He could swear, the temperature itself fell a few degrees after those last chilling words spoken by Dahler. Novák's face clouded over, visibly. He was reliving all that as well, through Dahler's testimony.

"But it was when they began digging the pits that we knew that something horrible was coming." Dahler paused. "We were right. Dante's *Inferno* soon appeared to be a child's play compared to what Moll organized there. The Sonderkommando were digging in sunshine and rain those days, until nine pits – fifty meters long, eight meters wide, two meters deep – were dug out next to Bunker 5. Inside, Moll constructed a device of sorts, which was supposed to direct the fat dripping off the burning corpses back into the fuel to ensure an efficient, non-stop operation."

Dr. Hoffman swallowed. It wasn't the first testimony he'd heard from an SS man. He was present during the trials in Nuremberg. He heard Otto Ohlendorf himself talk. However, suddenly, he wished for Dahler to stop, just to stop talking before the image would be forever branded into his mind. No wonder Dahler didn't wish for

Helena to hear all that. The psychiatrist himself wasn't sure how he would be able to tolerate it any further.

"Together with crematorium ovens, those nine pits made it theoretically possible to burn an unlimited amount of bodies, without stopping; every single day, double-shifts – day and night—"

Intentionally loudly, Lieutenant Carter cleared his throat and groped for the glass of water almost spilling it in the process. What appeared on Dahler's face in response to that was supposed to be a grin but it came out so grim and crooked, it could hardly pass for such.

"Yes. That was precisely our reaction as well when we saw the pits with our own eyes." Suddenly, he was looking at Novák – a long, sorrowful gaze full of remorse and agony. The Slovak held it and nodded slowly. Something passed between them that moment – something profound and meaningful, yet impossible to decipher for anyone who wasn't bound together by that common horror they both lived through – the perpetrator and the victim.

"When you say, 'our reaction,' who else are you talking about, Defendant?" the Chairman asked.

"Rottenführer Gröning, the Kanada accountant. He didn't believe me when I told him about the pits. He wished to see for himself. We went there, into the field, at night. There were only flowers everywhere; there was a meadow right behind the Kanada detail and the two bunkers. For some time, we waded through those flowers and I, myself, began doubting what I had told him for there was not a chance in the world that someone could transform such a beautiful, blooming meadow into a death factory in the course of a few days." He went silent, then continued. "They had floodlights there though. We saw the pits all right. We both had been in Auschwitz much too long not to understand the meaning of all such preparations. The next day, Gröning asked for a transfer to the front."

"What about you?"

"I wanted to. I almost did."

"Why didn't you?"

Dahler gave a small shrug, with a guilty smile in tow. "I couldn't leave Helena there all by herself. Who knew what they were planning afterward, Höss and Moll? We were losing the war. The Reds had just liberated Majdanek. Who knew if Höss would order to liquidate all of the prisoners after he was done with the Hungarians?"

"And what was your plan in the case of this happening?" the Chairman asked.

Another shrug. "To try and run, I suppose. There were a few successful escapes before that… I don't know. I didn't have a plan if I'm entirely honest with you. I don't know what I would have done if such an order came through. I wouldn't have been able to protect her anyway. I just wanted to stay with her, I suppose."

Hoffman smiled. Dahler's honesty was almost endearing.

"When did the transports begin to arrive?" the Chairman asked.

"The first one arrived on May 16."

"Did you serve on the ramp at that time?"

"No. They would have made me but I got myself out of that duty." Dahler was smiling slyly now.

"I thought you said it was impossible not to obey direct orders under Höss."

"That is true. But I didn't openly disobey orders. I simply stole enough things from the Kanada and ensured that I got caught red-handed, for the Political Department to put me into the bunker on disciplinary charges for an entire month. I have submitted the document confirming this to the court."

Hoffman caught himself grinning as well. The Chairman was reading the mentioned paper. He shook his head but a smile was playing on his lips, as well. "A crafty thing to do," he commented under his breath but loudly enough for Dr. Hoffman to hear him. He chuckled softly.

"You were released in late June?"

"That is correct. But I was still 'banned' from the ramp for the entire month of July as well – they didn't trust me with the Hungarians' belongings, they said. Again, exactly what I was aiming for. I can't confirm my not being involved with serving on the ramp though. I have no witnesses to give you any affidavits in this respect."

"You do." Novák suddenly gave his voice. "I can confirm this, Your Honor. He didn't serve on the ramp in July. I was there every day, escorting people to the gassing facilities. I didn't see Herr Dahler there. Not once."

Chapter 30

Franz

Auschwitz. Summer 1944

The sky itself grew dark with smoke. Suffocated by the reddish clouds, the pale sun struggled to get through the columns of fire just to die before reaching the west. We hardly saw it nowadays. We became a nation of twilight.

The pyres had been burning for two months now, daily and nightly. Moll had introduced two shifts to ensure continuous operation. *An engineering genius, no less.* Rumor had it, the old man Höss would promote him soon for his efficiency and inventiveness. *Who else would think of using human fat as fuel?*

I took another swig from my flask, cringing at the taste of confiscated brandy. So, there was still brandy in the world if they kept bringing it with them. There must have been an outside world too, from which they came, where people took their breakfast that didn't taste like charred human flesh and went to work along streets that weren't surrounded by barbed wire and manned by watchtowers outfitted with machinegun posts. I regarded the sandwich which I took from the canteen this morning after pushing my breakfast around my plate, unable to swallow a single piece, brought it to my mouth but couldn't eat it either and threw it to my Alsatian instead, who wolfed it down in two beastly gulps.

The mutt was not mine per se. He belonged to one of the specially trained dog handlers. However, after the fellow had gotten himself into the infirmary a few days ago – officially, with the flu –

but, unofficially, with a nervous breakdown, after he began seeing dead people standing in front of his cot at night and then, during the day also – and since I had the same kind of dog at home, this poor beast was assigned to me as I'd know how to handle him.

The dog, Rolf, lolled his tongue out and regarded me with his amber eyes, no doubt grateful for the unexpected treat. I rubbed him behind the ear, pretending that it was my Prinz. *Hopefully, I won't end up like your previous handler,* I thought to myself as I lowered to the ground next to the dog. I hadn't seen any stiffs yet but my appetite was as good as gone and the SS doctors here muttered among themselves that it was *one of the first signs.* Also, unofficially. Officially, the SS men, the hardened Teutonic Knights, didn't suffer from such things as weak nerves brought on by the ungodly view of mountains of human corpses. They suffered from shrapnel wounds and enemy bombs but never from any sentimental feelings. That was the official Party line. The unofficial... oh well. What good would it really do, to contemplate such philosophical questions?

I gulped some more brandy. In the July heat and in the absence of any food in my stomach, it went straight to my head. I thought it to be a good thing. Much better than being sober nowadays.

"Down," I commanded.

Rolf was lying down before I knew it. He was a good dog, well-trained and smart, with a strong back and muscular sides on which he allowed me to rest my head. With his hind legs framing my shoulder, with a sweet blade of grass in my mouth instead of a cigarette – they had reduced our rations again – I could close my eyes and pretend that within a fifteen-minute walk from here, the inferno wasn't raging. Closer to the ground, the smell of the burnt flesh wasn't as strong, sickly-sweet, and thoroughly nauseating. Our uniforms stunk of it. Our hair stunk of it, even after a good scrubbing. Our food reeked of it. The dog's fur under me reeked of it. My eyes were red from all the smoke. Officially, Teutonic

Knights didn't shed tears for their enemies, nor did they feel pity for themselves.

The trouble was, it took me much too long to realize that I wasn't one of them.

"Dahler! I knew I'd find you asleep here, you miserable escapist!"

I snorted softly at the insult and lifted myself on my elbows. To be sure, Gröning could afford to have that idiotic grin glued to his face these days, as his request for a transfer had just been granted. The lucky devil was heading to the Western Front within the next couple of weeks.

"What else is there to do?" I sat up, lazy from the sun and brandy.

"Your job."

"I am doing my job. I'm guarding the perimeter."

"Shouldn't you be standing like a good soldier, with a rifle slung over your shoulder instead of snoring like a bastard?"

"What for? I have Rolf for that. He'll alert me, at once, if anyone approaches."

"He was snoring like a bastard, too, when I approached."

"He's only trained on the inmates, not SS men."

Gröning only shook his blond head. He couldn't really say anything to that. We all have always been a little envious of the dog-handling squad. They could lounge in the sun and nap all day or play with their mutts without a care in the world. Only when the transports came did they straighten their uniforms and put on serious faces, just like their dogs that strained on the leashes and snapped their teeth at the new arrivals. As soon as the ramp was empty, they would be back to their playing and napping. There were a few degenerates who amused themselves with setting their Alsatians on the prisoners just for the thrill of it but thankfully, they were the minority. The majority only wished to sleep and shirk duty.

"So? Are you packing your suitcase yet?" I teased him and nodded in gratitude for the offered cigarette.

We sat next to each other facing the camp. Behind our back, columns of black smoke were rising from the pits until the sky itself was charred with it. In front of us, smaller columns of smoke were shooting towards the blue dome. All four crematoria were gulping down their victims with the insatiable greed of ancient beasts. For some time, we smoked in silence, poisoning the air with our own smoke. It appeared as though the entire world was on fire these days.

"I won't miss this place," Gröning spoke at last.

It took him quite some time to admit it, to even utter it out loud, even though he knew it very well that I would be the last person in this camp to report him for it. He was of the same age as me, twenty-two. Our generation wasn't quite sure as to what to make of itself as of recent times. It was easier for the idiots; they raised their arms in snappy salutes – *Heil Hitler, little soldier! No defeatism among the German ranks!* – and walked right under the Soviet tanks with four hand grenades tied together. It was also easier for the calloused bullies; they hanged the ones who began thinking for themselves, off the trees and lampposts and wrote, *"I am a traitor of the Reich,"* on the cardboard signs, with which they adorned their former comrades' necks.

It was the hardest for us, who grew up in a world that only had one master race; which drummed it into our heads since school how our lives belonged to the Führer and the Fatherland; how the orders must never be questioned, for our loyalty was our honor and our honor was our loyalty and some other utter bullshit to that effect... Until one day, when we looked around and saw what we did and were suddenly so very terrified of what we had become that no words would ever suffice to describe that cold horror that now resided in our hearts, which we weren't supposed to have in the first place. Our hearts, just like our lives, belonged to the Fatherland. They only had the right to beat, for it – all else was treason.

"You will miss this place as soon as you see the front with your own two eyes. Though, in your case..." Trying to joke, I even pulled the glasses, in their tortoiseshell frame, off his nose but the jest and the horseplay came out as pitiful as it gets and I returned his glasses, with a sigh, before he even asked for them.

"You saw the front already," he said, unoffended. "Would you rather see it again or stay here?"

"I asked for a transfer in 1942. They didn't grant it."

"Mine neither but that was two years ago." He obliterated me with a wave of his hand. "We were winning the war then. Now, they can't afford to be so selective. Ask for a transfer now and I guarantee you, the Old Man himself will sign it for you, even with your wounded knee. They take thirteen-year-old snotty-nosed kids from *Hitlerjugend* into the ranks now, or the grandfathers who must be old enough to have fought for the Kaiser in the 1870s. Surely, they'll snatch you at once and particularly with your combat experience."

"One doesn't need experience, to get a bullet in his stomach," I replied evenly.

He ignored the treasonous statement. "Even more so! Go to the Kommandantur; I'll watch your post while you're at it. Then, we'll go to the front together!"

I only stared ahead of myself without moving. *I ought to go,* I told myself, *I really ought to… If I do, this all will be over within mere days. In mere days, I'll be rocking on a train next to Gröning; he will be reading one book or the other and I shall be gazing out of the window and see people – living people and not walking skeletons whom we had starved to near death – and fields in which the fires weren't burning.*

I regarded my nails, the grass matted around me – anything just to escape Gröning's reproachful look.

"You won't go, will you?"

Slowly, I shook my head.

He didn't ask me anything about Helena. He had never openly asked me about her – he silently disapproved of such a relationship – but only sighed and shook his head again, much like one would at a stubborn child.

"What's the plan then?" he asked, as if the logical question would bring some sense into my head. He was very *logical*, Gröning. I was *the sentimentalist,* according to him.

"I'm staying here."

"To the bitter end?"

"To the bitter end."

"I think you're making a mistake."

I smiled, amused by such a suggestion. "You know, for the first time in my life, I'm actually certain that I'm not. For the first time, I feel like I'm doing the right thing."

"Your right things landed you into the bunker twice in the past few months."

I shrugged. "I didn't mind. It was cool and quiet in there and didn't smell like smoke."

"Just don't end up being shot for something stupid, will you?" He was back on his feet again, brushing the weeds off his uniform. "We're almost done with this rot. It would be stupid to die now. A really stupid, pointless death."

I waved my hand around. "What's the meaning of all this then? Is this not stupid and pointless? Why are we murdering all these people, if the war is lost at any rate?"

He walked away before I could say something even more treasonous that he would never report but equally didn't wish to hear.

He was the logical one, Gröning. He wasn't a vicious anti-Semite like Moll and didn't approve of the killings in a brutal manner but he thought of his own skin first and one couldn't quite blame him for that. I watched him go, with infinite longing for the days when I only thought of my own skin too, when the world was black and white, when the Jews were the enemy, and when my uniform didn't stink of smoke and death.

Chapter 31

Franz

The new fellow was barely eighteen, with cheeks hardly touched by the razor, gangly and patriotic. He was sent here straight from training, in Munich, he said and threw himself at his new duty with the true fervor of a freshly brainwashed idiot. By noon, already my head began aching due to all of his shouting and running around the warehouse with the efficiency of a chicken that'd just had its head chopped off. Growing more and more annoyed, I signed to him to come over.

He even saluted me with that fresh-out-of-school salute. We, the old guard, hardly bothered bending our arms at the elbow as of late. Our *Heil Hitler* had also lost its enthusiasm quite some time ago. Unlike this new greenhorn, we uttered it indifferently. It tasted stale and moldy on our wind-bitten lips.

"Just what are you doing with those poor wretches?" I motioned my head in the direction of the inmates. Confused and mildly alarmed, they kept throwing anxious glances in my and even Wolff's direction, unsure of what to make of all this newly introduced shouting.

"We have so many things to sort with all these transports, Herr Unterscharführer." He gestured helplessly around. "I'm only urging them to work faster so we'd catch up with Herr Kommandant's plan…"

I snorted softly under my breath. I had the most profound conviction that Herr Kommandant's only plan included organizing himself a passport with a new name in it and evacuating his villa with all the stolen goods before the Allies came. I considered breaking the news to the new fellow but noticed a *Hitlerjugend Sieg Rune* for special distinctions he proudly displayed on his breast pocket, an earnest Party loyalty look in his pale blue eyes and wisely decided against it.

He was right about one thing, this earnest *Pimpf.* All around the different warehouses, mountains of belongings grew as high as the roofs; inside, there were only narrow trails left in between the tightly stacked suitcases and baby prams. One of the warehouses had been remodeled into a permanent storage facility; the trucks that used to transport all belongings with commendable efficiency to Germany were, for the most part, commandeered for the war effort; the diesel was in short supply and Germany itself was so relentlessly bombed that they needed medical supplies or coffins much more than all of these clothes.

"They all have been working in this Kommando for years now. They have their own system that they're used to and you're only upsetting it with all your incessant slave-driving and shouting. They won't work any faster than they physically can. Let them be."

He had already opened his mouth to bring up one argument or another, quote some insufferable postulate perhaps – most likely he'd been informed about my political unreliability upon arrival – but then shot a sidelong glance at my "Wound Badge" that I had brought from the Eastern Front along with my limp and only saluted again. At least combat experience carried some weight for them so far. If it hadn't been for that, the snotty-faced sod would be writing a report on me in the Old Man's office within an hour. And in spite of all I had said to Gröning, I didn't fancy one little bit landing in Bunker 11 once again. It was cool and quiet there and they fed me just fine but the mere thought of not seeing Helena again turned me cold with horror.

She glanced up quickly from her sorting table. I caught just a fleeting ghost of a smile on her face – in gratitude for curbing the new fellow's enthusiasm, no doubt – and then it was gone before I could warm myself in its light. We stayed away from each other since our arrest in May, as much as it was possible for both of us to bear. I didn't bring her into my office anymore and neither did she speak to me unless addressed first. Before releasing me, Schurz muttered something to the extent that *he really ought to have shot the wench instead of releasing her* and I suddenly wasn't so sure whether I wanted to put his goodwill to the test with further defiance of the racial laws. And so, all of our interaction had ceased to rare looks, exchanged when no one was watching and an odd *I love you to death,* also whispered in passing.

Rolf found himself on the wrong end of my affections, instead and soon grew lazy and tender from all the back pats and ear scratches and half of my rations fed to his growing belly. He was as good as mine now. His former handler was not coming back anytime soon, they said. They said he was in some good clinic near the Alps.

"Herr Unterscharführer!" The greenhorn again. I turned to him, obliging him with a politely bored smile. His face was flushed but he didn't gasp for air after his sprint. The *Sieg Rune* and the Sports badge were well-deserved then. "Dr. Mengele was asking for you. He says, he needs you on the ramp. The new transport has just arrived and they're short-handed with the SS staff."

July heat was raging outside and yet, I was suddenly cold, almost on the verge of trembling at the mere mention of that hateful name.

"I'm not allowed on the ramp." I tried worming my way out of the duty, which I had not the slightest inclination to perform. Perhaps, I should have joked about the Old Man and his new passport. Perhaps, the bunker was not such a bad affair after all.

"You are now. He asked for you specifically."

"Why me?"

He hesitated before answering. "He said he has a lot of cattle and you're good with the whip." He grinned. He thought the joke to be amusing, no doubt. He liked me now, the newfound respect reflecting in his eyes.

I set off before I could comment something vile to that, which I would later regret. I still had Helena to see to and whether I liked it or not, landing myself in more trouble with the authorities would not help me in the slightest.

The ramp was in wild confusion. It swarmed with people. A moaning, sweat-drenched sea of bodies that hardly parted, even at the sight of the viciously barking Alsatian. *They hadn't had water in days,* they pleaded. *The children needed food.* Their elderly sat on the ground, resigned and almost already dead. Moll was not there, only Dr. Mengele, outfitted in an immaculate uniform as was his habit, his black hair shining in the sun like an onyx crown of some underworld's god, eyes fixated on the crowd, searching, hunting for his usual twins or dwarfs, no doubt. I made a step toward him but he waved me off, much to my relief.

"I have the selection under control. I only need you to escort these people to the showers. I have only Sonderkommando men here and no officers to supervise them. Moll is supposed to be here but as you can see for yourself, he is not."

I looked ahead of myself, ignoring the crowd's moans and pleas. The *showers,* also known as Crematorium V, to which Mengele gracefully pointed with the tip of his whip, loomed up against the smoke-filled sky. The Sonderkommando fellow, with his sleeves rolled up, looked up at me inquisitively. I knew that this was where I had to begin speaking to the people, spinning the tales to pacify them, promising them cold coffee or tea after their nice, refreshing shower, lie convincingly about the children's camp to make them undress their children faster, lull them into blissful ignorance so that they'd go there willingly and didn't give us any trouble by screaming and pleading for their lives. But with the best will in the world, I couldn't open my mouth. Silent and grim, I motioned the column, doomed by Mengele's mere movement of the hand, after myself.

Murmurs began growing louder behind my back. Someone grew bold enough to shout a question about the smoke coming out of the showers. *Surely, showers didn't need any ovens, did they?*

Yet, I still marched ahead with stubborn resolution. *Let them start a riot. Let them know where we're going. Let them trample and maul us all. The whole affair could go to the devil for all I cared. None of us were leaving this place alive, a sudden revelation occurred to me. Might as well get it over with now.*

Alarmed by the growing unease among the crowd and my persistent silence, the Sonderkommando began pacifying people on their own.

"The smoke, that's coming from the heater, my good man; from the heater to warm the water for the showers." The familiar story began. "Surely, you don't want your elderly and your children to stand under ice-cold water. The water here is pumped straight from the wells and it's blisteringly cold, I tell you! They can catch a cold with the sudden change in temperature and such things are dangerous at their age. Who's burning people alive in the field? Who told you such a silly thing, my good woman? Those are bog fires that are burning. Don't you see how thick the smoke is? And the smell? That's the bogs! That's the smell specific to the bogs. There are so many bogs in Poland; you don't have that sort of thing in Hungary, I know. That's the specific smell of the bogs. They catch fire every summer. We've grown used to it by now. We hardly even notice it…"

An ugly smirk sat on my face. Well, that much was true, out of his whole speech.

Unterscharführer Gorges, Kommandoführer of Crematorium V, met me in front of the building with a grin and a friendly handshake.

"Ah! The reinforcements!" He beamed at me. He was tan and gleaming with health. "Would you do me one last little favor? We are terribly out of people, as you can clearly see."

"Yes, Mengele told me and you all do have my sympathies but I really ought to be back in the Kanada." I made a move to leave but he clasped my sleeve before I had a chance to escape.

"The truck for your Kanada is being loaded as we speak," he rushed to reassure me. Indeed, a Red Cross truck – a pacifying sight for the new arrivals' eyes – was backed and parked carefully right in front of the double doors from which a passage led into a changing room so that no one would see what exactly was being loaded into it – the belongings of the ones who had just been gassed and who were being burned, now, in the crematorium, in the exact same building. *Water heater, my foot.* "It will only take up ten minutes of your precious time. The driver will give you a ride back and I shall be forever in your debt. There's more where this came from."

His hand brushed my pocket ever so slightly but I'd grown used to such gestures by now. With a chilling lack of interest, I wondered what exactly he dropped into it; gold, diamonds, or dollars. I contemplated taking it out and shoving it back into his hand but now, at the sight of the approaching end, it was unwise to make enemies and Gorges was no brute, unlike Moll. One could negotiate with him when the occasion called for it. *Sod it, I was growing* logical, *like Gröning.*

I forced a smile onto my face and gave him the wink of a co-conspirator. "I don't need a bribe to help out a comrade in need but one day, I shall take you up on your word. Perhaps, you'll be able to help me with something."

"You only need to say the word, Dahler."

"I will. What is it that you need?"

Several people strayed away from the column and began collecting water out of the puddles on the ground. The puddles came from hoses, with which the Sonderkommando cleaned the corpses of the foam, blood, urine, and feces inside the gas chambers. They were in such constant use that the ground around the crematorium itself was soaked with water, running from the hydrants. Gorges allowed them such a pitiful last favor and didn't even order them back into the line.

The elderly sat on the grass, shielding their heads from the sun with their handbags or newspapers. They even took newspapers with them. They were Hungarians, the city people, for the most part. They could have very well been *Reichsdeutsche* – they looked exactly the same, well-mannered, well-dressed, much too timid to start any revolt. Now I understood why Gorges had no qualms on their account. He'd gassed far too many of them, since May, to know that these people wouldn't give him any trouble. They went to their death peacefully, placated with the reasonable explanations offered by the friendly Sonderkommando and the SS. He beamed again, utterly satisfied with himself.

"One last favor." He stepped closer and spoke close to my ear so that the people wouldn't hear his words. "All six ovens are full but there's still a batch of stiffs left to burn and we need to put these people in there before they start putting two and two together, eh? Sitting on the grass and thinking doesn't really benefit the order of things here. The Kommando have already cleaned out the chamber itself and stacked all the stiffs outside, behind the screen. While they're finishing loading up their belongings onto the truck, escort the Sonderkommando men with those remaining stiffs outside to Moll's detail, will you? I'm a bit swamped here, as you can see and it's against the rules to let them go alone, without an SS man's supervision."

"Naturally," I replied evenly.

"Rules are rules." He spread his arms in a helpless, apologetic gesture, breaking into yet another sunny grin.

"And orders are orders," I muttered before turning on my heel and proceeding towards the back of the crematorium. I still noticed how his smile faltered after those last words of mine.

The tall, solid, 3-meters-tall camouflage screens, protecting the unsuspecting eyes of the new arrivals from the ghastly picture of the pits in the field that lie a mere hundred meters from the crematorium, were also Moll's invention. Much like the flowers he had made the inmates plant in front of the crematoria before the Hungarian action went into full swing. And much like cheap decorations, they opened the ugly truth to one's sight as soon as one stepped behind the screens and came face to face with the Grim Reaper himself. There were enough corpses there, some already stacked one on top of the other, some were laid out in neat, ghastly rows as the dentists were busy wrenching gold crowns out of their mouths, to assure me of his presence somewhere near. Three Sonderkommando men were so consumed by shearing dead women's hair, they failed to notice my presence, much like the ones who crouched by the corpses, searching their orifices for hidden valuables.

The Sonderkommando corpse bearers, who sat on the ground next to the "cleared" corpses and smoked, jumped to their feet at once and tore their striped hats off their heads before freezing to attention next to the handcarts. I guessed those were used for the transportation of the bodies.

But it wasn't the stacks of arms and legs hanging helplessly off their sides that made the breath catch in my throat at once. Three young women, as naked as on the day they were born, huddled together behind the Sonderkommando men's stiff backs.

"What is the meaning of this?!" I shouted at the inmates, anger rising in me at once. Rolf growled and pulled on the leash, still tightly secured in my hand. A raw lust for destruction arose in me, along with the desire to set the dog on the bastards.

They exchanged alarmed looks, blinked uncomprehendingly and then, as though remembering the young women, began talking all together at once.

"It's not our doing, Herr Unterscharführer!"

"On Hauptscharführer Moll's orders!"

"He was just here before the last gassing—"

"These three begged him to be killed at the same time—"

"He ordered not to gas them—"

"He ordered to take them down to his detail as soon as we go there—"

"It was him, he made them undress so that the clothes wouldn't be ruined…"

"We wouldn't touch them, Herr Unterscharführer! You may ask them yourself—"

"We only waited for someone to escort us, Herr Unterscharführer…"

My face must have softened enough for them to breathe out in relief and stop their protesting.

"Well, I'm here now. Let's go," I grumbled.

The bearers picked up the handles of the wheelbarrows and the women reluctantly stepped onto the path to which I motioned. Thus, our ghastly funeral procession began marching toward the raging inferno.

Dante really had no imagination when he was describing his hell, let me tell you. Boiling pits of lava with demons shoving sinners into them with pitchforks? How grotesquely fantastic and improbable. How almost beautifully gothic and fear-of-God inspiring.

Here, the main demon wore a white summer uniform with a Cross with Swords – *for the distinctive service to the Reich,* no less – and shouted his insults at the fire stokers who didn't turn corpses in pits fast enough for his liking. Under the mournful looks of the elderly men in their watchtowers (I still wonder what they were making of all this, brought into this hell not by conviction but by conscription; former farmers, for the most part, or injured frontline soldiers like myself, all of them of our fathers' age), Moll strutted along the length of the pits with his Alsatian at his heel and instructed Jewish stokers on how to burn their own kin more efficiently.

The heat from the raging fire brushed my cheeks even though we'd barely made it half of the way along the path. The women must have felt it too or began recognizing that it wasn't wood that the SS were burning in those strange pits but human bodies. One of the bearers prodded the girls gently in the backs, urging them forward. The young women were slowing them down and the bearers didn't fancy facing Moll's wrath in the slightest. There were rumors that he had shoved someone alive into one of those pits for angering him. No one knew what precisely occurred but as a result, no one wished to get on Moll's wrong side from then on.

I wiped the sweat that broke out on my forehead, either from the heat that was growing more and more intolerable with every step or from nausea that was rising in my stomach. I kept swallowing with difficulty but the back of my throat was suddenly dry as though wiped raw with sandpaper. The women stopped altogether, positively refusing to take another step. I left them to their own devices.

Now, I'll just force myself to walk up to that pit, report to Moll that his bearers and women are here, turn my back on all this business and let him do whatever the devil he wants.

I should have gone with Gröning to the front.

I should have caught that shrapnel into my guts and not the damn knee and died like a hero instead of...

"Herr Hauptscharführer!" I surprised even myself with how calm and collected my voice sounded and how crisp and snappy the salute came out as soon as Moll turned around and faced me. He nodded his approval at such excellent military bearing as he called it. His freckled face was pink and glowing from the heat. Tongues of the red-blue fires reflected in his glass eye, gaily dancing on its unseeing surface. The other one, the good one, observed me mischievously. "Allow me to report; the bearers are here with the bodies cleared for cremation. The rest shall be escorted by Unterscharführer Gorges as soon as he finishes with admitting the new arrivals."

He nodded in satisfaction. The good eye was now regarding Rolf who sat patiently at my feet – a mirror reflection of Moll's Alsatian.

"Beautiful dog."

"Thank you, Herr Hauptscharführer. He's a very good dog."

"How is he with the prisoners?"

I hesitated before replying, unsure of what he expected me to say. "He… keeps them in line, Herr Hauptscharführer."

He grinned deviously. The glass eye began unnerving me with its unblinking stare. Just to escape its incessant ogling, I tried looking past him but now I was boring my gaze directly into the stacks and stacks of corpses and I grew lightheaded instead. I swallowed once again, tasting the bile in the back of my throat. I closed my eyes – to hell with what he thinks – but they were still there, in front of my closed eyelids, their bodies turning and moving of their own volition as though coming alive as soon as the flames touched them.

"You seem a bit pale, Unterscharführer." Moll's voice cut into the nightmare, mocking and slightly amused. "Are you all right?"

I forced myself to blink my eyes open. My hand brushed my pocket instinctively. A flask was hidden there, so close and so out of reach.

"I'm a bit warm, Herr Hauptscharführer."

"I should think so." His hyena's chuckles were far louder than the ringing in my ears.

One of the stokers stood boring his eyes into me. I recognized him despite the waves of heat distorting his features. Andrej Novák. Slowly, intentionally slowly, he reached into the stacks and stacks of bodies and began prodding at them. The sizzling noise where their bellies burst, torn open by the fire, the ghastly movements of their partially-charred arms raising, by themselves, as though in mocking salutes, as the muscles stiffened with heat; their skin covered in blisters that kept rupturing and leaking human fat that fueled the fire even more and lit it white – he wanted me to see it all, to face what exactly my kin was doing to his.

Wild screaming pierced the air around us. The SS men were driving the women closer to the pit with the muzzles of their guns and crude shoves in the backs. Encouraged by Moll's chuckling – everyone knew he got his kicks from such disgusting things – his underlings began pushing the women forward with even greater enthusiasm until the poor creatures tore away from them and ran like frightened deer toward the barbed-wire fence surrounding the area.

"Not so fast, my little chickens!" Moll was in his element now, the fire dancing in both of his eyes. "Go get them, boy! Atta boy!"

His Alsatian caught up with the women before they could reach the fence, his teeth snapping at their heels and tearing into their bare flesh. The dog rounded them up, much like a sheepdog would his herd and began pushing them back toward his master. Rolf made a high-pitched noise, shifting from one foot to another next to me, clearly agitated.

"Set him free!" Moll urged, laughing like a Satan. "Let him have his fun, too!"

My hand coiled around the leash even tighter, before I knew what I was doing. In fact, I didn't feel my body any longer. It had suddenly grown so light that the wind could have picked it up and carried it away. The ringing in my ears grew so loud, the women's screaming barely registered in them. They huddled together, bleeding from their torn wounds and trembling viciously, with their entire bodies, despite the overpowering heat around us.

Moll licked his lips as his only eye stared at their tear-stained, petrified faces. Slowly, he reached for his gun and tugged onto his uniform trousers to hide the bulge straining them. His breath was heavy with excitement. "Just look at it! Look at it well! In a moment, you'll burn exactly like them!" He shouted, spraying the air with saliva.

At last, accompanied by the laughter of his SS men, he took mercy on them and shot them one by one, shoving them into the pit with his boot right after. I turned away and vomited all over the ground and my boots before dropping to my knees. Agitated, Rolf kept licking my face and hands, whining and pacing around me.

Apart from that whining and the crackling of the fire, not a sound could be heard around. Suddenly, the whole world grew mute. I wiped my mouth with the back of my hand and slowly roved my gaze around. Hostile, disdainful faces stared back at me from above.

"You're a disgrace to your uniform," Moll commented calmly, as though stating a fact. "I thought you'd have a better stomach for it, after the front."

For what? For death? For murder? I wished to ask him but my voice was suddenly gone as well.

Moll called somebody over. "Get him away from here and take care not to bring him back. Pathetic weakling."

A pair of hands pulled me upward surprisingly gently. It was an inmate, a Slovak doctor. I recognized him even through the haze still blurring my vision. In silence, he escorted me out of that hellish scene, supporting me all the way to the crematorium for I staggered unmercifully, like a veritable drunk. Rolf trailed next to me, his leash dragging on the ground. From time to time, he nudged my hand with his wet nose. I kept wiping the sweat off my face angrily. The sweat and the tears…

In the crematorium, the Slovak doctor had his own entrance on the side of the building. Apparently, his dissecting room, newly set up by Dr. Mengele, was there. He sat me down onto the corpse slab and asked me politely to wait there. I was lying down when he returned with the syringe.

"What is it? Phenol?" I jested grimly.

"Would you like it to be phenol?" he retorted, without much emotion and rolled up my sleeve.

Rolf sat up next to the slab, eyeing him with suspicion. I reached down and rubbed his ear with the other hand until he relaxed again.

"Would you?" I tried to sound mocking but it came out rather pitiful. The pathologist looked at me with reproach and rubbed the injection site before folding my arm at its elbow.

"Hold it tight for some time."

"You didn't reply to me."

"No, I wouldn't," he sighed eventually. There was something pacifying about this room, something oddly calming in the sound of the instruments clinking on the metal surface, in the clean, sterile smell of the disinfectant. I closed my eyes once again. My limbs were growing heavy with sleep, along with my eyelids. "I gave an oath to Hippocrates. I would never do harm to anyone living."

"What were you doing in the field?" I muttered.

"I look for certain deformities that may interest *Herr Doktor*." It was clear who *Herr Doktor* was. "He likes autopsies performed on those and sometimes ships particularly interesting cases to Germany, to one scientific institute or the other."

"For what?"

"For what? To prove how degenerate and racially inferior the Jewish race is compared to the Aryan."

"Is it really? You're a scientist…"

"Of course not. Those are common deformities that occur in every race."

"That's what I thought. The science is rigged. Just like the press, the history… We have nothing to trust anymore. Everything is a lie…"

"Don't speak, please," he pleaded with me, placing a warm palm onto my shoulder. I was saying all sorts of wrong things and his suddenly protective attitude would have amused me if I weren't so apathetic, with a growing numbness in my body. He must have felt it too, the fact that I was almost fully under the effect of whatever sedative he gave me. His fingers pressed into my shoulder slightly. "That young woman who you brought here two years ago and who got sick with typhus later… Is she still alive?"

I smiled softly. "Yes. Of course, she is. I'd never let anything happen to her…"

"There's still hope for you then, young man."

I wasn't quite sure whether he really said it or if I only dreamed his words.

*

January 1945

The columns were ready to set off on their last journey. The roar of the approaching Soviet artillery had grown quiet for the night. It was wiser to abandon the camp under cover of darkness.

Kommandant Höss was the first one to go and he took care to make off as early as the end of July. He evacuated his entire villa, where his family used to live so lavishly. It took two whole train cars to bring all that plunder to Germany.

All three crematoria had been demolished with explosives in November. The Sonderkommando took care of the fourth one, burning it down after their standoff with the SS earlier that month. Most of them were shot, in retaliation but the remainder were still alive and firmly set on staying that way. None of them had identified himself as a former Sonderkommando member during the last roll call that took place not two hours ago. The men were not stupid. They knew what fate awaited them had they done so. What was left of the camp administration were quite clear on the question of "evidence." Everything must be burned and buried. First, the paperwork and then – the witnesses.

With two pairs of warm, fur-lined boots carefully concealed under my overcoat, I kept searching the column for Helena and her sister. It was ready to depart, in fact, the beginning of it had marched out already. At last, I found them, or to be exact, Helena found me, clutching at my overcoat at once and positively refusing to let go. I doubt she heard me instructing her to put on the boots before they would start marching and it would be too late. There were clear instructions to the SS escorting them to shoot everyone who fell behind, indiscriminately.

"I'm staying here with you."

That was all that she was repeating with the obstinacy of a madwoman, while her sister Rózínka was changing her footwear as one would do with a helpless child.

"Leni, I am not staying in the camp." I tried prying her frozen fingers off my coat but to no avail. She kept clawing at me with more desperation. At least, the inmates next to us took care to look the other way, thoroughly pretending not to see the unraveling scene. "I'm going to the front along with the newly formed division. No SS man is staying in the camp."

"Take me with you then."

"To the front?" My smile resembled a wretched grimace if anything.

"I can help. I can bandage wounds…"

There will be no wounded where I am heading, only dead bodies. I wanted to tell her but that would only make everything worse.

"Helena, here's my mother's address in Vienna." I shoved the note into Rózínka's hands instead of hers. Rózínka was in a much better state of mind than Leni. "As soon as you walk out of here, Unterscharführer Gorges shall take you to a village – we have already agreed on everything. He'll leave you there to wait for the Soviets. When they come – it shall only be a day or two, maybe less even – show them your tattoos and tell them you're escaped inmates. They shall take you to the Red Cross, or their nurses will sort you out… In any case, you shall be taken care of. And when this whole affair is over with, go find my mother. She will take you both in. She's expecting you. And when the war is over, I shall come and join you. You won't even notice how fast the time will pass."

I cupped her cold cheek for the last time. It was time for me to go but she still clung to my overcoat and cried and cried and begged me to take her along as though she had not heard a word of what I had just said. It was a good thing that Gorges appeared in time and tore her off of me a bit too forcefully and nodded with a solemn look to my question, "You shall keep your word, won't you?"

I knew he would. It wasn't even the heavy bribe with which I had lined his pocket. The war was as good as lost and helping two Jewish women "escape to safety" would look mighty good on his new POW's resume.

The column marched on. Helena kept twisting in Gorges' forceful grip and looking at me until the darkness swallowed them all, leaving only the flattened snow and an occasional corpse here and there. But I still stood and stared after them until the whistle blew, gathering us, the remaining defendants of the Reich, into a new "regiment." An entire twenty men, against the advancing Russian army.

Chapter 32

Germany, 1947

The court hearing was over. Dr. Hoffman, Dr. Hutson, and Andrej Novák stood outside the Magistrate's building and smoked. The setting sun cast its golden shadow onto the ruins that lay in front of them. Among them, gilded shadows of the dead stood.

"May I ask you a question?" Dr. Hoffman turned to the Slovak.

"I imagine you have quite a few." Novák smiled. It suddenly occurred to Dr. Hoffman that it was the first time that he'd seen the Nazi-hunter smile.

"Why did you withdraw your charges as a co-plaintiff?"

For some time, Novák just smoked in silence, squinting at the sunset. "I changed my mind," he finally replied, with an almost astounding nonchalance about him.

"About charges?"

"About Dahler." He looked at the psychiatrist. "He saw me in that column when we were about to be marched out of Auschwitz. He saw me and yet he didn't point me out to his fellow SS men, even though there was a special order on our account. He didn't mention it during the hearing and I still wonder why."

"Didn't want to sound like another Gorges?" Dr. Hutson proposed.

The Slovak gave a small shrug. "Perhaps." He looked ahead of himself, his expression pensive. "I never knew him as a person. Only as a uniform, an SS man and they were all the same to us, more or less. Killers. Torturers. Heartless bastards, in general." He paused. "That day, in July 1944, when he made such a mess out of himself in front of Moll, I thought he was simply stinking drunk. Pissed to the point where he couldn't even stand. The SS drank a lot, you see. It was one of their favorite pastimes. I thought that this was the reason behind his behavior."

"You don't think he was lying to the court, describing that day?" Dr. Hutson narrowed his eyes slightly, his face pulling to a wry grin.

Novák waved him off. "I remember very well what I was saying in the beginning. That he was a liar through and through and he'd say anything to save his skin. I said it because I wanted you to jail him for as long as it was possible. I didn't know if he was actually a liar. I didn't want to know. I didn't want *to get to know him* as a person." He shook his head. "No, I don't think he was lying. You don't lie convincingly about such things that turn your stomach when you just think of them. One can't lie about something of this sort and get away with it."

"Are you satisfied with the verdict?"

"I am. I knew he'd most likely be acquitted due to the low rank, the birth-date amnesty, and the absence of personal participation in the crimes and I only persisted with the charges because... I just wanted him in jail. Doesn't make me an exemplary citizen, I suppose?"

"You have every reason to want to see an SS man in jail," Dr. Hoffman said.

"Yes, but... see, that's the point of it. How does my seeing him only as a uniform make me different from him, who only saw all of us like vermin before someone finally came along and opened his eyes? I suppose I needed someone to open my eyes too. Someone has to stop this cycle of hatred. We all need to become better men. He made his first step when he saved Helena and didn't report me to the SS. I may as well make the second and let him be. He's punished already, punished for the rest of his life with his wife's state. It's him who'll have to look at her daily and realize that it's his kin that did this to her."

"He'll take good care of her," Dr. Hoffman said softly. "He won't abandon her."

"I know that," the Slovak agreed surprisingly easily. "I saw him with her. Another reason why I changed my mind about him. Though, I must admit, changing one's mind is never easy."

"No, it's not."

The door to the Magistrate's Office opened and Franz Dahler stepped outside, holding onto his wife. Still a bit pale but beaming nevertheless, she moved past him, hugging the folders, with papers, to her chest.

"Did you get your Denazification Clearance stamped?" Dr. Hoffman asked, smiling at the couple, in spite of himself.

The Austrian nodded and hesitated before offering his hand to the psychiatrists. After both shook it, he lowered it hesitantly, as though in respect to the Slovak. It was Novák who smirked slightly and offered him his palm first. Dahler grasped it at once and shook it thoroughly.

"I don't know how to thank you, Herr Novák."

"You don't have to."

"Please, allow me at least to ask for your forgiveness for everything. I didn't get a chance to say it properly in the courtroom… I really, truly am sorry for everything that I've done to you personally and to every single person I've wronged. I know that it's all just words and it's much too late and surely won't bring anyone back—"

"It's all I wanted to hear," Novák interrupted him with a soft smile. "Trust me, it does mean a lot. Doesn't change anything for the past but means a lot for the future."

"Is there anything I can do, perhaps? Anything…" In vain, Dahler searched for the right word.

"Yes, you can. If, in the future, you see a teenager shout a racial slur at someone, stop him, pull him to one side and explain to him where you served and how such slurs led to the slaughter of millions. If you see a newspaper article denying the Nazi crimes, write one countering it and tell the people exactly what you've witnessed. The hatred, the racism, the xenophobia didn't miraculously disappear with Hitler. They're all still very much alive and kicking and it's up to us to do something to fight them. If you want to do something for the victims, don't stay quiet about the past, please. Talk to people – young people most of all – tell them the truth as you saw it. Talk as often and as loudly as you can. Many people will deny our, victims', experiences. They shall say we invented it all to suit our agenda or some such. They will deny the existence of the gas chambers and the crematoria. They will deny our own memories. But they will surely listen to an SS man."

Dahler smiled sadly. "I doubt the ones who you have in mind shall listen to an SS man who betrayed his own kind, in their eyes that is."

"Still, Mr. Dahler. Talk. Whether they will listen to you or not, just don't be silent. None of us should ever be silent in the face of injustice. The victims need people to talk for them, otherwise, it's much too easy to pretend that they never existed."

Dahler nodded slowly, solemnly. "I will. I will talk, Herr Novák. I want to apply to the University to get my education at last. If they accept me, I shall talk to the students, if the administration allows it. And I shall write to the newspapers. You will hear my name again, I promise. I will be talking until you get sick of me."

Novák broke into chuckles, looked at Dahler's sleeve, and then clapped him a bit awkwardly on his shoulder. There was a veil of mist in the SS man's eyes. Dr. Hutson gave his colleague a dig in the ribs.

"Thank you for everything, Andrej." Helena stepped in front of her husband and, after promptly depositing all of the papers into his arms, enclosed her fellow countryman in an unexpected embrace.

"I'm sorry for dragging out the court session for so long." Novák reddened in spite of himself. "I was honestly trying to help."

"I know you were. And you did. Just not like you thought you would." She beamed at him.

"Will you be all right?"

"I will be very much all right, yes. We are applying to the same University. I will be writing a lot, too."

"You? You will be attending the University?" The Slovak looked her over incredulously.

"Well, as long as Franz and I go there together, it shall be all right. The University will do us both good." She hesitated before asking, "May I have your address if that's all right with you? I should so love to stay in touch and write to each other."

Novák glanced at Dahler expectantly.

"Don't look at me." Franz grinned. "I'm not the one to grant any permissions here. The more things Leni does independently, even such insignificant ones as writing letters to her friends, the better for her."

Dr. Hoffman couldn't agree more. "You should apply for the psychiatry faculty," he called to Dahler. "You'd make an excellent therapist."

The latter only waved him off. "I'm too dumb for that."

"You have excellent instincts for that. At least consider it."

"Perhaps, I will."

The surviving lampposts came to life and blinked their yellow eyes open. The sky was quiet without bombers tearing through its cloth. Amidst the ruins, children called to each other and to passing American GIs, asking them for gum.

A warm grin broke on Franz Dahler's face. "What a fine evening it is today," he said.

"Let us not forget how lucky we are to be alive to see it," Novák added softly.

"Yes. Let us never forget." Helena nodded solemnly. "None of this."

A Note on History

Thank you so much for reading *The Girl in the Striped Dress*. Even though it's a work of fiction, most of it is based on a true story. Helena Citrónová (Kleinová in this novel) indeed arrived at Auschwitz with one of the first transports from Slovakia and was signed up to the Kanada work detail by the Kanada Kommandoführer Franz Wunsch (Dahler in this novel), in which she worked, up until the liberation in January of 1945. The circumstances of their meeting are true to fact; she indeed was scheduled to die the next day and only the fact that she was told to sing a birthday song to Franz saved her life. He was so touched by her singing that he immediately ordered to take her off the "selected" list and assign her to his Kommando instead. The following development of their relationship (the love note he gave her and which she destroyed; the scene in which she refused to do his manicure for which he threatened to shoot her; the fact that he saved Helena's sister Rózínka from the gas chamber; the fact that he hid Helena in the Kanada detail while she was sick with typhus and cared for her until she got better; the parcels he smuggled to her via sympathetic guards and *Pipel* boys; Helena and Franz's arrest after someone reported them to the camp's Gestapo; the final scene in which he gave her and her sister warm boots and instructed them on how to find his mother in Austria) are all also based on Helena's and Franz's interviews and testimonies, given to the BBC and during Franz's trial. Franz's life story, his wartime service, his transfer to Auschwitz after his injury are all also based on true fact. Their story is mentioned in both H. Langbein's study "People in Auschwitz" and L. Rees's "Auschwitz: New History."

To me personally, the Holocaust is an extremely sensitive subject, so while writing this novel I tried my best to keep as close to reality as I could, only using creative license where no survivors' testimonies could be used and where I had to use my author's imagination to fill in the blanks. The timeline of events, most historical figures, the complex camp hierarchy and the functioning of different work details are all true to fact and their descriptions are based on survivors' memoirs and historical studies.

The Denazification Tribunal procedure (its structure, members, history, and background) is also based on historical fact. The program itself was extremely complex and had to undergo multiple changes throughout the years. The German courts were indeed replacing American Military Tribunals starting in late 1946 – early 1947 with the Americans acting only as supervisors from that time on. The backlog of cases was such that a lot of POWs and former Nazis indeed escaped justice and got off without a charge but only with minor restrictions imposed on their professions (no public office, no positions in the education or press were permitted for a certain period of time, etc.). You can read more about the program and the way a Denazification Trial was conducted in Spayd and Insanally's study "Bayerliein: The Denazification Trial of Rommel's Chief-of-Staff, and Panzer Lehr Division Commander Generalleutnant Fritz Bayerlein" and also F. Taylor's study "Exorcising Hitler."

Most of the historical figures mentioned in the novel are also based on real Auschwitz survivors and SS men serving there. R. Höss, who is considered *the* Kommandant of Auschwitz despite the interruption of his service there, was indeed removed from his position during the investigation of the corruption in Auschwitz (conducted by Dr. Konrad Morgen and his staff in 1943, as described in the novel) and replaced by Kommandant Liebehenschel. The personality of Liebehenschel and the changes he introduced at once (he indeed toured the camp right after his appointment, spoke to the inmates, strictly prohibited the Kapos and the officers from abusing the prisoners, removed the so-called "standing cells" which the Auschwitz Gestapo used during Höss's time as a Kommandant and introduced a system of rewards to the prisoners) are all based on survivors' memoirs. H. Langbein, a former Austrian political prisoner in Auschwitz and a historian, has an entire chapter in his study dedicated to the comparison of the two Kommandants. Both Höss and Liebehenschel were tried in Cracow after the war and sentenced to death by hanging, for crimes against humanity. Höss's personality I also based on what I read about him from his own memoir that he wrote in captivity, "Death Dealer."

Franz's comrade Oskar Gröning (the name was not changed), indeed worked as an accountant in the Kanada detail until his transfer to the front was finally approved in 1944. He arrived at Auschwitz in 1942 and, after witnessing the cruelty reigning there firsthand, requested to be transferred to the front immediately but that request was denied. He was indeed mostly a desk person and wasn't charged with any brutality towards the inmates, however, he was still tried as an accessory to murder in September 2014, found guilty of facilitating mass murder and sentenced to four years of imprisonment but died on March 9, 2018, before he could start serving his sentence. He gave multiple interviews to the BBC, some of which were made into documentaries, such as "The Accountant of Auschwitz," "Auschwitz: the Nazis and the Final Solution," "The Last Nazis."

Gerhard Palitzsch was actually the first Auschwitz Rapportführer, who was indeed accused of appropriating inmates' valuables and of having sexual relations with a non-Aryan inmate during the investigation of 1943. As a result, he was transferred to Brünn and later, in June 1944, he was thrown out of the SS. His further fate is unknown, though, he is considered to have fallen during the Battle of Budapest.

Aumeier, Hössler, Moll, Voss, Gorges, and Grabner are all real people who served in the SS in Auschwitz during Helena's incarceration there. Hössler, nicknamed by the inmates "Moshe Liar," was indeed infamous for his sleek manner with the new arrivals and the stories he would spin in order to pacify them. While writing his eerie addresses to the new arrivals, I mostly relied on the memoirs of one of the Sonderkommando survivors, Filip Müller ("Eyewitness Auschwitz"), who witnessed Hössler's talk firsthand.

Unterscharführer Gorges, who was the Kommandoführer of Crematorium V, and Oberscharführer Voss, who was in charge of all crematoria before Moll replaced him on Höss's orders right before the Hungarian *Aktion,* are also described as they were presented in Müller's memoirs, "Eyewitness Auschwitz."

Otto Moll, unanimously remembered by the inmates and fellow SS men as the brutal and fanatical slave-driver, torturer, sadist, and murderer, was indeed placed in charge of the Hungarian *Aktion* by Kommandant Höss, who returned to Auschwitz in May 1944; the change of the command in the crematoria, the construction of the pits behind the crematoria, the camouflage screens, the scene with the three women brutally executed by him personally, and also his appearance and personality are all based on the Sonderkommando survivors' memoirs, who worked under his charge. Moll was indeed one of the few people awarded, by Himmler, with the Cross with Swords for distinctive service to the Reich. He was tried in Cracow after the war and sentenced to death by hanging.

Maximilian Grabner was indeed the head of the Auschwitz Gestapo, who was later tried in Weimar for corruption and unsanctioned murder of inmates at the so-called "Black Wall" – the wall, by which many prisoners died by firing squad, on Grabner's orders. It was situated near Block 11, the punishment block. After the war, he was tried for crimes against humanity, found guilty, and hanged in January 1948.

As for the inmates, some of them are real people (such as Mala Zimetbaum, who worked as an interpreter and a courier in Auschwitz before her escape with her beloved, Edward Galiński, as well as the inmate known as Dayen, who was said to be a former rabbi and who was in charge of burning books and documents left from the new arrivals) and some are fictional characters based on real people. For instance, the Slovak doctor who helped Helena. He is based on Dr. Miklos Nyiszli, who worked as an inmate pathologist assigned to Dr. Mengele. His living quarters and his responsibilities are all based on Dr. Nyiszli's memoir, "Auschwitz: A Doctor's Eyewitness Account."

The Kanada work detail, its structure, organization, and functions are all described based on the survivors' memoirs. It was definitely considered to be the most desirable work detail since the inmates had comparatively bearable living conditions (they lived in the complex itself and were allowed to have mattresses, pillows, bed covers, etc. in their barracks), were permitted to take showers that were also installed next to the warehouse, and allowed to keep their hair and wear civilian clothes. They did work under the supervision of male SS guards, both male and female inmates together, which was not the case with the regular camp in Birkenau, where the inmates were strictly separated by sexes and where women from the women's camp worked under the supervision of female SS wardens (most of whom began arriving in the spring of 1942, along with the first women transports from Slovakia). The idea to appoint "antisocial" German inmates (mostly it meant prostitutes) as Kapos belonged to Himmler, who ordered Kommandant Höss to implement it at once. Maria Krupp is the collective image of such a Kapo. It was mostly women who worked in the Kanada Kommando under Franz Wunsch's (Dahler's) charge.

The Sonderkommando (the inmates who worked in the gas chambers, crematoria, and burial pits) was also considered an "elite" kommando since they, just like Kanada inmates, were allowed certain privileges. They also had separate living quarters from the rest of the inmates and were more or less prohibited from interacting with them since the SS didn't want any details of the crematoria operations leaking out to the general population of the camp. They also had rather comfortable bunks, plenty of food and drink in their living quarters (SS camp leader Aumeier later characterized the members of the SK as "hulking, well-nourished Jewish inmates"; Tadeusz Joachimowski, who was a roll-call clerk in a section of Birkenau, provided the following description: "When I went to Block 3 and entered the room occupied by the camp elder and camp Kapo, I saw a big table with a cloth of white linen at which about twenty Jews from the Sonderkommando were sitting. Karl Seefeld put platters with choice ham, sausage, fish, and other foods on the table and those around it enjoyed the feast. After-dinner treats included chocolate and an assortment of fruit." – H. Langbein, "People in Auschwitz" – and were permitted to wear civilian jackets and sometimes even civilian slacks. The SS tolerated their appropriating food, alcohol, and even valuables from the dead inmates and the Kanada solely due to the fact that no one else would do the job and therefore the SS felt that the SK had to be compensated somewhat for the horrors of their profession. The difference between the Kanada and the SK was that the members of the SK were summarily liquidated every four to five months, with the exception of only a few members and a new team would be gathered, in order not to keep witnesses alive for too long.

The description of all five crematoria is also all based on survivors' testimonies and historical sources. Crematorium 1, the walls of which were constantly crumbling, which was the reason why the corpses were at first buried in the open field behind Bunkers 1 and 2 (which served as gas chambers) called The Little Red House and The Little White House, was situated in Auschwitz; Crematoria II, III, IV, and V were later constructed in Birkenau. They combined the crematorium facilities, the gas chamber, the SK living quarters, and the Kommandoführer's office and became the main extermination sites starting in 1943. Bunker 1 and Bunker 2 were former farmhouses which were transformed into gas chambers before the construction of the four crematoria; they were much smaller in size and only had a small changing room and hatches in the ceiling into the gas chamber itself, through which the gas was dropped by the SS medics. The new crematoria were much more complex, had changing rooms much bigger in size and with multiple signs in different languages that were placed there to pacify the new arrivals and persuade them that they were indeed only taking a shower. Inside the gas chamber, they had special "gas columns," through which Zyklon B was lowered into the chamber by the SS medic. They also had elevators to deliver the bodies faster, from the basement into the crematorium upstairs. You can read more about it in F. Müller's memoir "Eyewitness Auschwitz," which also includes their detailed plans.

Trucks with the Red Cross were indeed used to deliver the gas to the bunkers and to transport inmates, who didn't pass the selection. The members of the SK also had to shave heads of the corpses and extract golden crowns, which were later melted into gold bars and delivered to the Reichsbank. The hair was said to be used for the socks and belts of the Kriegsmarine, for felt boots, mattress stuffing, and upholstery.

Burial pits behind the bunkers indeed had to be dug out and the bodies burned in the fall of 1942 since the ground around them became poisonous and began contaminating the waters in the vicinity. Later, in the same field, the pits were used for burning the bodies during the so-called Hungarian *Aktion,* just as described in the novel.

The food given to the inmates (including bromide added to tea and coffee), the monthly "disinfection" procedure (including the solution used for the inmates' hair), the clothes the inmates wore (including the differences between the so-called "elite" prisoners and regular ones) are all based on the survivors' memoirs. You can read more about it in H. Langbein's study, "People in Auschwitz," and in R. Gelissen's memoir, "Rena's Promise."

The so-called *Muselmänner* (extremely emaciated inmates who seemingly lost all will to live) and the scene with their selection by the SS doctors is based on H. Langbein's memoir of his time in Auschwitz.

The camp orchestra and their appearance are also based on survivors' testimonies.

Jehovah Witnesses and their refusal to handle anything military-related is also based on true fact, just like the so-called *Pipels* or bum-boys and their "relationship" (one can only use the term very loosely here) with the homosexual Kapos.

The inmates could indeed receive Red Cross parcels (as mentioned by Helena) starting in the Fall of 1942. First Aryan, and then Jewish inmates were permitted to receive parcels from Red Cross and their homes, however, they were opened by the camp's post office and some things were taken out before delivering the rest to the inmates. The inmates were allowed (and, in fact, even ordered) to write postcards to their relatives and friends; most likely so that the SS could enrich themselves even more after an inmate would ask for a parcel to be sent to their name or, a more sinister motive, to get their relatives to come to Auschwitz willingly. Auschwitz was indeed called Waldsee on cards dated 1944.

A part of the Sonderkommando did organize a revolt in October 1944, blowing up Crematorium IV and burning one of the SS men alive in the oven (as described by Franz Dahler in this novel); the revolt was suppressed and 451 Sonderkommando men were shot, as a consequence. Filip Müller was fortunate to survive it and later described the event in his memoir.

*

Every survivor definitely experienced Auschwitz differently, however, every single one was scarred by it to a greater or lesser extent. All of the people who were fortunate to leave the camp alive brought with them certain psychological traumas that stayed with them for their entire lives. Among such traumas, Stockholm Syndrome (still undiscovered in 1947, yet described more or less accurately by the fictional psychiatrist, Dr. Hoffman) definitely played a big role. Forced into the position of a virtual slave, an inmate often turned to anyone who was in a position of power and could offer assistance in case that inmate's life was in danger. It's only natural that bonds began forming between the captor and the captives, who were so desperate that they were ready to do anything to gain the captors' favor to survive.

Whether Helena and Franz's relationship was actually a case of Stockholm Syndrome or whether she indeed fell in love with him, we all can only speculate. Among the general brutality of the camp, their case is certainly an exception to the rule. However, the fact that the SS man could change under his beloved's influence from a "natural Jew-hater" (as described by one of the survivors) into someone who began helping the inmates and tried to get out of ramp duty by any means possible (the scene where he vomited while escorting the people to their death is also based on a survivor's testimony, Ernst Müller) testifies to the idea that love is always stronger than hate and that even in the most brutal conditions, a person can undergo the most drastic change if only that person chooses kindness over violence, which is always a conscious choice. As an author, I cherish such stories the most and particularly today, when we, as a society, could really use some compassion and kindness towards each other. I hope that Helena and Franz's story touched you just as it touched me after I first learned about it. Thank you for reading!

If you still have any questions left or would like to proceed with further reading, feel free to contact the author via Goodreads or Facebook – I'll be more than happy to provide you with answers and further reading material!

A Letter from Ellie

Dear Reader,

I want to say a huge thank you for choosing to read *The Girl in the Striped Dress*. If you did enjoy it, and want to keep up to date with all my latest releases, just sign up at the following link. Your email address will never be shared and you can unsubscribe at any time.

www.bookouture.com/ellie-midwood

Thank you for reading the story of this truly remarkable woman. I hope you loved *The Girl in the Striped Dress* and, if you did, I would be very grateful if you could write a review. I'd love to hear what you think, and it makes such a difference helping new readers to discover one of my books for the first time.

I love hearing from my readers—you can get in touch on my Facebook page, through Goodreads or my website.

Thanks,
Ellie

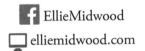

EllieMidwood

elliemidwood.com

Acknowledgements

First and foremost, I want to thank the wonderful Bookouture family for helping me bring Helena and Franz's story to light. It wouldn't be possible without the help and guidance of my incredible editor, Christina Demosthenous, whose insights truly bring my characters to life and whose support and encouragement make me strive to work even harder on my novels and become a better writer. Thank you Kim Nash, Noelle Holten, Ruth Tross, and Peta Nightingale for all your help and for making me feel welcome and at home with your amazing publishing team. It's been a true pleasure working with all of you and I already can't wait to create more projects under your guidance.

Mom, granny – thank you for always asking how my novel is doing and for cheering me up at every step. Your support and faith in me make this writing journey so much easier, knowing that you always have my back and will always be my biggest fans. Thank you for all your love. Love you both to death.

Ronnie, my love – all of this wouldn't be possible without you. Every time you meet a new person, the first thing you say about me is "my fiancée is a great novelist, you simply must check out her books!" I always grumble that you're embarrassing me with all that attention, but inwardly I'm so very grateful for you being so very proud of me. Thank you for all your support and for putting up with my deadlines and all that research information I keep dumping on you. You are my rock star.

A special thanks to my two besties, Vladlena and Anastasia, for their love and support; to all of my fellow authors whom I got to know through Facebook and who became my very close friends – you all are such an inspiration! I consider you all a family.

And, of course, huge thanks to my readers for patiently waiting for new releases, for celebrating cover reveals together with me, for reading ARCs, and sending me those absolutely amazing I-stayed-up-till-3 a.m.-last-night-because-I-just-had-to-finish-your-wonderful-book messages, for your reviews that always make my day, and for falling in love with my characters just as much as I do. You are the reason why I write. Thank you so much for reading my stories.

And, finally, I owe my biggest thanks to all the brave people who continue to inspire my novels. Some of you survived the Holocaust, some of you perished, but it's your incredible courage, resilience, and self-sacrifice that will live on in our hearts. Your example will always inspire us to be better people, to stand up for what is right, to give a voice to the ones who have been silenced, to protect the ones who cannot protect themselves. You all are true heroes. Thank you.

CPSIA information can be obtained
at www.ICGtesting.com
Printed in the USA
LVHW021318050322
712646LV00015B/1350